Stopover at World's End

Stopover at World's End

Artimidor Avennay

A Comic Fantasy Novel

STOPOVER AT WORLD'S END
Copyright © 2024 Artimidor Avennay

To request permission, contact the publisher at
art@artimidor.com

This book is a work of fiction. Names, characters,
businesses, organizations, places, events and
incidents either are the product of the author's
imagination or are used fictitiously. Any resemblance
to actual persons, living or dead, events, or locales is
entirely coincidental. The world is not going to end.

Independently published
Hardback ISBN 979-8-8634-6066-6
Trade paperback ISBN 979-8-8634-5969-1

First paperback edition: January 2024

Typeset in Minion Pro
Edited by Kate Nascimento and Emma Parfitt
Cover and interior art by Santiago Iborra
Map by Artimidor Avennay

To the smallest person

Preface

If there's an ultimate bummer, it has to be an apocalypse. Fair enough. Putting a damper on things is what apocalypses do, and being thorough about it is what discerns a proper cataclysm from a wannabe. One wouldn't expect anything less from the Big A. Better not to have one around. Not in your particular universe anyway. Big A? Big no-no.

On the upside – and yes, there's one, even to the ultimate bummer – apocalypses are as rare as they're deadly. Which is also why we tend to dismiss the possibility of one happening, no matter what. That is, nobody expects the End of Days to pop in for a visit. No official calendars mark the event, no kings or queens are privy to insider information, no town criers are likely to announce the thing. Expect no advance notice to make you rethink your shopping trip. So why bother?

And let's face it, even if there were subtle tip-offs from a supreme being, veiled in cave etchings or prophetic parchments from days of yore, something that hints at the exact date and time when things will fall apart once and for all – well, good luck with that. If there were such a thing, the scholars would call it outright fake, and move on. They'd rather analyse fossils.

Some nutcases have an inkling, or so they claim. Those who hear voices and cover their walls from top to bottom with messages from beyond – warnings and threats, sprinkled with prospects of a life after life, or a lack thereof. It's just that one loony rarely agrees with another, and so – loonies exempt – when the End came to the world known to its residents as Aenyros, nobody saw it coming.

Yet come it did, the Big A.

And with it, all of Aenyros's grand empires were swept away. Aspiring kingdoms, declining ones, and the so-so ones too. Among the also-rans was Zarrafanda. Maybe they should have known; by all accounts, the Zarrafandans were pretty nuts.

Before its demise, Zarrafanda was a tiny, vibrant human domain, located someplace in the heart of Aenyros's largest continent, no threat to anyone beyond itself. It was a picturesque spot, colourful and quaint, as any well-intentioned travel agent would put it, and not too bothered about its negligible role in the grand scheme of things. The Princedom, as it liked to refer to itself, preferred a quiet life, snugly tucked between more imposing features on the map, and celebrated that very fact as one of its main assets. Sure, now and again, the bastard son of a neighbouring kingdom with ambitions of his own chose to raid what little land there was... and was repelled, persistently. But apart from such nuisances, nothing earth-shattering ever happened in Zarrafanda. Not before the quakes. But the quakes came only shortly before the world as a whole went belly-up, with Zarrafanda smack in the middle of it.

Just as well. People don't have time for the End of Days. Everyone's used to their established routine. They have plans for the weekend. They go fishing. Or rock climbing. Or do some competitive nose-picking. And because things have gone on for days and days, and then even more days, a not uncommon way of thinking is that it's more likely than not that whatever there is will continue as it has always done: the sun rising and setting, maybe with enough rain in between to inspire the obligatory rant about the weather seers getting it wrong again.

But the actual End of Days? Ludicrous! That's not a conversation anyone's likely to strike up at breakfast while buttering toast. "Would you pass me the jam?" one might prefer. Only come teatime are some ready to ask the bigger questions, like "Fancy another biscuit?"

Chapter 1

Sound Soothsaying

At the beginning of the very end, Thimble was like most people: assured of everything there was, and a fan of biscuits.

When the world headed south and Thimble with it, he had long outgrown his name. By then, he was a full-grown halfling, his chestnut-coloured curls complemented by thick, fluffy sideburns. His front teeth still sported a gap you could drive a horse and buggy through, but never mind. The gap added a certain rakishness to his grin – or so he imagined. And that wasn't the only thing he imagined about himself, by the way. Deep-set in his mind, bedded on fluffy daydreams, he bore a conviction that his humble little self was destined for something big. No, not size-wise, of course. Rather he was banking on fate to come a-knocking someday, somehow, any way it chose, in need of a halfling. Even so, when it made its move, he was taken aback. His destiny barged in with the apocalypse in tow.

But before we get to the end, let's start at the beginning.

One Folkday morning, Thimble was dilly-dallying around Weaverring market square. The Grand Clock Tower's hands pointed to the hour of Lightthrive and, apart from the sun climbing the sky in the most unspectacular way conceivable, nothing much was going on. The giant dial was advancing at a snail's pace towards breakfast number two. A quarter of an hour crept by, then another, and a third after that.

Thimble's stomach growled. He fancied a mug of hot chocolate.

For a while now, his slight frame had not moved an inch from his favourite shady corner. He was twiddling his thumbs, just watching... watching. Had he stepped out into the sun, early passers-by would have seen a trim little guy, with a mint-green cardigan stretched over his pot belly, short gingerbread-brown pants, and a neat cape thrown around his shoulders. All part of the package. Neatness went a long way, Thimble knew. It went the same distance in fair trade as in thieving, and thieving was the kind of unfair trade Thimble was in. People rarely demanded instant refunds from him once they'd been pickpocketed; they couldn't imagine such a cute individual being mixed up in that sort of thing. They were much more likely to focus on any shifty-looking fellow standing about. So whenever he could, he made sure somebody else was nearby to take the blame while he quietly slipped away.

None of those misconceptions would happen anytime soon in the early hours on a Folkday. Burly peddlers were still moving crates and unpacking their junk. Potters arranged jugs, dyers spread their clothes, herb women strung up spices. As of yet, the only customers hunting for greens were maids. The more well-heeled aristocracy wouldn't deign to stroll about the place before midday. Tough times for a self-respecting cutpurse trying to make a living.

The rag-and-bone man came clop-clopping by. He sat on his box, beaming. It was one of those smiles that succeeded beyond measure to brighten up other faces too. It was uncanny. No matter one's mood, you had to smile along with him, or with the smiling lookers looking at him, and in no time, wherever one pointed one's nose, smiling faces littered the street. Happiness everywhere. Like a *Chain of Lightning* spell leaping from person to person, only more uplifting than deadly.

On a side note: Nobody would have believed that the rag-and-bone man was a sourpuss at heart, nor that he hated the people grinning at him. But hate, he did. Some are born with a proverbial spoon in their mouth, but the rag-and-bone man's welcome gift on the day of his birth hadn't been cutlery — it had been a smile. "Nothing we can do about it," the healers had declared. And hence, ever since the unfortunate fellow with that grin etched on his face was old enough to contemplate the circumstances, he had started off his days grumpy. He'd just need to graze a mirror with a glance, and he'd had enough of it already.

Clop-clomp-cloppety-clomp.

After the rag-and-bone man and his magic had clattered past, Thimble wiped his smirk away and jammed his hands into his pockets. A discordant whistle came to his lips, but he had to stop it right there. It was a myth that whistling made people look innocuous; whoever had thought that up hadn't considered that it drew attention too – even more so if one couldn't carry a tune in a bucket.

So for a while, he just cast languid glances around him. Then he spotted the caravan at the end of the lane. *What's that about anyway?* he thought, and ambled closer.

The caravan was parked in the shadow of an elm, a shabby thing with a makeshift chimney, curved wooden steps and sandy paint flaking off in most places. But in its ramshackleness also lay its fascination. *Must belong to one of those Black Butterfly rovers,* Thimble thought. A hand-painted sign on the door revealed it to be the domain of a certain *"Madame Elga"*, and the crude crystal ball carved into it promised all sorts of intrigue. Beneath the sign, a poster announced:

Soothsaying and more! ONLY this weekend! Learn about your future NOW before it's too late to be foretold!

Oh! Someone was coming!

Thimble's intrigue doubled when he saw her. She was young. Dainty. He could also see – and hear – the little jingling pouch at her side as she rapped on the wagon door. At length, the door creaked open and she was given entrance.

Curiosity might have killed the cat, Thimble knew, but as halflings were far from feline, he decided he would take his chances. And so he slipped over to investigate the three things the early hours had brought him: the blonde, her future, and – as a business interest – the pouch.

A few heartbeats later, his nosy self was already balancing atop a crate outside the caravan, eavesdropping on the beauty's reading.

"…Really?"

"Why, of course! And full of promises!"

A tiny halfling ear pressed closer to make out some more of the scraps drifting through the window.

"Oh dear, oh dear…" That must have been the blonde: she chimed like a bell.

"But let's see the rest!" The other voice was its own thing: smoky, scratchy, and a-quiver with suspense.

Thimble dared to peek through the half-open shutters and beheld the voice's owner whose body was hunched like a gargoyle over a little table, where three tarot cards were laid out. The crone's blade-like nails, capping long bony fingers, moved over the cards as if about to carve a turkey. They flipped over two more from the deck; the first showed a warrior in a chariot pulled by two sphinxes, the second a man and a woman in the nude, holding hands in front of a sunrise. The cards were added to the row already on the table, completing a set of five.

Straggly hair swung forward, copper earrings clinked and a gasp escaped the rover's wrinkly mouth. "Ah… You're one of the really, really lucky ones. *Great* things lie ahead, my dear! *Great* things!"

"But… Madame Elga…" The blonde looked at the cards that held her future. "Doesn't that one" – she pointed at the card that showed a rat skeleton swathed in a shroud, standing erect and wielding a scythe – "mean something… unpleasant?"

Thimble had glimpsed the Death card too. It was the Rat Queen, otherwise known as the Reaper's Bride. His eyes had travelled back, though, to the blonde's flowing hair undulating over her shoulders like moonbeams. He gazed at the delicate curve of her back, her willowy figure, the snub nose, the soft glimmer in her entrancing eyes… He shook his head. Actually, no, he didn't see any eyes, or a nose for that matter. Looking at her backside had its downsides. But what he otherwise missed, he chose to appreciate in his mind's eye. What he *did* see for certain was the beauty's pouch. She had placed it on the table right next to his window. Nothing imagined there.

"Yes, yes, that's the Rat Queen, alright," admitted the soothsayer, her only remaining tooth glinting in all its golden splendour. She was so ancient-looking, her features so caked in make-up, it seemed like a solid layer. "But don't be silly, sweetheart! Every kid knows that the Rat Queen really stands for *change*. Something has to go, something new comes along, and blah, blah, blah." Like a spider on stilts, her claws clacked towards an ashtray and the wrapped bundle of fuming weed waiting there. A long puff later, swirls of smoke danced about the limited caravan space.

Her visitor gave a polite ladylike cough, and then coughed some more in a much less ladylike way.

"Want my professional opinion?" The rover blew out more smoke. "The Rat Queen's little more than a glorified Knight of Cups in drag. Bit more dramatic looking, you know."

"So it's... um... nothing ominous then?" the lady ventured apprehensively.

"If I say so."

"And you're not just... saying so? It's a vile thing. With a scythe!"

The crone levelled a cold stare at her.

Even Thimble felt the tobacco going to his head now. Maybe it was the resultant lightheadedness that inspired him, or the thickness of the cloud, or the mere thrill of it. Whatever it was, temptation got the better of him, and he seized the opportunity by reaching through the window to—

"What *exactly* does it all mean?" The lady's high-pitched voice cut through the veil of fumes, unaware of any unlawfulness occurring under her nose, or a tad to the right of it.

There was the slightest of jingles. Billowing smoke took the pouch's place as if it had only been waiting for Thimble to make his conquest. Done. He weighed the coins in his hand. Instinct was quick to remind him to make himself scarce at this point. But he couldn't just scamper off now, could he? The prediction part of the reading was yet to come, and he was a sucker for listening in on all things fateful.

"Let's go through the cards one by one then, shall we?" the crone said, her finger on the Rat Queen. "Here… this one tells me you'll emerge from our session a changed gal. That's all there is to it, no need to overthink happenstance. Wheel of Fortune's next: you'll soon… very soon… come into the possession of money."

"Oh! How exciting!"

"The third one here is Ordeal. Now, that's some kind of trial, test, or what have you. And after that: the Chariot, meaning victory, of course. And the last one, that's the Lovers. So, let's say, roughly, there will be a struggle, but you'll weather hazards and hardships, etc., etc. And at the end, your Mr Wonderful will be waiting. The knight in shining armour."

"Really? A true knight? Shining armour and everything?"

"Hey, maybe he's not a knight *as such*, but certainly in… er… spirit, even if his armour, or whatever he's wearing, might need a little polish. Fate's a bit more complicated than that, but that's the gist."

"Can't you be any more specific, Madame Elga?"

A sigh escaped the brittle lips. "Meh," the rover moaned. "Let's see if I can get a vision too then…" The crone's eyelids slid down and her hand travelled over the cards, fingers jittering. Maybe it was part of the act, maybe it wasn't. "Yes, I can see something… It's… his steed! I behold…" She hummed ominously for a moment.

"Yes?"

"A white horse…"

"Ah, I *adore* horses!"

"The sun is setting and… there's a figure at the horizon…" The fortune-teller's misty voice rose to a dramatic crescendo. "He's riding towards you… and you're waving back. Now you're running… yes… to greet him… He's respected and revered, my dear. Quite a character!"

"You can read all this in the cards?"

"*Between*, sweetie," rasped the crone. "*Between*." She had opened her eyes again, and now she clasped the lady's wrist to pat her mousy hand with her own bird-of-prey claw. "It's like reading between the lines. Only with cards." Her spindly forefinger dropped to the empty spot between the Chariot and the Lovers. "It's right here. With a bit of divinatory training, you'd see it too." The crone flicked some tobacco ashes into the tray. It looked very much like the upper half of a human skull.

"And *when* will this man… come around?"

"In due time, cupcake. In due time."

The lady clenched her delicate fingers. "But you didn't see, like… people marching?" A tinge of anxiety flitted over her face. "Kettledrums and such? Trumpeters, pipers?"

"You want a musician? Someone who plays in a band? You've got the wrong idea. I'm not a dating agent."

"No, no… It's not that. It's just that whenever I meet someone, bad things start happening. I've seen it. It's like I'm the eye of the storm of all things evil! A whole war might break out around us! Who knows?" The blonde wiped a tear from her eye. "It was like that before. Twice! Curse that megalomaniac Vensk and his crackbrained raids! With the luck I've been having, I could meet the one and the next day would be the end of the world."

"Ah, poppycock!" The crone flicked her hand. "The world's not going to end. I would know. I'm in the business."

The lady sighed, regardless. "You wouldn't mind if I get a second opinion on this? From someone with, say, a scrying stone?"

"Whatever. Got one of those myself, but the weather's bad in there today, see?" A fright-inducing nail jabbed out, pointing at a crystal ball among other paraphernalia atop a curiosity cabinet in the corner. Sluggish grey mist writhed as if trapped within. The vapours bore a suspicious resemblance to cigarette smoke, Thimble noticed, which might have been sucked through a crack in the glass and found no way out. Maybe some sort of magic was keeping it inside. Every swirl looked like a silent cry for help.

"Anyway…" The crone collected the cards. "That will be three coppers for your Johnny. Cash only." The tone conveyed finality, like a portcullis rattling down. "Oh, and one more for the extra vision." She held out a claw as the tobacco stem sagged from her lipstick-spoiled mouth. "If you please… Madame Elga needs her beauty sleep."

"Of course!" said the lady and went looking for her money. However, she couldn't locate it at first, and then her brief search was interrupted by a sharp snap outside.

Followed by a pained howl, which turned seamlessly into cussing.

The shutters of the caravan flew open. "Oh, my dear! You hurt?" asked the lady.

A bottom-rubbing halfling looked up at her.

"I... um..." Thimble started, then reconsidered, at a loss for further explanations. His breath came quicker. It struck him that while one hand was busy with rubbing his behind, the pouch he had pinched featured prominently in the other. A pink pouch, with ruffles on top. With what were presumably the lady's initials embroidered onto it. An accessory uncommon among halflings, males, or a combination of both. Details like these hamper first impressions.

"This... er... must be yours?" Thimble mumbled. That was shortly before his mouth dried up. He hurled the evidence up to the dazzling blonde, and before the beauty with her brilliant future had time to react, he had picked himself up and taken to his heels as if chased by a swarm of hornets with no good in their hive mind.

Dratted conscience! Thimble thought as he panted and bustled through Weaverring's alleyways. An absolute stunner glances at him just once, and what happens? He gets *stunned.* As though caught by the death-darting eye of a basilisk! Only this one made him return his well-earned loot instead of kill him outright. Of course, loot is a thief's living, and so, in a twisted way, it *was* a death-glare after all. "Dratted conscience!"

Still running, Thimble vowed to work on that issue. And while he was at it, he also vowed to ignore the next blonde he came across, however beguiling she might be. Blondes were up to no good. Always had been, always

13

would be. Everyone knew that for a fact. And he should have known it too, considering his fatal fling with Flocksi Brimbottom back in Willwold-on-Glee. There was something Netherworldly about blondes.

Back in the wagon, the rover crone was more interested in the coins owed to her than the trail of dust the halfling had left behind. "Well?"

The demand didn't quite reach the lady's ear. Bemusement had entered her face and was running all over it. "Oh..." she moaned, once a bit of reflection had caught up with her. "Some sweet halfling, that one, wasn't he? And so humble!"

The fortune-teller took a contemplative drag.

"I... must have lost my pouch..." the lady mused, "and what do you know? That shy little fellow found it! Didn't want a single coin, not even a kiss as a reward for such brave honesty... Oh, the poor, poor, confused thing! Climbed that crate so valiantly to get my attention, fell in the effort, hurt himself, and all on my behalf!"

A wry smile contorted the crone's features. "That's the Wheel of Fortune sorted for you then, love." She chuckled.

"The Wheel of Fortune?"

"Got your money, hon, didn't you?" Smoke gushed from the corners of the fortune-teller's mouth. "You're fast cashing in on predictions, eh?"

"But... but... that was my *own* money!"

The rover's smile vanished. "Piece of free advice: next time, don't lose it first." She stubbed out her cigarette. "Anyway, it's still four coppers. Pay up, and when you meet your Prince Charming, tell him Madame Elga says 'Hi!'"

Unrelated to the halfling's misguided attempts at making his wrongdoing right, two city guards were dealing with the real thing. Sergeant Broadtoe, a well-rounded, moustached officer with a bowl haircut, and his partner in crime-solving, Constable Nives – younger, less rounded (but working on it) – were investigating an alleged offense at the far end of the market. Issue at hand: the disappearance of gnomes.

"That would be… abduction," Sergeant Broadtoe muttered, confused. "Mass abduction!" He aimed a querying look at the constable. "Is this even our department?"

"No. *Gnomes*, officer," the buxom woman at the stall insisted, "the garden variety."

"Garden gnomes?" The sergeant twisted his neck to peek from under his haircut at the gnome-deprived world.

"All gone! It happened between *two blinks!* Gone! Two dozen of them! Now what do you think of that? Well, I'll tell you what *I* think!" And Mrs Buxom told them exactly what she thought, in as many words as she could think of, her two chins wobbling merrily along.

She paused for a gasp's length, a point at which the officials might have gotten a word in, but the opportunity – tiny as it was – passed unchallenged.

"From *my* stall, officer!" It poured down on them again, Mrs Buxom's arms flailing about as if her mouth was puppeteering her limbs. "And, if one wants to believe *her*, they also took some from that smug cow's stall across the street, and *that* woman has no business peddling them anyway, let me tell you! *I* was here first. *I* sold them gnomes first, *I* made good business!"

Sergeant Broadtoe began to bounce up and down on the balls of his feet.

"Top-of-the-range gnomes, too! Sell like hotcakes, them gnomes! And if I may be so frank—"

"Thank you," someone should have inserted at this point, and yet didn't.

"Let me tell you something else! That cow dared to accuse me – *me,* of all people – of having stolen hers! Do I look like someone who goes about stealing gnomes? Why would *I* need gnomes? *More* gnomes? *Common* gnomes? *Ugly* gnomes? Who says it wasn't—"

"THANK YOU!" a sudden, bloodhoundish roar put an end to it.

Mrs Buxom gaped at Sergeant Broadtoe, shell-shocked.

The words still rang in the sergeant's own ears like cannon fire. True, he had a temper, but it was usually well guarded. Unless he was prodded, and prodded, and prodded again. There were days when the prodding started early in the morning, when it sounded like a nagging wife. Days like this one.

A moment of dead silence later, the sergeant lowered his hands, folded them over his chest, and when he spoke again, his tone had considerably softened. "That's plenty," he whispered, almost with extra politeness. "We'll get a separate statement from Mrs Cow, I mean, the other lady you mentioned, ma'am. No need to further elaborate."

Mrs Buxom nodded, or quivered. It was difficult to say which. She took to fanning her rosy face with her fingers.

"So, *garden* gnomes," Sergeant Broadtoe jotted down in his notebook, enjoying the enforced calm. He could almost hear his own thoughts again, whether or not he liked what he could almost hear – which was that the case didn't look like the breakthrough opportunity he needed to advance his career. "We're talking clay things, right? Lawn ornaments, that sort of thing?"

"Yes. Yes, officer." The buxom woman's tone was low as a whimper.

"About... two dozen, was it?"

"Or thereabouts."

But, of course, Mrs Buxom couldn't leave it at that. Noiselessness wasn't in her nature, and she soon lapsed back into chat mode, harping on in any number of directions – from standard gossip to wild speculation and back, taking tangents left and right and detours in between. Before the officers knew it, she had mentioned a third cousin's hunt for a wedding dress, though according to Mrs Buxom it was doomed from the get-go anyway – the wedding, not the dress. Gnomes had no role in it, she said, but who knew? Who could really say what went on with those gnomes, and who they'd been involved with?

Constable Nives intervened. He did the only sensible thing and, as he had learned recently in a witness training workshop, involved a second, equally garrulous female bystander – an acquaintance of subject one, which he had no difficulty borrowing from the gathering crowd – thus neutralizing the rambling into background noise.

Leaving the women to their chatter, Nives looked up at the sergeant, who wasn't only broader but also taller than him. "Mayhaps a concerted operation of the Dwarven Underground Movement, Sarge?" he pondered aloud. "Typical DWUM stuff, I reckon. The DWUMs are very protective of anything dwarven."

Sergeant Broadtoe pulled his subordinate closer. "Is that DWUM thing even real? I thought people just picked on the little ones, and so the little ones created a sort of urban myth to threaten the bigger ones."

"Isn't this an indicator? Missing gnomes?"

"You're saying that these DWUMs steal gnomes? Why would something called the *Dwarven* Underground Movement steal *gnomes?*"

"*Dwarves* are the ones with the beards and pickaxes," Nives said. "Right?"

"Right."

"And yet everyone's putting figurines of their likeness in their gardens for personal pleasure. And guess what they call them? Gnomes! It's warped, to say the least. It's racial misrepresentation. Outright offensive, especially in this day and age. Put yourself in the shoes of a dwarf!"

"Hmm…" Broadtoe tried to wriggle his thoughts into a dwarven half-boot.

"How would *you* feel if someone moulded you out of clay and then made the thing wear, say, a tutu?"

An image swam up between them.

"I… er…" Broadtoe couldn't say anything. "O-o-hmm…?"

"It's disrespectful and exploitative, I'm telling you, Sarge. Dwarves don't put human-shaped things in their underground mushroom patches and call them mine elves."

"Guess not," Broadtoe admitted with a shake of his head. "Maybe you're on to something here after all. Now, let's assume—"

Something fast and mint-green darted past.

It seemed to be a person, a small person. It zipped into the next-best back alley, quick as a hare. The most well-timed dash in dash-history it wasn't, and it was easy to grasp why: dwarves, gnomes and halflings are all different races, but a superficial glance might lead one to suggest that they're all about the same size. And superficiality was all there was time for, eliciting a spur-of-the-moment-accusation from Mrs Buxom and Mrs Cow and shouts of "Thief! Thief!" directed in the vague vicinity of the speeding blotch.

A connection to the Dwarven Underground Movement hadn't been confirmed, and the case probably wouldn't have held up in court, but the charge had been made. Valid or not, the accusation echoed through the street. "Thief! Thief!" everybody yelled, mostly because everybody else did. Dogs yapped in solidarity; a few ducks quacked. In less than no time, half of Weaverring demanded a proper chase. After all, the officials were around. They had seen the blotch too. The situation demanded urgency.

Sergeant Broadtoe and Constable Nives took off. They lumbered after the suspect – one a little quicker than the other. The day had started so well! Fresh blueberry pie from the Waftwell bakery and a leisurely patrol to work the pie off. But then they'd been rousted by the gnome stuff. Inconvenient, yet manageable – a standard inquiry, destined to be filed away by lunch. After that, all this shouting. All this plodding on the taxpayers' behalf.

"Over there! There he is!"

"In the name of the law!" the watchmen panted.

They must be mad! Thimble thought. *Altogether!*

Then he thought less and ran more. He bobbed and weaved through the alleyway. He ducked and bounded around stalls. Merchandise hit the streets. Trashcans were sent rolling. Dogs growled and stray cats hissed. He skittered around corners, climbed a fence or two and almost got caught, not by the law, but in a labyrinth of linen hung out to dry. It was a hoot and a half for the watching townsfolk.

For his part, Thimble was mostly confused. He hadn't even got any loot on him, and now he was on the run. Moments like this made him question his line of work. And also… his identity.

"Stop right there, dwarf! *Dwarf! Stop!*"

CHAPTER 2

Thirst Things First

Speaking of dwarves…

In the same town, three lanes away – at the corner of a tiny square where the Fullfarrel Thoroughfare crossed Thinglefang Street, just opposite the local temple and next to a big fancy dolphin-shaped fountain – a grungy door was set in a no-less-grungy sandstone building. Both, building and door, would have looked altogether inconspicuous if it weren't for the fellow leaning against the wall. And no, a dwarf he was not. He was tall. Also black-maned, square-shouldered and bare-chested. A brawny fellow.

But if one were to get past the guy, one would come across a flight of stony stairs spiralling down, down, and farther down still into a nebulous dimness, into a dive well deserving of its name. With a bit of patience, one would be able to make out glimmers of candlelight seeping through the wall of smoke, marking tables scattered all over the place. And *there*, nursing a tankard of dark ale in the farthest corner, sat Bormph. A stout, keg-chested, red-haired exemplar of, yes, dwarfkind.

Bormph was *not* part of the DWUM, the notorious Dwarven Underground Movement – in fact, he didn't even know what it was supposed to be moving toward. In this particular dwarf's thinking, advocating a dwarven agenda aboveground would rather make you part of an "aboveground movement" anyway. Not that Bormph wanted to be part of any such group. He was a lone mover. If he wasn't moving, he was mostly an ale-nursing, sitting dwarf. A simple fellow who preferred a sharp axe over politics, and shiny, chinking coins over all that up-and-coming rustling papery nonsense.

Bormph shifted in his chair, turning his tankard around and around. He was twitching like a dwarf maiden who had just spotted the first evidence of fluff growing on her upper lip. Anxiety and excitement were both giving him a hard time, sentiments Bormph didn't even know could be combined.

He cleared his throat. "Thing is, I'm new to this."

"Likewise," slurred a hoarse voice somewhere in front of him, emanating from a wraith-like figure.

The candlelight tried its best to illuminate the two of them, but wasn't very convincing. A gnarled hand peeled itself out of a frayed robe sleeve and felt its way towards the nearest mug. Once it got ahold of the glass, the stranger raised it to his scraggly grey beard and gulped it down.

"You got handed that leaflet too?" the dwarf asked the robed fellow, and the other nodded. "Says here: 'Inspired by the Prince himself.' Naturally, I was curious as to what he was up to this time, our royal basket case." He underlaid it with a nervous cackle. It has to be said that one rarely hears nervous cackles from dwarves, and for good reason. "So I said to myself, 'Well, why not? What's there to lose?' Looks as though like-minded people are out there, so, you know, I might as well see if, and how, and with whom, and well…" Bormph ran out of words. He was more a man of action.

The fellow on the other side of the table nodded along. He was a bit difficult to read in the half darkness, especially with his eyes well hidden under the broad brim of his pointy hat.

"Anyway… want to give this a try?" Bormph straightened up.

"I'm all yours," returned the other, leaning a tad to the right, as if this position contributed significantly to keeping the world in balance.

More beer and another shot arrived for Mr Greycloak. The barwench's gaze went back and forth between the two, winking alternately at each of them and waggling her eyebrows as she collected the used glasses. Her red lips curled upwards. Then her hips sashayed back towards the bar.

"How does this all work?" the pointy-hatter asked from the shadows, disrupting the dwarf's straying thoughts. He reached for the shot in front of him, and missed. He closed one eye to eliminate the dancing glass, reached out again, and looked a little happier when he caught the remaining one.

The dwarf indicated the back of the menu. "They've… uh… prepared questions. To… erm… help us along."

"Very queer… But s'alright with me. What's they wanna know?"

"'Name'," read the dwarf, then answered himself. "Bormph. Not to brag, but I'm Bormph of Clan Shumgulth." Pride coloured his voice. "Second-born of Sommghalt the Steady, in the line of the Sculpting Stonebeaters of Swoth."

"Good for you, beating those stones and everything," Mr Greycloak said in a congratulatory voice. "I'm…

Winewing." The geezer paused and thought some more on that. "No, no… It's… Wingvain, I guess? Well, I'll get back to you on that one." Whinewaeyn paused again. "Oh, and if you've got to know: I haven't beaten any stones yet. 'S it required?"

"Um… no. Next… 'Age'. Pushing a hundred and forty on my side. You?"

"Ah, I'm not pushing anything anymore, stonebeater. Shouldn't lift either, that's what the healer says. 'S my back." Whinewaeyn pressed the shot of liquor against his facial area, fumbling around to find an opening.

"I see, right." Bormph's fingers drummed on the table. "Well, let's make this a little quicker. 'Race'," he rushed to the next question. "Now guess what? I'm a dwarf."

"Thought as much, to be honest. Regular human here. Never fancied a change."

Bormph added that answer to his collection of doubts. "And… 'Describe yourself.' So… As for my assets, well, I'm the muscular type. Strength, endurance, that's my thing. Also, I'm in it for the money. There, I've said it. So sue me."

"Sue… erm… suit yourself," slurred Whinewaeyn. "I do… Now, what was it? The whizzy kind. Yup. Call me a wizard, if you want. Not a *lizard*" – he raised a cautionary forefinger – "but a wizard, mind you! Entirely different thing. I do stuff with staffs."

Bormph was already at the next item. "'Tell each other when you discovered that you were g—'" His breath choked off. He must have read that wrong. When he started again, it didn't go any better, though. A quick scan of the questions further down made him baulk even more. He stared at the mage, a lump rising in his throat. "Whdd…g."

The old man looked at him, owl-eyed. "Wh-d-d-g?" he asked back, tentatively.

The dwarf read some more, to himself this time. The half darkness helped obscure a sudden redness taking over his features, rivalling the ginger hair.

"Now this is awkward…" he mumbled, his eyes darting here and there. He couldn't help but notice a few things around him now: two bald-headed blokes sitting at the next table, gazing dreamily at each other as they sipped their colourful cocktails; a table further away a feisty fellow caressed the hand of… a not-so-feisty a fellow; and from the bench at the other end of the room, a handsome young squire right now subjected him to an extra-slow blink…

Bormph's chair scraped back. The dwarf bounded to his feet. For a brief moment his panicked eyes met those of the barwench, who beamed back at him, like a beacon from a trusted shore, as she wiped down the counter. When she turned to tap more beer, darkness descended on him again and he became aware of at least two dozen pairs of eyes on him! *Male* eyes! Eyes eyeing him. Eyeing him up, and down, and all around…

"Listen, you filthy old codger!" The dwarf's hand shot forward, clutched the wizard by the collar and gave him a good shaking. "I'm not that kind of guy! *I. AM. NOT!*"

"No?" It was a weird thing to hear, apparently, and the rashness of it threw the old mage off. As he endured some further shaking, he tried to figure out what kind of guy the dwarf was supposed to be, and then, based on that, what kind of guy he wasn't.

Bormph backed off again. Was the wizard as clueless as he'd been? He took a longer pull than usual from his tankard, ignoring the piercing stares he felt directed at him. He leaned forward and pulled the wizard closer.

"This… place…" he said, as low as he could manage. "It's not… what it appears to be."

"N-oh?" Whinewaeyn hiccoughed.

"No!"

"Threep-throlly-thrum-throb, my good dwarf! How would you even disguise such a thing? Any idea what it… *is?*" The wizard cocked his head and looked down his nose at his red-bearded companion as if he had been challenged to answer a trick question. A wild guess popped into his mind: "Is it… an enchanted forest or something?" He swung round to investigate the potential trees nearby and almost slid from his seat. "What tipped you off, stonebeater? If it's an enchantment, it's a damn good one. How about we try a counterspell? Where's my staff?"

"Listen!" hissed the dwarf. "What do you think this place is, mage? *Why* are you here?"

"Um… Same reason as you?"

"Answer, wizzer!"

"Er… Looking for men, no?"

"Men, eh?"

"For dungeon action, that sort of thing." Whinewaeyn swayed gently, but tried to keep his eyes fixed on the dwarf.

The mage wasn't helping. The idea that he might have stumbled into "dungeon action with men" made Bormph's hair bristle, beard included. This was getting even too bizarre for a battle-trained warrior who thought he'd seen everything before.

"For ad-ad-adventuring?" Whinewaeyn put forward as a final offer. He gave the dwarf an obtuse look.

"Hold on..." Patting his pockets, Bormph's clammy hand fished out a piece of paper and shoved it under the wizard's nose. "This is the thing you've come for, right?"

Having trouble finding your sort of fellow to party with?
Looking for a partner for those special adventures?
Starting to get a bit desperate?
Then visit us at the newly opened
Adventurous Companions*.*
Your new favourite pub to meet up with the likes of you.
No questions asked.

"Why, yes! And *I* didn't ask any questions," the mage threw back at him in reproach. "*You* did, stonebeater!"

Bormph shook himself. "This is no place to find yourself a party for some good old sword and sorcery venture, you old sot! It's a dating affair with an advertisement problem! Can't you see, wizzer? Look! Have you counted the broads in here?"

"Nah," slurred Whinewaeyn. "What a cartload of balderdash you're peddling, dwarf! My eyes are all open, and there's not... a... sing..." Realization came slow, but it made it. Romance was high, he found, the lights low, smoke clouds thick, and – apart from the wench who had served them – there were no other women to be found. The mage's bloodshot eyes widened. "Noo-*ooh!*"

"Yes!"

The old geezer grabbed the mug in front of him and knocked it back in one go. He managed it without missing this time, but only because the dwarf's tankard happened to be in the same place as his imaginary one. Shreds of bawdy songs swirled through the wizard's head, songs belted out by sweaty, muscular men swaying to and fro, arm in arm.

Yet there was still more in store for table four.

The door banged open, and a green blob-like figure came whirling through it. The blob scurried close to floor level like a Thakuthian sand devil, short arms flailing, cape and curls flying, heading for a corner, where the devilish thing dove under a table and pulled the lower end of a wide robe over whatever passed for its head.

"Ahem..." Whinewaeyn let out.

He shifted uneasily in his seat. Then experience set in. In his inebriated condition he was used to seeing things that others contested, and so he reverted to his tried and tested solution: pretending that nothing had happened. Only in this case, the supposed figment of his imagination reared its fuzzy head one last time, wheezed and puffed, and went "Shhh!" shortly before it vanished again. Up close, it looked nothing at all like a sand devil. Sand devils had horns, not curls, and no sand devil he'd ever made acquaintance with had worn a cape.

Two seconds later, the city watch showed up.

"Nobody move!"

Temporarily, this had the opposite effect; unrest rippled from table to table. Illegal substances were taken care of – drowned in beer, swallowed or slipped into a mate's pocket.

"Nobody... MOVE!" Sergeant Broadtoe blared again.

Then movement ceased.

Constable Nives, a bit out of breath, laid out the facts. A thug was on the loose. A dangerous fellow from the Dwarven Underground Movement for all they knew. Sought for all kinds of heinous crimes short of murder. He'd probably shaved his beard to disguise himself.

There was a murmur of surprise, irritation and apprehension.

"Strange place, and strange games they have here," tutted Whinewaeyn. "Grown-up, uniformed men playing hide-and-seek!"

Bormph wasn't sure what to make of it. Not so much about the men in uniforms, but more about a fellow dwarf hiding from the authorities. A dwarf in need was a dwarf to heed.

"I *think*… I saw something," Whinewaeyn whispered to him. The wizard leaned to the side, pulled up his robe and found a quivering Thimble underneath. "Nah, you're not a dwarf!" Whinewaeyn established. "If you are, they haven't fed you properly, and your face hair's all fallen off."

Thimble snarled, "I'm *not* here!" and pulled the end of the robe back over his head.

"'S in denial," Whinewaeyn reported back to Bormph. "Even about being here. Now that's a hell of a confused fellow! He needs help."

"Don't—"

"Guaaaaards!" yelled the mage.

Then he got kicked in the shin.

The howl that escaped him was shrill and intense and turned a few heads, the watchmen's among them. They eyed the wizard slipping from his bench, reeling in agony.

"What's going on here?" The moustached official clomped closer. "What's with him?"

"Badgers on broomsticks! You blind, eye of the law? He's hurt!" Bormph rearranged his face into an imitation of a concerned expression. "Has a penchant for drinking, see?" He leapt to his feet and pulled the frail wizard out from under the table. "Now you burst in and yell at him, and the poor devil topples over and harms himself!"

"Ag-ag-ag-…" Whinewaeyn produced, segueing into a wail when Bormph's hand began to pat his lower leg. At the same time, the dwarf pointed at the mage's head.

"Owww!" Whinewaeyn shrieked again.

"See? Fell on his head in the excitement! There's blood in his hair. Not pretty, that!"

"You're making this up!" Sergeant Broadtoe alleged. All he saw was a dwarf. And they were after one.

"I'm telling you, he needs a healer, quick!" Compassion almost oozed from Bormph's ears.

The mention of blood was an exaggeration. There *was* some liquid on the scraggly-bearded geezer, stemming from ale abuse – an outrage in itself as far as the dwarf was concerned. But when Constable Nives stooped over to inspect the thrashing wizard's head, the difference was impossible to discern in the dim candlelight. *Guarding 101* hadn't specified a proper course of action in case of unrelated grisly incidents interfering with standard policing procedures.

"There's a temple on the other side of the street," the barmaid suggested helpfully, proving she was as well informed as she was well formed.

"Ow-ow-owwww…"

"I'll get him over there then," Bormph offered.

"Halt!" bawled Broadtoe, in keeping with handbook instructions. He gave the dwarf a once-over. "You don't happen to have anything to do with that shaven DWUM guy we're after, do you?"

Bormph stumped closer. "Look," he started, "any decent dwarf wears a beard." Then he pointed at *his* beard to show that he was decent, beard-wise, and that whoever they were looking for apparently wasn't. He reasoned with them further that his beard, to which he was still attached, had been around for more than an hour already, and the barwench was charming enough to corroborate his account. Lastly, Bormph reminded the guardsmen that even if he were an accomplice, he would flat out deny it, but *because* he brought this very point up of his own accord, he couldn't possibly be involved – for if he *had* had anything to do with whatever they were looking for, he'd only complicate matters by mentioning a thing like that, and who'd want to create unnecessary complications? "Well, I certainly don't," Bormph concluded, and the guards simultaneously scratched their heads at that.

"Besides," Bormph added with nonchalance, "if you keep discussing the art of beard-braiding with me for any longer, you'll have the wizard on your conscience." He let his argument simmer for a bit. "You know, if the poor fellow checks out here and now, there'll be questions, lots of them, and paperwork and overtime. Oh, and guilt. It's the guilt especially that will gnaw at you for the rest of your lives. Now, I could help you out there and shift the guy for everyone's sake, or we play it your way, slow and deadly. Just saying."

Sergeant Broadtoe and Constable Nives briefly exchanged glances. "Alright, then. Shove off, dwarf, and do what you must! We've got work to do."

Bormph dipped his helmeted head and let a few coppers tumble onto the table. "May the Stonefather watch over you!" And then he was off, wizard in tow, the oversized robe providing proper floor-sweeping padding for his old bones.

Further down the corridor, well out of sight of the bar-room, a mint-green figure crawled out from its hiding place. Close to suffocation and riding a wave of nausea, Thimble gasped for air. His eyes met the glare of the stout dwarf.

"Hey, what the—" Bormph planted his hands on his hips. "You aren't a dwarf *at all!* Not even a shaven one!"

"Sorry," Thimble said, and sneezed. He reached into his back pocket and pulled out a handkerchief to polish his nose. Then he introduced himself.

"Name's Bormph," grunted Bormph in response, as if he'd been named to match his grunt. "And now you can tell me why the heck you're running like an ox from the slaughterer."

"It's all a big, big misunderstanding, I swear! I'm nothing but a petty thief, honest!"

Bormph wrinkled his nose. There was something troubling in a rogue pledging honesty, more so if he was being honest about it.

"This time I haven't even stolen anything!"

"So the city guard is just out and about for the exercise?"

Thimble shrugged. He dusted himself off.

"And I kicked the old daft wizzer in the shin for *that?*" Bormph said.

"You what? I thought *I* kicked the wizard in the shin!"

Dwarf and halfling traded uncomfortable glances.

"Ow-ow-ow-owww…" Whinewaeyn squirmed. Then his tone and message abruptly changed. "You lousy savages, good-for-nothings, scourge of the elderly, you…" There was more of this sort, a *lot* more. In fact, the mage was only beginning to rummage through his treasury of verbal abuse, from which he dredged up quite a few gems. They radiated in all their abusive glory.

"Rants just fine," Bormph diagnosed. "Can't be life-threatening,"

"But maybe we should still get him to the temple, after all?"

The dwarf growled. Everything considered, leaving the old geezer on the doorstep, drunk and shin-kicked – twice! – bordered on impolite. Even a petty thief and a surly dwarf could agree on that.

So they hoisted the mage up, propped him between their shoulders and hauled him off again, his feet dragging behind. The wizard wasn't really built for a jolly drag by a dwarf half his size, or a halfling with not even half of the dwarf's strength. It wasn't the shin-friendliest way of transport either, judging by the wizard's howls, and when the three climbed the steps out of the dive they'd all accidently found themselves in, they made a rather pathetic sight.

Out in the fresh air again, they took a rest: Bormph and Thimble from dragging and Whinewaeyn from whining.

The beefy fellow was still there, daunting like an obelisk, arms crossed and a sword dangling from his belt. At first, he didn't seem to take much notice of the two vertically challenged newcomers and the ailing mage glaring up at him. His stare ahead was dutiful and grave.

Bormph exhaled a couple of times to catch his breath, and his eyes climbed the giant's imposing build. "You the bouncer for this questionable dive?" he ventured.

"Bounce... er...?" The barbarian twisted his face. "Ramrok no bounce. Ramrok stand still." Then he went back to focusing on doing just that, keeping his two feet firmly on the ground.

"Ramrok, eh?" Bormph wiped his forehead. "That your name? Or are you talking about somebody else?"

"Ramrok name. Son of Remrok, son-son of Ramrek."

"Not very creative name-givers up north, eh?"

The question was met by a blank, sullen-eyed stare.

"Waiting for someone?"

"Uh-huh," the barbarian muttered. A moment of what might have been reflection went by, after which the giant bent forward and took a closer look at the dwarf. "You not him?"

"Me? Him? Who'd that be?" Bormph gave back, surprised.

"Market man give me this. Job thing." The giant pulled a piece of paper from his belt and handed it over.

Bormph recognized the leaflet right away. Someone had scribbled a note on it: *Show up at the entrance near the fountain later this morning. Bring your mighty sword!!* The last two words were underlined.

Bormph looked at Thimble, and Thimble at Bormph, and then both of them looked at the broad-as-a-barn-door fellow pushing his eyebrows together as he gaped back at them.

"Sellsword, huh? Well, you've brought your two-hander," Bormph noted, inspecting the massive weapon dangling from the barbarian's side. "Good boy!"

"Hrmph." The barbarian's chiselled face brightened a mite from the statuesque expression he had perfected while waiting.

Bormph slipped Thimble a telling glance. "Dumb as a doorknob…" he muttered under his breath. But instead of a chuckle, Thimble gave him a strange look back, which made him rethink. He hesitated. "Erm…" He had to get something straight, *very* straight. "Just so you know… We, I mean the wizard and me, the both of us, we were in there purely for business relations. Nothing else."

"Sure," Thimble whispered back. "Mum's the word. I'd be more worried about the age difference… You must be over a hundred!"

"*Other* business!" the dwarf snarled. "It was just… an ill-chosen location, halfling. That's all there is to it!"

Thimble nodded, but backed off. "Certainly."

Bormph turned back to the barbarian. The guy had hands like a pair of cymbals and pecs as sturdy as steel plates. His two-hander alone exceeded the dwarf in height.

"Say, Ramrok," he asked him, "if *I* had a job for you, would you do us the honour of carrying our poor friend over there?"

Thimble glared at the dwarf.

"A job for your *sword*," Bormph clarified, knocking on the blade. "That one."

The giant looked at the dwarf as though the half-size was as slow as a sack of potatoes.

"Carry wizzer, get job," the dwarf simplified. He pointed at the archway on the other side of the square, framed by two white marble columns. Rows of cypresses extended to the left and right in front of the building housing Novotroth's sanctuary.

"Carry wizzy. Get job. For sword," the barbarian repeated. "This one." He knocked on his weapon. "Ramrok like."

And because everybody liked it so much, Bormph snatched up the wizard's hat and staff, Ramrok picked up the mage like a bundle of brushwood and, with Bormph in the lead, they started for the temple.

Thimble overtook the barbarian. "What job would that be, dwarf?" His curiosity was piqued.

"Want one too?" Bormph's eyes swivelled sideways. "I'm putting a party together. Adventure stuff. *Traditional* adventure," he hastened to add. "For fame and fortune, gold and glamour, that sort of thing. Anything with treasure involved." A gleam shimmered in his eyes.

Could be a harmless daydream, could be madness, Thimble thought.

"So far I've only got Mr Muscle; but the way I see it, you're already on the run and looking for a change of scenery."

Thimble considered himself a rogue in training, but he wouldn't mention that fact first thing in a job interview – maybe not last thing either, or at any point in between. He had lost two mentors so far: one due to the teacher's short temper, the other to the law during a botched two-man operation, and let's leave it at that. Thimble's breakthrough hadn't come yet, but he appreciated a vision, and someone who'd tell him what vision that was.

"I'm in."

"Very well then, halfling," Bormph said, and in a low mutter added, "Now all we need is a wizard other than that Whineling fellow. Someone who knows a spell or two, and can remember his own name."

CHAPTER 3

Heavenly Helping Hands

The scent of lavender wafted between the columns. It felt like the refreshing surge of an ocean compared to the sweaty den of vice they had just left. Even Bormph was struck by the contrast as he ambled quietly through the light-flooded halls. Thimble, on the other hand, observed the welcoming smiles of the virginal dazzlers flitting about. What went on in the head of the big fellow galumphing behind them and doing all the work was anyone's guess, but some things must have been hard to miss even for a savage – like the fact that Novotroth, or "The Dancer" as the fifth god of the Hyleian pantheon was known, preferred his Hands of Mercy female and able-bodied. *Cleansing rituals were true charity,* Thimble thought.

Already he had spotted a particular exemplar of the blonde species gracing the premises, a radiant creature in a figure-hugging bluish linen, a sun-sky combination on two long legs. At which point, an imaginary voice weighed in. *Only an hour ago, you swore off all things blonde. For-ev-er. No take-backsies. Remember?* The voice sounded rather thin, though. Almost unintelligible. Ignorable, one might say.

Thimble gawked.

The blonde embodied everything he wasn't: female, elven, tall, supple, and just the right amount of exotic for a halfling. That hair alone! It was a single, flowing entity of golden silk, dropping deep onto her back, where it swirled and swayed as if it had a life of its own. Every gazelle-like move she made was a far cry from the lousy rogue crashing through crates. When he caught what he thought was a hint of a smile in his direction, he'd already picked up the sound of wedding bells... Then again, maybe that was just because an actual wedding was taking place in a side wing. Whether the peals were real or not, it was on the barbarian and bare-chested eye-catcher that the gaze of daintiness incarnate came to rest.

Thimble glowered up at the giant, decidedly unsmiling. She wasn't just looking at the wizard in his arms, was she?

"This way..." The blonde breezed past him like a fleeting dream. Before he knew it, another Hand of Mercy had taken over, a raven-haired priestess, who ushered the party through an archway into the infirmary. Now that the blonde was gone, Thimble felt a little betrayed. *It's better that way*, said the voice in his head.

Whinewaeyn's ailing soul was put in a cot and propped up against a heap of pillows so that his ranting could continue in the utmost comfort. The raven-haired priestess wiped his alcohol-soaked beard first and went on to rub lotion on his mistreated legs. Some svaq was brought in, a gnomish sober-making concoction, and the wizard gulped it down like booze. One slight disappointment for bystanders was that the Hand of Mercy skipped their famous healing dance. She had questions, though.

"So... what happened? Who did this?"

"Long story." Bormph said.

"Uh-huh," Thimble agreed. "*Very* long."

A strong hint had been dropped to leave it at that. But in sanctuaries like Novotroth's, where time comes to a standstill, long stories are all the excitement.

"Go on," the priestess said, set to listen while salving and swathing away.

"Well, it was like this…" No doubt, Bormph was about to tweak the account a little, when—

"They kicked me!" the wizard squealed. "Both of them!"

He followed up with a fresh verbal excursion, which became so intense that the priestess had to call for help.

The halfling's heart skipped a beat in his tiny chest when the blonde reappeared, only to sink like a millstone a moment later. While he'd learned the fragrant beauty was a mind-smoother, she had no doubt overheard the news that he happened to be a mage-kicker, and no brownie points were likely to be earned from that.

"Stay away, you two," she ordered, and began to rub Whinewaeyn's temples.

This calmed him down a bit. Already the cussing showed subtle hints of increased sophistication – like references to their specific races and sizes. The mage slurred less too, thanks to the svaq. Not that it made the insults more printable, but there was some headway and, after a time, his swear-word repertoire was exhausted.

"Why would you kick this poor, poor fellow?" the elf demanded, looking daggers at Bormph and Thimble. "Look at him! He couldn't hurt a fruit fly!"

There was a telltale pause. No short answer suggested itself without mentioning a thief running from the law, and meeting up in a gay bar.

"Oh, he *could* very well hurt a fly if the fly was asking for it," Bormph said instead. "I'd stake my beard that he swatted a few gnats in the broiling nights last summer. Don't be fooled by his guileless looks. I'm sure he'd go for a beetle or something much larger too, if need be. He *is,* after all" – he went for the broader picture – "a mighty wizard!"

Bormph waggled the old man's staff and held his pointy hat up as if to imply that the frail geezer on the bed was the next Ghargetram the Gruesome. What he kept to himself, however, was that all he'd seen the old bag of bones actually do was make liquor disappear. But to the dwarf's surprise, the mention of the old drunk being a wizard elicited a somewhat magical reaction nevertheless…

"Archmagus?" the raven-haired priestess cried out all of a sudden. "Is that you?" And then – to everyone's bafflement – the young lass hugged the old boozer! Just like that.

The wizard's eyes opened. They were open already, but he had been too busy grousing to do any proper looking. So he opened them again, this time for real. "Why, if it isn't… Amjelle!" he croaked, tears welling up and coursing down his crinkly cheeks.

"Archmagus!" sobbed the healer. "Master Whinewaeyn!"

"Amjelle!" the mage croaked again. "Amjelle, dear!"

"I didn't recognize you at all with your unkempt beard and those tatty clothes…"

"Oh, and I couldn't see… because of… because of all the pain!"

Even the Fervid Fiddlers of Fay Street would have been no match for the rampant sentimentality sweeping the infirmary. Turned out, the old geezer had been the lass's tutor a few years back, in her time at the Studyarium of All Things Magical.

"I quit elemental magic to join the Order of the Four Chalices," Amjelle said to the wizard. "I thought being a cleric would be more fulfilling."

But the fact he'd been her tutor was only one part of the surprise. The other was that the priestess had called her former teacher "Archmagus", and one really ought not to use such a word lightly. Not unless the subject in question indeed had some substantial arcane magic up his grimy sleeves…

"Did you two hear the same thing I heard?" Bormph mumbled to Thimble and the brawn-manifestation while healer and mage hugged it out.

"If you heard what I heard," said Thimble, "then yes, I guess."

"…" thought the barbarian, agreeing in principle.

"They threw me out of the Studyarium," Whinewaeyn told them when the healer pressed for his story. His head was clearing more and more under the svaq's influence, and the slurring was on the retreat. "The Grand Wizards' Assembly retracted my teaching license and took away my best wands! Good grief! All for doing my work! I was researching in my study, working on an *Explosion* spell, when—"

"An *Explosion* spell?" the healer interrupted. "Hasn't that been done? Isn't that just a" – Amjelle searched for the word – "you know, an… explosion?"

"No, it's not. Oh no! That's what *they* want you to think, my dear," Whinewaeyn said through gnashed teeth. "I was looking for a spell *meant* to cause an explosion, whereas all known spells that go by the book are just spells that don't try very hard. Every amateur can cast explosions! Even the great spellweavers and scholars like Agheltraph II or Mashin Drorkt messed up proper spells to get a decent blast. It's not right! They're all fizzles with a whoomph!"

"So... you wanted to cast a proper one?"

"I certainly did!"

"And?"

"Why, it worked! With bells and whistles. Blew the roof off the Studyarium."

"I heard about that!" Thimble chipped in. "Some crazed—"

"Blew the bloody roof off!" Bormph threw his hands up.

"It was all *proper!*" Whinewaeyn insisted. "Worked much better than I could ever have anticipated! And what did I get? Not so much as a 'Thank you!' Their loss." The wizard clenched a feeble fist and thrust it in the air towards the Studyarium. He was still a bit disoriented, so he tried a couple of directions to make sure he got it right at least once. At last, drained of energy, he dropped back on his cushion.

A smile brushed over Amjelle's lips.

"Ah, let's face it," the geezer said, lying back with his eyes on the ceiling. "I'm kaput."

Amjelle reached out to pat the wizard's wrist. "Oh, you shouldn't say such a thing, Master Whinewaeyn!"

Glassy eyes fixed the young healer. "Thought I'd do something that matters now instead. Join a party, maybe," the wizard mumbled, "and go on an adventure... see the world, travel as far as Land's End... make myself useful one way or another, one last time, and *be someone!*" A glimmer of something larger than a rambling mage reflected in his gaze, something equally indeterminable as it was grand.

His sobriety was almost frightening, Bormph found. As a dwarf he had been raised to keep a stony face, whatever may come, but now he gulped, suppressing a tear. The wizard almost sounded like someone who hadn't deserved a double-kick to the shin.

Whinewaeyn stretched his battered leg. "You know, ever since I was a little wizling, I've imagined myself doing something you read about in the myths. Something like outwitting a darkmage, prying a mighty artifact from the clutches of some vile beast or bustling from a crumbling building as I" – he paused for effect – "save the world!"

"A bit clichéd, no?" Bormph muttered, rubbing his eye.

"Anything better on *your* bucket list?" Thimble turned up his nose at the dwarf – a little bit, at least.

There was an awkward silence.

"Well, what's keeping you, Archmagus?" Amjelle asked, breaking it. "Go out and do it! Now is as good a time as any."

"Just look at me, dear!" Whinewaeyn waved the thought away. "I'm a wreck! A wash-out! A has-been, a might-have-been and a never-will-be! The world doesn't need saving anyway. And if it did, it's a young man's adventure. Someone else will have to find the few lost treasures that are still left: the Rings of the Zingerlings, the Belt of Quaelt or Knoth's Collapsible Staff of Enlightenment! Still… wouldn't it be great to pull that one out whenever you feel, you know, dumb and dusted?"

"It's *done* and dusted," Amjelle said.

"Is it now?" Whinewaeyn feebly turned his head. "If we only had that staff…" Eyes squinted, he looked into the distance, but his thousand-yard stare only got as far as the infirmary wall, a mere couple of feet away. What had started out as a misty-eyed gaze thus became much more limited and mundane. It was weirdly fitting, though, given what he'd been saying. And a little sad.

Amjelle put her hand on her former master's shoulder. "Archmagus! You *have* to follow your calling. Better late than never. Look at me – when I realized that elemental magic wasn't for me, I quit. I walked away and became a Hand of Mercy."

"How's that working out for you?"

"Well, as you can see, I do something useful with my life now."

"Is that all you ever dreamed of? Being locked up here in the temple? Rubbing ointments on dumb and dusted drunks?"

"I…"

"Ah. You hesitate, my dear." The mage coughed the cough of a wise man, who endured old age like a ramshackle hut puts up with the wind sighing in its rafters. "I know you well enough, and I always thought you were more of the adventurous type."

"And what am I supposed to do with that? See the world *before* I go into healing?"

"Anything else to see besides the world? You might as well start there."

Now the tides had turned. The question appeared to make the healer drunk with emotion. She brushed a strand of long hair back behind her ear and stared at the mage with wide eyes, a bit lost and helpless. "It's not all roses being a daughter of Novotroth, true. And you're right. I left the Academy to see the temple, just to do something else, but… I haven't seen the world yet."

"So go together," said the golden-haired elf on caressing duty.

A flash of amusement crossed Amjelle's face. Then her brow furrowed again. But, before she could say another word, the elf beat her to it.

"Can't have the wizard go alone. *Vallanía vallanát,* as we wood elves say, *náh macadáns.* 'The Eternal Dreameress dreams. But She's not the one to choose.' So choose. You're blessed with choice. Choose your heart, Am. The Dreameress dreamed you one."

"A mage and a healer?" Amjelle's lips turned up in a smirk.

"And if you need an archer when hunting for ring-things or whatever, I can hold a bow," the elf said. "I left the woods to learn about the other races, but I can do that anywhere."

Amjelle's smirk widened. "You want to learn about foul-breathed zombies, Sylthia?"

"Half as bad with a healer around and some rose petal spray in the back pocket."

Amjelle broke into a giggle. "Now, what kind of party would *that* be? An old geezer and us two for support? That's dodgy!"

The elf tittered along, and the snicker travelled back and forth playfully between the two of them until even the wizard was infected and snorted with wheezing laughter. The others present thought this was no joking matter.

"Ahem…" came from the back of the room amid the merriment.

The giggling trickled away.

Bormph stomped forward. "You know, if you need strong men to protect you pretty lot, there's a bunch *right* here. In fact, we've been meaning to put together a party anyway. It's only that events got in the way." The dwarf's callused hand stroked his long ginger beard as if to make him more presentable. He stuck his chin up, put his chest out, and motioned to Ramrok to join him. It was more chin down for the towering barbarian, but his steely chest didn't need any special introduction. And Thimble? *Fair maiden protection?* he thought. *I'm all for that!* And so he scurried to the barbarian's side to complete the picture, even if it ended up notably uneven, with two half-pints – one broad, one thin – flanking a mobile, ceiling-scraping battle station.

"I'm with the dwarf," Thimble announced, in the hope that some of his neighbours' presentability would rub off on him.

The blonde elf eyed the halfling. "You're trained to wield an axe too, little one? You don't look it."

"Ah… erm… no," Thimble sheepishly shuffled his feet. He clasped and unclasped his tiny hands. "Not exactly." He was a firm believer in quotas, though, when it came to partying. Basic balance in group composition was important. Like, for each heaven-sent creature there ought to be one male halfling – and in this case, that ought to be him. "I-I would be the one to handle more… delicate affairs," he got out in the huskiest voice he could muster. It was meant to stress his sensitive traits, but the red glow in his cheeks immediately betrayed such ambitions. "I-I have an eye for things and people. That… that subtle h-ha-hand—"

"Rogue material," Bormph shortened Thimble's embarrassing flirtation attempts. "Question answered? Now, how about it, ladies?"

"Those two kicked me in the shins!" the wizard croaked defiantly, if a little more muted than before. "Both at the same time!"

"I footed the bill for your booze too, gramps. Besides, it was only meant to be *one* kick," Bormph maintained, "which is only half as bad, considering."

"We're much better at kicking monster asses!" Thimble blurted out. "You'll see!"

Ramrok grunted, rolling the thought over in his head. How big were those donkey-monsters? And how would a halfling kick one? But wherever they were, however they had come into this world, whatever they were up to, Ramrok vowed to himself, he'd be game kicking them out of it.

"How about it, Archmagus?" Amjelle quit shin-rubbing and put the ointment on the nightstand, with a sense of finality. "It was your idea to begin with. A party is nothing without a magician."

Wise words, Thimble thought. A piece of wisdom that applied to children's birthday parties and adventuring alike.

An air of the unknown, the scent of peril and discovery, filled the infirmary. Gazes wandered from person to person, over beards – unkempt and grey or braided and red; over tiny facial details – like the dimples in the halfling's rosy cheeks, or the dreamy healer's eyes, or the remarkable blandness in the barbarian's expression; over tight and stalwart masculine chests, and their round and firm counterparts; and over a concerned crease cutting into the elf's forehead as she caught a brazen halfling checking her out.

"Ahem!"

Thimble snapped out of his daze.

"Well?" prompted Bormph.

"Well?" It went around from mouth to mouth.

"Well," said the wizard too, with a smile flaring up. "Got something else to toast with, aside from that dreadful gnomish brew?"

The elf suggested tea could substitute for spirits.

"Then make some of your finest," Whinewaeyn declared, giddy all of a sudden. "Let's drink to seal the deal." He raised his mug with the last drops of svaq. "We need gear, my friends… horses, tents, weapons and provisions!" A surge of energy gripped his old bones, recalling the excitement of a teenager at his first romp-a-domp dance with the village beauty. "We might follow up on that precious tip I got the other day, after all…" He tapped the side of his nose with a finger as his eyes shifted left and right. His voice lowered. "It's about a cursed crypt not too far away. Ancient and untouched. Needs cleansing. We could clear out the unholy undead in exchange for an artifact or two. What do you think?"

Bormph issued a little grumble, if only to himself. He had hoped for something more original. But how many treasure hunts started big? The most important thing was how they ended.

"Alright, then," he said. "Let's take it from there. It's a fine day for adventuring."

Yeah, right.

The sky outside had other plans. As if on command, the picturesque idyll of perfect azure dotted with errant white tufts gave way to a much less agreeable grey. The clouds stocked up in numbers, flocked together, and the sky grumbled and churned as rainclouds rolled in over Weaverring, their peevishness mounting. A cool breeze sprang up. At first, only a hushed windy whisper snuck through the town's crannies, but before long the boughs were creaking too. Banners flapped on masts. Crows struggled in flight.

Tap, tap, tappety-tap… Scattered raindrops dripped gingerly on the shingles. A peal of thunder ba-boomed and the rain's pace changed to a steady *pitter-patter*, drumming on the roofs. Soon enough, the water came down in sheets, pelting the cobbles, sweeping through the streets. What started out as a bit of wind was on its way to a full-blown gale, which rattled on window casements, sent parasols flying and blew flurries of extra freshness up unsuspecting skirts. By the time the hailstones joined in, there was nobody out in Weaverring's alleyways anymore. Lightning flashed; thunder rumbled.

The abandoned market stalls resounded with a *clinkety-clonk*, and the caravan down the street returned its own version. *Clankety-clunk*, the trashcans rolling about answered, and occasionally they *clonkety-clinked*.

Even the flowerbeds around the village fountain contributed to the clinks and clonks, along with the fondly tended greens and rockeries in the well-off town quarters, since the occasional garden gnome peeked out between the rose patches.

Gnomes were, no doubt, the latest craze. So much so that one didn't even require a garden to have one around. They were a welcome addition to the family: handy, quiet, jolly companions, rain or shine. They never talked back, weren't moody and, unlike the house cat, wouldn't insist on being fed. Hence, more than a few balustrades were decorated with gnomes too, where they spread merriment by just being around. Quite a few had even made a career for themselves inside, acting as bookends. Most commonly, however, they stood on the doorstep, looking out at...

Actually, a certain Mr Gnome at the last house at Lame Crane's Lane wasn't looking out at anything anymore. He couldn't, for the simple reason that he was no longer in the spot where he'd stood for the past three years or so. Same thing with that lute-playing dwarf lookalike at Bards' Park, and the potter's otherwise ever-present little friend who used to reside next to the rose bushes. Gone, gone and... gone.

Now, when gnomes start disappearing from the potter's ground, something has to be in the air. It couldn't just be the whirlwind in the thorn trees, could it?

No, something was brewing out there, and it wasn't just the tea in the Novotroth infirmary.

CHAPTER 4

Vanishings, Visions, Vagabonds

Elsewhere, while the bad weather bothered somewhere else, carnival reigned. The place was the Zarrafandan capital, and the partying lasted long into the night.

Dimmerskeep had been aptly named a few years earlier by Prince Dymmling, when he'd been bitten by the renaming bug. Formerly known as Sagesfort, the city lay cradled between the sparkling Grand Lake to its west and the ragged Thourgethrum Mountains in the east, at whose foothills the Prince's palace was also perched. From there, it overlooked the town's sprawling sea of colourful gables, jutting steeples and twisting streets, all adding to the impression of a somewhat cobbled together townscape growing in all directions, a bit like weed, but weed with a certain charm about it.

The feast rattling the town at the moment was Mish-Clash, dedicated to the celebration of the differences between the sexes. An odd event, by all standards. The bunting and parades were only the beginning: with the passing of the hours, tempers usually began to stew, and by the time the sun went into hiding and the festive paper lanterns were lit, the rough and tumble was in full swing.

Anyone surprised to get a bloody nose during the festival surely knew very little about it.

Of course, nobody but Prince Dymmling could've had devised a thing like Mish-Clash. To give him credit, he had meant well. For the three days of the carnival, women were supposed to dress as men and men as women – an exercise intended to encourage a better understanding of the opposite sex. The festival might even have helped a smidgen in this regard if only this exchange of clothing had been decreed mandatory from the get-go. Making it optional was a recipe for disaster. The Festival of Understanding effected embarrassment, mistrust, suspicion, conjecture and accusations, combinations of which often culminated in screaming matches, bar fights and the occasional mass riot sweeping the streets. At times it was difficult to discern the parade from the brawls. One might say that the idea had got a little out of hand.

Or had it? The magic word was "reinterpretation". Reinterpretation allowed for the tumultuous scenes to be seen as a bonus, symbolic of the battle of the sexes. The scuffles livened everything up, both relationships *and* street life. It wasn't long before visitors from all over the continent wanted a piece of this unique ruckus. Redefinitions of relationships in the wake of Mish-Clash became part of the tradition, and the people embraced it. Some didn't mind a sound thrashing either, for their own reasons. So yes, Mish-Clash was fascinating, revolutionary and risqué. And so it had become a cult favourite.

Maybe the vigorous celebrations were the reason certain circumstances remained unnoticed on a night where bad weather was somewhere else.

But when sunup came…

Early in the post-Mish-Clash morning, the Prince of Zarrafanda himself shimmied out on the parapet of his palace in a sapphire-blue, tight-fitting gown, endowed with a prominent bust. Lace embroidery and sparkling jewellery covered his neck and wrists. The impossible wig would be better left unmentioned (too late now), though the scarlet lipstick smeared over the lower half of his face at least complemented the wig in terms of misguided taste. The other noteworthy thing was that the Prince – or the Princess, depending on how one wants to look at it during a festival like Mish-Clash – failed to spot the palace's east wing tower. He blinked and looked again, but found nothing of the sort.

His Royal Highness staggered back, mouthed something inaudible, rubbed one eye and then the other, turned this way and that – all of which did nothing to improve the situation.

He quickly ascertained that the tower wasn't just hiding someplace behind another edifice, nor that it had lain down, inebriated after a turbulent night. East wing towers rarely played hide-and-seek, and they didn't drink, let alone the hard stuff. Even in his current extremely hungover state, the Prince knew these things for a fact. No, the tower insisted on being outright gone. Every single brick of it. Very much unlike its western equivalent, which drew attention to a gaping lack of symmetry by being accusingly present.

"We've been robbed!" His Temporary Ladyship blared from his lipstick-mistreated mouth. "WE'VE BEEN ROBBED!"

It was enough to get some groggy townsfolk out of their beds and the nobles on their respective balconies to see what the commotion was all about. Some of them found out, in a particularly hard and abrupt manner, that they were missing something too.

Their balconies had deserted them.

Strange things had gone on all over the Princedom that night.

A shepherd by the name of Tjillmer, who had been watching his flock in the Peet Hills, could've attested to that. Had he seen a tower marching by? No, but boy, had he seen things!

The sun had already set when Tjillmer sat by the campfire, smoking stuff he'd been slipped by his friend and drinking buddy, Brand. Brand was a sorcerer's apprentice at the famous Studyarium of All Things Magical, and the shepherd was very proud to have a mage as friend. Even more so because Brand was a pioneer. He was an alchemagist.

"Wanna be part of it?" Brand had once proposed.

Tjillmer had failed to see how a humble shepherd like himself would be any help with something as important as a mage's work. But then Brand's argument had swayed him. It went like this: "Just try these magic mushrooms, and you'll see!" And ever since, Tjillmer had been smoking magical vegetables for scholarly purposes.

"Alchemagy's a brand-new way of doing magic!" Brand had explained to Tjillmer's look of incredulity. "It awakens the dormant magic in everyone, Tjilly. There's dormant magic in you too. You don't need no wands or anything. It's a spirit thing."

"Tastes funny," Tjillmer said to himself as he tried the latest patch on that fateful Mish-Clash day. These new ones produced more smoke than any he'd tried before.

After another puff, Tjillmer *saw*. He saw hills heave and dip like ocean waves, and so real was it that he gripped his crook for fear he might get washed away; he saw sheep do hoofstands, as if preparing for a travelling circus; he saw a cliff – a huge, tipsy one – turn into a kite; and he watched the night sky pull nearer to take a closer look at him. He even *heard* things he'd never heard before: trees barking, and Stinky – up to then as talkative as any other guard dog – taking a stab at advising him on romantic matters. A luminous maiden with wings dropped by too when the evening wore on, relating a story about an impending falling star, but he sent her away. After all, he was busy experimenting, and she said not to worry and that she'd try her luck with the next group of shepherds she came across.

It all made sense. Especially the barking trees. Looking back to his pre-mushroom days, Tjillmer now wondered how it could be that trees had so much bark and yet had held their tongues for so long. Maybe it was because they had no tongues. Or maybe it was because Stinky had been communicating with the wrong end all this time.

Tjillmer took a nap then, but was startled awake later in the night, roused by saliva dripping onto his face. Stinky was one of the things he awoke to. The other was a marvellous picture show: gigantic images jittered all over the horizon – images of raging seas, exotic jungles, mist-shrouded mountainsides and fields, of wyverns cruising in the air amid a flock of seagulls, and of tuna raining down on a fish cutter.

The visions flickered at a frenzied pace. They flared up like lightning, illuminating the scenery in one instant and then disappearing in the next. Instead of the rumble of thunder, there was a maniacal buzzing and humming as though the sky was full of wasps. But it wasn't. There wasn't even half a bee.

One image showed a party of six badgering through the desert, and another one appeared with a shepherd and his dog watching a canvas stretching all over the horizon, which also showed a party of six badgering through the desert. It struck Tjillmer as familiar somehow, though he couldn't quite put his finger on why.

"Very nice. 'S the perfect ending!" he barked at his dog, congratulating him on the marvellous show and shaking its paw when it was over. "That's grand, Stinky! But now I need a wink of sleep, me dear. Not in the mood for cuddling today. Why don't ya have a chat with the elms if you fancy some company?" he said, and off he went to dreamland.

Baaaaaa, bleated a sheep.

When the sun returned to do its daily duty and Tjillmer awoke, he found that his sheep stood on all fours and the trees refrained from barking, Stinky didn't wish him a good morning, and the meadows were at low tide. His head was still spinning, though, as if he were on the high sea, and he'd held it fast for most of the day to keep it from drifting away. Yet Tjillmer still felt like a magician.

He'd have been even more convinced of that if he'd known he was being watched from a mountaintop far away, by someone who stared down at the valley with glazed eyes. Not acknowledging the daylight, the gnome steadfastly held his lantern aloft.

A flicker overcame the figurine. Then it vanished.

Odd? Odd, indeed.

Sooner or later, someone was going to have to sort all of this out – track down vanishing gnomes, unruly buildings (or parts thereof) and investigate unauthorized picture shows. Someone would have to get to the bottom, or on top, of whatever horseplay was going on, slay the beast, incarcerate the villain, and put things back in their rightful place.

But where to find such a hero?

Maybe in the Great Caeshian Empire up north. Many a paladin had earned his stripes there, and one of them might find his way south in time. Perhaps there was one just starting out in Great Caesh's ancient metropolis, Shaeggadynn, with its oily high-rise stone edifices, turning even the bluest of skies steely and sombre, its ornamented buttresses and steeples, pointed arches and gargoyles overlooking the narrow alleyways threading through stony canyons. A place of character, so the Shaeggies say. Quite a haughty one, just about anyone else would add to that, for conceit is on prominent display in the streets and worn like a title.

Let's zoom in and see who we have…

One promising candidate was knocking about the business quarters that strange day, staggering like a drunken mule with a big lump on his back. A passing nobleman took him for the local hunchback and was about to part with a coin, but the supposed poor soul would have none of it. He threw the charitable offering right back at his benefactor and called the man only-the-gods-know-what. Turned out that the hump dragging our candidate down was a bundle slung over his shoulder. The burden lent him the undignified posture of a slumped ape. It has to be said, he wasn't well dressed either, hence the mix-up: a scrap of light leather, a pair of torn breeches and a rusty dagger tucked in his belt was all he had on him. And his footwear, if one could call it that, was of notable shoddiness and allowed for his toes to be aired in plenty of creative ways. Not the look of today's hero as advertised. But perhaps good enough, if saving the world could wait for the morrow.

This soon-to-be hero shuffled into a shop.

Ching-a-ling! chimed the bell above the door.

The gum-chewing tomboyish brunette behind the counter – freckled, bespectacled and now a tiny bit miffed – snapped her book shut and blew a bubble as she looked up.

Pop! it went when he floundered in, the man and his bundle, at odds with the doorframe. After a few failed attempts, the idea hit him to step outside again. There, the stranger separated himself from his oversized load, shoved it sideways through the entrance and followed after it with a loud jangling noise as an accompaniment. Finally triumphant, the main lead of this clownish show staggered over to the counter, where the bundle eventually landed with a brash *thump!*

"Ugh…" Gwynn backed away a bit. A harrowing stench wafted in her direction. But a customer was a customer. "A… good day to you, er, sir. What can I do you for?"

"Hullo there," the stranger wheezed in a mellow voice. He wasn't bad looking at all, with wavy hair, blue eyes and stubbly cheeks that made one think he had carefully composed his features from a catalogue. The rest was the problem: the vagrant bit.

He fiddled with his bundle. "I've been exploring a forbidding place deep down below," he divulged while he was at it. "Fought vile creatures. Ah, it was ghastly."

"Yeah? Where exactly was that?" Judging from the reek, it could only have been in—

"The sewers."

"I see... Were you perchance hunting" – Gwynn switched to mock aristocracy mode – "for an expensive piece of clothing in alleged prior possession of a pretty rich lady or something?"

The smelly vagrant gave her a half-surprised, half-bewildered look. "You know what? That's *exactly* what I was doing! Was looking for a scarf, if you must know, a precious thing that fell through a grate up Witchthing's Street only yesterday, the lovely lady told me. How would you know?"

"Just a lucky guess." She had done it before too – the "send someone on a mission" exercise. It was a favourite sport in her clique, telling unwanted suitors to stuff their advances by making it appear like a challenge. Oh, would you jump into a well for me? In a lake? Wearing armour? And the pinheads who dreamt of a night of passion fell for it. Every. Single. Time.

"Wanna see? Haven't delivered it yet." The oh-so-courageous one pulled something from the stinking heap. "Ah, here it is! Look!"

Gwynn's face froze mid-chew.

It was a piece of mud-crusted cloth, or a chunk of fossilized dirt with some fabric peeking out in places, depending on how one looked at the messy "artifact".

"You must be so proud of yourself!" Or full, Gwynn thought.

"Oh, I certainly am." The stranger untied the bundle, rummaged about within it and produced a couple of old pots. He put them on the counter one by one with the utmost care as if handling porcelain vases imported from across the Burning Sea. "Killed about two dozen rats," he went on while unpacking, "with nothing but a dagger. Imagine that! Also a couple of slime-thingys, and nasty creepy-crawlies in all shapes and sizes. Besides" – he puffed up a bit – "I discovered a couple of odd symbols on the one or the other wall down there. Could be the markers of some secret society. Have to pursue that. Looks right up my alley."

Probably some brat's latest doodles.

"All of which, of course" – he made an expansive gesture – "is only the beginning of the adventures of me, Valerius Frilbo Stingswinger."

"Is that so?"

"It is, it is..." The stranger pulled a small mud-stained notebook from his pocket. "Adventurers are always in demand. Take tomorrow..." He thumbed through the pages. "Ah, here we are. Haunted mansion investigation. And after that I'll help some peasant search for his prize cow."

"At least you'll get some fresh air."

"I'll also be looking into a special remedy for a sick little girl over in Navgard, and a fisherman from Ka'damm has asked me to deliver a letter to his estranged son."

"The compassionate kind, I see."

Valerius Frilbo Stingswinger gave a little bow. "One does what one can."

"And so humble!" Gwynn wondered why everybody and their brother would entrust their troubles to some tramp on a mission towards self-fulfilment. She must have missed a bulletin on that.

"So, you see..." The guy shook his full mane. "I'm just here for the night before I'm off again to make the world a better place."

First the mysterious stranger routine, then the I'm-gonna-save-the-world-starting-with-little-girls scam. And now, to round things off, the subtle insinuation that he'd be available for a one-night stand. "Daft" wasn't her middle name.

"That's all nice and dandy, Mr Stingswinger, but what are we to do about *this?*" Gwynn gestured at the collection piling up on the counter.

"Ah, just valuables I found on my journey." The prizes he had fought the city's rats so ardently for were two ladles, an iron helmet with a hole in it, a broken lantern, a battered buckler (now foldable), a soaked spell book (unreadable), and dirty laundry in various stages of decay, which he seemed certain were not his lady client's size.

"How about an estimate?" he said.

"You want money… for *that?*" Gwynn gauged the pile for about half a second.

"Well, yes. It was tough enough to get it up here. The sewers are four levels deep! Now I have to make a few bucks to get myself a better dagger or something, and then the fun starts all over again. I'm half pack mule, half adventurer." He forced a grin.

"We're no animal shelter, and we're certainly not a charity. Did you even bother to read the sign outside?"

"Sign? What sign?"

"The one that you evidently missed. The one with the gilded bolt and arrow fixed on top that says 'Bolt and Arrow'? Hint: It contains some vital clues."

The stranger's gaze swept around. "You sell bolts? And… arrows?"

"Your wits *do* impress me, Mr Stingswinger." *Pop* went a bubble.

"Meaning... that's *all* you trade?" he said, aghast.

"Bull's-eye, yet again! First-class archery equipment. Sorry to say, but we're unlikely to branch out into kitchen utensils or lady's undergarments in the foreseeable future."

"Damn." The vagabond's face fell almost to waist level. "Why didn't you tell me *before* I got all this out?"

"Oh," Gwynn said innocently, "I guess we both were so busy appreciating someone's valiant deeds. Don't forget anything when you pack up."

The adventurer's mood changed within moments from talkative to peeved. He wordlessly shoved his treasures back into his bundle.

"You might try your luck in the gnomes' quarter," Gwynn suggested. Everyone knew that gnomes bought all kinds of rubbish. The garbage dump would also work, but she kept that idea to herself. "Or," she came up with a third option, "you could try the general store down the street. My friend there said something about a problem she needed dealing with the other day. Maybe you'd get a quest out of it too, if you enjoy that sort of thing. Just tell her I sent you, and mention a well." Amabell would recognize the codeword.

The vagabond nodded, tucked the last pieces of trash into his bag, then hitched it onto his back.

"Safe journey, Mr Stingswinger! Give my regards to the vermin!"

Mr Stingswinger. Even the *name* was lewd. She shuddered. Stingswinger, my ass!

And this – with more din marking the not-yet famous sewer crawler's exit – concludes our brief glance at one of the candidates for tomorrow's hero. Obviously, this one still has got a few things to learn before anyone bestows a knighthood on him. But could he be cut out for something bigger than hunting imaginary pieces of women's apparel in the sewers? Only time will tell.

The path to fame is a rocky road, they say. For some it's a sewer crawl. For others, a trudge across vast stretches of desert. Life deals all kinds of hands. Though, at times, one suspects that the dealer must have shuffled all the aces into *another* deck.

CHAPTER 5

Teatime Troubles

Mehhh...," Bormph moaned in Thimble's direction. Their tents already pitched for the night, dwarf and halfling were watching the day draw to a close. Desert crickets punctuated the monotony.

"Tell you something," the dwarf let out after a bit. "I'm not a sunset kind of bloke. Never have been, never will be. Sunsets aren't for dwarves."

In some ways, Thimble agreed. He was a halfling-hole fellow. Back in Willwold-on-Glee, at his mummins and daddins, he used to watch Sundrown from a little bench in front of his home-hole. He still remembered the smell of daddins's good-night pipe when he would slip back inside. But a sunset in front of a halfling-hole, which – as everybody knows – means comfort, could never compare to one seen from a flat, vacant plain that tried to fool you into taking it for a landscape.

Dust-filled desolation, that's all the Joghavri Desert was. No mortal in their right mind would pick the far reaches of a desert to watch night fall. If one was into sand, a beach would do. Beaches have cool water as well which deserts are notoriously short of. In the Joghavri, sand was the only thing one *could* get into, and knee-deep at that. Yet building sandcastles wasn't an option. It was just sun minus the fun. At least Bormph and Thimble had found a remedy against the baking heat…

"A bit more to the right, Rammy, will ya?"

The barbarian moved.

"Perfect. And now… just stay there!"

Strategically placed, his leathery-skinned manifestation of brawn was a welcome source of shadow.

In other news, the great adventure wasn't going so great. The long and short of it was that some drunk had scribbled vague directions on a napkin, which had ended up in the hands of another drunk – otherwise known as the party wizard. But to a boozing mage thirsting for adventure, the gamble must have sounded like a one-way ticket to glory. In the stark daylight of the desert sun, it felt more like a shot in the dark. Even the handwriting was shaky. The so-called map was a mystery of its own, full of illegible "hints", and still Whinewaeyn kept brooding over it, turning it every which way, confusing lines for stains and the other way round. And so, for three full days the adventurers looking for some action had been following what might or might not have been an arrow, all the while sweating buckets under the scourge of the desert sun, with the party's halfling faction getting way too much sand between their hairy toes.

Finally, at the end of their tethers, they had arrived at a sand pit. "That's it! The forsaken crypt," in Whinewaeyn's words. True, the pit was "guarded" by walking heaps of bones, likely held together by glue and lingering magic, and the late inhabitants wielded weapons alright, but the swords were as blunt as butter knives, and the corpses' memories of how to make use of them had left along with their spirits. Whinewaeyn conjured up a bit of a draft, and the crypt-dwellers, supposed overlord included, crumbled to dust. The zombies dropped a couple of coppers in loot, and that was that. They found a smiley etched into one of the coffin lids, with a note inside: *Thanks for stopping by! Please sign the guestbook in the alcove in the back.* After the disaster, Whinewaeyn declared that they must have entered the wrong crypt. "The other one, the one with all the treasure, has to be close by," he insisted. Everyone else was not so sure.

Now, an evening later, the motley party was back at square one. Bormph and Thimble had founded the can't-be-bothered-with-sunset-appreciation fellowship and felt some silent satisfaction that the celestial body was finally disappearing before their eyes. They had already seen more than their fair share of Joghavri sunsets.

"What're you doing, Curly?" Bormph snorted all of a sudden. He jerked to the side, and Thimble's arm got painfully yanked.

"Me? Er…" A halfling hand freed itself awkwardly from the dwarf's backpack.

"You fumbling again?"

"I'm not fumbling!"

"You are!" Bormph thumped Thimble. "Where I come from, it's called stealing!"

"But… that's because I'm the rogue here! I need the practice."

"I can tell!" Bormph was about to tell him a lot more, when—

Ahead, in the vast, limitless desert landscape, a shimmer rippled across the sands, scything through the insipid heat.

There was a *swoosh* too, curtailed by a hiss and an altogether misplaced gurgling noise. The sounds huddled together to form a discordant medley and seemed to describe a half circle.

"What's happening? What's going on?" Thimble looked frantically about, searching for anyone larger and more capable than him to deal with the situation. His eyes came across Ramrok.

The barbarian was chewing away on a crust of bread and a hunk of cheese. He cocked his square head like a puppy and squinted. When whatever it was kept doing whatever it was doing, he leapt up with his sword in hand and pointed it here and there, but the hubbub was everywhere and nowhere by now, not paying any attention to anyone pointing swords.

Tiny flashes sparkled left and right and somewhere in between. Dust swirled over random patches in the desert sand, not necessarily where the flashes occurred. There were no apparent gusts to fuel them. It was as if the desert had suddenly had enough of looking dreary and tried something else.

Then, as though flushed out by the omnipresent display of noise, a blur of movement washed over everything. Runes drifted across the skies – not unlike birds flying south. Out of the earth crept a score of cryptic glyphs that one might otherwise have taken for an emergency migration of beetles. The odd buzzing desert bug was around too when the things – apparitions? spectres? – chased them over the ground, but the real insects soon dug themselves into the sand again, accepting defeat against an insubstantial enemy. Wherever phantoms took shape, whether close by or on the horizon, they swam up, bleary and wobbly, some of them skipping about like sand rabbits during mating season, and winked out again.

"By Thock the Titan's toe!" Whinewaeyn cried out from his tent retreat. As a first measure, the wizard held fast to his hat and then… left it at that.

A cat that wasn't there meowed. A cow mooed. Invisible wings flapped. Horses neighed. At least the party's mounts were accounted for, and Amjelle and Sylthia rushed to keep them from bolting.

Next, a rumble joined the cacophony of noise, and when everyone turned, they found themselves watching a line draw itself into the sand a stone's throw away. Propelled by some unknown force, it wormed forward, and in its wake the ground buckled, as if something horrific was going to break through at any moment. Shortly before the sandy beast reached the party, though, it came to a standstill, and just lay there, frozen, shaped like a giant serpent. But no eyes, scales, or maw emerged. The sharp crest remained the thing's most frightening feature; it might as well have been a dune with an attitude.

And, by all accounts, a dune it was. It waited around for a long moment, then whirled away with a sudden gust, going to wherever dunes go. Maybe to visit other dune friends, or greener pastures. The conglomeration of noises petered out, and shortly before the riot had fizzled away altogether, it celebrated its demise with a roaring *PA-DANG!*

A dead quiet followed. Firm, insistent, desert-wide.

"What in the heavens," Whinewaeyn blurted out, "was *that?*"

"I doubt it was heaven-sent," Sylthia replied.

Amjelle – in her function as a priestess, and to be on the safe side – drew the sign of the Five in the air; she let her folded hands sink from her chest, the palms parted, described half a circle upwards and ended with them folded again over her chest.

"Is it just me," Bormph said from his down-to-earth perspective, "or did the universe just… burp?"

A horizon away, the sun went about its business. It was ignorant of things it hadn't seen with its own eyes, which – as suns don't have eyes – is perfectly understandable. The fiery orb had made progress during the incident and was now about to dip away into the Void beneath the world, leaving the sky awash with a spectacle of reddish threads. The famous Joghavri sunset suddenly regained some respect from certain party members. Its cosmic predictability felt comforting.

"Is it *really* over?" Thimble's small voice piped as he dared to take a peek from behind Whinewaeyn's robe.

The wizard made an uncertain gesture and resorted to tugging pensively at his ear. He wouldn't commit one way or another. Already he was brooding over a couple of protective spells in case the universe was to burp again, but his academic training on burp protection was vague.

"So, you saw that from down there too?" Whinewaeyn asked Bormph.

"You can bet your hat I did." Bormph's nose twitched a little.

"Because sometimes," Whinewaeyn informed him, "things get muddled in a magician's mind up here, you see. Possibilities and realities, real possibilities, possible realities. As do spells, words, spell words, wordy spells, the spelling of words…"

Amjelle locked gazes with Bormph as if to say, *"And he hasn't had a single drink for four days…"* Her eyes leapt back to the magician. "As long as you still remember that you cast spells with words, Master Whinewaeyn, and that just spelling words isn't enough, I guess we'll be fine. I trust you can still distinguish a fireball from a blessing?"

"Ah, I might be a bit rusty, my dear Amjelle," Whinewaeyn replied with a wink, "but when the time arrives to do my magic, I'm sure it will all come back. I'm just a tad... you know... how do they say...?"

"Forgetful?"

"Yes, yes, that's the word!"

Amjelle rolled her eyes. *Wizards!*

"Now where were we?" Whinewaeyn searched their faces. "Remind me."

"Here," Bormph said. "For the records, wizzer, a rampant dune paid us a visit. Brought its own runes and stuff, and a brass band or something."

"Ah yes, yes!" Whinewaeyn drew a sharp breath. "A dune. Rampant. Noisy. Visible from above and below. On the loose. Gone now."

"Could've just nipped out to call for reinforcements." Bormph hefted his shiny silver axe over his shoulder.

"Reinforcements?" Thimble squirmed, unsettled. "Where from?"

"From where-the-heck-should-I-know. Dune town?"

"So it was a *real* dune then," Whinewaeyn established.

"Dwarves lack imagination," Bormph growled. "If someone imagined it, it wasn't me."

"Yeah," a sonorous voice concurred. "Er... no," came after a slight delay. "Ramrok not do nothing." The barbarian nodded his head vigorously, added a shake, got confused, and stopped shaking and nodding. The muscled Northlander, bulk of a man but negligible as a conversationalist, sometimes had trouble expressing himself, especially when he tried several words in succession. He pushed his horned helmet forward to scratch the back of his head with his broadsword's hilt, then added for clarity, "You know what Ramrok mean."

Bormph watched the sweat drip from the barbarian's brow a little while longer before he turned back to the mage. "Here's an observation for you, gramps…" He cocked his head as he tugged at the wizard's grubby sleeve. Whinewaeyn bent down, and when he was level with the dwarf's face, Bormph reached up and pinched his nose.

"Ouch!" The wizard almost parted with his staff. "What was that for, you silly dwarf? Was kicking me in the shins not enough?"

"You're not dreaming either," Bormph deadpanned. "Got to cover all the bases."

Whinewaeyn, suppressing tears, eyeballed the dwarf. Dwarven pinches meant business. But at the same time his face lightened up somewhat. "Hmm, good thinking, dwarf. No dream, well noted." His gaze slid towards the rest of his fellow adventurers. "It was a bit spooky, though, wasn't it? That thing grew and then… went away. Like a ghost."

"A solid ghost?" Amjelle had her doubts. "And since when do ghosts come a-haunting at sunset?"

"Better than monsters," Thimble pointed out.

"Not so sure about that," Bormph said. "An axe will deal with those." He brandished his. "But have you ever seen a dune going for a walk before? Now *that's* spooky!"

They looked out into the desert where Sylthia was investigating the spot at which the dune had made its questionable appearance. The elf had dropped into a crouch, and her slim fingers slid over the ground, scrutinizing the sand that now stretched to the horizon without a single significant bump in between. After a while, she was joined by Ramrok and his bare chest.

"No traces of anything," Sylthia reported.

"Hrmph," the barbarian grunted. In a way, that said it all. When the barbarian stuck to just one word, he proved quite versatile. It was almost frightening how accurately he managed to encapsulate complex issues in a nutshell. Most of the time, people understood perfectly well what he was implying.

This time, Thimble almost blushed when he heard the barbarian's sweet talk. All that romantic innuendo packed into a single grunt… Fed up with the barbarian's insolent insinuations, he scampered after the elf and the cocky Northlander. "Hrmph indeed!" He aimed a reproachful look at the barbarian. "Of course there are no traces. Dunes don't wander around, nimrod!"

The giant looked puzzled for a moment. "Me Ramrok, Fumbler!"

"And I'm Thimble, nimrod!"

"Ramrok!"

"Nimrod!"

"Ramrok!"

"Nimrod!" insisted Thimble once more, but finally gave up. "Well, fine then. Have it your way, *Ramrok!*" He stuck his tongue out. "Nitwit!"

Ramrok wasn't familiar with tongue gestures and advanced vocabulary. But he was certain that he had taught Thimble his name, and his next grunt sounded satisfied.

There wasn't much headway on the dune front, though. Sylthia sat back on her haunches and shook her head. "Not the slightest impression." She stood, turning something over in her hand. "Except for… this." The others clustered around her. "Looks like a…"

"Beetle?" Amjelle suggested.

Sylthia blew dust off the object, which had the shape of a scarab with its wings spread out. "It's as stiff as a rock. Maybe fossilized. Could've been here for years. Only it's as hot as a stove." She cupped the item in her hands. "There's some sort of needle attached to it." She held the object out to Amjelle.

"Looks like a hairpin," the healer declared after giving it a polish.

"Dunes no hair," Ramrok muttered, perceptive as he was.

Bormph nudged Thimble. "Our very own font of wisdom."

The item was handed around, but no hairpin experts were forthcoming, and Whinewaeyn denied right away that it had any magical properties.

"Is it ancient? Precious? Let me see!" Bormph grabbed the scarab-shaped rock eagerly and rubbed it like a magic lantern. "There's something in its belly, I just *know* it! Elf, give me one of those." He reached into the quiver that dangled from Sylthia's back and pulled out an arrow. "There…" Once he had the surface scraped clean, he wedged the arrowhead under the lid he'd found on the scarab's back, pried it open and… a handful of sand trickled out.

"Gah!" There was more of a glint in Bormph's eye than in the hairpin.

"Just a piece of shiny copper," Amjelle declared, underwhelmed. "They probably sell them for a Dimmy-dime at Weaverring market."

Sylthia tried it on, nonetheless. "It's light, though. Shiny and fetching."

Sure is, thought Thimble, *with that elf attached to it.* He slotted the elf's new look into his ever-extending repertoire of daydream options.

Sylthia and her hairpin strode off. "We might as well have tea now," she said. "And by the way," she added, not deigning to glance at either Thimble or Ramrok, "you might as well stop being silly."

The both of them looked after her, slack-jawed.

Whinewaeyn, for his part, looked wizardly out into the desert, his thoughts clouded like a Mistdale hamlet on a particularly bad day. "Fascinating," he murmured to no one in particular, "and disconcerting. Most disconcerting. Disconcertingly fascinating. And fascinatingly disconcerting."

As he weighed his thoughts, he absently brushed an imaginary speck of dust from his robe, the way he always used to do before retreating for the night. He was a creature of habit. Only the speck wasn't imaginary at all this time. The wizard *was* covered in dust, hat included. The sorry excuse for a headpiece – formerly pointy and proud, now saggy and baggy – was decorated all over with souvenirs of the clumpy kind. Whatever they had experienced must have had some dust-raising, clump-spouting faculty. Hardly the work of a mirage. Tricks of light don't leave permanent traces.

And as the sand on him was real, Whinewaeyn could only conclude that the dune must have been quite real too. Unless it was unreal, but somehow capable of creating real dust… At which juncture Whinewaeyn's thoughts took a sharp turn and veered right out of his mind. He turned and shuffled tentwards. "Do I smell tea?"

What the wizard and the rest of the party didn't know then was that the journey ahead was about much more than a dune. The dune was only the tip of the iceberg.

Meanwhile, farther west, deep, deep down beneath the earth, a battle of life and death was underway.

The air crackled. Sparks flew. Spells flashed and fizzled.

At the very end of a labyrinthine tunnel system, a dark-skinned elven sorceress and her dwarven companion stood on a platform bounded by molten lava, wishing they weren't. Sizzling lava was one issue, the other was a dragon the size of a house – chimney included. Each of its innumerable scales was as large as the dwarf's shield, which, under these circumstances, barely deserved its name. Every time the behemoth moved, the ground shook, sending cartloads of loose sand drizzling down on them, and whenever the beast felt like it, it breathed a little fire too. The lich mounted atop it didn't help either. Incantations sputtered out of the living corpse, causing the air's energies to coalesce and form blazing missiles. Directed by the deadly rattle in the creature's hand, they left fuming craters wherever they landed.

"*Oouhm-goorosh!*" the undead roared, like a well with a message. One of its fireballs struck the ground.

Already grazed by several fiery tokens of disrespect, elf and dwarf saw their chances of survival dwindle. They weaved and dodged, but death, it dawned on them, was about to collect two more today, and it was going to be a fiery affair. Incineration by magical means was one possibility, ending up as the main ingredient in a dragon's barbecue another, and sizzling in a lava bath the third. Which would it be?

The lich and its dragon mount emerged from the shadows at the back of the cave and advanced on their prey. If the undead creature meant to grin, it didn't show, as there was no skin over the crooked set of teeth to back it up. The gem-studded amulet wrapped around its bone-stack of a neck, however, seemed to glint in mockery.

"We're done for," the dwarf yelled. He rushed forward to score a hit, but hesitated when he got too close, and his battle-axe sliced ineffectively through the air. "It's hopeless!"

"I know," the elf yelled back, her staff flailing just as wildly.

"What are we supposed to do?"

"Um…" the elf shouted, suddenly aware that some things sounded odd when yelled.

Grim determination was written over their faces. There was a nod, and one in response. They were in silent agreement. One last assault.

Dwarf and elf said their final prayers, each to their own god. Soon they'd find out who'd get full points in the belief department, if either of them would. The dwarf kept his fingers crossed for stone paradise; the elf wagered it was all about rebirth. There was, of course, also the risk of a double fiasco: death *and* the realization that they had both put their money on the wrong ticket all along. Could the prospect of eternal life just have been a bedtime story? Might the totals of their good deeds and transgressions not qualify them for anything worthwhile eternity-wise? And why do such questions always arise when the time for a serious think is in extremely short supply?

"Argggggh!" the dwarf's deep voice boomed.

"Aaiiiiiiiiiiii!" the elf's high-pitched scream joined in.

Kabooooooooom! A thundercrack. The lich's amulet flashed.

What should've happened didn't. What actually happened shouldn't have.

Weapons brandished, ready for anything – or so they thought – both elf and dwarf missed their rendezvous with death. It wasn't their fault. It was because of a sudden lack of opponents. In the place where the dragon and its rider had been, a certain shimmer hung in the air. That, and a fragile one-note sound, chiming away like a grandfather clock next to a cosy hearth. Which felt a tad off in a death-trap of a dungeon.

Speechless, elf and dwarf looked at each other, then…

…the tip of the iceberg materialized. Not just a proverbial one, but an actual iceberg. The tip of one, anyway. And even the tip of an iceberg is sizeable enough to fill a whole cave. And that's what it did.

The gigantic pyramid-shaped block grew out of the ground, just a few feet in front of the two opponent-deprived combatants. It glistened in the light of the lava pools, smooth and shiny, an immaculate, polished, spotless display.

"Look!" Catching her reflection in the giant mirror, the elf had spied something else trapped behind the frosty surface. Facial features, frozen stiff. There was a body too, though it was a small one. Dwarf-sized. Why, it *was* a dwarf! On a little… pedestal? "Wh—"

That's as far as she got.

The iceberg finally picked up on the sizzling pools in which it had partly materialized. It also noticed the hot vapour in the cave, and was reminded to answer to its nature and melt away.

On the bright side, the two adventurers beat the odds by escaping certain death by fire. The bad news: they drowned. With a gush, a swoosh and a flush Dormhelm

Humhammer and Ilvith Irwithswing adhered to their date with destiny and went on to meet their maker. Or makers.

In the iceberg's defence, it has to be said that it dropped by only briefly. It was unfortunate that its visit caused inconvenience to any observers present. However, the tip of the tip of the iceberg – which was all that was left of it – made off once again. An odd chiming set in, the air shimmered and wavered, and then it was gone. Anyone listening in, provided they'd managed to survive the encounter up until this point, might have heard a sigh-like sloshing, equivalent to an "Oops!"

CHAPTER 6

Further Fishy Things

Dear diary, Thimble scribbled, his tongue sticking out of the corner of his mouth. *Yesturday we had a visit from a doon. It woodn't stay. Made a lot of noyse too. The dwarf says it's a renegat* – he scratched that – *rainagait* – and that one too – *runawy one, exploring the lands. The wizerd says it's eether something magickal, or something else. I'm not so shure. If it's magick, it's a trik the rong way round. Becuz at first there was nothing. Then there was something. And then nothing again. Makes you wonder if there was something in between at all. A magickan, however, starts out with a bossome assistant, makes her disappear, and ends up with a bossome assistant again. There's always an assistant and her bossome.*

SPLOSH! A rogue droplet of ink seeped into the parchment, delighting in spreading out. Thimble cursed, tried to smudge the mess into an ornamental arc and failed miserably. Embarrassed, he flipped to a fresh page without prior sins: *Anyway...* His quill connected with the paper, but no idea came out.

It was still early in the morning as Thimble went over his impressions of the past day. No one else was up. There's always a chance for any thief to wind up behind bars at some point during a great expedition, so he had to prepare. Given the lack of pockets to pick in a cell, he figured he'd take a shot at his memoirs. Jotting down notes between adventures would help with this upcoming masterpiece. The only thing he was lacking was an exciting life. But be it as a master thief or a man of letters, he'd make his mummins proud!

Well. A random dune just wouldn't cut it, no matter how much noise it made. What he needed was some serious drama, even if it meant bending the truth a wee bit. Some fake drama, but *real* fake drama so to speak. Like a dragon in the crypt. Readers were keen on action: fights, chases, evil lords, the apocalypse looming, that sort of thing. He'd write an epic. Early on, he'd put in a big mystery, a hero, and a girl, and a few others, and then something would happen to one of them, to get the thing going. And towards the end, there'd be a big twist where—

A clamour outside broke his train of thought.

Quick as a whip, in the event that this was worth writing about, Thimble stowed away his quill and inkwell and poked his head out of the tent flap. Bormph was running around outside like a crazed bull.

"Over. There!" the dwarf panted in fragments. "Gone!" He came to a jerking halt and cocked a thumb towards the back end of the camp.

Thimble stared at him, confused.

"The elf!" Bormph flung about some more disjointed words. "Gone!"

"What do you mean 'gone'?"

"Gone – as in, gone away. Not here. Disappeared! Vanished! *Pfft!*" He threw up his arms.

Thimble deflated. No way. There was only one elf, and the elf was the one. Only a few hours ago, he had lingered at the girls' tent and listened to the titters of laughter inside, his imagination running rampant, and now…

He unwrapped himself from his tent flap and pushed past the dwarf. Ramrok had planted himself near the tent in question with all his muscles on display and a crinkled-up forehead, studying the sand. Through the opening, Thimble noticed Amjelle also searching the ground for hints.

Thimble shot Ramrok a dirty look. He didn't see eye to eye with the giant, and not only size-wise. "Was it you?"

The barbarian scrunched up his face.

Thimble pressed again. "On your watch? It was your watch, wasn't it?"

Ramrok nodded. "Ramrok watch, aye."

Thimble's mind seethed with images of Ramrok watching lithe silhouettes, undressing, through the tent. Peeping at a helpless fair elven maiden! Hah! Probably half-naked in the sizzling desert air… Disgusting! Thimble's fantasies neglected the fact that the nights were anything but hot in the Joghavri, and that he had almost frozen to death himself – while sneaking a look. In his mind, though, the elf's tent was much closer to a sweat lodge, hence the necessary taking off of clothes.

"You were peeking!"

"Ramrok? No peek! Ramrok watch."

"That's what watching is. Peeking!"

Ramrok shook his head. "Ramrok watch. Ramrok no peek."

"Peeked!"

"Watch!"

"Peeked!"

"What's all this?" a grumpy, cracking voice broke in.

It belonged to what could best be described as a shadow of a wizard staggering out of his tent, a fact entirely unrelated to the position of the sun. It was just that early in the morning. Hence Whinewaeyn was even less his usual self, and his usual self was a vague affair to begin with. Even the few zombies back in the crypt had overlooked him and focused on the one wielding the most threatening weapon – before they were struck by a bolt of lightning originating from an unassuming beanstalk growing nearby. Or so they thought.

That's also why Bormph, used to the wizard's idiosyncrasies, didn't startle when a tent pole next to him began talking in Whinewaeyn's voice. The dwarf simply snuck the shadow in tent-pole guise a sidelong glance to make sure that the mage indeed had sidled over, and yes, there he was, looking discomfited and drowsy.

"It's the elf," Bormph told the dishevelled mage. "Nowhere to be found. She's vanished!"

"I see." Whinewaeyn peered out from under the brim of his battered hat. "Had enough of those two squabblers already, did she?"

Thimble and Ramrok were still at it.

"Watch!"

"Peeked!"

"They only started quarrelling *after* she had disappeared," Bormph informed the wizard. "Not that I mind. The halfling's so distracted when the two are at each other's throats, it's the best time of the day to get my coins back. You know, he hides whatever he pilfers under his pillow. He's got a real problem there."

The wizard slipped a hand into his pocket and jingled the contents. For some reason, it sounded less jingly to him than it had a day before.

"Anyway, as for the elf…" Bormph sighed. "Who can blame her? We've made a dime and a half so far, and a worthless pin. No wonder she took off."

"Ah, the youth of today! No patience whatsoever. We were just about to—"

"Here's the thing, wizzer. It's not just *where* she is. It's the *how* too. We haven't got a clue. Just *pfft*."

"Oh?" The shape of Whinewaeyn's mouth held an extended O. "*Pfft,* you say?"

"*Pfft,*" Bormph confirmed.

"Puff of smoke?"

"Hey, old man, I wasn't there. She could've ridden off on a broom for all I know. Ask the healer whether she brought one. Her stuff's still here. The horse too. There are no sets of footprints in the sand and nobody noticed a thing."

The wizard looked even more befuddled than usual. He motioned to Thimble and Ramrok, encouraging them to take a break from their vibrant discussion. "All three of you were on watch last night?"

Thimble nodded, as did Bormph, and then Ramrok.

"Nothing unusual? None of you dozed off? No spooked horses? No pieces of landscape strolling by, that sort of thing?"

Ramrok shook his head, as did Bormph, and then Thimble.

Whinewaeyn gazed at the tent in question, his mind wandering. And then it wandered farther. The trouble was that once his mind went, he just went along with it – over hills, across dales, up the next mountain, into the clouds, the skies, the spheres, the—

"Hey!"

A violent jerk at his robe snatched him out of his reverie.

"Thought of something, wizzer," Bormph rasped. "Suppose the universe indeed burps on occasion? As we've witnessed." His furry eyebrows arched up. "Who says it doesn't also get hungry every now and then? And then, you know, it takes a bite…"

Thimble turned ashen at the dwarf's blunt rationale. The sweetest girl had been robbed from him overnight. But… who was to say that universes didn't have a sweet tooth? A shudder passed through him.

Even the barbarian shifted around uneasily as if he expected at any moment to be plucked away by the forces at large. He issued a roar and stomped about, brandishing his two-hander. The universe made no further move. Could be that it was still busy digesting.

"Universe or not, this is personal!" declared Thimble. "We need to *do* something for the gods' sakes! Anything!"

"Then stop arguing and accusing universes of snacking and whatnot!" Amjelle snapped from inside the tent to the male assembly outside. The healer was knelt next to what must have been the elf's last resting place, her long raven hair almost touching the ground as she bent down. With her healer's tool, a three-foot-long rod with a round glowing crystal at the tip, Amjelle drew a circle in the sand. She brushed back her hair as she looked up at everyone. "Keep your mouths shut! Or one of *you* will get gobbled up next!"

The party's non-healing faction stood as stiff as a collection of pokers.

Tap... tap... tap... The crystal on the rod, now enveloped in a shining halo of light, gently dabbed along the outline of the circle she'd drawn. *Tap... tap... tap... tap...* Each tap prompted wisps of magical energy to rise up from the ground. The swirling tongues grasped sand grains and swirled them gracefully through the air like flames dancing around invisible wicks. Soon, the whole circle had been covered and Amjelle was ringed by at least a dozen of her dancing creations. It was a weird spectral construction, a bit like lit candles on a ghostly birthday cake.

"*A'ha-ma-damm... q'tha phaw-namm?*" she intoned. "*K'tkt'ka-aa!*"

A "Huh?" escaped from Ramrok's lips.

Thimble leaned over to him and the big one bent down.

"She said, 'Cursed be the ones who say 'Huh?'"

"Huh?" Ramrok said. It took a few moments... And after one more extra moment following the few, Thimble's cheekiness dawned on him. His giant hand descended, and Thimble kissed the dust.

Meanwhile, magical discharge crackled in the air. When everything was in place, Amjelle stood, left the circle and let the spooky birthday cake sizzle on its own for a time. She returned with a quiver in hand and drew an arrow from it.

"*Tak-bash!*" The arrow landed inside her creation.

Thunder pealed and a spark of lightning flared, but only a homemade version of the real deal. A magical wind whipped up the insides of the circle with a loud *whoosh*, fuelled by the dancing swirls. The gust shot towards the arrow in the centre, propelled the object into the air and sent it spinning around. Whatever else found itself in the vicinity of the tent's centre buckled and twisted for a moment. In a flash, things snapped back to their original state as if sorry for ever having tried to be part of whatever was going on. In the blink of an eye, the arrow disappeared, only to be spewed out in another blink from a realm beyond the senses. The wind ebbed away. Whatever sand was still afloat settled. Everything looked the way it had before the little ceremony, except for the arrow, which was now levitating softly inside the circle, pointing in a particular direction.

"North-east," Amjelle announced. She rocked back on her heels.

The magic that held the object afloat dissipated by degrees, and the arrow, lifeless again, dropped onto the sand.

"Her aura is still linked to the arrows she used. Got to step lively – the link is weak!" Amjelle looked around as if to say, "What's the holdup? You wanted some adventure, now you've got it."

"This the best we can do?" Bormph asked. "North-east is sort of vague."

"Got any better ideas?"

Bormph hadn't, not at the moment anyway. Ramrok and Thimble needed little convincing. They turned on their heels, one lumbering, the other scampering towards their respective tents, and got packing. Bormph just scratched his head. The special effects had been eye-catching, but other than that he was dubious about any kind of magic that wasn't used as a weapon.

"Marvellous!" Whinewaeyn gazed at the arrow. "You see, I was wondering, dear... Speaking from the point of view of a magic user and a traditional caster, unfamiliar with the clerical approach, is there an auratic link between, say, *things* too? Consider the situations in a man's life – and a woman's as well, I presume – when two pieces of the same, yet separate, clothing decide to spend their lives in different parts of the cosmos."

Amjelle stared at him. The wizard blathered on.

"Like the missing sock dilemma. It's an uncharted area of research still lacking resolution. And this whole auratic *k'tkt'ka-aaing* with sandy birthday candles, could it find its application in... Amjelle? Dear?" The wizard's voice trailed off as he noticed that the healer's grey-green eyes were taking on a more bilious tinge the longer they were pinning him. "Just asking on behalf of..." he started again, but in the process of talking, the mage's mouth got the message too and took a break.

"We've got work to do. Here." Amjelle handed him what appeared to be a leathery rag with a handle. Its purpose wasn't immediately apparent. "May I suggest that you carry this, if you please, Master? Now buck up."

"Yuck!" protested Bormph, who just had to poke his nose in.

"Eurgh!" The mage subscribed to the same reaction. It reeked abominably. However, he didn't let it interfere with his innate politeness. "Why, thank you, Amjelle. Um... May I ask—"

"You tell me, Archmagus. It wasn't here yesterday, so let's just assume it means something. And I'll eat my shoe if we won't find out what someplace north-east from here."

So north-east it was.

Regardless of direction – be it north-east, south-west, south-east, or due north – the experience was strikingly similar: the smouldering heat was unrelenting, assaulting everyone indiscriminately. With no hint of a breeze, the air stood around like it had nothing better to do than kill time – and with the air being sluggish and time persistent, it was a stalemate at best. Blue and impervious, the sky looked on with neither the energy nor the means to chip in. Both land and sky had had millennia to complain about the prevailing dreariness they all were part of, but had come to a tacit agreement that it was too late in the game to plead for radical change.

Spirits waned. Only once in a while were glances exchanged and, rarer still, the occasional word. These glances were mostly reproachful and aimed at Whinewaeyn, to whom the party owed this trip to this wretched wasteland. Spoken words were few and far between – when one made an effort to come out, it turned sullen to match the glances. Other than that, nothing much happened, and a whole lot of it.

After half-a-day's ride they reached the Mound, the Joghavri's single known bump. While a landmark, it was nothing to write home about. The lack of a post office was excusable.

A few hours later, a watering hole was met with more enthusiasm. Bellies were filled, canteens and waterskins topped off. While they were at it, Thimble broke the monotony by putting a question to Whinewaeyn.

"Desert shifts?" The wizard assumed a sage air as he fastened a flask to his belt. "Well, I've thought about this quite a lot, little one, given our recent experience. I guess it's when there's sand – and there's always sand in the Joghavri – and yet, even in the hottest desert, there's an almost imperceptible circulation of air too. Sometimes, and other times a wee bit more, the sand gets moved elsewhere, to where it formerly wasn't. And so… the desert shifts. It's quite basic." The corners of his mouth went in different directions. "As to whether it helps explain our dune popping up out of nowhere, I was wondering about the time factor of that. Any insights from your side?"

Thimble stared at the wizard for a bit, then tried again. "No, *ships*. Desert ships."

"Ships? Why, they bear no relation at all to anything I've been talking about. Not that I can think of. You're talking what? Camels?"

"Well, yes," Thimble said. "I guess. Those horses with bumps and long necks and muzzles like sheep with oversized lips and teeth a bit like a hippo."

The mage knew what camels were: mounts that would have fared much better than horses in the desert sands. Another noted point for improvement.

"So what about them?"

Thimble wiped the sweat out of his eyes. "They call them 'ships' because of the sand, right? The sand's like the sea. But it's not… really… *sea*, the sand."

"Well, yes. I mean, no," confirmed and then denied Whinewaeyn. "What are you getting at?"

"Fish." Thimble gestured northwards. "If a camel's a ship in a sea that's *not* a sea, then what's a fish?"

The wizard's sore, sun-plagued eyes followed the halfling's finger. "What the—" Then his mouth snapped shut.

"Looks like tuna," Thimble said.

A couple of heads, horses included, bobbed up from their watering hole business and gazed into the haze shimmering a distance off. In the midst of sand, sand and still more sand, lay a sizeable silvery mass, recognizable by its basic shape as something fishy. When everybody shuffled over, as if hypnotized, to gaze at the wonder at close range, it became apparent that they were looking at more than just a fish. They were looking at two. And farther away there were even more! Actually, the closer to the horizon they looked, the more tuna there was, with less sand to fill the gaps in between. Then the stench hit.

Whinewaeyn choked. His face scrunched up, and as this by itself didn't do enough to stave off the smell, he resorted to holding his nose. "By the Wilful Wand of Wenx the Wizkid! This is revolting!"

Bormph – who had already pushed past him into the open fish field – looked about first, grunted in disgust second, then came to the conclusion third that the frying fish odour wasn't worth enjoying close up. He backed off, holding his nose. Amjelle on her part was quick to wave her stave and engulf herself in a cloud of tuna-neutralizing aroma – in which Ramrok and Thimble, neither of them fish lovers, sought refuge in.

And it wasn't just dead fish. There was also a blurry speck out there in the haze, which bobbed in and out of the rows of misplaced sea creatures like a skiff on a bed of waves. Until it didn't. Thimble blinked hard. There it was again, the speck, as if the desert had spewed it out elsewhere. The more he looked at it, the whiter and fuzzier it grew. It kept sinking into the unstable surface, but each time clambered back up again, plodding on until its clumsy journey ended right in front of the party. It wasn't a speck anymore by then. It had four paws, a neck, a mouth, and a fish in the latter, which it dropped at Thimble's feet.

"A cub!" Thimble tingled with excitement. "A *bear* cub!"

"You sure you've got that right?" Bormph eyed it with suspicion. It was as white as snow. "Doesn't look too healthy with fur that colour."

"Must be a polar bear."

"A pole-a-bear? And its pole would be where?"

"No, a pol*ar* bear. It's a bear, alright, but not a common one. I saw one in the princely menagerie once. White bears live *near* a pole, in the ice, and that's why it's snow white. There's one pole up north at Land's End, close to the Edge, and one down south as well, and these poles... they're enormous!"

"Now why would anyone put poles in the ice and turn bears white with them?" Bormph muttered. "I bet it's magefolk with too much time on their hands."

Amjelle threw Thimble a dubious sideways look. "You sure you're telling that story right?"

Thimble blinked. "But it's true. Can't you see?"

Bormph glared at the cub. "Why's this one here then? Shouldn't it be pole-a-bear-dancing up north or whatever? Is it on vacation?"

Thimble shrugged. He wasn't familiar with bears' migration patterns or holiday preferences. But this one looked as though it had lost its way. It was also as cute as a button.

"Well, I refuse to be surprised," Whinewaeyn declared as he watched Thimble and Amjelle take turns cuddling the regionally confused newcomer. He had certainly conquered at least a couple of hearts on the spot. Thimble gave him some water.

"He must be hot!" Amjelle squatted down, level with the cub. She got her rod of Novotroth out, drew a kind of cool air from it, in which she bathed her hands. She rubbed the coolness into the creature's fur, and the little fellow squeaked with delight.

"Can we keep him?" She held the cub up to the wizard.

"It's a polar bear!" Whinewaeyn argued.

"Right. But can we? As a pet. Other adventurers always seem to have rats or some such. If only as a mascot. For good luck."

"Amjelle, dear, adventuring is dangerous business. We've already explored an ancient crypt, fought monsters, and now we're on a serious rescue mission. Dungeons are full of traps, and who knows what's to come! If you had a rat, it might at least gnaw through a piece of rope, fetch stuff by squeezing through a gap under a door, things like that. And with a full-grown, trained grizzler, you'd break through enemy lines in no time. But this bear's… tiny … and white."

"We can't just leave him here!" Thimble was quick on the defence about tininess.

"Well, wherever he came from and wherever he ends up" – the wizard's gaze swept over the fish field – "he's not about to starve, is he?"

"Would you just look at him?" Amjelle asked.

Whinewaeyn did look. At the wiggling snout, and the wide, heartbreaking eyes. They say eyes are the doorways to the soul. Whinewaeyn entered through these double doors and could've sworn he heard them swing shut behind him. Everything turned pitch black. He suddenly remembered another expression: getting lost in someone's eyes. If only he knew the way out.

"It's settled then."

"…" Whinewaeyn mouthed wordlessly. And while he was still contemplating what exactly had been settled where and when…

The cavalry was coming. Literally.

A dust cloud rolled in from the north, zigzagging its way through the masses of dead fish. In due time, an actual train of horses emerged from it, a whole regiment, which drew nearer, nearer still, and eventually closed ranks around the party. Three dozen steeds circled them all in all, still sporting the vibrant plumes of the cavalcade in Dimmerskeep. Zarrafandans in official uniforms sat on their backs.

"The desert's busier than I thought," Bormph said with a sneer. "They better have a few answers too."

"Whoa!" With the command, the regiment came to a coordinated halt. After a slight pause, the men-at-arms lurched in mutual pain when the excruciating stench caught up with them. If they had ridden a tad faster and jerked to a halt more rapidly, they might have dropped from their mounts like flies.

Several pairs of eyes stared up at the riders, hands shielding them from the sun and holding noses. Almost out of reflex, the captain copied the idea, and the same motion went quickly through the rank and file. The soldiers' horses, lacking the opposable digits required, simply tossed their heads around impatiently, snorting and pawing at the sand.

Whinewaeyn lifted his hat in greeting.

"Stop right there!" the head of the regiment barked, less amicably – though holding his nose gave Captain Klampf's words a somewhat unofficial timbre. He motioned at the fish-littered desert. "I'm not aware that any fishing permits have been granted for this region," he squeaked, "magical or otherwise, wizard."

"Neither are we, Captain," Whinewaeyn squeaked back.

"So you aren't in the possession of a permit?"

"Why, you need one? Didn't you just say there is none?"

"Don't be cheeky!" Klampf warned shrilly.

"Say," Bormph chimed in, sounding more like a badger, "not to rain on the parade you seem to be having, Captain, but wouldn't it help your investigation if we were actually fishing?"

"Who's to say you're not?"

"Haven't got the equipment, see?" Bormph waved his axe about. "It's not wizardry either, at least not ours." His eyes shifted to Whinewaeyn. "No offense, but this one would have difficulty getting a dove out of a hat that he put in beforehand."

The mage gesticulated in silent protest, but Bormph ploughed on regardless.

"And I doubt I could lure even a sardine out of the sand just by knocking three times, Captain. But if I could, I'd pull chips out of thin air next, crispy on the outside and soft in the middle, to have something to go with it. And then we'd invite you and all your horsey friends for dinner."

"Well..." the captain thought aloud. He scratched his head with his free hand. "And how do we know you're telling the truth, dwarf?"

"Do we look that stupid?" Bormph's arms extended left and right in a futile attempt to measure the fish graveyard. "A bit excessive for a snack."

"What then is your business here?"

"Adventuring," Whinewaeyn squeaked, to which the cub in Amjelle' arms yelped.

"Found him," Amjelle volunteered as Klampf's brow knitted into a frown watching the bear wriggle about. "Out here. Among the fish."

"But of course!" Klampf mock-squeaked.

"Hrmph," Ramrok contributed, squeaking the loudest.

"What was that?" Klampf pinned the barbarian.

"Hrmph," Ramrok repeated with emphasis, still blank-faced.

Klampf turned to his fellow riders for support on a statement like that. The whole regiment of nose-holding, eye-shielding, befuddled-looking subordinates gawked back at him like loons on a field trip.

"What's your explanation for all this then?" He turned back to the party.

"Beats me," Bormph squeaked with a rumbling undertone.

"And me," said Whinewaeyn.

"We're all beaten," Thimble summarized.

It did little to reassure the captain. "Maybe we should apprehend you all, in any event. On the grounds of being around at a place and time like this, and for looking suspicious. It sounds like the setup for a joke. Why would a wizard, a polar bear and a savage grunting at authorities—"

A dull thud interrupted him. Heads turned. Swirls of sand rose up a short distance away, from a spot once empty but now occupied by something silvery, shimmering in the desert sun. The group's gazes were still fixed on the spot when the next errant tuna thumped into the sand a couple of feet away, gasping and flapping, before lying quiet.

"Or," Amjelle suggested, "maybe it's just the weather in these parts."

"Which stinks, apparently," Bormph grunted.

Murmurs rippled through the ranks.

"Erm… Right. Maybe so." Captain Klampf shifted in his saddle from one uncomfortable position to another and squinted up at the great, blue, fish-leaking yonder. "Maybe there are indeed other things at play here. Speaking of which… You haven't perchance seen a… Hmm, how to put it? You haven't seen a… tower?" His narrowed eyes travelled over the assembled faces. "A tower that would normally be attached to a palace's east wing?"

Questioning looks.

"His Royal Princeliness lost one," he specified.

"Got bored of standing around in the same spot, eh, Captain?" Bormph quipped. "No farewell note?"

No farewell note was confirmed, no motive apparent.

"Haven't come across a tower. But there was a dune," Whinewaeyn brought up. "Somewhere one shouldn't be, if that's of any help." By the look on the captain's face, it wasn't. "Really the dune came to us, was what it was, and before we found out what it was, it left again. If we'd only— Ouch!" He was nudged into silence.

"It wasn't *just* a dune…" Amjelle laid out the whole rest of the incident in fewer and much less rambling sentences.

"Huh," said the captain, when she came to Sylthia's unknown fate.

"Elf leave no trace," Ramrok boomed and squeaked simultaneously, which sounded the strangest yet. "Like dune."

The captain listened, but wasn't receptive to ideas of vanishing elves or sand dunes. "Sorry about your dune and the runaway lass, but we can't help you there. I'm sure you'll find one of the two soon enough. Now, absent towers combined with raining fish out of nowhere, that's different. That's a first. We've got our priorities sorted." In the background, another meaty thud sent more sand swirling. There was a certain regularity to the irregularities now.

Amjelle found herself tempted to thwack the cavalry captain with a fish. Would be a first too. She considered picking out a large one.

On the spur of the moment, she instead pulled Whinewaeyn's saddlebag open and drew out the mysterious leathery thing she had found back in the tent. "Maybe *you* can help us still, Captain. Seen anything like this before?" She held the thing out, and Klampf leaned down to take it.

Which was a mistake. Holding the item with both hands, the captain realized that his nose was free to sample the present desert aroma. What's more, the abominable stench of the thing he was looking at joined in merrily. And thus assaulted by the odorous equivalent of a combination of plague and cholera, he gasped, reeled back and dropped the thing like a hot potato. He pulled so hard on his reins that his sergeant surged forward to assist him.

"You alright, Captain?"

Nodding, his commander covered his nose again.

"Looks like a *knoo'boosh!*" exclaimed Sergeant Quinch, a man with a ratty face, as he saw the object close up, still wisely holding his nose.

"A *knoo'boosh*, Sergeant?"

"It's an actual thing?" Amjelle was excited to put a label on the rag too, metaphorically speaking.

"Sure. A *knoo'boosh*... That's footwear. Orcen stuff."

Amjelle flinched.

Bormph too. "Aren't orcs brutish, aggressive and rather repulsive? A race to avoid altogether? As far as I can remember, in the last war they promised death and destruction to everyone who's not an orc south of the Amcalladams…"

"Well, on the positive side," said the rat-faced man, "there's only a single orcen settlement left around here after the war. Thog'thok. It's on the Oc'potsh piece of land, a couple of leagues over there." He squinted into the northerly distance. "They're the prime example of reformed gruntlings. I was there only a while ago escorting the tax collector. They're just about the most adorable creatures one can imagine, next to teddy bears – hospitable, courteous, always willing to learn from humans. In fact, they enjoy human company."

"What about elves?" Thimble chipped in.

"I couldn't say with certainty, but I would assume…"

"They aren't cannibals, right?" Bormph growled. "A cannibal with table manners is still a cannibal in my book, whatever race he prefers."

"Nah…" The sergeant shook his head. "That was yeeeears ago." He stretched the "e" in "years" quite a bit. "They've all recanted that sort of thing! There was the one… oh, and that other… a very, very, very unpleasant incident, it's true, but the exceptions prove the rule, no? You really have to allow for a certain leeway when taking people like these back into the fold of society. Progress requires some sacrifices, no?"

Shortly after this exchange, a dust cloud filled with adventurers was heading north.

As if to mark the end of this brief get-together another tuna plummeted from above. Just a few days ago, the odds of a fish actually hitting someone in the middle of the desert had been close to zero; now, with three dozen riders covering a whole lot of space for an extended amount of time, the chances had increased substantially, although they were still pretty slim.

This plunging tuna picked the captain.

THUD!

CHAPTER 7

Plucked Princess Predicament

E arlier in the day, not too far away, life was good.

It always was until it was time to get up; things had a habit of going downhill from there. However, this time around, even with one's eyelids peeled back life *still* looked good – better than ever, in fact. Blinking didn't change a thing. The second impression only attested to the initial verdict. Everything looked… paradisaical.

She rose with a start.

A lush silken canopy enshrouded her. Swathes of shiny cloth studded with rosebud patterned embroidery cascaded down on all sides as a layered curtain, a strong vanilla scent exuding from it. In the middle of it all, there she was, sprawled out like a pig in muck – though the muck was made of goose-down cushions and satin sheets, a whole snow-white, cloud-like landscape between the four dark mahogany bedposts, the sentinels of her very own little realm.

She pushed back the covers, dove through the layers of lace and found herself in a perfectly round chamber. In the world beyond the hangings, a bedside rug welcomed her bare feet; all sorts of exotic animals and colourful whorls were woven into it. It was hemmed with red tassels and led up to an elegant, bow-legged dresser, with knobs of pure gold in the shape of lion heads. Atop it, ringed by an assortment of brushes, sat an open jewellery case, its gemmy contents sparkling from within.

And what a mirror! She stepped closer. The wall-sized looking glass showed a blonde, slender, pointy-eared figure in her undergarments with eyes that were widening by the minute. Aside from the giant four-poster bed, the mirror also reflected a nightstand, tapestries fashioned in an Eastlander style, and two shelves full of tomes and all manner of memorabilia. Next to the door, a suit of armour holding a halberd stood sentinel, joining the bedposts in their solemn vigil, and through an arched opening near the nightstand the bright sky was visible, lending the looking glass some of its blue. The only thing off about this otherwise majestic idyll was a scrap of cloth with a handle sitting in the middle of the floor, smelling awful.

At this point the elf's drowsiness bowed out, admitting that it couldn't possibly be involved in a dream anymore, and made room for a close relative, daze. Daze dabbled around with the given material for a bit, but eventually called for befuddlement. And together, Sylthia and her befuddlement decided, for a start, to listen.

Muffled grunts filtered into the privacy of the chamber. When she sidled over to the drape-framed window, the volume of the babbling increased. Until a booming bark shushed everything. A little while later, the grunts started again, a trifle subdued.

Sylthia drew the wine-red damask drapes further to the side and ventured a peek out the window. Down – quite a bit down – below, jittery green humanoids were milling about. Gruntlings. Not all of them were agitated. A pack of them stood observing the huge stone structure of a tower, not sure what to make of it, while others circled it cautiously. Now and again one of the lot gave off snarls as if to intimidate this masonry monster.

One gruntling dared to look up.

"*Kh'thum, phe'thun!*" he yelled, pointing.

Sylthia quickly withdrew from the window as soon as she registered several of the fearsome orcs staring back at her. Tusks decorated their jaws. Bones pierced their noses. Her skin began to crawl.

"*Uk-uk!*" There was a stir outside. "*Moogh-moogh! Woogh-nook! Coo-coogh pa-dook!*"

The elf understood not a syllable – though she had an idea what the pounding footsteps and clinking weapons echoing up the winding stairway were up to: no good. The grunting grew louder and more frantic, with bangs and clangs mixed in.

Sylthia grabbed a blanket to cover herself. A moment passed in which she wondered whether she had got her priorities right. To make up for it, she endowed herself with one of the gilded brushes for a weapon and rushed to bolt the door, but as soon as she got there, it shook on its hinges and flew into her face. The orcen way of knocking meant knocking things *down*.

"Have you no manners, barging into a lady's bed chamber like that?" she yelled at them.

Yet there was no forthcoming demand for etiquette lessons. Rather, the gleam of knives and cleavers amplified the affront. The brass nails on the oak clubs didn't glint so much, but looked like they could leave an impression regardless.

A throwing axe headed already for the elf. Sylthia swerved to the side, and it juddered into the nightstand. She was nimble but – no way around it – outnumbered, and more orcs kept pouring in.

"Anyone care to talk?"

Judging from the puzzled looks, the uninvited pack thought about it for only a second. A language issue? Probably not.

Sylthia lunged forward into a dive between two orcs. The suit of armour propped against the wall clanked noisily, toppled over and crashed onto the floor. The mess of metallic components clanked for a long time out of sheer protest at being treated in such a coarse fashion. Sylthia curled into a ball, rolled to one side and reached out for the lower end of the halberd from under the pile of armour, now it was short of an owner. With a yank, she pulled the pole towards her, got to her feet and held the axe blade topped with a spike in her opponents' irritated faces. As their reactions showed, this one had the edge over any brush.

"*Ko-ko-posh!*" grunted a green-skinned brute with a particularly long knife.

Sylthia swung the halberd forward. It kept the orcs at bay, but the doorway was blocked already by more unbidden arrivals.

With a lurch, she backed up. The pole was long, but space quickly grew short. Behind her, the arched window offered the only escape route, though the blue sky served as a helpful reminder that a hasty retreat by window generally works better closer to the ground.

"*Ko-ko-posh!*" The orcs advanced.

Pushed back against the opening, Sylthia's halberd entangled itself in a last-ditch effort to teach a meddlesome gruntling how to mind his manners. Beads of sweat trickled down the elf's nose, tickling irritably, when out of the corner of her eye, she noticed a nose-ringed orc of impressive size jostling through the throng. He made quite a sight with his dark, heavy cowl and the jingling chain of animal teeth wrapped around his neck, identifying him as a shaman. His enormous, claw-like hands reached forward and, to Sylthia's astonishment, pushed aside the weapons of his fellow orcs.

Three things happened then, in close succession.

For one, the shaman hollered something in orcish. Then, in the tongue familiar to the elf, he said, "No fear! We no want hurt!" Better still, the orcs listened, and abruptly stopped attacking.

The second thing that happened was that Sylthia, pitting her halberd against an orc's jagged spear, found herself on the receiving end of a violent backlash. Weapons parted, the halberd slid from her hands, and she tumbled back, grappling frantically for support. Her fingers latched onto a fat tome sitting on the windowsill and held on to it. Just not for long.

The book gave way. A drawn-out gasp of a noise changed halfway into something closer to a shriek as it left Sylthia's lungs. More importantly, she lost her balance and slumped – not very gracefully – right out of the window. The cessation of hostilities from the orc side did very little to help her under the circumstances.

The third thing that happened was that half a league away, Tjillmer the shepherd was chatting with his friend, drinking buddy, sorcerer's apprentice and self-declared alchemagical pioneer, Brand.

"So…" Brand began. "Experienced anything new last night when you smoked the magic mushrooms?"

"Oh, sure!" Tjillmer told him. "Some of the weird stuff even refused to go away."

"You're kiddin'. Like what?"

Tjillmer pointed.

A cluster of mud huts lay scattered about the landscape a fair way off, and among them rose something large and looming, a structure from which – right at the very moment Tjillmer stuck out his hand – a woman wrapped in a blanket was on her way out through the top window, screaming her head off.

"I'll be damned if that thing was there yesterday," the shepherd insisted. "And neither was that woman!" Then she was gone. Gravity had taken its toll. "Weird, isn't it?"

"Gosh! I can see it too!" Brand cried out. "It's a tower!" He looked in horror at it. "And this thing… it's throwing people out! This stuff is way stronger than I expected!"

At which point Tjillmer's alchemagy-dabbling friend suddenly had some doubts about dabbling in alchemagy. He repented his misdeeds on the spot, and vowed to change his ways to appease the gods from hence on. True to his word, before the day's end he had burned all his magic mushrooms and was on his way to Weith Abbey to become a monk.

And back at the tower? Where we've left things at a pivotal moment, hanging in mid-air? Unsurprisingly for someone in want of wings, Sylthia – now that she had exited the window kissing her chances of escape goodbye – plummeted earthwards, arms briefly flailing, with her life flashing before her eyes…

Nobody had expected a tower to pop up overnight slap-bang in the middle of an orc village, let alone an elf dropping out of it as soon as she had the opportunity –

certainly not the orc peon who had dumped a wagonload of hay behind his mud hut the other day. But as coincidence would have it, a full-grown tower made camp in his backyard, an elf tumbled out of it, and that heap of hay found itself in the right place at the right time.

Thwomp!

As it was a very prickly kind of hay and her blanket had abandoned her mid-flight, Sylthia's shriek gained an octave.

"There they are! Orcs!" Amjelle hissed. "Get over here!"

A dozen feet scrambled to hide behind a massive column of sandstone rock.

The pillar jutting out of the ground had been waiting forever for its chance to play a part in a grand adventure. This was it. Pillars of rock don't have exciting lives. Most wouldn't even call them lives, that's how bland they are. This specific pillar had, like most of its kind, been formed by the gradual accumulation of sediment over eons. However, unlike others, it had a unique shape, of which it was very proud in its own pillarly way, and yet it had "erosion into nothingness" written all over it. In a couple of eons, it would be gone. Suffice to say, a group of adventurers seeking cover behind its peculiar shape marked the pinnacle of its existence.

Bormph's head peeked out from behind it. He extracted his spyglass, and with it observed the goings-on atop the elevation ahead. What he spied were wattle-roofed mud huts with deerskin flaps for doorways, a couple of smouldering campfires and assorted skulls mounted on sticks. Some of these totems wore wigs, horns, sparkling chains; quite a few looked scary, others ludicrous, or both at the same time. There was an east wing tower too, lacking a building. It stuck out like a sore thumb.

Gruntlings were bustling about among the huts like ants.

"There she is!" Bormph announced when he spotted someone non-green in a totem-riddled area. "It's her, alright!"

The elf was in shackles by then, squatting on the ground at the back of the settlement, surrounded by a handful of cross-legged orcs. The mood seemed sombre. A nose-ringed shaman, draped in a thick cowl, flopped down in front of the elf, looking particularly noteworthy with his intricate beard which boasted the addition of some choice pieces of cutlery. At least he'd have the proper tools at hand in case of a snacking emergency.

Two more cowl-wearing orcs with less complicated beards flanked the shaman, probably hoping to get their own cutlery worked into them someday. The remaining four were garbed in colourful armour, patched together from the most diverse sources conceivable – maybe for protection and to hurt their enemies' eyes at the same time. Sylthia, comparatively, wore a simpler outfit: plain and scanty. Sensual, in Thimble's judgment. Less emotionally invested, one would call it a rag.

"What are they talking about?" Thimble whispered.

"You tell me," Bormph whispered back, tapping at the spyglass. "Next time pack one with a hearing aid, guys." He peered into the device again. "I see a cauldron. A big one."

"*Ou'p ti-doo? How-hoo?*" asked H'roc-Noc'sh, the cutlery-equipped shaman. The elf assumed from the way he held up his snout that he was the one in charge. "What you do here and why you do? *N'pee-wee oo-hop?* And why you bring tall home with you, non-orc?"

"Listen, all this is a bad joke…" Sylthia started.

"*Hu-ho? K'num ho?* Why joke and why make bad one?"

The elf groaned. She had only regained consciousness a short while ago in one of the mud huts, which had been stuffed with yet more damp-reeking straw – as if hay was an elf's natural habitat.

"It must be a misunderstanding. I never *wanted* to be here. It just *happened!* I don't even know where I am, and I don't carry towers in my travel sack."

"*S'pockee rook-took!*" What sounded like someone tapping a drum was actually a village elder to the head shaman's left. "Pointy-ears be lying!" He sounded adamant, and with one of his eyebrows always cocked, he looked a little devilish too.

"Where even *is* my travel sack?" Sylthia asked. "Where are my clothes? I've got no bow. No arrows, numbskulls! Can't you see?"

"*Rook-took s'pockee!*" came from the other side of the circle. "Lying pointy-ear is!"

"Why would I invade an orc camp all on my own? It makes no sense!"

"*Ghrab-ghrob t'a-lot!* To steal!"

"*Lo-oo-khey!* To spy!"

"And why would I do that without clothes and weapons?"

"*Mee-ow ow! Wow-pow!* Be you woman, be you weapon," the elder said. "*Owee rak-tak!* Womanses very dangerous! Most dangerous of all! Break heart. No trace."

"*Rook-tooks!* Liar!"

Sylthia let out a nettled sigh. "See, I was sleeping as peaceful as a lamb in some godsforsaken desert someplace, and the next thing I know I'm in that stupid tower of yours! You tell me why!"

"*T'k, t'k t'oc. T'g t'um!*" said H'roc-Noc'sh. Sylthia wasn't sure how. "No, no. Tower no orc. Tower be human!"

"Well, the last time I checked *I* was an *elf!* I don't know a whit about whose tower it is, and frankly, I don't care! But whatever is going on here, there's more of it out in the desert!" She went on about mysterious phantoms, a formidable din, runes flitting over the sand, and a dune stopping by.

While the elf was still talking, the orcs put their heads together, muttering under their breath. It sounded as if one insisted on "*Cuck-oo*" whereas another put a finer point on it, repeating "*Koo-koo-ka-choo*", over and over. None of it, she was sure, boded well for any elves around.

"Is there no one who believes me?"

"*U'oo,*" grunted head shaman H'roc-Noc'sh, who had mostly let the others speak until now. "I do."

"You do?" Sylthia felt a flush of relief. As long as the leader of the pack was on her side, she was safe. Right?

At this point, some notes on the Oc'potsh orcs.

The Oc'potsh are an offshoot clan of the Oc'motsh, one of the fiercest groups of gruntlings that ever roamed the lands south of the Crimson Peaks. The atrocities the Oc'motsh brought upon the various races – and even other orc tribes – were so gruesome that records are scarce for this reason. The less said, the better. Archivists assumed everyone knew that they were rotten to the core anyway and there was no need to rub it in. It would have made the annals look like cheap penny dreadfuls. Instead, they chose to let the orcs' crimes speak for themselves.

The crimes spoke until the Great Battle of Rak-a'tak at the foothills of the Amcalladam Mountains in 997, where joint human and elven forces destroyed the advancing army of this abominable tribe once and for all, broke its backbone and wiped it off the face of Aenyros. The few remaining orcs hid in the mountains, where there was nothing to torture other than some withered trees and sturdy rocks. Their natural demise was inevitable. One by one, the last pockets of Oc'motsh resistance were eliminated. The rest of the orcs ended up as the Oc'potsh. They changed a consonant, and that was the beginning of it.

Fortune shone upon them. After their surrender to the enemy, the orcs found support in an extraordinary man: Pons Galligler, Great Caesh's wealthiest philanthrope and professional dreamer. He later became known by the honorary name of Long P'orc, the Orcwhisperer. P'orc had a low voice, hence the whispering, but he also had a big heart and brought the case of reforming the remaining orcs to the court of Great Caesh. He also convinced the dwarven Stonelord Mough-da-Shoog of Burrowsbend to have mercy, and put in a good word for the orcs with Master-Moffle Miff of the city-state of Mynn, who never objected to anything anyway. Last but not least, he convinced the Prince of Zarrafanda, who could've been Miff's brother, and the elven council of the Thyael'ka'lar Forest. P'orc had such a soothing, comforting, reassuring whisper that it was capable of wiping away centuries of atrocities with a throaty "There's some good in everyone if we only believe it." The leaders of the western world had heart and believed him.

It had sounded like a good idea at the time. The Oc'potsh orcs moved south, got a tan and founded a settlement in the foothills of the Silvery Sickle mountains. It was located on the outer fringes of the Joghavri Desert, where they named it Thog'thok ("Placid Place"). They were taught manners, language and a bit of advanced politics by select teachers; they recanted murdering, torture and cannibalism and lived happily ever after, more or less. Some say more, some say less.

After all, there was an incident early on. It was reported that in a cultural exchange session P'orc had looked a tad too closely at some ancient orcen torture instruments. After the incident, he wasn't able to look at any devices anymore. His demise was for a good cause, the orcs insisted, and the least they could do was organize a vast funeral banquet for the big-hearted P'orc. To this day, the ambiguous nature of this event still gives rise to the exact same racial prejudices the great philanthrope intended to eradicate. Some things never change.

But even without P'orc, the civilized orcs project continued with the occasional challenge. The most recent case in point: an uninvited elven visitor with a turret in tow, who swore to high heaven that she had arrived overnight via unknown means, and certainly not by her own volition.

"*Ka-rumpf...* Well then," said H'roc-Noc'sh. "*T'k pt'ee!* No need be hasty! *Oc-wok? Bagh-ack-dum! Oc-wok-trok.* Make ancestor orcs decision? No. Own we make. Ancestors bad. *Hum-hum, dum di-dum.* Decision make like humans say we make. We good orcs! *Oc-okh!*"

Sylthia's sceptical ears perked up, which made them extra pointy. "You make decisions like humans? How does that work?"

"*Oc'motsh-potsh vote.* Elders vote."[*]

---

[*] The orcish and human terms for "vote" are of striking similarity. And for good reason. The practice of asking subordinates for opinions was

"You vote?" The elf couldn't hide her bafflement. "How... commendable!" The orcs as pioneers in democracy? Voting was still one of the latest and most progressive developments in politics, so spanking new that some human kingdoms had not even considered it in any seriousness. While it was widely agreed that voting was the future, common sense kept reminding current rulers that the future was always a day away, and so that's where they left the idea.

A smile lit up Sylthia's face. She wanted to express how much the notion was appreciated, that she held the firm conviction that a hint of democracy was essential towards advancing this particular tribe (and the orcs as a race), and that in the long run these concepts would nurture togetherness in the context of world community as a whole. But then an idea dawned on her, reminiscent of a snowball on a wintery mountain top, setting out to see what was down in the valley...

"*Uk rook-took s'pockee?*" H'roc-Noc'sh put the question to the others. "Who believe pointy-ears no tell truth?"

A couple of moments later, Sylthia's premonition was a thing of the past; an avalanche of crushing votes had rolled over her. The head shaman was outvoted, six to one.

"Hey!" she objected. "There's something wrong with your vote!"

The orcs counted again. But, according to the democratic principle, numbers don't lie. Sylthia, so far ardent supporter of the said principle, went off it then and there.

---

entirely alien to the Oc'motsh before they turned Oc'potsh. So they simply adopted the human word, and had they ever written it, which they didn't, because they couldn't, they'd have done it in italics.

"*Oc troc t-ok.* Council has spoken," H'roc-Noc'sh announced, unblinking. "Human way, good way. Now… punishment."

"But—"

"*Kak'tak?* You want torture?"

"Course not, I—"

"*Okh.*" And that seemed to settle the matter.

Sylthia was shoved back into her mud hut, locked up and given more time to spend with the cartloads of hay she had not ordered the last time around. Her only company was the heavy tome that had triggered her tumble out of the tower window and, needless to say, the two hadn't been on the best terms since. When she was alone with the villain, Sylthia threw it in a wide arc across the room. She felt a little better after that.

A few moments later, her head cocked to the side. From where she was sitting, it almost looked as if the book wasn't quite where it was supposed to be. It rested, the pages spread-eagled, propped up against the wall, and yet it seemed to have partly entered it. Which, of course, was absurd. So she hitched herself up and looked again. Same thing.

Leaning over, Sylthia carefully pulled the book out of the wall in which it appeared stuck. It slid out, smooth and quiet, as if to tell her – without making any fuss about it – that she was losing her mind.

She checked the walls. The floor. The straw. No secret panel or trapdoor answered her knocks, no magic gate offered its services. And when she flipped the book open, she only found a couple of ham-fisted drawings of what might have been a cow's head, a rooster lording over a muckheap, and a rout of pigs wallowing in mud, some of the images crossed out. The rest was full of symbols upon symbols that she had never before seen in her life, with odd diagrams and abstract sketches interspersed here and there that professed even less artistic merit than the ones at the front. At least the rooster looked like a rooster, third leg aside.

All things considered, she was at the orcs' mercy, trapped and imaging things. Great.

Outside, the *kh'pha'phts* – traditional Oc'potsh waterpipes – were served, and deliberations on the elf's fate commenced as they smoked.

"Elfling no want torture," the head shaman reminded everyone. He almost seemed to regret it as he inhaled through his mouthpiece. Reform entailed uncertainty in areas that had been clear cut in days past. Reform was challenging.

"We good orcs," a shaman colleague grunted, blowing some smoke. "No do torture."

"*We* no want torture, *she* no want torture. But vote say, she liar."

"Human ways, stupid ways," one of the elders rasped sagely. Murmurings echoed his wisdom.

H'roc-Noc'sh, hands on knees, struck a defiant pose. "But we vow, we do human way!"

"Human ways, stupid ways!" It was a chorus by now.

A sigh rattled through their leader's cutlery-laden beard.

"So we keep elfling?" an elder asked. "Locked up?"

H'roc-Noc'sh took another puff. "If keep we do, and humans find out, they say we take elfling. We be bad, bad orcs. Like ancestors."

"So we let go elfling?"

"Elfling be liar. Vote so say." The head shaman grunted with irritation. "Liar tell lies. If let go we do, elfling tell lies. We be bad, bad orcs."

"*Always* we be bad, bad orcs?"

H'roc-Noc'sh growled and sucked on his charred pipe in the hopes of drawing some inspiration out of it.

Eventually, a heavy blanket of silence descended over the circle and made itself comfortable. Nobody objected. The totems around the elders conveyed a knowing air, but whatever yesterday's spirits would have to say on the matter, they never audibly spoke up. For a while, the orcs glanced at each other and hadn't a thing to contribute. Their faces were masks of awkwardness, much like the totems, only they still had some brains to grapple with their predicament. Leadership was required. When nobody knew where else to look, all eyes returned to the one presiding over the circle.

The massive cranium of the head shaman had dropped to his chest, his beard cutlery clinking. Eyes squeezed shut, he was in deep contemplation. The weed was cooperative, the tobacco was doing its work. It made things less complicated, blurring the lines between problem and solution. The dizzier he felt, the lighter his mind, and the lighter his mind, the more easily it freed itself from his body. It floated away and cruised about, looking at the trouble from all sides.

H'roc-Noc'sh finally rammed his fist into the soil. "Elfling be problem *here*," he grunted as his spirit reported back from its excursion. "Elfling be problem *there*." A claw-like nail stabbed in the air in the direction of the world at large. "Elfling be problem *anywhere*." A long, pregnant pause followed. Then, light at the end of the tunnel: "*Elfling* be problem."

"Elfling be problem," everybody agreed.

"We get rid of elfling!"

This time, it wasn't the head shaman who had spoken. But the obvious solution was up for grabs with the fumes enlightening receptive heads, and one of the elders merely had to pick it up.

The orcs looked at each other.

"We get rid." H'roc-Noc'sh rose. "We get rid, and elfling not here and not there. Elfling not anywhere. Elfling gone, problem gone." He put his foot down. "We good orcs."

"How?"

Some ancestor blood must still have rushed through his veins when the head shaman rasped in reply, "We… *eat!*"

"We eat!" Now there was that chorus again.

The idea resonated instantly with everybody around the circle. It was so simple and self-evident, it almost hurt. It might have had the one odd moral flaw, but other than that, it was… palatable.

If only the elf was their only problem. "What we do with tower?" someone demanded.

"We take desert sand." H'roc-Noc'sh peeked through the heavy fumes writhing before him. He watched the smoke as it curled up into the twilight of the falling evening.

"And then?"

H'roc-Noc'sh's tone was as flat as the Joghavri. "We bury."

West Wing Woes

"Name and profession?"

"Glampatch E. Zaengdaengler. Fireworks specialist."

"Please take a seat, Mr Zaengdaengler. Address?"

When the man had given his address, the clerk dipped his quill into the inkwell, shoved his round spectacles back for the umpteenth time that day and glared up at the haggard figure opposite him. "Insured, I presume?"

"Yes, of course. In my line of work, you know…"

"And there was an occurrence you wish to report?"

"Ach, I'm afraid there was."

"Balcony?" The clerk gave it a shot. "This is the non-balcony line." He pointed with a leery frown at the other queue populating the vast Dimmerskeep town hall foyer. The other line wound around a complicated pattern of red cord towards one of his colleagues, extending back to the entrance and beyond. Only the obscure cases landed on his desk. That is, once he got rid of those lawless balconeers, who hijacked his queue to cut the line.

"No, not a balcony," Glampatch E. Zaengdaengler said. "It's about firecrackers, bottle rockets, cracklers. And flares, missiles, flaming wheels, sky flyers…"

"Pyrotechnic stuff?" The clerk scented a pattern like a sniffer dog. A trace of smugness stole over his freckled face. He'd have loved to make a career as a private investigator, and not have to sit around all day feeling like a sketchy character in some pulp mag, created for the sake of filling a couple of paragraphs to advance the plot. He was young. He was smart. He had potential.

"Well, yes, pyrotechnics. That's what it is. As I said, I'm a fireworks specialist," the man repeated patiently. "I was hired for the Mish-Clash closing ceremony by the Prince himself! Alas, due to the dire circumstances…"

"Yes, yes, of course." The clerk nodded as he finished filling in the "missing objects" column. "Flaming wheels, sky flyers… Anything else… less flammable?"

"Ach, I almost forgot! There was one Willy the Weeder."

"One Willy the what?"

"One Willy the Weeder."

"And what would a Weeding Willy wee… er… be?"

"It's one of those little figurines one puts in the flower beds, you know? A birthday gift for my dear wife, see, and I tucked it away with all the other stuff until the big day. And now they've got my Willy too."

"You allege someone took it?"

"Well, yes," Glampatch E. Zaengdaengler said, confused. "That's why everyone's here, right? Things have disappeared."

"I gather you secured the material? So that nobody would tinker with it?"

"Of course. All the explosive stuff's gone from a storeroom I locked myself! Double and thrice, I swear!"

The clerk narrowed his eyes. "Was that double or thrice?"

"Pardon?"

"Double *and* thrice, I heard. If you locked that storeroom of yours thrice, you must have locked it double *first*. So why even mention it?" The bespectacled man wore no hat to adjust knowingly, no trench coat to bury his hands in, nor did he have a rolled piece of tobacco hanging from the corner of his mouth. But he felt as though he had all of that in spirit, and in spirit the thick biting smoke almost made him tear up. "Now was it *double* or *thrice*, Mr Zaengdaengler?"

"I... I... It's only an expression, isn't it?" the other gasped. "I... ach... I reckon one could say that I locked the room just once then. But firmly. *Very* firmly."

"Just once?" The clerk cum detective leaned back, tapping his quill on the tabletop. "Once is half as much as double, and only a third of thrice. Actually, once is a long way from thrice, Mr Zaengdaengler. Once is hardly locked at all, wouldn't you agree?"

"Um, erm, well, it could've been locked... *better*, I guess?"

The quill got to work again. "Hardly locked at all." The clerical detective looked up, staring at his client with an unwinking eye.

"Erm... If you say so, Mr... Um, Mr—"

"Minver. Mincling Minver. But this isn't about names, eh?"

"Yes, Mr Minver. I mean, no." Sweat pearled on the haggard man's forehead. "I... I..." The drops coursed downwards with determination.

"It's almost as if you have something to hide, Mr Zaengdaengler..." The clerk's reedy voice had suddenly turned throaty, threatening. "Have you?"

"Why…? What? How…?" Glampatch E. Zaengdaengler's pop-eyed stare found itself confronted with the menacing eyes of the clerk, peering through his spectacles' lenses.

"I presume the Prince paid you in advance?"

"Ach, yes. The Prince always pays in advance, Mr Minver." For a moment there was firm ground. "He's very gracious. May the gods bless him… and his ways."

"But your services aren't required now," the clerk reminded him.

"No, the closing ceremony was cancelled. Too bad, that is."

"So the Prince *owns* the firecrackers, and you were merely storing them for him, up until the day they'd come into use."

"Th-that's right."

"And yet now your firecrackers have all of a sudden evaporated into thin air." Mincling relished the words as they rolled from his tongue. His eyes glinted. "Without… a single… *crack.*" As he arrived at the last word, it sounded like the snapping of someone's neck. "How… convenient."

Unease spread across Mr Zaengdaengler's face as the insinuation hit home. Combined with the clerk's maniacal conduct, he began to fear for his life.

Mincling leapt to his feet. The immediate result, on account of his limited height, was that he vanished beneath his desk. A temporary impression. The next moment, heaving himself up on the table's edge, feet clambering onto the chair, the pocket-sized man reappeared like a phoenix rising from the ashes. Propped up on his outstretched arms, he now loomed over his client, who had curled up into a ball in his chair.

"Maybe someone *made* things disappear when an opportunity presented itself, Mr Zaengdaengler?" he let out. "A tower, balconies, fireworks… Who'd notice, right? Do you know what happens with frauds when the Prince is in a bad mood?"

Glampatch E. Zaengdaengler, honest businessman, pious believer in the Holy Quintity, who had never missed a single Prayday mass in the past fifty cycles, faithful husband and adored father of two teenage daughters – Glampatch E. Zaengdaengler, to whom the thought of scamming another human being had never occurred in his whole life – slid from his chair. "Ach, I… I'll make sure to check ag-again in that storeroom, Mr M-M-Minver," he stammered and hustled out, almost tripping over himself.

"You do just that," the clerk yelled after him. "Remember, I have your name and address!"

The foyer fell dead quiet.

It took a bit, but eventually the murmuring picked up again. Some used the buzz to abandon their line and rush out.

For the umpteenth time plus one, Mincling Minver prodded back his spectacles. When his call rang through the hall again, it was as crisp as a whiplash.

"Next!"

A few streets away, up Dymmling's Hill, the Prince's palace loomed over the city. Preparations for a busy evening were already underway in the West Wing. While it was west of the main building, the West Wing had invariably been front and centre when it came to Zarrafandan politics – even more so since the east wing tower had gone absent without leave. Now the fate of a relative was at stake.[*]

Over the years, the West Wing had seen its share of drama: the labour pains of policy-making and the death throes of half-hearted ideas; heated disputes before, during and after the implementation of measures; all kinds of political excitement, agitation, controversy, conspiracy and ballyhoo. From time to time, an angry mob had brandished pitchforks and threatened to burn down the premises – business as usual in the world of plotting, double-crossing, back-stabbing and intrigue.

But as of late, politics had shifted to party hats and an evening of card games once a week. Thanks to the Prince. Before he came to power, nobody could figure the Prince out, not even the age-worn King Thorgwold. When he abdicated in favour of his son, the latter's peculiarities came quickly to the fore, until each and every last citizen knew: The Prince had bats in his belfry, squirrels in the attic, owls in his loft. A whole menagerie. And yet, the Prince loved his subjects – the men a trifle more intimately, as speculation had it. Which shouldn't have bothered anyone. And yet it did. It bothered those who took a shine to same-gendered townsfolk, and it did so because they worried about their agenda being associated with a Prince who was stark raving mad.

His father, the Geezer-King, couldn't quite follow these developments. In his old days, he grew increasingly

---

[*] In contrast to the West Wing, the east wing's role in the Princedom's history had been negligible – unless one counts the much lauded chicken curry prepared in its kitchen. The chicken curry, however, tasty as it was, had not been enough to earn the east wing capitalization. There'd been a vote on the issue. The motion was rejected.

convinced that his son was his daughter. And, as any father does, he also believed that his daughter would do as fine as the son he never had when he handed over the throne. Well, Dymmling the Third soon showed his mettle.

"Dimmy the Pink" started off by renaming the Kingdom to "the Princedom." That had "zing". He also abolished the use of ermine for royal uniforms on the grounds of his favourite pet being a rodent, and championed the so-called "Velvet Revolution" instead, declaring velvet the prime fabric of royalty, nobility and every other self-respecting citizen. Furthermore, he devised the Mish-Clash festival and issued the famous Alternative Decree, reminding the world at large to "Just be gay."

This illustrates why the Prince needed advisers. Damage controllers. Someone to point out that the Alternative Decree was "non-binding" and that the room left for interpretation was "deliberate". It was more of a thought-provoking suggestion than a compulsory mandate, an... alternative. Being grouchy or straight or both was *not* against the law of the land. "Not yet," the Prince tossed into conversation when the matter came up at numerous parties. It won him a barrel of laughs, albeit not always for the same reasons.

Hence the rise of the "princelings" – observant courtiers, clarifiers and full-time worriers when it came to matters of succession. While the Prince slept snug as a bug in a rug, the princelings had the nightmares their sovereign skipped. When the Prince's flushes of asinine inspiration went full-force around the bend, they tried to distract him, or else told him, "Great idea, Your Majesty. Let's take this off your hands. This just needs some time." It even became a strategy to encourage fresh nutty notions in order to delay the execution of any decrees that were a mess-in-progress, pending interpretation. As such, the Prince's inspirations could be consigned to the mires of oblivion, where they sank, quietly and thoroughly.

The counsellors had been busy ever since Dymmling the Third insisted that his favourite rodent, a white gerbil by the name of Ruffles, was to get her own throne right beside him. His Majesty was adamant, despite all their concerns. "But *I* am the Prince! And I *want!*" – and so he got. It was one of those things that kept him from getting into other blunders.

As far as effective governing was concerned, the Prince exhibited a pretty *laissez-faire* attitude anyway. A *what-do-I-care* approach, as his princelings put it. While His Majesty tended to matters that caught his fancy – like working towards a velvetier Princedom, experimenting with make-up choices or painting the Dimmerskeep town fountain in garish colours – his subjects were left to their own devices. As a consequence, the most influential townsfolk had taken affairs into their own hands and self-regulated away to their heart's content, ignorant of the objections brought forward by considerate heads of the intelligentsia.

The system worked. Everyone knew their place.

The congress of influential people worked to maintain the natural balance: the princelings, the commander general, the principal merchants, the heads of the craftsmen guilds, the scholars, and Archbishop Vynnfield gave his blessings. Even Shady Shoo, patron of the underground and ensurer of its seediness, in charge of protection services and the proper alignment of the horizontal profession, was a ruling congress member –

reason being that a confidant hailing from the other side of the law provides a divergent angle. No doubt, having an in-depth conversation with an assassin *before* any action is taken spares a life, the hassle of disposing of a body, covering tracks and an investigation. All sides win. "A few coins every other day keeps the coroner away" went the worldly wisdom originating from the crooked alleys of the Harbour Quarter. Shady Shoo served as a reminder of the importance of upholding established traditions.

So it came to be that the princelings arranged meetings in the West Wing. "Congress" was scheduled for every Brewday evening, the third day of the week, and took place in the interludes between rounds of the Princedom's most popular card game, Knucklebuck. The presence of the Prince wasn't required, since he wasn't playing with a full deck anyway. Others covered his absence, and sometimes the decks were even fuller than full or marked by the royal gamekeeper. A correlation between the outcomes of the game, the stakes, and the policies that Congress agreed on was a natural consequence.

This time though, things differed. This was an impromptu get-together. It wasn't even a Brewday, and the Knucklebuck decks were resting. Instead of an evening of entertainment, bargaining and blackmailing, the assembled parties had gathered to deal with the Big Unknown. Even His Royal Dimness had shown up in the West Wing to defend the east wing tower's honour, whimpering like a puppy.

"Gentlemen. Prince." A stern-looking giant of a man nodded at the assembly from the far end of the polished mahogany table. Aside from a look of concern, he wore a well-trimmed beard and a silver breastplate, all of which, with differing degrees of subtlety, added to the impression of a man representing law and order. When he peeled a mailed glove from his hand and tossed it onto the table in front of him, the animated talk in the room hushed.

"You've all heard the news…" The giant's voice penetrated the tense air, as gruff as a battering ram in full swing. "The situation's dire."

The whole room stared transfixed at Royt Montrakhán, Commander General, Valiant Defender of the Realm, Keeper of Military Secrets, Bear of a Man, Voice like a Battering Ram. The shock of his blunt words percolated through the gathering of minds. It trickled, and in response a murmur began to rise from all corners of the giant conference table, or rather – considering its oval shape – from all its curves. As the murmur rose, volume joined in, and they had a ball.

"Isn't that a… rather sweeping assumption, Commander?" asked a much less impressive voice, riding the murmurs' wave. It belonged to a plump and balding man, owner of Brommrog & Brommrog, Zarrafanda's leading shipping guild – Lord Alkam Brommrog, a heavyweight in more ways than one. His face was as well rounded as the sums he shifted on a daily basis from one account to another. "Just because a couple of decrepit bricks disappear from the face of the earth and a few careless balcony owners break a leg, we shouldn't get carried away. Perhaps builders had better check their materials!" His quip sent ripples of nervous laughter through the assembly.

"Silence… *Silence!*" A voice like the general's never failed to leave an impact. I fear that some of us," he shot back at Brommrog, "fail to see the bigger picture… Let me help you." The commander pulled out a piece of parchment tucked inside his armour. "Vanishings reported so far are as follows. First: the palace's east wing tower."

Prince Dymmling's sorry self winced. He was seated at the side of the table, wearing a cap he had borrowed from the court jester. Maybe because it jingled.

"Search parties are underway, Your Highness," Montrakhán boomed in a slightly more comforting tone, but the Prince's snivelling and jingling went on nonetheless. "Also, we're missing seventeen balconies, about three dozen cuckoo clocks, a few bookcases including contents, twenty-six left boots" – the murmur rekindled – "fourteen horned helmets, each of which had one horn missing before they went missing altogether. Also unaccounted for: one hundred and sixty-nine clay gnomes, and their number is growing by the minute. Furthermore unlocatable…" – he turned the page over – "unspecified lengths of fencing, a well, a creek and its riverbed near – rather *once* near – Wayman's Warden and a handful of dunghills from the farmsteads around Weaverring. Among the most unusual cases: An old lady, Mrs Swisham, claims her cottage was stolen the minute she left to buy groceries."

Disquiet at an advanced stage seethed in the room.

"And, in case anyone needs proof closer to one's vest… Should you be wondering about the whereabouts of your *Fairy Maiden*…" The commander general levelled a look at the heavyset merchant, and Lord Alkam Brommrog pricked up his ears at the mention of one of his largest ships. "Messenger pigeons delivered the news that she has been found, crew intact, up a giant mahood tree in the Wending Woods, a hundred and fifty leagues from the nearest body of water. Evacuation is underway as we speak."

Just as his ship had vanished from the sea, Brommrog's overbearing grin was plucked from his fat face. His once rosy cheeks turned waxen and his pudgy hand clasped at his thick neck.

"Gentlemen…" The commander general glanced around. Faces stared back at him aghast. With mounting details, the agitation became palpable. "This is an assault against the Princedom."

"What does it mean?" someone cried out.

"Inconceivable!" protested another.

Whispers made their rounds. Voices talked over each other. "Outrageous!" "Hiding bits 'n' pieces, and whole buildings…" "Parts of the landscape? Now who'd do any of that?" "Who *could?*" "Who *would?*" "And why?" "Must be magic!" "*Powerful* magic!" "Foul magic!" "Gnome magic?" "Someone's playing Ding-the-Diddle with us!"

"Is it Vensk?" A distinct voice surged above the others. "It's always Vensk, isn't it?"

Once brought into play, the name kept bobbing up around the table like a piece of foul fruit drifting in the current. Vensk Stormraiser, bastard son of the former Emperor Mishka of the neighbouring kingdom, Aermerlyn. He had his reasons for vengeance, it was said. The world had been mean to him, or so he was convinced, and it was going to pay for it. Ignored as a successor to his old man, Vensk had been battling his half-sister Lysna for years from his underground fortress in the southern goblin mines of Groo'cae'tran. His whole being was devoted to reconquering Aermerlyn with his army of goblins, and the tiny Princedom of Zarrafanda just happened to be in the way. For the past year, things had been quiet, suspiciously so.

"But Vensk's not a magician!" a reedy man with a bushy moustache and thinning ashen hair objected. It was Master Gnorf, the head of the Barbers' Guild, and the opinion he harboured was shared by quite a few along with his fashionable haircut. "Vensk's not even bright enough to fill out the application forms for the Academy. Vensk's a peasant, who led a rebellion of fork-wielders, and when that was quashed, he rallied those abominable goblins round himself."

"Only the gods know what they see in him!" someone issued from the backbenches.

"Why, it's utter fear. It's fear that there's so much of that bastard around," said someone else, an unveiled reference to the man's notorious abdominal girth.

"Although," another pointed out, "not an inch of him has anything to do with magic. It's as Master Gnorf said."

"So he must have *hired* a mage," Baron Robart of Gryphonsaerie argued, "one as barmy as him. Who can do, you know…"

"Barmy stuff? Lots of it? With gnomes? And towers?"

"There's no such mage!"

Arguments passed back and forth. But even the attending authority in the field, Xoormrax the Elder, Archmagus Emeritus, considered himself confounded. As a wizard bent with years but nonetheless with a repository of anything that resembled a spell under the sun, he offered some speculation. "If it's magic at all, then it must be arcane in nature. Ancient. Potent. Legendary, to be sure." He lapsed into a contemplative pause. "Could be a big joke too. But if so, who has the means to make one of that size?"

Brommrog squirmed in his seat. With each passing moment coins were slipping through his fingers. "I doubt," he said, agitated, "that the *Fairy Maiden* just missed the sea and sailed into a tree because the captain read the chart wrong."

Xoormrax's brow furrowed. "If I hadn't seen the effects with my own eyes, I'd have considered removing a whole tower without a trace outright impossible. Maybe it's transdimensional distortion on a large scale. Never been tried in this day and age. What bothers me most is the multitude and seeming randomness of these phenomena. Could be the disappearances are the mere side effects of black wizardry of yet unknown proportions. But if we're sat here in the middle of the side effects, what then, I ask, would be that magic's actual focus?"

"Side effects... middle of... question mark," Princeling Klimbish scribbled. He'd been tasked with taking the minutes of the West Wing meetings, which usually meant filling his pages with Knucklebuck scores. Not this time.

"Unless..." the wizard mused, looking over at the archbishop on the other side of the table. "Unless, Your Holiness, it might be more like... divine intervention?"

Archbishop Vynnfield, a lean man with the eyes of a ferret, wasn't going to contradict that. He thought divine intervention was far more widespread than most assumed. Every time he sent a little prayer heavenwards on minor business and got what he wanted, he liked to imagine one of the gods had directly intervened in his favour. It worked almost every second time.

"Nothing is impossible for a god, indeed." The archbishop nodded with a solemn grace.

"And yet, *why* would a god intervene?" Xoormrax followed up.

"Who are we to question the gods?" The archbishop held his upturned nose even further aloft. "The One giveth and the Other taketh away, Archmagus." Personally, he'd have wished Prince Dymmling away to whatever unknown place the east wing tower had gone to. Better luck next time.

"Not of one mind, your gods, eh?" Shady Shoo croaked from the other end of society's spectrum. "Riddle me this, then, Archy…" Shady's voice came from someplace deep inside the obscurity of his cowl, as hoarse as a consumption-plagued chain-smoker's. "Let them gods have some towers, fine. But why would them fetch gnomes, cuckoo clocks 'n' shoes? We've got our own thieves, y'know! Do a marvellous job too!" Among other things, this was a matter of professional honour.

"True…" Xoormrax agreed on the principle. "Some might accuse your gods of stealing," he directed at the bishop.

"The gods move in mysterious ways, my sons," said the archbishop, pulling out his undefeatable argument. With his thin hands folded in front of him, he let a dismissive look linger on the shade that was Shoo. "Gods certainly don't steal. They may… retract… bits of creation, if it's their want."

"Yeah, those garden gnomes aren't for everyone," someone remarked.

"But the gods, they *made* none of it," reasoned Achmadan Fynn, guild master of the artisans. "Humans did!"

"Trouble is," said Shady Shoo, "them gods gave humans a mind o' their own, and ne'er thought they was gonna use it to make ghastly things like cuckoo clocks!"

"What blasphemy!" the archbishop cried. "The gods are infallible!"

And with that the muffled chatter returned in full force, punctuated by various utterances of outrage.

"Gentlemen, please! Please!" the Commander General Montrakhán's voice rumbled. A messenger bustled up to his side, saluted and left a missive before being off on his way again. Montrakhán skimmed it, then read the message out loud. "The captain of the guards out on tower retrieval mission in the Joghavri reports fish raining from the skies."

"Oh dear, oh dear, oh dear!" Hushed voices picked up again. "Signs 'n' portents!"

"Fish 'n' ships!" Brommrog sensed a cosmic connection somewhere.

As did the next man, Normi Stargazer, royal astrologer extraordinaire. "The time has come!" The doomsayer let his fateful words loose amid the kerfuffle and they sailed like a vessel chased by the gale. "It's as I've seen it! It's written in the stars!"

Montrakhán gave the astrologer a hard look. "As far as I remember, you've predicted the End of Days before."

Normi, baldness in gnome shape with one eye that tended to wander from the other, seemed to have grown an inch with his pronouncement. He craned his neck in the general direction of the commander general, notwithstanding the fact that his eyes didn't quite align, generally.

"Yessir, General," he conveyed to the area somewhere over there. "I have predicted the End of Days before. And isn't this proof of how right I was, now that the signs are heaping up?" Normi goggled around, savouring the many eyes that were fixed on him, the one with the clear eye when it came to the apocalypse.

Montrakhán tugged thoughtfully on the rough hairs of his beard. "But, according to your predictions, wouldn't it have happened about ten years ago? And then eight or so? And the last time was – what? – three?"

"Ah, yessir, General. Very mindful of you to notice and keep track of the observatory's progress! But how could I expect a non-professional to understand? It's not just that the stars have to be in conjunction. Which they *are*, of course, *again*. Our methods are very complex, based on numerology and related scholarly approaches like calendric science, horology—"

"Numerology, eh? That's your main thing?"

"You might say so. After all, in the end it all comes down to numbers. Especially the number seven to be exact, for everything in the universe is related to instances of sevens. Maybe you've happened to notice that fact?"

The general couldn't say he had. So, instead, he said, to be constructive, "And what do you do with your numbers?"

"We add, subtract, multiply and divide. That sort of thing. And once we're done, we arrive at a conservative estimate regarding, for instance, the occurrence of an apocalypse. If I may elaborate… First, there was the constellation of the seven-pointed star of stars. It was, to be truthful, an eight-pointed star, but we didn't know that at the time due to a cosmic nebula obstructing point number eight. Still… considering the seven-pointed star, the seven days of the week were devised, and our kingdom… I mean Princedom," he quickly corrected himself, with one eye at their dejected, fool's-cap-wearing ruler. "Our… Princedom… only has three provinces now, after His Magnificency discovered that three was a nicer number, but it had four before, and four plus three is seven if you take a holistic approach. And we astrologers *always* look at the whole rather than the parts. It all developed from there. Important events like births and deaths, wars, revolutions, inventions – they all happen in patterns, it's said. Patterns of seven."

"Some say so, eh?"

"So say some."

"Even down to the hair growing on people's heads, I've heard."

"There's a school of thought on that too," Normi said politely. "Astrology covers *e-ver-y-thing*, yessir General. The phases of the moon determine the growth of plants, fingernails, and, yes, hairs. If you're in doubt about when to water your pot plant or whether an appointment with Master Gnorf makes cosmological sense, let an astrologer cast your horoscope. Or the pot plant's, for that matter."

"Well, you stargazing lot have been wrong before. Multiple times!"

"Six to be exact!" Normi said cheerily. "Now it's number seven! You see, it all depends on *when* you start counting, *what* you count as an event, *how many* events you count and *in which way* you align and correlate them. If events aren't seven years apart, just consider a margin of a year or two for safety, or instead of the actual event, use the moment of the idea's inception or – in case the moment lasts longer than a year – its end. It's a system that has developed over the years and is now close to perfection!"

"Right in time for prediction number seven?"

"Precisely!" The astrologer's uncoordinated eyes gleamed, a broad grin illumining his face. He couldn't have said it any better. He felt he had just recruited a high-ranking supporter of his life's endeavour. The recognition he had always craved was finally coming his way. Too bad the end of all things was riding its coat tails.

"The gnome's right. It's... happening!"

It was more a mewling than anything, accompanied by a soft tinkle. Heads turned. The voice was unmistakable, especially when it came to lamenting. It was the voice in charge.

Prince Dimmy the Pink rose with all the enthusiasm of a sleepwalker. "It must be... the *apocalypse!*"

His Majesty's glazed gaze revelled in regions nobody could follow, and yet he seemed to have drawn a profound vision from that far-off place. All eyes were on him now, on his rosy velvet blouse and the pearl necklace winding twice around his neck, both attempts unsuccessful in strangling their abuser. Eyeliner added a particular undefinable something to the minute man's personality, the cone-shaped earrings did their share too and the flamboyant red, blue and green jester's hat completed the look.

The bells on the fool's cap jingled ominously now, as if heralding the prophecy – as if the Prince in his ludicrous attire, uttering those fateful words, was none other than the Harbinger of Doom.

Ding-ding ding-a-ling, the bells went. *Ding-a-ling, ding...*

"Ah, yes, Your Majesty." General Montrakhán nodded to his ruler from the head of the table. "The apocalypse, you say... Thank you for your input!" The drawl in his delivery added weight to his words, and to their ambiguity.

One of the princelings cautiously pulled His Majesty back down into his seat, where he remained for a while unmoving, in fairyland until further notice.

But the thought had been put into everyone's head. Once more a vigorous babble of voices swept through the West Wing, more incited, confused and urgent than ever. Terror, exasperation, griping and swearing each took their turn. Not even the most recent Knucklebuck tournament with its associated tax collections at stake had caused such tumultuous scenes.

Disquieting questions reconquered the room. "What have we done to deserve this?" "We're doomed!" "We're all gonna die!" "Judgement has come!" "Gods! Have mercy on us!"

"You're all wrong!" A soft-spoken but weighty voice broke through the hullabaloo. "This is *not* the apocalypse." When the wizened, silver-haired man spoke, everyone fell quiet. Reybold Quillwich's long beard alone commanded respect. "Drivel about the apocalypse has filled the libraries for ages," the realm's leading scholar said. "And guess what?"

"What?" it echoed.

"The apocalypse *still* hasn't happened!" Quillwich fed the thought to the crowd.

"That's only because prayers have prevented the worst," the archbishop assured him.

"But this time it's number seven!" Normi blurted out. "It's proof!"

"Proof that you're obsessed with it," Quillwich barked back with the authority of a local wise man. "Let me tell you: When the Oc'motsh came over the Amcalladam, all and sundry knew the end of all things was about to happen. As it was prophesied by whoever. So it was talked about, prayed against, and believed in. There was to be a Battle of Five Armies, according to some fairy tale, and it would be the very last one, but only four armies showed up. Pity that.

"And after that? Came Xarradash the Eternal. To wage his war too, of course. Well, turned out he wasn't so eternal after all. And, to put the record straight, if he'd succeeded, getting enslaved by a megalomaniac is hardly an apocalypse in the broader sense. It's an apocalypse for *some*.

"The plague gave up one day too, realizing what an awful lot of people it would have to do away with, and when the floods came in 756, they were only half as bad as the plague. So, come the turn of the millennium, here we were, waiting for the comet. Well, it hasn't shown up yet. The world's still here. And the only thing that has gone to naught, is all the prophesying."

"Morals have too," someone coughed in the back. "And it's a shame! If the world ends, it starts with morals. With morals going down the drain who says it hasn't started already?"

Quite a few murmured in approval.

"Either way, it's gonna end one day, isn't it?" Shady Shoo reasoned. His thoughts ran along practical lines, befitting his business, and this included unavoidable premature partings.

"Maybe the apocalypse is just… late?" Head Princeling Klimbish suggested, anticipating a princely notion. "Like when the sun rises in the east and it's morning over *there*, but not yet around here. And then the sun moves, and it's morning here. Could be the same with the apocalypse, taking its time to get into gear. Maybe it already started with the turn of the millennium? With the morals going down. With all this skirt-cutting."

In a heartbeat, the doomsayers were at it again, like vultures wheeling over a carcass.

Quillwich gritted his teeth. Those who lived common lives lacked the eye for the subtleties of ivory-tower thinking. But be it as it may, if mankind had to come to an end here and now, he at least would know what *not* to call it, and in a twisted kind of way, it gave him strength enough to face a possible impending demise.

A strength the commander general lacked. Montrakhán was wondering whether the apocalypse was going to be his demise, or whether all this talk about it would finish him off before then. Either way, he saw himself in the casualty column. Pondering this, he leaned back in his chair and stared out of the West Wing's arched window, the discussion raging around him more than ever. With the tinkling of His Majesty's bells riding the tumultuous tide, night had already snuck up on Dimmerskeep and, for the first time in years, the general found that the jagged silhouettes of the dwellings outside leaning into each other against a full moon had something comforting, something romantic about it. Nostalgia grabbed him and made him feel all warm inside. Ah, the magical scent of the end times!

Though he could've sworn the moon had just changed colour.

Montrakhán blinked. *Had it?*

CHAPTER 9

Pitching Peculiar Plans

Moments earlier, the same moon – only a tad younger – shone on a dwarf-sized figure whiling away the hour. The stout figure was assisted by a pillar of sandstone rock, which had provided cover for a whole party of adventurers earlier in the day. That was reason enough for the stone to be pleased with the day's accomplishments, or the last century's, for that matter. Its metaphorical appetite was whetted. World domination suddenly felt like a viable option.

Bormph straightened up. Having answered nature's call next to the ambitious rock, he waddled back towards a skeletal tree, which was occluded by the veil of darkness, but would show up if he only walked far enough. Forty-seven steps later, he had certainty that the tree was still there. Nothing exciting ever happened on guard duty. The reserved sounds of his armour as he walked proved the evening's highlight. *Clink-a-clink, clink-a-clink,* they went, followed by a short, thoughtful pause at the end of the stretch when he turned heel, then a *clack-a-ta-clack* took turns with the scraping of boots on stone. Ah, the excitement of turning around! Then he was off again, clattering away in the opposite direction, back towards the pillar and its dreams.

A brisk wind gusted up and shook Bormph to the bone. He cursed the night a little for its lack of hospitality, and found that working up some minor rage helped with keeping warm, so he swore some more for good measure.

Activity over at the tower had simmered down to a couple of half-witted orcs huddling together around a campfire. They drank, grunted, bawled and burped, and then started all over again, varying the order. From time to time, one of them tottered over to the mysterious building. At first, the dwarf thought they were just fascinated by the human ingenuity displayed by the tower's construction. But after further observation, he reconsidered. The gruntlings had an inane need to prod the stationary giant in their midst, howl insults, charge at it head first or – as an astonishing alternative – embrace the naked stone. Their brains didn't seem to be much involved in these approaches. Bormph wasn't sure, though, whether a whole clan of gruntlings would be fool enough to be fooled by a handful of adventurers. *Any minute now*, he thought.

Clink-a-clink. Bormph paced back. *clink-a-cl—*

He stopped dead.

Before him, in the gloaming, he saw something sketchy, blurry. It appeared to be a hovering, cloud-shaped phantom, about a quarter of his own already limited size, if that. More longish than tall. He waited for the shock to subside, after which the wafting motion turned into a bumbling walk. The white cloud had grown legs, and paws.

"…!" Bormph mouthed wordlessly, searching for a name.

The bear cub ignored the two-legged bearded creature and circled past him, skedaddling into other parts of the darkness. The dwarf clinked after the little rascal, more quickly now, cursing under his breath.

"Wait! By the Stonefather's mighty anvil!"

He caught up with the escapee, grabbed him by the scruff of his neck and shook him thoroughly. The cub gave a whimper.

"What are we supposed to do with you anyway, pole-a-bear? Maybe we should just let you get back to that pole of yours... Would make things much easier for everyone, no?" He tried an icy, slit-eyed glare, but it had no effect on a bear used to the cold. On the contrary, it was the dwarven warrior who thawed.

"Alright, fleabag. Have it your way!" Bormph shuffled back to the tents, ruminating on whether there even was such a thing as pole-a-bear fleas, when a muffled *thump!* blended with the armour's gentle clinking and disrupted his flea-infested thinking.

He froze. The noise sounded like anything but a traipsing orc. Weighty, thuddy, and it didn't repeat.

Now that he stood still and listened without the sound of his own footsteps interfering, the thump echoed in his mind. It was as clear and bright as freshly washed linen, if linen was a noise. This time, the bear – who was writhing in his arms – had nothing to do with it. With a moment's delay, Bormph decided that the time would be about right to... startle.

Bormph startled.

He whipped round. The cub slipped from his arms, and a freed hand jerked towards his weapon.

Out of the half-darkness, a faint gleam reflecting the moonlight caught his eye. It wasn't much, only a soft flicker among the shadows. Barely illuminated, and partly hidden behind a high, sloping mound and a copse of gnarled trees, Bormph discerned the outlines of something sizeable. The magnitude of the silhouette came close to that of the other hill, but it was rough and jagged in shape. A sand dune it was not. And it hadn't been around a moment ago.

Bormph advanced on it, until, about halfway there, his boot struck an angular rock in league with the darkness and, quick as a flash, the earth rose to greet him. He found himself flat on the ground, pebbles bouncing in all directions, his axe blade a handspan from his nose.

Bormph turned his head. Heavy gasps whistled in and out of him. Already he could picture the gruntlings springing to their feet and storming the camp. But the Stonefather must have had an eye on him, as things remained quiet... Disaster, avoided by a hair's breadth, had backed away. It might have stuck around a little while longer, though, somewhere in the surrounding darkness, just in case.

The cub studied his beardy companion. The bear's ears flattened back, unsure whether he was supposed to join the silly game, then decided not to. He sat, licked his paws and watched as the dwarf finally scrambled up.

Bormph rubbed his elbow, figuring he had done his share of daily push-ups. A quick check through the spyglass was in order. The bawling in the distance went on as usual. Only a single orc was lurching about, casting a querying glance into the night. Bormph stood rigid for a moment as the orc tilted his head in his direction but he soon realized that the gruntling was just struggling to stand upright. There he went, the orc, careening into a bush in his drunken stupor. He had to be rescued by his mates, and nursed back to their grunting, bawling and burping activities with the help of more rum.

Bormph turned away. He had a mystery to attend to. Each step guided by more careful deliberation than before, he eased his way forward over the rocky surface until he reached the mysterious object. It stood calm and quiet, towering before him and beckoning his curiosity forward as if expecting a visitor.

Wood. The dwarf's hand drew back.

A pile of chests? Barrels? Supplies, maybe? There was something papery too his hand could seize, but his mind still had trouble visualizing. Little stalks – rods? canes? wands? – were bundled together with cords, and a pungent odour stung his nose. He produced a box of matches from his pockets and lit one. As the red head flared and crackled, Bormph rushed to cup the flame with his hand to shield it from the wind and the orcs on the lookout. He stepped closer.

A mountain of boxes, that was indeed what it was. Wicker baskets too, with sticks protruding from them, sticks topped with… little cones? Further in the back, crates upon crates were stacked together, some held shut by metal clasps. And somewhere among them… two eyes. A stare that pinned him to the spot.

Bormph recoiled, expecting the stranger to lunge, and yet he didn't. The little guy just stood there, weapon in hand, quiet as a mouse.

Bormph raised his match again. On closer inspection, the stranger's weapon looked more like a rake, and the fellow leaned on it with a wide grin. He was pot-bellied and white-bearded, with a fleshy nose and a twinkle in his unmoving eye. There was also that pointy hat. This was a gnome. A clay gnome. With a soft shred of sackcloth wrapped around the bottom half, held tight by a piece of cord. Bormph's least favourite bear cub vigorously sniffed the unbidden guest up and down.

"Would you get out of the way, you pestering—" The dwarf did a little two-step stagger to avoid another fall. He clutched a crate. "Why is it that in a world as wide as this, you have to be exactly where *I* am?" Bormph railed under his breath.

Meanwhile, exploiting the dwarf's distraction, part of the tiny flame he held declared independence and sought out further combustible opportunities in the close vicinity. Disaster – which, until now, had been waiting in the wings – was quick to offer companionship.

L-A-M-P... Bormph was too busy deciphering the chalk scribblings on one of the boxes to notice when the new alliance between flame and disaster formed. *Lamps? What kind of lamps?* He shifted position to read the rest of it. No, actually, it spelled *G-L-A-M-P-A-T...*

Ssshhh...

It was the smallest of sounds, at first.

Sssssssshhhh...

But it kept getting more intense. Intense enough for a dwarf to pick it up.

Fearing a snake hidden among the crates, Bormph leapt to the side, the sound now more of a sizzle than a reptile's hiss.

Sssssssssssssssssshhhh...

"What the—"

At the edge of the pile, a tiny flame had made an alternative home and announced the fact with a mild flash. A small campfire sprung up, as comfortably warm as it was massively disquieting.

When Bormph put out his match, the pile was already busy doing its own thing. Smoke billowed up. The idea of a little bit of illumination had just gone up in flames.

"Cudgels with cream! How—"

A wall of heat pushed Bormph back, singeing his beard. The sizzles multiplied in volume. No snakes were involved, after all. Just fuses – a whole bunch of them, burning away happily. Wherever he looked, tiny sparks nibbled their way up towards the top end of the sticks, which reeked of… brimstone. That's what that smell was!

A rocket whizzed into the night, wailing like a tortured cat, black smoke trailing behind. Then another lifted off.

There was a *whoomph*, and a massive flame roared up. Sparks flew. Almost the whole pile was suddenly ablaze. Within seconds fiery tongues licked at the stars, and the smoke mushroomed.

Bormph, soot-blackened, admired the mess for a moment then ran for his life.

Cracklers burst, whole rows of them. Overhead, explosions thundered through the wasteland. New, colourful stars sprinkled the night. Firecrackers cracked, flares flared, sky flyers flew skywards and unfolded into the glistening shapes of phoenixes and vague lookalikes of Prince Dymmling. The flaming wheels started burning and turning, spinning and spouting. The bulky boxes first fumed, then boomed. The eruptions could be felt two towns northwards and one west, and in an underground dungeon no humanoid had set foot in for centuries, a colony of bats went bananas.

Even Whinewaeyn, a sound sleeper, jolted from his rest. One reason might have been repeated shock waves that had blown the party tents to smithereens. Another was that

Bormph had barrelled up to him, coughing through a cloud of thick smoke.

"Change of plans!" he improvised.

Back in Dimmerskeep, the West Wing was peeved. It missed the Knucklebuck tournaments with their swift and merciless decision-making, where all pressing issues got wrapped up before midnight. All it took was a winning hand. Now an apocalypse had dropped in unannounced, stolen a close relative from eastwards and mucked up the natural order. The apocalypse wasn't playing by the rules. It hadn't even deigned to disembark for a Knucklebuck game to deal with matters fair and square, West Wing–style.

As it was, hapless card players had been left to face a faceless foe alone. A plan still hadn't shown up yet. Maybe it was too late in the day or someone had mislaid the invitation or it was too short a notice.

Midnight passed. The witching hour commenced.

Only then did the Harbinger of Doom snap out of his trance-like state and take matters into his own delicate hands. Another day, another decree, that's how Prince Dymmling III operated, and if further decree-making was about to be hampered by the world going south, the world had another thing coming. He vowed to rise to the challenge and earn himself a new title: Saviour of the East Wing Tower. That, and Redeemer of Man, Elf, Dwarf and Halflingkind, and whatever other kinds there were. He would even redeem the not-so-kind kinds along the way.

Ding-ding-ding-a-ling!

The Prince shook his head as he picked himself up, and the room fell quiet. He was still a tiny, wispy creature, still conveying a message in hat form, but a self-confident urgency was now speaking out of him, and it was waving with his finger: "Let's put an end to this travesty of deliberations. It's *measures* we need!" *Ding-ding.*

Fools made it all look so easy. Fools certainly got people's attention.

"First…" The Prince turned to his head princeling. "Remind me, Klimby, what was that thing our dear archbishop suggested? You know, the… clerical thing?"

"Um…" Klimbish hastened to flick through his minutes. As he couldn't come up with anything worthwhile on the spot, he deferred the question to the next princeling in line, and from there it went to the one sitting next to the next princeling, and the frantic search of all three of them together eventually arrived at a speculative "Was it… *pray?*"

"Indeed!" His Majesty's eyes lit up. "Splendid. First, we pray! Let's make it a priority! Take a note of that."

"We… pray?" the princelings echoed back. Not even they were sure they had heard that right, let alone the archbishop.

"Yes. Among other measures, of course."

"Have we established the *existence* of the gods with certainty?" interjected Quillwich, sage and apocalypse-redefiner. He was afraid to tell anyone else, but – as every proper philosopher should – he had doubts about even his own existence, let alone the gods'. Unlike the east wing tower, the sage's proverbial ivory tower hadn't moved. "What about the other races? The various tribes? They have other gods! How do we know which are the real ones?"

"Archbishop?" the Prince asked, conceding, "The wise one has a point."

Archbishop Vynnfield straightened up. "If I may correct you there, sage… It goes without argument that there's *only* the Holy Quintity of the One, the Other, the One In-Between and Those-Flanking-Them-All. That's because the Holy Quintity's the right religion."

"But then there must be something wrong with your praying," the Prince said, "if the One, the Other, the One-In-Between and Those-Flanking-Them-All reward you with an apocalypse."

"Er... um... There's always the prophecy, Your Magnificence."

"Prophecy? What prophecy is that?"

"As is written in the scriptures," the archbishop said with a rush. "When the end draws nigh, the saviour will come and redeem us. If we believe in him, so it shall happen."

"A bit simple, this redeemer thing. Are you sure about it?"

"Faith is not trigonometry, Your Highness."

"And why would it be?"

"Exactly."

Prince Dymmling stared at the archbishop with some frustration and raised his pinkie finger. "I'd rather have you set up a committee."

"What... Me? Now? Why, certainly, Your Majesty. What for, may I ask?"

"To gather representatives from various creeds and pray around the clock for deliverance to any kind of god we can think of, common or not."

"But—"

"With any luck," the Prince continued, "we'll get through to someone who runs the whole show and makes such a mystery of it. They'll appreciate the effort, take pity, and you can all thank me for thinking about it."

The bishop was still stammering.

"Aye. It's a long shot," even His Majesty had to admit, "but the longer the shot, the sooner we ought to try, no?"

Nobody dared to speak against such reasoning. Whatever the Prince devised, there was always some method in his madness. The archbishop bowed obsequiously.

With a swing of his hips, Prince Dymmling switched from one pensive pose to another. "There was another thing. Something our Despicability Shoo suggested..."

"Them gods musta gone bonkers," said Shady Shoo flatly. "Won't help praying ta gods gone bonkers."

"Let's consider that for a moment, then," said the Prince as if he knew a thing or two about the subject.

"Your Majesty!" the bishop protested. "The gods cannot possibly—"

"We've merely suggested one approach, Your Grace," the Prince corrected him. "But wouldn't you admit that, according to the Holy Quintity's teachings, we're all made in the image of the gods?"

"So it's written in the scriptures." All the same, the archbishop was in two minds about this one. The times when he had doubted his faith as a youngster came back to him with the full force of a sledgehammer. The sight of the Prince gyrating before him, as if riding a wave, setting up ludicrous committees while he was at it, hammered it in. Shifting, rocking, swaying was the Prince's natural way of being on two feet. Could the gods have created *this*? This, this—

Ding-ding. "Are you insinuating that the scriptures got it wrong?"

The archbishop peered at the tiny man under the jester's hat. "N-no, no... Of course not."

"So we're in agreement that if a man may lose it, a god may too."

"Er…"

But suddenly it dawned on the archbishop, and the scales fell from his eyes. Hadn't the Prince just explained *himself*? But of course. This misguided excuse for a ruler must be a divine aberration. As was everything else that happened these days, the bishop figured. Could it be true? That not even the gods were infallible? That they might be as imperfect as their children? As flawed as… a certain prince they had created? And, he realized, wasn't it also ingenious? The notion made the gods even more loveable, for in this new light they appeared so… so… human. So close, so familiar! Here he was, and all it had required was His Royal Dimness to open his mind and explain the teachings of the scriptures to him…

A surreptitious smile tugged at the bishop's features. *Prince Dimmy, creature of the gods…* The thought was brand new to him, and it felt… exciting.

"Let's dig through all the myths and legends we can find," His Royal Highness pronounced. "Get the whole church on it. Everyone who's not praying. Make it plain: we're looking for mentions of gods off their rocker!" One nail-polished hand landed firmly on the Prince's hip as the other ran over his pearl necklace. "You got that, Klimby?"

"Off… their… rocker," Princeling Klimbish repeated, scribbling.

"Good. If we have to cure a god, so be it."

The reactions were a bit reserved there. One reason was that something occurred to the one or the other at this point: there was no denying that madness was a common trait among the gods. In the scriptures, everything started off hunky-dory but once the One and the Other had three children and it came to the creation of further descendants, things inevitably got incestuous first, and then embattled. With too much love around, jealousy poured in, power struggles erupted and the ensuing legends ran rampant with hare-brained schemes and the machinations of one divine being working against another. When one god created the first element, Wind, the other made Earth, just out of spite. Fire turned out to be the first weapon, but already Water had been conceived to douse it. Then the first children, the titans, came into play, and they stomped about the place like the louts they were, brawling, ripping landmasses apart, forging volcanoes and unleashing floods. Once the races emerged, they too took a leaf from their role models' playbook – and sowing discord and perpetuating madness were written all over it in big letters. Gods off their rockers? The question was more like, where to start?

But Prince Dymmling, his bells jingling with enthusiasm, had already moved on.

"As for the magic angle…" The Prince brought his fist down hard, and yet, the massive oak table, underwhelmed by the exertion of force from a flyweight, allowed only a meagre *thunk*. "Should foul magic be at play, natural, intentional or otherwise, if the world is being altered because of it—"

"Technically," Xoormrax the Elder jumped in to specify, "*any* spell is world-altering. It's simply a matter of how much."

"Then all you need to find is the one spell that can alter it back, and by the same amount." The Prince subjected the mage to a penetrating stare. "I want you, Archmagus, and all your sages and as of yet useless colleagues, to delve into anything arcane nobody has tried for decades. No, make that millennia. Anything and everything that has the potential to work against this... this... universal, unannounced cheekiness!"

"Dark sorcery too?" asked a voice from the back.

"But of course. You have my express royal permission. Gather all the dabblers in your art, the conjurers, the thaumaturges, the alchemists, the sorcerers, what have you. Research and experiment away, and speedily. I want *results!*"

"I must protest!" the archbishop intervened. "The gods—"

"Will forgive us, if we save the world. And even if we don't. It's their job to forgive. If they don't forgive us, something's wrong with them, and in regards to that—"

"See plan A." Princeling Rimfish finished the thought and knocked confidently on his quilted jerkin.

Prince Dymmling jingled, then took another turn through his mazelike thoughts. "What else have we got? How about... diviners?"

"Diviners, Your Majesty?" The scribe's eyes snapped upwards, trying to untangle that one. "I take it you mean soothsayers?"

"Soothsayers, yes. Won't we want to know what awaits?"

"So... we should just *ask* soothsayers?"

"Soothsayers, seers, prophets, the common tea-leaf reader, what have you. Call them what you like, as long as they have an idea about the looming apocalypse."

"And if they do?"

The Prince spared his princeling a knowing glance. "Then we'll ask them what's beyond it, and how was it averted?"

"Ahhh…" A collective gasp ran through the assembly.

"Have I got this right, Your Majesty?" Klimbish poised his quill. "By finding in-the-know seers, we'd be able to trick the apocalypse out of existence by looking *behind* it?"

"Precisely." Prince Dymmling nodded. "Then, when we know, we'll apply that knowledge. It's simple."

"But… but it wouldn't be a real apocalypse if we could simply look behind it."

A few supportive murmurs made the rounds.

The Prince, however, didn't flinch an inch. "If it's the real one, we're done for anyway. If it just looks like one, the seers will see us through."

Hidden away in his wise man's corner, Quillwich flashed a smile, alarmed by how sound the argument seemed to him. He was no believer in the apocalypse, neither was he sure whether the future lent itself to a reading. But from a philosophical point of view, Quillwich enjoyed the existential irony of bending reality back onto itself in such a constructive way. He almost regretted that he hadn't come up with the idea himself.

"You must be aware there are a lot of charlatans out there," the princeling cautioned. "Fake seers…"

"Skip them." The Prince's voice cracked with impatience. "Anyone who only predicts the end is useless." It so happened that he glanced over at Normi as he spoke the words.

"I…" The royal astrologer extraordinaire peered around like a sheep ambushed by hungry wolves. He saw things, sure, but he didn't feel much like a seer. More like a well-informed gazer. "I-in seven years' time, Your Magnificency," he stammered, "I mean… *after* the end of the world… something else will happen. Most certainly!"

"Right, Normi," a deep voice boomed. General Montrakhán didn't bother looking up. He had been cleaning his nails with a dirk and making little sense of any of the discussion. "Seven years *after* the end of time, *something* will happen."

Normi nodded vigorously. "I'll keep watching the skies then."

"You do that," said General Montrakhán, with little enthusiasm.

Shady Shoo volunteered to handle the seers. "I knows a strange rover woman or two down at the River Quarter," he breathed from inside his cowl, where his shifty eyes… shifted. "I'll have a look 'round, Yer Majesty."

"Please do, Shoo." The Prince's eyes roamed about. "Anything else we might have missed?"

Another princeling raised his hand. "What about the other kingdoms, Your Majesty? Like Aermerlyn and Great Caesh? If the world ends here, it will get to the rest in time too. Unless it's a regional apocalypse, but I'm not sure there's such a thing."

It was agreed that they should get in touch with any leaders who would hear them.

"Oh, and one more thing…" The Prince cast his gaze about to find his official defender of the realm chewing lackadaisically on a dried fig. "In case the abominable Vensk *is* in fact behind this, Commander… Commander?"

Commander General Montrakhán swallowed hard and almost choked.

"You listening?"

"Aye, Prince Dimmy, er… Your Highness!" General Montrakhán sat up.

"We have to be prepared."

"Aye, Your Majesty. Of course. Prepared we have to be."

"Be so kind as to rally the troops then, will you? We might have to launch an attack against Vensk sooner than you think."

General Montrakhán gulped. He was a practical man. His hope that praying to the gods – any gods – was going to result in instant salvation was limited. Unearthing ancient myths and mystic secrets to get a straightforward answer? More conceivable, but unlikely. Finding the ultimate spell to intimidate the apocalypse? Hardly. Tricking it with seers? Nonsense. Support from Aermerlyn or Great Caesh? Hmm… The Prince's reputation preceded his requests, and it always wore a jester's hat. There was little else left.

The general felt the skin prickle on the back of his neck.

CHAPTER 10

Threefold Trap Trickery

Whinewaeyn found himself sitting bolt upright, stricken with a coughing fit. Above him, fireworks painted radiant blooms onto the night sky. The air carried the stink of a Netherworldly pit seething with gaseous vileness. When a round, bearded face peered through the tattered tent flap, the wizard blinked at it. Chances were, there was a connection between the face and all the rest of it.

"Remember when we talked about diversion and distraction?" the face was asking. Actually, shouting was more like it. "A DI-VER-SION! Remember, gramps?" Bormph had difficulties placing words between the firecrackers going off a few dozen feet back. "To lure… the gruntlings… away! Remember?"

"YES!" Whinewaeyn shouted back as he exhumed a vague memory from the recesses of his mind, weighed down by a thick carpet of drowsiness.

"THIS IS IT! Hear?" Another rocket zigzagged behind Bormph, illustrating the point. "Started without you!"

"Dwarf! What about the thing we discussed earlier?"

"What was that exactly?"

"That we have to be extra careful. Cook our meals by magical means, things like that. No open flames, no smoke, no... *detonations?*"

"Ah... yes, yes, it's coming back to me now, wizzer. It's just that things got a little... out of hand, to be honest. I'll explain later."

Another voice rang out. Female, angry. "What in the name of Novotroth came over us to hire this *maniac* of a DWARF?"

Amjelle's bloodshot eyes, wreathed in a hair-do fiasco, joined the mage in looking irritated. Soon after, a mumbling, bleary-eyed barbarian crawled out of the ruins of his own tent, and a halfling from his.

Amjelle rounded on Bormph. "You were supposed to keep watch! What part of 'standing guard' was the difficult bit?"

"Spared you a shift, healer. The wizzer and I have just agreed to proactively initiate phase two. Get your things!"

Whinewaeyn offered only a blank-faced look and flinched at the sound of yet another explosion.

"Oh, and by the way, this is yours." Bormph scooped up the terror-stricken cub hiding behind his boots and put him in the healer's arms. That kept her quiet – for the moment.

Amjelle quickly tucked the polar bear into her backpack, so that only his head peeked out, and buckled it on, while Bormph turned to the other staring faces.

"Need an invitation? No time for dilly-dallying!"

Already a commotion had seized the settlement. Orc after orc, tiny and large, unimpressive or imposing, peered from their straw-thatched huts. After a slight delay – just long enough to spout out "What?" (or "*G'n?*" in orcish) –

the fighter in them awoke. The fighter said, "*Get hold of a weapon!*" And what orc would argue with their inner fighter? Bright torchlights flared from every corner of the village. Shamans barked commands. A band of extra-fierce-looking warriors quickly gathered and set out into the blazing night, scimitars and cleavers brandished.

"Now, if there are no objections, I intend to cast *Fog of Obstination*," Whinewaeyn volunteered.

"*Obfuscation*," Amjelle corrected him.

"As I said." The wizard looked at her as if she was hard of hearing.

Amjelle skipped the debate, instead readying her crystal-topped stave and motioning to Ramrok and Bormph to draw their weapons too.

Everyone stood prepared, yet the mage was still busy thinking. "A case could be made for *Thieving Winds* too. Or *Void Breath*." He wavered for a moment. "Nah, *Obstination* is about right. One of Khalvach's discoveries. And after that, a trifle of *Wizard's Eye*, hmm? See the irony there? That's a spell by the infamous Irmash, Khalvach's archenemy. Doesn't ring a bell? The one who swamped the Plains of Psheesh? Ha! A Khalvach and Irmash combination, it's almost like…"

Bormph had to suppress a serious grumble. "Would you *please* get on with it?"

"But of course." A little huffy, Whinewaeyn readjusted his hat. Standard wizarding procedure. "Dwarves and their patience!"

Behind the wizard, Thimble squirmed. The clatter of armour on the move drew closer. The rattling gasps of the approaching gruntlings amid the fireworks gave him the jitters. He could've used a cuddle just like the polar bear cub, preferably from a blonde elf. But as the elf had to be rescued first, he was trapped in a vicious circle.

At last, an incantation ran over the wizard's lips. He repeated it over and over. Eyes closed, Whinewaeyn held his staff at arm's length in front of him, and after a few moments of concentration, the wood jolted to life. Vibrations rattled the piece of wood, sucking blue-grey wispy threads out of the air, and the magic strands won that way wrapped around the staff like cotton around a sewing spool.

The wizard's eyelids fluttered open.

After adjusting his hat again in hopes of good luck, he levelled a stern stare at his staff. The wispy strands unwound and, as they did, thickened into a billowing mist. The wavering mass, black as night, drifted away instantly to enshroud their immediate surroundings – rocks, trees, underbrush – and their own shapes as well. Forth it rolled, the artificial darkness, exploring, while the skies continued to serve an unabated potpourri of booms and bangs, spiced up every now and then with a particularly ear-splitting blast that shook everyone to the core – friend and foe alike. The darkness skirted the nearby rounded hills, headed like a tidal wave towards the mud huts dotting the elevation ahead, and dutifully swept everything in the way under its cloudy rug. Assisted by its foggy friend, night regained dominance. Only the tower rose above it all, bathing in the moonlight like a lighthouse amid a roiling sea – or a painting of one, given the slow silent motion of the gloom draping around it.

In reaction, orc grunts sprang up everywhere. The settlement was abuzz with confusion. One by one, their torches died, snuffed out by the spreading magic.

All the while the valiant party of adventurers kept tiptoeing forward, making their way towards the enemy's lair, bumping into each other almost every second step. But not for long. The dark had grown too dense.

"Time for the other one!" Amjelle's whispery voice entered the fog-infested gloom, but Whinewaeyn seemed too preoccupied with sneaking to notice that nobody could see a thing, himself included. "The *other* one!"

There was a long pause.

"The other *spell!*" Thimble spelled it out.

"Oh!" Somewhere in the shadowy soup, Whinewaeyn fumbled for his staff. "I had a suspicion I'd forgotten something, little one. Something I, you know, shouldn't have... er... forgotten." The rummaging continued. "But that's only because I remember other things. I tend to think. Funny thing, I was remembering the discussion we had the other day about forgetting."

Another long pause. A very, very long pause. Too long a pause.

"Master Whinewaeyn?"

"Yes, Amjelle dear? Wasn't there something we were about to—"

"Cast the spell!" came at the mage from various directions.

"Oh. Right you are! So... First, we need a reagent..."

The wizard's silhouette, barely visible to anyone except those who already knew where he was, pulled a phial from its side, and Whinewaeyn dipped two knobby fingers into it, extracting a pinch of powder. While he mumbled a few syllables, his hand found the tip of his staff and the powder coated it with a faint cerulean glimmer.

"Touch this. Everyone." The staff reached into the darkness. "One after the other."

Bormph went first, and the glimmer travelled from the wood down onto the dwarf's fingertips, whereupon it vanished. Whinewaeyn tapped the staff, and the glimmer flared up once more. Amjelle picked it up next, and so the procedure was repeated for everyone around.

"See anything?" Whinewaeyn inquired in a low voice.

They all nodded, each of their own silhouettes now standing out against the black curtain swirling around them. More importantly, they also now recognized the shapes of the orcs. Some of them were still stumbling through the darkness in varying directions, disoriented as they were. Others remained rooted to the spot, gaping. It might have looked like pure confusion, but those orcs were, in fact, considering their options. Stories of hoary lore haunted their minds, myths about the Great Darkness that would one day descend upon them to swallow everything there was. Hardly a single gruntling had taken such tales literally, trusting they were a figure of speech. But now that the figure of speech had dressed up in its nightgown, the prospect of the swallowing bit had begun to bother even the fiercest warrior. Strangely enough, the tales hadn't mentioned anything about the Great Darkness celebrating the occasion with firecrackers…

"See anything?" Whinewaeyn asked again.

Everyone nodded to each other in the affirmative.

But they also saw the wizard shaking his head. "No, no, this isn't working at all. Everything's still as pitch as charcoal. Something's altogether wrong, can't you see?"

"Ramrok see wizzy," muttered Ramrok.

"No need to rub it in. Working on it."

"Archmagus, we *can* actually see," Amjelle clarified.

"All fine," Thimble confirmed.

"What's the problem now?" Bormph cracked his knuckles. "You gone blind, wizzer?"

"Well, that's odd…" Whinewaeyn babbled on in an undertone, regardless. "I know this spell like the back of my hand." There was a pause. "No, I know it *better*," he said, after realizing he wasn't sure he would be able to pick out the back of his hand from any given selection. "Hmm… Maybe it's just that *Obstination* worked too well, if there ever was such a thing. Maybe I've obstinated more than *Wizard's Eye* can handle… I've got to look at…"

His mumbling dwindled away. Then there was a gasp. A moment later, the blue-green glow flitted over his knuckles again.

The answer to the wizard's problem had dawned on Amjelle already. Mind like a sieve, that wizard. "Don't say you forgot… yourself?"

Whinewaeyn didn't say it, but that's what it was. There they were again now, right in front of his eyes: Bormph, Thimble, Ramrok and Amjelle, plus the cub peeking out of her backpack – their outlines, at least. And everyone but the cub were shaking their silhouetted heads.

"This way, Confusius…" Bormph sighed and crawled forward towards the first mud huts. "Stick close to me!"

"Captain?" Two polished boots thumped together. "Here to report!"

Captain Klampf's head jerked up from the map spread over the makeshift table before him. "Yes, Sarge? Any news from the scouts? What's going on?" His eyes met Sergeant Quinch's, who stood to attention at the tent entrance, looking alert.

"Our outriders report no enemy contact, no casualties," Quinch stated. "Whatever it is, it's too far away."

Klampf folded the pair of compasses with which he'd been marking potential east wing search areas for the day to come. He looked flummoxed. "We're in the middle of nowhere, Quinch. Who's attacking whom?"

"Well, it appears not be an attack at all."

"No? What's it then?"

"If you'd allow me to make a guess, Captain, I'd say the Oc'potsh orcs have staged a bonfire with some accompanying pyrotechnics."

Captain Klampf pushed his compasses away and rolled up his map. "But that doesn't make a lick of sense, and you know it!" Irritation edged his tone.

Quinch's expression turned tortured, as if he'd been working on dislodging a stringy piece of meat stuck between his teeth for hours with no success.

"Orcs celebrating with fireworks?" Klampf barked. "They haven't even heard of such a thing! Rubbish, Quinch. Not in a week of Praydays!"

"Of course, Captain." Quinch fell silent for the better part of a minute as he watched the captain pace about. "But, you see, Captain, if I may... I always wondered about that particular saying. What about Praise Week? Happens only *once* in a dozen cycles, and only in Weith Abbey, but... one might say, it is, sort of, in a way, more or less... just like it. Like a week of Praydays."

Klampf eyed his sergeant. Then he drew himself up, walked past his officer and pushed the tent flap back. He peered out. More muffled detonations bubbled up in the distant night sky like gas rising from a celestial mud bath.

"Orders?" Quinch asked. The faraway flashes wouldn't let up.

"Saddle up, Sergeant. We're riding out."

Sergeant Quinch snapped the captain a salute and dove out of the tent.

Under cover of the velvety mist, the party advanced, edging around the awestruck orcs. Some stood quiet, others mumbled to themselves, grappling with the concept of the Great Darkness coming for a visit. A few stammered mantras. Even the fiercest warriors stood paralyzed, at a loss on how to make the thrust of a blade count against a shapeless foe. A shaman or two tried to conjure up a magic light source, but they might as well have tried to set water ablaze; their efforts died in muffled puffs.

Mud hut by mud hut, Bormph made way toward what they had identified as Sylthia's prison cell, the rest trailing after in single file. Together they angled across a yard. At one point, a half-grown orc poked his head out of a door with a swath of fog tearing right in front of him. Thimble flicked a pebble at him with his slingshot, which sent the orc right back inside, and that was that.

They came across more serious company a bit later – in spite of all the camouflage. Only a breath away, a green face oozed out of the darkness – grim, leathery and fully matured – staring Bormph right in the eye. The surprise was mutual. The orc must have been as flabbergasted when something red and bearded had swum up from the black mists. But the shock lasted only for a second. The orc was at the brink of a grunt, a roar, anything to—

He didn't get any further. Before Bormph could bring up his weapon, the urgency of sounding the alarm had faded from the gruntling's face, and his expression gradually slid from consternation to drowsy-eyed detachment. Even though he stood right there, he was miles away too.

"What are you waiting for, dwarf?" Amjelle snapped.

Bormph twisted around and was almost poked in the eye by the healer's rod. In the gem at the end of it, a mesmerizing soft amber vapour rotated very, veeery slowly, almost viscously, like honey going for a spin. *Faaasciiinaaatiiiing,* thought Bormph, and forgot where he was and why he was and what was what. The healer's punch to his chest brought him back.

"Would you pray look *away,* dwarf?" Amjelle hissed. "Better keep an eye on *him.*" She pointed over at the orc.

"Erm… As you say." Bormph, alert now, turned back to the green creature.

"And how about you do the honours, so that we can move on?"

"The honours. Certainly. Coming right up!"

Thock! Bormph's axe handle clashed with the orc's head and the creature dropped out of sight.

Otherwise, the operation was swift and smooth. The hut with the elf inside was easy enough to identify thanks to a hideous mask grimacing from the door, giving them the evil eye without even having a proper one on display. Aside from the mask's empty eye slits, only a guard hung around, staring into the booming night, perhaps waiting for the Great Darkness to reap him away with a bang. Rather a dull thump than a bang later, darkness descended over this orc's senses too. Ramrok wiped his hilt clean, and Bormph, who had volunteered to cushion the fall, disposed of the dazed gruntling in a tangle of bushes.

They were almost there. They stole around the back to get to the door and... were short of a key. Apparently, one of the first things the orcs picked up on their way to civilization was how to padlock a mud hut.

Thimble time. The party's designated rogue saw his heroic moment approach with seven-league boots, and a jingle later had produced his burgling gear and was off working on the lock while the others stood guard.

"Hush," Amjelle had to remind him, and Thimble tried to jingle a little less as he poked about in the heavy brass lock.

Right away, one of his tools broke. *That's fine, don't you worry,* his shady instructor had told him once. *The lock recognizes a challenger. It's a token of appreciation if it breaks your pick. It tells you: we will work this out together. Respect me, and in turn I'll respect your efforts and let you in.*

Thimble growled. Another lock pick had bent out of shape, testing his patience. As it was, the lock kept recognizing its challenger. Almost too respectable, this lock was.

"You darn-blasted, ruddy crap-thing!"

A tinkle issued from the mechanism, then a much more serious metallic clatter. Another tumbler had snapped into place, proving once more that sometimes a little sweet talk does wonders.

Clonk... clink... cli-clonk... And there it was: the triumphant sound of freedom. *CLACK!* Thimble eased the door ajar and ducked inside.

The observers held their breath. But instead of the squeals of an overjoyed elf, all they heard was a hearty whack, and the little rescuer keeled over back into the doorway, stiff as a board.

Sylthia peeked out, white as a ghost. A strangled cry pushed through her throat as the weighty tome slipped from her hands. "Er... whoops?"

In the head shaman's hut, the air was so thick with tension that an unsuspecting person might have bumped into it.

H'roc-Noc'sh had to know. He sat on his patchwork floor mat, tossing chicken bones into a circle sketched in the dirt in front of him. Had he missed all the subtle hints announcing the Great Darkness? And now that it was here, was this it?

He first counted the holes in the tiny thigh bones, examined the exact shape of each bone's shaft, where they touched, the distance they held from each other. Then he moved on to focus on the bigger picture, observing the figures the bones formed together, the triangles, the "X"s, the lines, their positions in the context of the whole. The bones spelled trouble, sure. They always did one way or another. It was all a matter of degree. But still he could see no mention of the Great Darkness.

A bluster outside rent the shaman's concentration. The tent's entrance flaps were abruptly pushed aside, and the knoo'boosh-wearing foot that burst in crunched the prophetic chicken bones, sending bits and pieces flying all over the floor mat.

H'roc-Noc'sh, wild-eyed, glared up at the unwelcome guest, a burning rage creeping up his throat. He was about to unleash something... ogrish.

"*G'sh'z!*" first grunter Gh'porth grunted, apparently not at all bothered by the divinatory bones he had just trampled on. "It's over! *T'um gloum!* Men bring darkness!"

"*K'wha?* You sure?" H'roc-Noc'sh's hulk of a body jolted up like a catapult. The cutlery in his beard glinted menacingly in light of the hearth fire, and his venom-green eyeballs smouldered with rekindled fury. He seized the other orc by his nose-ring. "*K'wha?*"

"*Wha'k'wha!* Sure be sure!" grunted his first grunter. "Men with horses come from east. Many, many men. Armed men."

Now H'roc-Noc'sh let out a primal shriek. It was a screech somewhere between anguish and ire, starting out at a low guttural roar and ending in a penetrating howl rivalling the force of a pack of moon-appreciating wolves. All the while, he shook the other gruntling like an apple tree until he realized that taking it out on the messenger wasn't the way humans had taught him to deal with frustrating news. But... was that a good thing? Were humans a good thing?

"*K'ak t'um!*" H'roc-Noc'sh thundered, which loosely – very loosely – translates to something like "To the Netherworlds with humans!"

The first grunter stammered something back, but it was lost in all the shaking he was subjected to.

H'roc-Noc'sh pushed him away. "Trap be!" he raged.

Gh'porth nodded fervently, or possibly he was just still jittering.

"Men want test orcs," the shaman grunted, putting together the pieces. He stomped around in circles like a caged animal, dispersing his foul-reeking breath. "Tower they send... Put in elf, yes, elf. No human... Ha! Men want fool orcs!" His frenzied steps came to an abrupt halt. So did his robe swishing in his wake. "Trap be! Now men come punish orcs!"

The first grunter, regaining his senses, fished from the shallow pool of orcen ruminations and picked out the obvious catch. "Human ways, stupid ways."

"Humans light night with fire," H'roc-Noc'sh grunted on. "Humans make Great Darkness. Humans frighten orcs. Humans on horses come. Humans be orc end."

The first grunter growl-howled in agreement.

"We orcs. Orcs no cowards," the head shaman rumbled, and pounded his chest with his enormous fists. "Orcs fight!"

When Thimble came to, he found his head cradled in Amjelle's lap. A bright light dancing above him had called him back.

"Uhmgglmpf," he garbled. "Glompth. Whagada-woof?"

The light moved away, and he felt delicate fingers kneading his temples. A familiar scent – the combined fragrance of coconut, mango and sea breezes – washed over him, rounded out by the sensation of soft lips touching his forehead. When the blur hampering his vision eased off, he saw Sylthia's silken hair rise from his side, framing her milky features. His little halfling chest heaved in bliss.

"I'm sooo sorry," the angelic voice breathed.

"Phphtph… T-t-that-tata-thop's al-righst," Thimble slurred. Eyes still half-closed, he was savouring the damp remnants of the kiss, with his mouth stretched into a big, dimpled smile. That spirit of his was up there somewhere, playing tag with the heavenly voice. More words drifted by like puffs of clouds, light and fluffy. Blearily, he forced an eye open.

"They were threatening to make a meal out of me and everything," Sylthia explained. "I just had to—"

"Taaag! You're it!" Thimble announced triumphantly.

"Quiet!" Whoever issued this coarse command sounded less playful. "Listen!"

When Thimble looked up, he saw heads swivel away from him.

"Where's we?" he babbled, still woozy, but snapping out of it, one realization replacing another. He pushed himself up on his elbows. "What's gappening?"

"Psssht!" hissed Bormph. "That dratted cell's where we are. Had to get in. Orcs outside. Lots and lots of 'em."

"All gone!" the usually tight-lipped Ramrok contributed unexpectedly.

"Gone already?" Bormph looked up at him. "Then we—"

"*Boom* gone. *Magic* gone," Ramrok clarified. With a subtle toss of his head, he signalled to pay attention to the goings-on at the other side of the barred window.

"*What?*" Bormph climbed a hay bale and peered out himself.

The giant hadn't lied. The fireworks had ceased. And the ghostly swaths of murkiness, once swirling thick and fast, were shrinking away as urgently as town hall clerks upon hearing the chime for lunch break. To Bormph's horror, the first torches had already flared up again outside, and nothing told them they were not supposed to. Grunts surged; feet shuffled. The dwarf pulled his head back.

"Guess what, wizzer? Your ruddy spell's worn off!"

"Naturally." Whinewaeyn sounded not the least bit surprised. "Aerokinetic depletion," he added analytically. "Now in advanced stage."

"Whatever," Bormph muttered. "Just do it again! *Hokum-pok'em-oakham...* Just say the words and get on with it!" The dwarf's eyes darted back and forth between the wizard and the disquieting scene unfolding outside. "Go on, gramps! *Quick! NOW!*"

"Ah, you see, stonebeater, while an understandable request, it's…"

"Yeah?"

"…a technical impossibility."

"*What?*" Bormph's helmet almost fell off.

"It's a common, albeit misguided notion that wizards can do magic…" He paused, and Bormph waited patiently. There had to be more. "…just like that."

"So you *can't* do magic… just like that?"

"It's like this: wide-ranging, long-persisting massive magic manipulation – category A archmagery material – at some point runs out of the energy that feeds it. That's just basic elemental redistribution for you. *Obstination* in particular. It's a paradigm of all-encompassing wind incantation, one might say. Complex and tricky to cast, yet rather fickle in the long run, good intentions aside. In point of fact, I'm surprised it worked a treat back there. Owes itself to the crisp night air, I would sup—"

"Suppose I don't particularly care how you cast it the last time and whether it's fickle, well-intentioned or eye-pleasing," Bormph rumbled. "We need it *now*, wizard… *Again.* If you're looking for fresh air, just wave your staff out the window for the Stonefather's sake, and get on with it!"

"Now *that* I could do." Whinewaeyn tugged thoughtfully at his beard, once, twice, and much slower the third time. "In principle. But now in particular? See, that's where I have to say no."

Bormph just stared at him.

"Actually, there's another common misconception, very closely related to the first one. Which is that magicians do miracles. We don't. And the more it looks like one, the more draining it is." Whinewaeyn waved a knobby finger under Bormph's nose. "Ever heard of the Law of Auratic Equilibrium? Probably not, by the looks of you. But as things stand, in layman's terms, our magical resources – that is, the focal point through which the elements are realigned – are, well, exhausted. You might say: *I'm* exhausted." He shrugged. "For the moment. Give me half an hour and—"

"Splendid," Sylthia broke him off. "Just splendid."

Bormph slumped on a bale of straw. "And of all the places we could be right now, we're trapped in the prison we broke into."

"The door is still unlocked, actually," Amjelle reminded everyone. But as she moved towards it, noises right outside gave her a start, and she flung herself against the wall to shrink back into the shadows. A general scurrying towards whatever walls there were ensued.

Sounds of gravel crunching under footfalls trickled in. Three hooded heads carrying guttering torches bobbed by, caught up in a lively discussion. Shamans… They'd come across the orcs drowsing in the bushes any minute now.

"Who started this?" Amjelle needled when the orcs were gone. She aimed an indignant glance at Bormph. "The fireworks, I mean. How did you even get hold of those?"

"Your cub led me to them!" Bormph shot back. "They popped up in the middle of nowhere. All I did was manage the aftermath."

"Oh, sure, they just popped up like that. It was the cub who blew things up!"

"But it's true! He might be a Netherworldly spawn for all I know, what with him parading through the desert and everything."

"Which of you lot is the head of this whole operation anyway?" Sylthia snapped. "Have any of you numbnuts actually thought this through?"

Bormph's nostrils flared. "How would I know that an archmage can't cast magic when you need it? It would all have worked out! And who told you to knock out the Thumbler? Without that, we'd—"

Before long, the barbed comments escalated in a full-fledged row, a screaming match in whispers and hisses. Bormph railed against Whinewaeyn and Whinewaeyn against Bormph in return, and Amjelle lashed out at Bormph, and Sylthia against Whinewaeyn and Bormph, and Bormph against Sylthia, and Ramrok harrumphed at everybody. Only Thimble claimed halfling neutrality and resorted to stroking the cub. He had made up his mind to call him 'Snowflake', if it was the last thing he did.

"As I suspected, Captain. Fireworks," Sergeant Quinch reported as he rode up to his superior.

The regiment was skirting the area they had determined to be the source of the racket, and the source of the racket was a heap of unattended pyrotechnics on the last legs of enjoying itself.

"Fireworks. So it is." Klampf put it out officially and let it rest there, along with the disturbing, inexplicable other discovery they had made: a singular tied-up garden gnome at the centre of the spent explosive mess with an ear blown off. A depraved sacrifice? A freemasons' figurine? A warning from the DWUM?

"There's more, Captain." Sergeant Quinch led his horse around the pile of cinders fuming profusely in all colours of the rainbow. A pungent odour filled the air. "A quarter of a league west, we've found what appear to be tent fragments."

"Tent fragments?"

"We believe so, yes. And horse tracks, for another thing, in all kinds of directions. We've also discovered pawprints in the mud. A bear's, apparently. It's all very odd."

"A bear's?" Klampf repeated. "A bear on a rampage?"

"*Tiny* pawprints, Captain."

"A tiny bear on a rampage?"

Pfft! A last rocket gave an unmotivated farewell, leaving behind a scatter of debris, a foul smell and the memory that it had been a blast.

Captain Klampf drew a long breath. "So what might be the purpose of such… tents and fireworks?"

"Camping? Festivities? Fun? Forgetting about the daily routine?"

"On the face of it, these rockets are out here in the wilderness by themselves, Quinch. There's nobody around who looks particularly pleased about it. No more than I am." He shot the figurine a disparaging look. "And what's with that gnome? Just look at his grin! He's mocking us!"

"Uh… There must be an ulterior motive then, Captain?" Quinch suggested.

"That would imply that it looks like one thing, when it's about something else. This doesn't even look like something."

"Then the motive isn't even ulterior. The motive must be right at hand."

Klampf's face went rigid. He bunched up a fist so tight that his knuckles turned white. "Someone must have *wanted* us here. It's an orchestrated set-up, and a blatant one too."

Quinch looked around hastily, scanning the hills. "Vensk? It's always been Vensk down here in the south, hasn't it?"

"How about that wizard we met over in the Joghavri?"

"The fisherman who wasn't?"

"That's him, Sarge. Him and his merry band." Klampf chewed his lip for a bit, then spat. "Dodgy fellow, wouldn't you say?"

"They were just adventurers, no? Treasure-seekers, I gathered. Probably fell for Old Wholford's scam. For all I know, the drunkard's still peddling maps to anyone stupid enough to buy one off him. A few skeletons in the Joghavri for sure have one of those…"

"Who says they were adventurers?" Klampf asked.

"Well, *they* did. Though the wizard looked a bit dorky to me. The whole rag-tag lot were a bit off, actually. Like a troupe of carnies. Come to think of it… Didn't they have a white bear with them?"

"Hah!" Klampf exclaimed. "That, and a fancy story at hand about some missing lass in orc territory. And that's right where we are now."

"To be accurate, Captain, it was *us* who suggested that there might be a connection between the lass and the orcs, on account of the *knoo'boosh*, that disgusting reeking shoe."

Klampf shook his head. "What if it was part of their plan all along? What if they got the *knoo'boosh* from the orcs in the first place? What if they're all conspiring together? These so-called adventurers, the orcs, the DWUM, Vensk? What if their head dork is powerful enough to move a tower? Perhaps their initial plan was to direct us here, and when that didn't work, they went for more drastic measures to lure us here? Like… fireworks?"

Quinch pulled a face. "I beg to differ, Captain. What a weird plan that would be. And if this *were* a set-up, then where's the attack?"

"Captain! Captain!" A rider came in shouting. "It's here!"

A hubbub of voices sprang up from the ranks scouting the area.

Klampf sat up and veered his steed around. "What is, Corporal?"

"The tower! Look!"

Captain Klampf, with Sergeant Quinch at his side, surged forward after the corporal.

Some distance away, surrounded by a sea of black mist against an otherwise moonlit sky, the east wing tower – lacking its wing – greeted them. As the fog tore apart, it exposed simple mud huts around the perimeter of the edifice that was the odd one out. An unreal sight.

Real enough though were the gruntlings clustered in front of the village, and the others that pushed after. They kept coming out of the woodwork – on foot and on carts, wearing grim expressions and matching battle gear, with weapons brandished. And now that they saw the humans circling, they started ululating maniacally, driven by a pace dictated by frantic drum beats. The orcs started towards them.

Klampf gritted his teeth, nodding to his sergeant. *Well, there you go, tower thieves! As you wish…*

His thoughts transitioned into a defiant yell: "*Chaaarge!*"

CHAPTER 11

Mislaid Moments Mystification

Dear diary, Thimble scribbled, only to pause again and watch the glistening ink dry. *Guess where I am?* He waited a bit, and when he heard nothing back, his quill got scratching again. *In a prizon cell! In a prizon cell I broke into. Outside are man-eating orcs, and in hear everyone's at everyone elses throat. Its a madhouse! Lucky you that you've no ears.*

"Fight. Big fight." The voice rang out hoarse and hollow. Thimble glanced up. It was the big one's.

The bickering had paused for a moment. Everyone stared at Ramrok, waiting for the giant to contribute something offensive to the discussion from his measly vocabulary, beyond stating the obvious. But the barbarian turned out to be the most civilized person in the room. Now that he had their attention, hands folded over his chest, he returned to peeking out of the barred window.

"Ramrok say fight," the giant insisted, with his bottom-of-a-barrel voice. "*Orc* fight. Out there."

That did the trick to hush everyone.

Talk to you later, Thimble quickly scribbled to his diary.

They picked up shouts outside. Heavy battle gear clacked and creaked and clomped past them and away. Drumbeats joined the shouting. The first guarded taps soon broke into a frenzied rhythm. Horses neighed, wargs howled, orcs roared, cartwheels rumbled.

A spine-chilling howl pierced the night, and moments later was answered in the same fashion from the other end of the settlement. Agitated grunts welled up. Torches were waved. The pounding of hooves and clashing metal streamed in from a distance, the noise of bucklers cracking upon impact and arrows whirring through the air.

"It's a battle!" Bormph rasped. He looked out from the cell's corner, incredulous. Another group of orcs darted past and dove into the gloom's embrace.

In no time, the immediate area around the prison had cleared out. Bormph, climbing on top of a bale of hay, and Whinewaeyn, hunching, stuck their noses through the bars. There was nobody outside anymore who might have found the presence of some extra prisoners suspicious.

A bolt of lightning lanced through the darkness half a mile away.

"What are they up to?" Sylthia peeked out too.

"Do we *have* to know?" said Bormph. "Let them have their fun."

"Ramrok say go."

"We might as well…" Whinewaeyn agreed.

"Where to?" asked Thimble.

"Um… Out?" ventured Whinewaeyn.

"Good idea. And then?"

"Away."

It sounded like a plan. Murky in details, but rich in ambition.

Bormph pulled a mental map from the back of his mind and tapped a mental finger at the symbols marking the most prominent elevation. There was only one prominent elevation: the Silvery Sickle. "How about… we go out back? Towards the mountains? Easier to hide there."

Everyone agreed.

The door opened a crack, and Bormph peeped out. The gruntlings were nowhere in sight, not at the moment anyway, but the rhythm of the drumbeats shook the air, stirred the street dust and made his beard twitch. He looked back over his shoulder. "Anyone who wants it all in writing first, just in case?"

A moment later, Bormph found himself on the doorstep, shoved into fleeing position. Apparently, the majority had deemed an evaluation of the situation from the outside necessary, and had the dwarf appointed to take care of it.

Things turned out well enough, though. Bormph remained in one piece for the better part of a minute, and so the rest of the party set off after him. They rounded a corner or two and scurried northward, with Thimble in charge of scouting.

Unlike the front of the village, where the action was in full swing, the back was closer to a ghost town. Indeed, the array of skulls spiked on poles that populated it looked quite dead. Due to their age, lack of voice and extremities, they made no effort to sound the alarm when the intruders crawled past. The two live orcs Thimble and company *did* chance upon weren't much better either. The bewildered-looking gruntlings seemed to have planned to ride out whatever was going on behind an overturned cart – hardly testament to the proverbial orcen dauntlessness. Ramrok stepped in, seized the two of them by the collar, and clonked their heads together. It would remain the only incident. They slid from shadow to shadow and were out in a jiffy.

Once the party passed the last hut, they broke into a run. The pounding heartbeat of the war drums, the clangour of battle and the far-off flickering of the torches dwindled in their wake. Little by little, the lowlands dropped away, and ahead the peaks of the Silvery Sickle reared up in their fierceness. Clouds scudded behind the moonlit crests, apparently in a hurry too.

"You know, with a proper plan, we'd have our horses now," Amjelle said as she puffed up the mountain path. Shaking off possible pursuers by putting a mountain between them sounded alright in theory. Now, on foot, with an actual mountain in play, the plan's inadequacies came to the fore. Amjelle threw a sharp sidelong glance at the dwarf.

"Yeah..." Bormph threw a look back up at her in return. "And if my hammer were a sword, I would be a Caeshian lord, now would I?"

"What hammer?" Amjelle tried to follow the dwarf's logic for a second. "You've got an axe!"

"Looks like it."

Bormph double-stepped as he trotted on, trying hard to keep up with Ramrok. The barbarian strode in front, ploughing through the night like a shipwrecker wyrm parting the waves of a particularly foreboding ocean.

The moon was full, but its light didn't flood all parts of the treacherous trail winding uphill. The mountain seemed to have been unaware of any such lighting requirements when it had formed into its current shape a couple of millennia prior. And, likewise stubborn, the moon refused to move even a handbreadth. On occasion, a boot stumbled over a protruding root lurking in the twilight because of it. Thus caught between this millennia-old animosity, the party struggled up the badly illuminated path.

"What's going on down there anyway?" Amjelle asked when they were three-quarters up a slope and took a short rest. "Aren't the orcs supposed to live reformed lives now? And what do they do? They abduct people and wage war in the middle of the night!"

"Exactly," Sylthia agreed.

Bormph stuck up his nose. "How did the orcs get hold of you anyway, Blondie, without leaving any traces? That's what I can't wrap my head around."

"Me neither," Sylthia said, because she couldn't, and went on to explain that she had woken in a tower, in a lavish bed, only to drop out of a window and then be accused by the orcs of having put the whole thing there. "Every single brick of it. That's what they said: *I* put it there."

"The whole tower?" A look of disbelief washed over Thimble's features.

"And, just for the record, you definitely didn't?" Bormph had to ask.

Sylthia shot the dwarf a dark glare.

"Well, how would I know?" Bormph said in a wheezy voice. He knew that most elves could do some magic on the side, and he had always found the ways of elves suspicious on principle. Apparently, the orcs had too, so he could relate, even if orcs were not to be trusted. Every dwarf knew that. But now that he thought about it some more, Bormph had to admit to himself that dwarves were suspicious of anyone who wasn't a dwarf. And most of the time they were suspicious of other dwarves too, even family. Dwarves were a suspicious lot.

"What's with the polar bear, Am?" Sylthia felt entitled to a question too, especially when the little fellow peeking out from the healer's backpack tried yet again to make a meal out of the elf's beetle hairpin. "Where did that come from? Don't tell me you just happened to find a polar bear in the desert!"

Amjelle loosened the strings of her backpack and let Snowflake out. A story about lots of fish, a cub, and a thud wanted to be told. She was only halfway through when she was interrupted.

A faint crackle fluttered over the mountainside.

The noise was brief, of a sputtering, frizzling sort, teetering on the cusp of being heard at all. It felt out of place up on a mountain trail. In the sound's wake, something – or was it everything? – appeared to be shifting. Or was it? Bormph could've sworn it was the mountain as a whole that moved, but that perception collided with his firm belief that if there ever was a thing a dwarf could rely on, it had to be a mountain. The mountain was a dwarf's staunch companion. Yet, only a moment ago, his eyes had led him to believe that the rocks had softened, blurred into a kind of haze, had stolen away for a second as if bereft of substance, steaming like his Aunt Thrumgasia's boulder pudding fresh from the stove.

Bormph rubbed his eyeballs. He squinted up the semi-moonlit trail, trying to separate the rock-solid truth from the trappings of imagination and a craving for dwarf pudding. He sensed the elf step past him to get a better look too.

A flicker of movement ahead had drawn Sylthia's attention. "Someone's up there," she said in hushed words, her eyes not leaving the spot. "Look!"

Outlined against the night sky, figures stood at the top of the mountain trail. A whole bunch of them!

Thimble stood back, as did the elf behind him, so the halfling wound up in front of her again. He considered his accidental role as Sylthia's protector for a moment. Maybe it was fate. But for some reason, he felt his toes curl and the colour drain from his heroic self. Out of the corner of his eye, he saw Sylthia pull an arrow from her quiver. His fingers followed the suggestion by clasping the dagger at his side. He swallowed hard.

The guys up there didn't particularly move like orcs. More like roaming brigands, outlaws returning to their hideout from waylaying unsuspecting adventurers... Who else would prowl about in the middle of the night in this godsforsaken neck of the woods – or the cleavage of the mountains for that matter?

The strangers – all different shapes, different sizes – were climbing up the trail, as they were. One stood out. For an instant, the moon revealed the biggest fellow's naked torso, the cone-shaped iron helmet he was parading around, and something enormous glinting in his hand that suggested he'd make anyone a head shorter if required.

Thimble looked over to their own tree-high fellow and saw Ramrok's hand jerk to his side. There was the faintest of noises when he drew his two-hander. Still, the scraping was loud enough to attract unwanted attention.

The big fellow, then the whole rest, turned back at them, all brandishing their weapons. There were six of them altogether – plus a tiny creature, which peeped out between the strangers' feet, a white, furry something, a—

Snowflake darted towards it.

Sylthia stared after him. It was among the oddest of things she had ever come across; the others had a polar bear too! But that was only half of it. She also noticed a certain familiarity in the shapes before her in the twilight, and when some moonlight fell on the battle axe wielded by one of them, she recognized its design. It had all the markings of a Swoth armourer, almost identical to the axe Bormph was holding. In fact, as the moonlight revealed some more, even the stout warrior wielding it looked like... like a Swoth dwarf. Actually, he looked *exactly* like Bormph.

The elf's eyes travelled over the other faces.

She let out a shriek. "This cannot be..."

Right in front of her, Thimble thought the very same. He shied backwards, where the desired repositioning of his heel coincided with the preferred location of his favourite elf's toes.

"Ouch!"

Something zipped over Thimble.

Sylthia's arrow had bolted through the night towards the figures and...

Everything shifted and jittered. Ahead, around, beneath, above. The image of the strangers – or were they? – wafted away into nothingness.

"Foul magic!" Bormph cried out. "Accursed and vile!" He stomped ahead towards the spot where the apparitions had fooled them only moments ago, as if he could just pull one of the spooks by an ear from its insubstantial hideout.

"Show yourself!" he bellowed at whatever wasn't there. His words got lost as they bounced around and eventually tumbled down the mountainside.

Whatever wasn't there stayed where it was.

The rest of the party caught up with the dwarf, their weapons still at the ready. But the figures were gone. They looked this way and that, and then at themselves, which was when a faint grinding noise sprang up from somewhere behind them – a sound very much like the very, very cautious drawing of a sword. But not cautious enough.

Ramrok whirled around first, flourishing his two-hander.

An odd chill stole over them when they looked down, and it travelled from left to right through each one of them, irrespective of size, race or gender. There they were again, a short distance back, coming up the mountain path – those mysterious figures, all six with a polar bear cub at their feet, gawking back up, as slack-jawed as they were looking down. Each one of them was alarmingly familiar. The barbarian down below already had his two-hander drawn and was now waving it about, and the others – dwarf, wizard, healer, elf and halfling – were readying their weapons too.

Everything available drawn, both sides froze. Except for the cub from below, who started towards them.

The elf below shrieked. "This cannot be…" An arrow broke loose from her bow and twanged uphill.

Everything shifted and jittered. Ahead, around, beneath, above.

There was a faint crackling, a sputter, then a clinking as of metal hitting stone. When they ventured a peek downhill again, all they saw was the trail wending away into the distance.

Sylthia hunkered down and picked up an arrow. She turned it round in her hand, inspected its head, shaft and feather fletching. If it wasn't hers, it very much looked like one of hers. She let the arrow slip back into her quiver, completing their number.

"Did you just...?" Whinewaeyn began, then began again. "Did you just shoot at... us?" He glared at the elf.

Sylthia glared back, stammering. "I-I..."

"Creepy," the barbarian issued a deep-throated comment, and that's just about how Thimble and Bormph assessed the situation too, but not in so many words.

"Let's get out of here," Amjelle whispered.

Marching, climbing, at times tripping over whatever was in his way, Thimble asked himself what they were running from – the orcs or themselves, or both? And the next question was, what was worse? The other questions buzzing through his head were *who* he was or was not, *where* he was or was not, and *why* everything was as it was. All of this made his tiny halfling self hungry. His stomach rumbled. And as for his legs, he had felt them still a while back, but now that he wasn't so sure of himself anymore, he was even less certain whether his feet had made it all the way.

Ramrok, in comparison, had brought his whole body, maybe because no deep thoughts dragged him down. His mind was blank, and in blank minds everything was always tidy. Quite contrary to the minds of wizards like Whinewaeyn. Whinewaeyn had an attic of a mind crammed full of junk nobody ever needed; when he went looking for something, he risked getting lost in the process.

The most practical of them was Bormph. He left the hard thinking to somebody else and focused on deciphering the weather-worn waymarks around them. At some point the path forked. A practical decision was required. Left or right.

Bormph made his case. "Got to be the one less travelled. Steeper, rockier. Hazardous all around. We have to keep pursuers off."

He said it as if it was a good thing. The things the dwarf mentioned were precisely the reasons why no one took that path... That's what Thimble thought anyway.

Be that as it may, they continued trudging up and up the Silvery Sickle's rocky slopes, squeezing themselves through tight spots between moss-covered boulders, travelling alongside ravines and navigating windswept ridges. And, for respite almost, they marched through bleak patches of stunted pines. While Whinewaeyn saved his magic, Amjelle had convinced her rod of Novotroth to serve as a torch substitute, and whatever dangers the path ahead had to offer – gnarled roots, slippery stones, lurking chasms – all things terrifying became a little less so in its soothing light.

Speaking of light: daybreak soon showed up, and it was early. There was nothing unusual about the sun being an early riser – it was part of the job description – but this time the whole dawn operation seemed overdone. In Thimble's judgment, it came right after midnight. But what did he, who was used to the comforts of a snug halfling-hole in Willwold-on-Glee, know about daybreak high up in the southern mountains?

They made it to a rope bridge spanning the dark maw of a gorge. The planks were broad, but the ropes that made up the handrails looked flimsy at best. Dark waters churned down below, furious and untamed. Above, for lack of other toys it might whisk away, the stiff breeze rattled the suspended slats and tugged at the ropes with a vengeance. The bridge endured the windy embrace with an arrangement of creaks and groans that sounded borderline obscene.

Right in front, a peculiar-looking cluster of rocks drew Amjelle's attention. She squinted at it, and in turn it was noticed by Bormph as well.

"What're you looking at?" the dwarf asked as he sat down on an uprooted tree trunk to readjust his footwear.

"Ah, you wouldn't know," said Amjelle, assuming that no warrior dwarf had ever set foot in the Weaverring art gallery. He wouldn't even have heard from the famous post-war masterpiece sculpture by Aqu'ruma "Quinchy" Ph'tang, which was a cluster of rocks with a disproportionally large humanoid head attached to it. Like this rock.

Quinchy's masterpiece, as any art-savvy person knew, was a comment on mankind's big-headedness, pun intended. The sculpture also expressed man's affinity for war through the massive club it stood perched on. The occasional gallery visitor, oblivious to fine art tropes and metaphors, would take the statue for nothing but a troll – which it looked like, of course. And yet, the social commentary went straight over the heads of the common gallery visitor, who was more excited about spotting a monster. "Walk past quickly, or it will come to life!" the society ladies would mumble among themselves under their breath. Blame pop art.[*]

---

[*] "Pop art" is art with a twist. Take Wendy War-Mole's famous one-time installation "Three Red Dragon Eggs". It turned out that the exhibited objects *were* three red dragon eggs. To the "oohs" and "aahs" of high society, three real drakelets popped out at the opening event, thus ringing in a new era of shock and awe in the art scene: pop art.

Amjelle smiled knowingly at Bormph, before she answered the dwarf's continuing wondering looks. "It's an art thing," she said, as she kept appreciating the stone. She remembered how some know-it-all had even tried to enlighten her about the biggest-headed trolls, the adamants, said to be the grisliest of them all. Unlike the common stone variety, adamant trolls rose *with* the sun, and early museum visitors felt compelled to keep their distance. As if Quinchy would have used a live troll! As if Quinchy was a pop artist!

Meanwhile, a ray of light slanted over the lowest peak of the Silvery Sickle. It peeked through the boughs of the handful of pines huddled together on an elevation that overlooked the rope bridge, and then, curious as it was, scuttled closer to greet the gathered party. The beam settled on the pile of rocks in front of them, where it felt wanted, warm and wonderful. For a moment.

A shuddering scream tore through the mountain idyll. A scream of a culturally interested healer facing a reality check in an unexpected place. A bit banshee-like.

The part of the stone pile that looked like a head stirred. Two rocks in the bulk flared, catching the fires of life like dying embers stoked by a strong breeze. With a bleary moan, the pile straightened up.

The irony was that Amjelle became petrified in response. Her crystal-topped stave flickered and died.

"Uh-oh," Thimble gasped. The group back-pedalled as a unit, save for the stone-still Amjelle. Sylthia and Ramrok had to pry her from the awakening heap.

A crust of grit and grime crumbled away from the thing's rocky surface. What remained when the dust had settled, was a shiny black creature, glittering in the morning sun with an iridescent sheen. It scrambled to its feet and rose and rose. Once the creature was done with rising, it had bulked to a height more than thrice the size of its largest onlooker, who was no less than a human giant. The giant was dwarfed in comparison, and the actual dwarf present was sort of brownied. Still, the beast didn't even reach its full size; it stood bent forward, propped on its knuckles, and the monster's head, which Amjelle had appreciated before, was almost as gigantic as its torso, with eyes as large as bucklers.

"Toooooll," rumbled the troll, gravelly, blood-curdlingly. A few scattered teeth protruded from the black hole of a mouth like tombstones. "Deeeath ooor toooll!"

"Hrmph!" Ramrok wasn't having this demotion to dwarf. "Ramrok choose death." He advanced wielding his toothpick – at least, that's how it must have looked from the troll's point of view. Brownie-sized Bormph, challenged by the barbarian's show of force, wasn't going to stand idly by either and charged with him. Sylthia nocked an arrow and fired.

There were two tinkles, and a sound like the shadow of a tinkle.

After that came a thunderous *WHOOOOMP*, and the uprooted tree trunk Bormph had been sitting on only moments ago landed between the attackers, now firmly in the rock-monster's massive fist. The ground shook, dust whirled up and loose boulders trundled into the abyss.

"Toooll!" The talking abomination was in no mood to be trifled with. It positioned itself in front of the bridge. When Ramrok lunged at it again, the creature sent all six and a half feet of solid muscle back with the flick of a stony finger, and the barbarian ended up sprawled on the wayside like spilled milk. Bormph collected his helmet. Time to refine tactics.

"The troll wants toll," he reported back to the watching Whinewaeyn.

"It's a common thing, I gather." The wizard eyed the colossus, who eyed him in turn with a stony stare. "Never understood the concept, to be honest. Same with dragons hoarding treasure. Not big shoppers, either of them. When did you last see a troll at the butcher's? If I were a troll, I'd prefer the meat wandering by. Saves the hunting trouble, and you get the gold anyway. You see what I'm saying?"

Bormph snorted. "I see that you're not helping, wizzer."

"How about a different route?" Whinewaeyn proposed. "This one looks expensive."

"TOOOOOLL!" The troll's voice rumbled like thunder. He grasped a piece of man-sized rock and flung it over their heads. It landed a short distance behind them, between two boulders, wedging shut the narrow passage they had come through. "GOOOOLD!"

"And yet, he seems insistent we travel *his* way," Bormph pointed out.

"Why, the troll's a blackmailer!" Whinewaeyn rifled through his beard as he looked for a thought. The troll watched their arguing with interest.

Ramrok had an idea. "Wizzy do wizzy work, no?"

"The big one's right." Bormph patted the barbarian's thigh. "How about some wizarding at this point? Right in time before our lights go out, something… flashy? We're out in the open, and you must have got your auras together by now, gramps?"

"Oh, yes," said Whinewaeyn, "but… it's an adamant troll, isn't it?"

"Sure is." Amjelle had learned her lesson.

"What of it?" said Bormph. "A bit resilient to good old physical attacks, but now that we've established that, it's your turn to—"

"The fellow's made of obsidian," Whinewaeyn clarified. "Obsidian negates light and magic. What's it they're teaching in that mason's school of yours anyway, stonebeater?"

Bormph gave the wizard a frazzled look.

"Every mage of course knows: with that troll's mass of obsidian, I'd say we can probably forget about spellcasting for about half a league around it. Let me demonstrate!"

The wizard pointed his staff at the troll. Everyone automatically stepped back.

"No need to worry," he assured the creature, who had turned an inquisitive eye at him. And an inquisitive fist, wrapped around a tree. "Just casting for the sake of argument."

Incantations flowed from Whinewaeyn's lips. The troll's huge eyes curiously followed his actions, but the tip of the staff didn't catch on. Scraps of darkness writhed viscously around the wood, but fizzled out, flaking away and leaving behind not so much a spell as the stench of foul eggs.

"Bleeergh…" went the troll.

Bormph held his nose and glared at Whinewaeyn's told-you-so face. "So you knew that it wouldn't work," the dwarf rounded on him, "cast it nevertheless, risk getting flattened by this monster, and now you're out of aura, *again?*"

"Magic won't help us here anyway." Whinewaeyn was much calmer about it. "So if we don't make it, we won't need any more."

"Or," Bormph said, "we could've used the little time we've just wasted to think about a way out that actually *does* work and still have magic as an option for whatever hits us next."

"Stop it!" Amjelle cut in. "What if we pay up? I mean… just this once."

"GOOOOLD! Want!" The troll had heard a keyword.

"But we haven't got anything!" Whinewaeyn faced the troll. "Last dungeon, no good, um, Mr Troll," he said, raising his voice. "Little gold… er… One moment, please!"

They huddled together and dug in their pockets for some change.

"Surely you've tucked away more than this, little one?" Whinewaeyn reminded Thimble, when the halfling produced just a few copper coins.

Thimble, crimson to the ears, shelled out a couple more.

"Okay, that's four gold pieces, half a silver, seventy-six coppers and two buttons." Whinewaeyn prodded the meagre pile around in his palm, but found no gem hidden among it. He held up what he'd got to the troll. "That enough? What's the fee we're talking about anyway? Any discount for parties and the elderly? And there's no way halflings have to pay full!"

The troll huffed, keeping a stony face – which was something he was particularly good at – and went on to pound the ground impatiently with his club. "Biiig TOOOOLL!" he rumbled, not being overly specific. "Want. Or breakfaaassst."

The wind kicked up, intoning a dirge's prelude.

"YOOOU fooor breakfaaassst… Fiiirst!" the troll boomed. He seemed to have taken a liking to Amjelle.

"What's with the fixation with eating adventurers these days?" Sylthia complained. She had considered skipping becoming dinner last night as a success, and now this.

"Oi! OI! Excuse me?"

A new voice drifted by. Necks craned round to look for it.

"Been here for a bit," the voice piped up again. "Not to sound impatient, but can I get served first? If this is going to take quite a while…"

The troll cranked his massive head around too and found a curious bear-headed figure waiting on the other side of the bridge. It leaned on a closed multicoloured umbrella, waving with one of its claws.

"Ooone aaattaaa tiiime!"

"Oi! No offense, but I'm in a hurry!" the irreverent bear-headed figure pressed on. "Would it be awfully inconvenient for you if I just go ahead and pay on the other side?"

"Noooo!" growled the troll. He had his principles – and a main course. First come, first served. He swivelled around once again, back towards the party, more determined than ever. "Breaaakfaaassst!"

Faint but insistent squeaks sounded from the bridge. The beast jerked its monstrous head back.

Against better advice, the speaking bear was already on its way over the slats, his stride brisk and confident. The closer the bear got, the more it looked just like a skinny fellow packed in multiple layers of clothing, with a raddled fur coat on top. The bear head, post the demise of its former owner, surveyed the ensemble from above. Without it, the fellow would have been about a head shorter, which made him far less intimidating and somewhat closer in height to a midget.

"BROOOAAAAAGH!!" the troll blurted out, somewhat nettled. This time he turned his full hulking body – which took him a moment or two – and stepped onto the bridge himself. The strained construction complained noisily, and yet the little man in bear's clothing and his shoddy umbrella marched on. When he reached the middle of the bridge, he stayed put.

"Yooou disooobeeey, yooou deeead!" roared the troll.

"The loony's mad," Whinewaeyn declared.

"So? Let him," reckoned Bormph.

"Troll be back," Ramrok said, putting things into perspective. They trooped over to the edge of the bridge and watched with tense anticipation. The face-off between the moving pile of stones and his challenger would begin any moment. And, most likely, it would be over before they could blink.

"Anything we can do from here?" Amjelle asked, getting panicky.

Sylthia shrugged. "I couldn't even tickle that thing with an arrow, Am! And magic's out too, so…"

"We could cut the ropes?" Thimble proposed, rocking nervously on his heels.

"With the madman on it too?" Sylthia was against it. "He might be mad, but…"

Ropes and planks creaked under the troll's weight as the monster lurched towards the overconfident stranger.

"Tell you what," Bormph said. "We wait till the big one has clobbered the little guy, and *then* we cut the ropes."

"And how would we get over there without a bridge?" Amjelle ignored the casualty angle for once. She offered a silent prayer to Novotroth, though, blessing the confused. Good advice was on vacation.

The troll had reached his unlikely opponent by now. "YOOOU DIIIE!" Fury blazed in the ember-like eyes. A fist holding the tree trunk rose sky-high.

"Oi!" squeaked the tiny figure, peering up like a bad idea facing crushing inevitability. "Come and get me!"

Thimble cringed from a distance. It was such an inept thing to say to a troll when he was about to smite you, even for a loony. An entry for a "famous last words" collection this wasn't. It also dawned on Thimble that the time to close his eyes was right about... *now*.

And yet he didn't. It was no different than Veggie Winfried's cart crash the other week, with melons bouncing all over the cobbles and tomatoes spattering on passers-by – carnage nothing short of the Great Battle of Rak-a'tak.

He thought better of it and covered his face with his hands...

...and then peered through his fingers.

The troll took a swing with its tree. "UUUUUAAARGHHH!"

His tiny opponent took a step back and mumbled some gibberish. That's how it sounded anyway.

There was a soft *ding*. Not a big and flashy thing, just a *ding*. Or a *ring*. A *bling* maybe. At any rate, an altogether unexpected thing.

Thimble blinked under his windblown shock of hair, and then blinked again. Something round and shiny – he couldn't quite fathom what – had appeared out of nowhere next to the troll's head. Presently, it took a free fall.

Tiny as it was, even the behemoth registered it and stopped in mid-motion. "Oooomgh?"

A few seconds later, a soft splash reached up from the waters below.

"Oi!" Mr Bearskin yelled. "There it is again!" He turned the umbrella in his hand by its crook, so that it pointed over the bridge's ropey handrail at the opposite side.

He must have mumbled some more, because there was another *ding* or a *bling*. Again, something round and shiny slipped out of thin air. It had a long neck… Or was it a trunk…? Certainly, whatever it was had no wings, for it plunged downwards, much like its companion had done before.

The troll rolled his head around in irritation.

"Careful there!" His challenger wasn't the least bit fazed. "Or the next one will get you…"

Another mumble, another *ding*, and one more object fell out of nothingness.

This time the troll's enormous arm jutted out, swinging its preferred weapon of rowdy customer destruction at the troublemaker with scary precision, and it landed a direct hit! The thing – for it must have been one – vaporized on impact. It shattered in multiple hollow-sounding, fragile noises. Bits and pieces sprayed all over the canyon.

The troll roared triumphantly. Until he realized that his own momentum had made his massive body careen to the side. From there on, the creature had some trouble shifting his weight back. The troll tilted over the ropey handrail and gawped into the churning waters below. Then, from this precarious position, the head took over and – weighty as it was – led the way for the rest of the monstrosity and his tree trunk to topple straight downwards.

A surprised ongoing roar echoed across the gorge, ricocheting off the cliff faces as it made for the depths. It found its end in a splash, literally drowning it out, and the obsidian troll, who had dropped like a stone, sunk like one too. The wind howled its take on a dirge.

The stranger, not a hair on his bearskin harmed, waved merrily at Whinewaeyn and company. "Hoy, folks! Thought I'd spare you your fee, eh?"

CHAPTER 12

Gnomes 'n' Goblins

H as he…?"
  "Did he just…?"

"Was he really…?"

Unfinished sentences made their way around the party. Only Whinewaeyn counted his marbles in silence, mouth hanging ajar.

Sylthia gave the dwarf a gloating grin. "The loony you wanted to get rid of just made you look like a fool, didn't he?"

Bormph bit his lip, forced a thin smile, that was in any case hidden in his facial hair, and grunted something too low to catch. What sounded like a grouchy grumble to the untutored ear was in fact a mix of mild displeasure and genuine bemusement laced with a whiff of sympathy. Though only another dwarf would know a dwarf's grumble from a dwarf's grumble.

The six of them clumped over the planks to meet their unlikely hero, Snowflake plodding alongside them, cautious on the wooden slats.

"I don't know how you did it… um… mighty midget," Whinewaeyn said by way of greeting once he had reached the middle of the bridge, "but I reckon you've saved our lives…" He doffed his hat to the stranger, who barely cleared the wizard's chest, extra head included. "Name's Whinewaeyn. Wizard." He introduced the others as well.

The little man lifted his bear claw in acknowledgement and eyed Snowflake with curiosity. The cub had padded ahead to investigate and now stuck up his nose at him, snuffled a bit, and then – as if he had seen and smelled enough – turned tail and slunk behind the wizard's robe.

Ramrok clucked. "Ho-ho. Bear-wearer give bear creeps."

"I'm Tsynnslin." The stranger bowed and smiled affably. "Tsynnslin T'shnolt. Pleased to meet you." His voice didn't sound like a hard-boiled troll hunter's, more like a clerk on an adventure holiday. The stranger shoved his extra skull back, revealing the weathered face of a prow-nosed gnome, with a goatee and bushy white eyebrows thick enough to store smaller provisions. The rest of his head wasn't as fortunate when it came to hair growth: his higher-than-high wrinkly forehead led up to a desperate patch of white curls holding up a semicircular line of hairy decency at the back of his head. His tiny eyes twinkled back at the party.

With introductions out of the way, the first thing on Whinewaeyn's mind was, "So… what was the trick there?"

"Picked that up somewhere," the gnome said, noncommittal.

"Good for you. Not that you look like a magician."

"Maybe that's because I'm *not* a magician?"

"No?" Whinewaeyn's pointy hat flapped around in surprise. "And how does that work, conjuring without magic?"

"Professional secret."

Whinewaeyn eyed the little person quizzically. "Are you one of those... shamans or something?"

"More a something than a shaman."

The wizard rubbed his nose. Wind whistled around him. "In case you didn't know, obsidian foils any well-meant spellcasting. It's sort of reflective in a non-thinking way."

"Pays off not to have to rely on spellcasting then, eh?" The gnome had an answer to everything, but certainly guarded his secrets. He also seemed to relish the wizard's ignorance. "I'm more, say, a mystic," he revealed at last, lifting his chin and his wind-beaten goatee to the wizard's face. "That's what you scholars would call it anyway." He let the bear head sink back onto his half-bald skull. "Let's walk and talk," he offered, with all four of the eyes on his head peering back at the party. Only two of them sparkled with life, the others delivered the cold, steady stare of a predator regretting its last excursion. The combination felt a bit disconcerting, especially considering the little man had just annihilated a full-grown magic-resistant monster by doing little more than raising a finger.

The gnome started strolling back to the side of the bridge where he'd arrived, using his umbrella as a walking stick to tap the planks, and the party tagged along in his wake, buffeted by the winds.

Whinewaeyn jerked a thumb behind them as they were walking. "Didn't you want to cross over, gnome?"

"No, not anymore. Got what I was looking for."

Whinewaeyn glanced at Amjelle, but all she could do was shrug.

A few steps behind them, Bormph noticed something protruding from the stranger's backpack. It had the shape of a night cap, but it didn't bend like one when it bounced around. So he looked closer and found it to be the headpiece of a figurine, worn by a... clay-made gnome! A gnome carrying a gnome? Bormph was still pushing his thoughts about it here and there when Thimble prodded him from his right.

"What's that anyway, a mystic?" Thimble's face was blank.

"You tell me." A shrewd glint reflected in the dwarf's eyes. "Someone who... mystifies? On a professional level?"

Sylthia asked the gnome instead.

Two of Tsynnslin's four eyes rolled up, looking back at her. He smirked enigmatically. "Aye, a valid question, elf. Well, we mystics busy ourselves with figuring out the universe. Not in a way any dabbler in the arcane arts might, mind you. Gah, the spellweavers are fine with taking what's there and rearranging it into something else they're more comfortable with. They take auras and elements and bundle them into explosions—"

"Now let me tell you something, gnome..." Whinewaeyn put up his finger, but was immediately shushed by Amjelle.

"You might say we study things," the gnome went on when she asked again. "All kinds of things." Tsynnslin paused, waiting for the whole group to catch up. They had arrived on the other side of the gorge.

"What kind of things?" Whinewaeyn forgot about explosions for now.

Tsynnslin brandished his umbrella and pointed to nowhere in particular. "This," he said, then he pointed elsewhere, which made just as much sense. "And that..."

But as the gnome stabbed some more random holes in the air, it became apparent that he was trying to indicate *everywhere*, which must be the sum of all particular nowheres, Whinewaeyn realized with a little delay. The wizard felt a bit smarter now, but just as lost.

"Mystics explore every tiny little something," the gnome carried on. "And the big somethings too, for they're made out of the tiny ones. I'm interested in whatever lies beyond the things we know, or think we know. What's the nature of a thing? Where do things come from? Where do *we* come from? And where are we going?"

"Yeah," Bormph wheezed, catching up. "Been wondering about that too, gnome." He'd looked up the serpentine trail they'd started to ascend, and it had worried him. "Where *are* we going, bear-wearer?"

"Follow me…" Tsynnslin said simply. "Now that I've found you, I have to show you something."

"Found us?" Whinewaeyn's expression couldn't decide where to settle. "You must have mistaken us for someone else, gnome! We're just passing through."

"Oh, I don't think so."

The six of them traded glances. None could make rhyme nor reason of any of the gnome's talk, and Bormph for his part had made up his mind that the gnome was a loony. A loony who knew how to deal with adamant trolls, granted. A rare breed of a mountain gnome loony then, but with enough tripe in his head. A hermit loony, a screw-loose recluse. He might push them off a cliff anytime just to see whether they'd fly. The thought became more urgent when he realized at the upper end of the trail that the gnome had indeed led them to the brink of a cliff…

"Look!" Tsynnslin called out, and they did. Apart from Bormph, a solitary dwarf afloat on a sea of suspicions, who only glanced over the edge from a very, very safe distance.

Bormph provided his spyglass though, for those who dared to gamble on having a glimpse and thus putting themselves at greater risk of a shove into the abyss, courtesy of a murderous mountain-dwelling gnome.

Thimble, always the curious one, volunteered – not for a push, but for a peer through the spyglass. The device revealed the early morning orc village in all its bustling glory, plus the addition of the notorious tower, or rather four-fifths of it. The orcs were dismantling the building from top to bottom, brick by brick. Some gruntlings loaded the extracted bricks on carts, and human horsemen directed the bizarre efforts.

"Why, it's the Zarrafandan cavalry!" Thimble cried. "They're forcing the orcs to pull down that damn tower!"

"Aye, so it is…" Tsynnslin nodded. "I saw fireworks from my cavern up here, and then the fighting began."

Amjelle took the spyglass from Thimble's hand. "Looks like the fireworks brought them right there to help us out."

"Perfect timing, then." Bormph gave a smug grin.

"Don't be so sure." The gnome extracted a piece of ragged-edged paper from the leather jerkin he wore under his fur coat. As he unfolded it to poster size, the official Zarrafandan seal became prominently visible. "Have a look at this notice. It has *shmodork* written all over it."

The paper changed hands.

"What's *shmodork?*" Thimble asked, peeking at it.

"Gnomish expression. Combo-word," Tsynnslin explained. "Stands for, let's say, a dire situation. Points out bad prospects. Also used for cussing. And there's 'orc' in it, for emphasis. Orcs invariably spell trouble, and that's what we've got here."

Whinewaeyn smoothed the poster out and read it aloud.

"'WANTED: This man.'" There was a sketch of a geezerly figure with floppy headgear, a beard, a staff and an overarching bedraggled look. "'On suspicion of tower and fireworks theft, deception of authorities, incitement of orcen revolution, possible DWUM involvement and general apocalyptic conspiracy,'" he read. "'At large. Presumed dangerous. Operates with dwarf, barbarian and halfling accomplices (one each), also a dark-haired female and a white bear cub. One thousand gold reward, a hundred and fifty more for each extra henchman, cub excluded. Signed Prince Dymmling, 8th of Fallen Leaf 1004.'"

Thimble whistled through the gap in his teeth. "*Shmodork*, huh?"

"Why, how—" Whinewaeyn boiled with indignation. "What are they thinking?"

The paper was handed around.

"Look like wizzy," said Ramrok.

"Looks like us," said Amjelle.

"Looks like a forgery," Bormph snarked. "See the date? That's two days ahead! What's the meaning of this, bear-wearer?" He traced the edge of his axe-blade with a thumb as his scowl deepened.

"Curious..." One of the gnome's bushy eyebrows described an inquisitive curve. "You don't have any recollection, do you?" His paw gestured at the path beneath their vantage point. "What exactly *do* you remember from when you disappeared climbing the slope down there?"

"When we... wait. What?" Whinewaeyn wiggled his pinkie in his ear, just in case something was clogging his hearing.

"Disappeared. You heard me. I watched you. From up here."

"Twaddle! We didn't disappear. We're right here. Aren't we?" The wizard looked around for confirmation.

"But you've skipped a couple of days," Tsynnslin said flatly.

"No offense," said Bormph, "but you've been up here way too long, gnome. You're seeing things. Or, you don't. Or didn't. Or whatever. Must be the mountain air. Let me tell you, the mountain is meant to be lived inside, deep down under, not outside, up here. That's where you high-plain gnomes get it wrong."

"How'd you explain this then?" The gnome's umbrella tip indicated the goings-on on the plain below. "The tower has already been dismantled about one fifth, see? You're telling me the orcs did all of this in the past hour or so?" He let the thought sit for a while, then his umbrella moved on to point at the faint outlines of the moon against the breaking dawn. The shape was that of a perfectly round biscuit with a bite taken out. "It was full when the Zarrafandans arrived, when the skirmish started, and when you fled up here."

They remembered. Muttering filled the air.

"What happened to you down there?" Tsynnslin pressed. "When you went up? Something *must* have…"

"Ramrok see… Ramrok," the barbarian ventured at last. "Winewing and Thumble, and little boiler-bear from desert."

"Yeah," Thimble said. "That was us! We saw… ourselves!"

At that point Amjelle told the gnome everything – what they had seen up that path, or thought they saw anyway, and how Sylthia had disappeared for no apparent reason, which was also why they were there in the first place. She also told him about the dune incident, and the fact that they hadn't an inkling what was going on with any of it.

"So…" Whinewaeyn summed up, "what *is* going on?"

"Good question, wizard. Good question. According to the Zarrafandans, the apocalypse maybe." Tsynnslin inhaled sharply. "And what's worse, I'm not sure they've got it wrong this time."

"The *what?*" Thimble couldn't believe it.

"Pocalpyps," Ramrok repeated, the way he had heard it.

"The End of Days," Tsynnslin clarified. "There are, indeed, certain indicators. And, if we believe the Zarrafandans, you're involved."

"Ah, twiddletricks! We'd know about that sort of thing," Whinewaeyn said with confidence. "Er… Wouldn't we?"

"I thought so." Tsynnslin had already turned his back to the cliff's edge and was descending the incline they had come up. He beckoned them. "We better continue talking elsewhere," he said in a hushed tone. "It's not safe here, and I haven't been looking for you all these days for nothing."

"Now what do you mean by *that?*" Bormph muttered, irritated. "And what's all this apocalypse business?"

"Follow me," was all Tsynnslin was willing to say for now. They slipped through a natural stone arch formed by two portentous rocks jutting out against each other.

"World-ending stuff's usually exaggerated," Whinewaeyn said as they threaded after the gnome, "and it's mostly Vensk and his goblins who are behind such silly talk. Don't believe any of it. I would wager—"

"Ssssh!" Tsynnslin held up a hand. When everybody had got the message, he motioned to make haste. "Goblins or not, the way I see it," he whispered to the wizard, "you don't have much choice anyway. You've got to save the world with me, or perish in the attempt." It felt like a strange choice of words, but it did also promise some excitement.

"Well. We're between adventures anyway," Whinewaeyn replied casually. "Oh, and fresh out of provisions too. Got any?"

A couple of days earlier, south of the Joghavri.

Thromp-da-glomph pulled the reins. His pony whickered wearily, slackened its pace and came to a halt.

Thromp had the look of an orc sitting there on his mount, albeit a rather small orc. But an orc he wasn't. Goblins are tinier, softer-skinned versions of their racial relatives, with bat ears, healthier teeth and hawkish noses. But when they bake in the sun for a whole day crossing a desert – which makes the backside sore and even the most docile creature grouchy – the orc in the goblin really shines through.

Thromp leaned over the pommel of his saddle, craning his head here and there. He sensed that something was wrong. The large eyes in his sunburnt face rolled over the whole mountain range before him, and his flexible goblin ears turned about exploratorily.

The Groo'cae'tran Heights, with their craggy peaks, grey crevices and the occasional waterfall tumbling from a precipice, reared up even more intimidatingly up close than from a distance. The black hole leading down into the bowels of the mountain was in plain view from here too, right where it used to be. But no one else was around; there was no hellhound barking, no sentry basking in the sun, no poster that said something to the effect of *"Wanna end up as mincemeat? Apply here!"*

Official courier or not, Thromp was worried. Only a single signboard had stood its ground, reading *"Mine."* Ever since Vensk Stormraiser had taken over the abandoned Groo'cae'tran tunnels. That single word was more than a location marker. It had developed into something of a bullying-sibling-handling-a-last-slice-of-cake situation. Something possessive.

Urged forward, the pony trotted closer to the tunnel entrance. The day was hot. No comparison to the scorching Joghavri heat Thromp and his taxed bottom had endured for the past day or so, but hot enough to gleefully look forward to the damp darkness inside. Thromp slid from his saddle, tethered his mount to the next tree at hand and untied his satchel.

"It's me!" he yelled into the black hole.

Nothing but an echo came back – and not even that sounded sure of itself.

"Well, I'll be off then, Knooble." The goblin's hand petted the pony's flank. "Back in a minute. Will get you some water." Then, a bit queasy from his long ride, he slopped bow-leggedly towards the opening.

"Courier reporting!" Thromp tried some other variations on a greeting as he scampered through the tunnel, but was met with only more ominous quiet once his own echo had subsided.

Suddenly, as if lit by an invisible hand, a whole row of torches in their wall brackets sparked to life. This wasn't how Thromp remembered it.

"Anyone ar—"

A metallic, unexpected, *cl-* noise underfoot made Thromp quickly re-evaluate the situation. A moment later, when he was still in the process of re-evaluating, the sound made more sense. Extra information had been added. The sound had transformed into a full-fledged *clack* – a *clack* exactly like a pressure plate's signature feature.

All oiled up and prepared, the mechanism got to the matter it was constructed for. To the triggering *clack* sounded two synchronized *clicks*, one for each hatch flapping open – a standard feature of model PLA-T/cla1-cli2, available at any well-stocked armoury specializing in dastardly devices. It was a trap.

"Whaaahhhh!" Thromp screeched as he lost ground.

Next thing he knew, he was sliding down a winding chute, bouncing around like a lone potato in a Northman's broth. The ride lasted about half an eternity, after which he nosedived into what felt like an underground dung heap. Darkness enveloped him.

It took a while until the numb Thromp came to. The first thing he did was splutter a handful of dung-muffled expletives. Attempts at wriggling out of the oozing slime, however, only greased him up even more.

Like a swamp-monster, he wobbled to his feet and limped forward. A faint light beckoned ahead. He knew it to be the glow of shimmering glimmerlings, self-illuminating mushrooms common in the Groo'cae'trans. Following their luminous haze, Thromp stumbled along into the unknown until something clanked. Again.

Model PLA-P/cl-zing17 got into gear with a snap and a zing.

An arrow swished past. It missed by a hair's breadth.

The goblin jerked his head to dislodge some dung from his eyes so as to get a better idea of what was going on. In the process, he took one more step, and—

There was another *clank*, another *snap*, and – no surprise now, really – one more *zing*. This time an arrow drilled into the satchel Thromp held, more by accident than intention. Half-blind, half-immobile, he flung himself to one side.

Clunk-clunk-clunk.

Phut-phut-phut-di-tutt... A whole barrage of arrows swooshed over Thromp's head. At least ground level appeared safe.

He pulled down his ears and, shielded by his satchel, wormed his way forward.

Pressure plate after pressure plate triggered. One arrow after another whooshed overhead and, outwitted, bounced off the tunnel wall opposite.

Clunk-phut-clink... Clunk-phut-clink... Clunk-phut-clink...

Struggling, wheezing, groaning, with his heart in his mouth, Thromp reached the end of the trap-riddled passage, where he was greeted with one more *clunk*, followed by a corresponding *phut*, an arrow twanging by, and the obligatory *clink* on the wall. After that, heavenly silence. The ground had run out of pressure plates.

Thromp let his breath slow and deepen. He closed his eyes and for once was happy to rest his dung-decorated head in plain dirt. It felt like a cushion. A smooth, peaceful, squashy cushion. Complacency descended on him.

But it was a short-lived repose. Thromp cocked his head. Everything around him seemed to move in the gloaming... No, that couldn't possibly be. *He* was the one moving, he deduced momentarily. He was skidding down a soaking wet slope. And fast!

With a large-scale splash, he cannonballed into a body of water.

Thromp surfaced, choking, spitting and sputtering. The water was ice-cold. But at least the bath helped get rid of most of the dung clinging to his joints. For some reason, though, he was surrounded by half a dozen floating logs drifting about. Their presence all the way down here raised a few questions, but for now he was happy to have them. Weak and weary as he was, he paddled closer to the largest piece of wood and heaved himself up onto it.

Half a second later, Thromp made a spine-tingling discovery: the log wasn't a log. He was riding something… living! It could only be… an alligator!

His heart stopped. But just for a little bit.

It got pumping again when it occurred to him that alligators and freezing water didn't go well together. Alligators in subterranean lakes? Unheard of! White toads perhaps, or schools of sliverfish, or – as for bigger creatures – ice raptors, maybe? Raptors even looked a bit like distant cousins of crocod—

By the time the thought had taken shape in his mind, Thromp knew that he was riding an ice raptor. And that's when he screamed for all his little goblin self was worth.

There was a resolute knock.

The super-heavyweight human mass, also known as Vensk Stormraiser, flinched. The prominent gold chain around his neck shifted noisily, on account of the effort its wearer was making to roll around on the assortment of blankets he'd been reclining on for the past thirteen days. The plan was to end up facing the massive double door of his luxuriously furnished underground residence, but it was no easy feat. After a bit of back and forth, the operation was aborted. Vensk chose to roll just his eyes instead, keeping his body in a more stable position.

"Enter!" he attempted to call, but ended up with a hoarse caw instead. He stared over at the entrance like a frightened animal, his gaze dull and vacant.

No, Vensk Stormraiser didn't sound like someone who could raise a storm at all, not even a breeze – bodily functions exempted. And he had never looked the part with his pudgy build either, a circumstance on which he had considerably "improved" over time. He had a tempest for a hairdo, though; maybe that's where his impressive-sounding name originated. But now that he'd lost most of his voice and measles danced over his already pock-riddled face, the extra-large-framed Vensk was almost a case to feel sorry for. Almost.

One of the bronze-faced cedar doors creaked open and a thin creature scuttled inside.

"Sorry to disturb you, Master…" The words ventured gingerly across the room. "A visitor has arrived. I fear his business cannot wait."

"It can't wait until I'm well?" Vensk croaked.

"No, Master. If I may…" The goblin dragged in another green-skinned creature, who was jittering like a leaf and dripping dirty water all over the place. The goblin's voice dwindled to a whisper. "Don't get any closer, Thromp. Master Vensk has been sick for days, and it's highly contagious. At first, he was sort of proud to be the only adult in the known world to have the measles, but then he realized that, well, he had it."

"What are you two scheming about over there, K'lhonk?" Vensk muttered, his voice trailing off into a cough.

"Nothing, Master. I'll leave you two to it, if I may, and see to cleaning this mess up. Oh, and I'll fetch a towel too." The goblin's footsteps departed, sloshing through puddles.

"Who're you?" Vensk barked from the pile of blankets that loomed over the remaining goblin. "Identify yourself! And why are you wet like a dog and reeking of dung?"

"Th-th-thr-thromp-da-glomph, Master," Thromp stammered and hung his head.

"You any relation to my messenger?" Vensk squinted at him. "His name's much shorter, but you look very much like him."

"I-I-I a-a-am your messenger, Master," Thromp insisted. "Th-thr-thromp-da-glomph. And I-I-I have a message."

"You positive you're not an imposter? How did you get all drenched like that by riding through the desert? *Answer me!*" Vensk, propped against a heap of pillows, held up a stubby-fingered fist and wobbled a bit sideways. What was meant as a threatening gesture looked more like an overturned beetle coping with its plight. "And where are my guards, who should be protecting my life when an assassin comes a-knocking in Thrompy guise?" Vensk groped for the bell at his blanketside and, feeble as he was, knocked it over. It tinkled ineffectively and rolled to safety into a corner.

"Master Vensk, it really *is* me," Thromp pleaded. "I-I-I came through the main entrance… Then dropped down into a pit! The guards fished me out of a raptor-infested underground lake. I-i-i-t was horrible!"

"Oh, yeah? And why is it that you didn't use the delivery entrance, courier? Eh? *Eh?*" The mound of a man winked at him. "You know the 'main' one…"

"W-w-what …?"

Vensk paused his struggle against the pillows and blankets, which made him look like an impossibly broad-bellied galley churned by a heavy sea. "Why are you talking in stutters, Thromp?" he croaked. "Don't you know?"

"Kn-n-ow what, Master?"

"That we've made modifications. A back entrance."

"A back entrance?"

"And then we changed the back entrance to the main one and the main entrance into a death trap." Vensk sniffed. "Security reasons."

"Oh."

"All part of an ingenious plan, Thromp. Top secret project." Vensk's two-layered chin relocated a tad closer to the goblin. It allowed him to rest his gaze on the tiny creature without any unnecessary eye rolling. "But why make a test run through something you don't even know about? You aren't the winner of our raffle."

Thromp shifted from one foot to the other, creating a fresh puddle to drip into. "Um... It seems I was ill-informed, Master."

"Impossible. Didn't you get the message?"

"Um... Who would message the messengers, Master?"

"Oh!" Vensk puffed. "Good point! It's like this whole who-guards-the-guards-thing, isn't it? Only with messengers." He pondered a bit. "Hmm... I reckon you've found a flaw in the system, Thromp."

"Erm... Just doing my job." Thromp's lips curved into a wry smile.

"What bothers me a bit is that you survived..."

"Er, pardon, Master?"

"I mean, a thing like that shouldn't have happened."

"No, certainly not. Oooh no."

"If one single lousy untrained goblin courier can survive stumbling into our trap accidentally, what about a crafty murderer with a wit as sharp as his blade? Or a whole regiment of enemies plotting to smoke us out? Imagine that, Thromp!"

"I—"

"The traps have to be doubled, improved and made deadlier. I will get right to the planning. Thank you for your feedback." Vensk rolled around excitedly, his weakness waning with the new ideas floating through his head. "That will be all."

"Erm… Master Vensk? The reason I'm here—"

"Oh, you have a message, right? Love messages! Let's hear it then…"

A mop with K'lhonk hiding behind it showed up in the doorway and got to business. "Don't mind me, Master," he said, as the strips of cloth squeaked over the flagstones.

"It's about those reformed orcs," Thromp started, "and the Zarrafandans, I guess. And elves. All of them. Strange things are happening." Between sentences the goblin rubbed himself off with the towel K'lhonk had handed him.

"Zarrafandans? Elves? Strange things?"

"Well, the strangest thing is a huge tower in Thog'thok."

"The orcs are building a tower?"

"It's not that they're building one," Thromp said. "It just *showed up*. Ready-made. With the Zarrafandan coat of arms on the front door. All of a sudden it was there, overnight. Like lightning out of a blue sky, only it was a tower out of a black night."

K'lhonk, the mopping goblin, stopped mid-squeak to digest the news.

"Don't be silly, courier," Vensk snapped.

"I saw it with my own eyes, Master," Thromp insisted. "Mayhaps an observation tower. Mayhaps something as to harbour more wizardry in. Orcs moved in and out, around and about. There was also a gathering of all the shamans and an elf – a female one – the day after. She may be the one behind all this, probably a powerful spellweaver."

"Orcs, a human tower *and* an elf?" Vensk's hair stood on end. It did that all the time, but now had a good reason to. "If what you say is true… if they can make one such tower, who says they can't make a whole lot of them? They might fortify the whole Silvery Sickle that way, and the Peet Fields too…"

"I'm afraid there's more."

What colour was still left in Vensk's face now drained even further, accentuating his measles spots.

"You see," Thromp said, "as I was on my way southwards to report… I saw a cavalry regiment scouting the fringes of the Joghavri. Thank the gods, they didn't spot me or have me followed. But something's afoot, Master. Something big."

"Fits with the Zarrafandans spreading rumours," K'lhonk chipped in from the back, throwing Vensk a sardonic look. "Rumours about you… planning something big."

"Who says we aren't?" Vensk rumbled. "Zarrafanda first, that's the easiest part, then Aermerlyn. I'm the rightful heir anyway, and then—"

"Ah, you're missing the point, Master," K'lhonk interrupted. "Can't you see that they're using such rumours against you?"

"Against me? How so?"

"Well, they put them out. And by accusing you, they sway everyone to join them before it's too late. They get the orcs on their side, the most potent wizards, the elves, and what have you, and together they entrench themselves around the Joghavri… They forestall your ambitions. They won't wait until you're ready! They'll attack before *you* act!"

Vensk's fever rose by the minute. He was infuriated enough to bounce into a stable sitting position. "Gosh! You're right, K'lhonk! An alliance! They're forming an alliance! I should have known that those pesky humans wouldn't reform the orcs out of sheer charity… And they've been far too friendly with the elves of the Wending Woods." He began to snivel. "How has it come to this? Why didn't we infiltrate that dratted orc village earlier on and recruit them for our cause? We could have been about ready to wreak havoc on Zarrafanda…"

"Well, Master," K'lhonk, propped on his mop, reminded him, "we've been regrouping ever since our last… erm… unfortunate attempt. It's not that we—"

"Quiet, K'lhonk," Vensk snapped. "I might be ailing, but my memory is not. If I hadn't been troubled by the measles, as rare and remarkable as this is, another raid on Zarrafanda would be long underway by now." He paused, and his eyes began glazing over as he stared at his two visitors: a dripping courier and his second in command, a goblin with a mop and a bucket spouting unhelpful advice. "Unless…" he then mumbled, "it's… destiny. Destiny unfolding… You know, as they say, an omen."

Thromp crooked his head towards his fellow goblin, then back at Vensk. Listening to the oversized one was often like listening to the wind: lots of whistles and incoherent howls, and before you knew it, the storm was upon you.

"An omen, yes," Vensk slurred, taking a liking to the idea. "The measles, the fever, these strange thoughts chasing through my head..." His gaze became ever more distant.

Mop-wielder K'lhonk audibly cleared his throat, but Vensk rattled on.

"If it weren't for the godsgiven measles, we'd have done just that. Launched a painstakingly prepared, well-thought-out raid, got our hands on some supplies and a couple of weapons maybe. We'd have captured a loaded nobleman here, a damsel there, and someone would have paid the ransom. A solid, common raid. Just a wee bit of decent mischief. We would have done all that, wouldn't we?"

"We certainly would have." K'lhonk's head bobbed up and down in agreement. "As we've always done."

"But I see now where we went wrong before. The fever has cleansed my mind," Vensk proclaimed darkly. "It has purged all the nonsense about 'Small is safe' and 'Look before you leap.' The Zarrafandans expect rational actions, and guess what?"

A sudden unease gripped K'lhonk and Thromp.

"We're not so obtuse as to give them what they anticipate! Ha-ha!"

K'lhonk squinted suspiciously at his master. "What else do we have to give?"

"All-out war!" Vensk roared. "With everything we have. Attack, they say, is the best defence! When you're up against a wall, you make your best moves."

K'lhonk and Thromp stared at the big immobile feverish lump rolling around on his blankets.

"A pre-emptive strike to pre-empt pre-emptive strikes! A strike the likes of which that sorry excuse for a prince has never seen before. We'll put an end to all strikes with one striking stroke!"

"Couldn't it be that you're overthinking this an itsy-bitsy bit, Master?" K'lhonk cautioned. "If you're a mite feverish, I'd be happy to tuck you back in, so that—"

"You do as you're told!" Vensk snarled. "I want all my captains right here within the hour. We must be quick and efficient. We've got an invasion to prepare for."

K'lhonk clutched his mop. "Did you say 'invasion', Master?"

"Invasion is implied in 'all-out war'. We must go all out here, and" – he indicated somewhere northward – "over there too. You don't think we're capable of an invasion, K'lhonk?"

"Er, may I be frank?"

"You may, K'lhonk."

"To be honest… er… no."

"Then that's *precisely* what we're going for." Vensk gave a hollow laugh. "If not even *we* believe in it, we'll have the drop on them."

"But… but…" K'lhonk grasped for some string of coherent thought. "You might as well say, Master, that nobody would expect an attack by an army of ducklings either."

Vensk rolled forward. "No ducks! I am the Chosen One! Now clear off! Go and instruct the captains!"

"Um… erm… Yes, Master." The goblin took his bucket and Thromp's wet towel, and excused himself with an abject panicky bow.

"And you…" Vensk groped for a word.

"Th-th-th-thromp," shuddered out of the goblin still around. "Th-th-th-romp-da-glomph." He was jittering afresh.

"Yes... Thromp... Return to the Sickle! Inform our outposts to stay vigilant while we prepare our army for the great assault. Tell them to muster all our forces up north. They'll soon have to cause a distraction when our goblin army advances."

Beads of perspiration gathered on Vensk's brow. The manic eyes beneath glimmered. Vensk's instincts as commander-in-chief had been awakened, and the measles, maybe intimidated by the person whom they now had to deal with, seemed to be making themselves scarcer already.

"Thog'thok and its tower will fall, and from there we'll march right into Zarrafanda, and then onwards." He dropped back into his pile of pillows.

"Ah, yes, Master," Thromp quivered. "Of course, Master." He took a step back. "Er, Master?"

"What is it now?"

"May I inform the other messengers about the delivery entrance? I guess K'lhonk can show me where to find it?"

"Sure, Thromp, sure," Vensk moaned. "Oh, oh, and that reminds me! Tell K'lhonk to come back for a moment, would you? Now that we're at war, we'd better put a few traps in there too. Just in case."

CHAPTER 13

Auras and Artifacts

The present. Somewhere around the Silvery Sickle.

After a short journey, Tsynnslin and company reached a hole in the mountainside. It was large enough for everyone, or at least it would have been if it hadn't been overgrown with brambles, thistles and ivy. In its present state, only a gnome could really pass through without a hassle.

"Ouch!"

There were more brambles and thistles than ivy. Dogged ones.

"Ouch, ouch, ouch!"

The mesh of greenery had caught itself a wizard. A robe became ripped, the victim was fuming, and foul language echoed across the mountainside. An assortment of fire and ice spells was unleashed until the forces of nature ceded defeat to the elemental onslaught, supported by non-magical sharp blades. After a few healing spells to treat the victorious combatants' scratches and scrapes, the party entered the throat of the cave, ushered by the gnome's torch into a stone-littered passage.

The tunnel wormed its way about a quarter of a mile into the rock, sloping down then up again, after which it curved backward for a bit. Eventually the passage gave way to a cavernous space. Books lay stacked in one corner, scrolls and parchments peeked out from chests and wicker baskets in another, and various maps were laid out on the floor in between, held in place by handfuls of rocks. The most remarkable thing about the snug abode was that the display of cosy scholarly comfort was illuminated by the soft glow of morning light spilling in through a sizeable aperture overhead, which made the cavern feel as much an outdoor space as it was a study. Aside from the literature and cartography, a wagonload of junk – ropes, knives, animal skins, rolls of cloth – lay tossed about helter-skelter in the not so apparent parts of the cavern. The natural features of the gnome's home consisted of a forest of stalagmites that stretched across the vast expanse, the occasional pool of stagnant water, and bat roosts in the darker recesses overhead.

The most prominent feature, to which the newcomers were invariably drawn, was the central stone circle. Inside, a metal pole was mounted over the remnants of a fire. Hanging from it was a cast-iron pot with a ladle offering the prospect of cooked food.

The gnome and his guests settled down. Bormph tugged off his boots and shook a mound of dirt out of them; Amjelle took to stitching up the wizard's bramble-torn rags, which he insisted were his only and, therefore, preferred robe; and Sylthia tended to her rumpled hair after the wind had had its fun with it over at the bridge. Thimble spent some time envying the wind. Ramrok drew some unwanted attention when his stomach gurgled, giving off the types of noises a zombie might make when launching into a speech.

"I'm on it, I'm on it," the gnome promised, quickly producing a bundle of dry wood and shoving some twigs under the iron pot. From a makeshift larder somewhere in the back of the cavern a few tins were foraged, and the fire was rekindled.

The special of the day turned out to be whatever-the-gnome-could-put-in-it stew, prepared in the must-be-good-as-long-as-it's-hot kind of way. The main ingredients appeared to be chunks of onion, an odd assortment of puckered potatoes and other vegetables of the undefinable sort, seasoned with excessive spices to give a sensation relatable to taste. To add to the excitement, Tsynnslin promised a few pieces of squirrel lurked within, waiting for someone lucky enough to find them.

Cupfuls of self-brewed grommgrog were poured out too – a potent alcoholic beverage that coloured unprepared faces beet-red within seconds. Thimble's face took only half a second and then called it quits. Amjelle and Sylthia skipped a sip altogether and focused their energies on keeping Whinewaeyn, a practising teetotaller, sober instead. What the one or the other missed, Ramrok and Bormph quaffed in their stead.

Already as they spooned up the pulpy stew, the visitors had a closer look around. An oil lantern hung suspended from a protruding rock somewhere farther in, a coat rack displayed a straw hat and featured an umbrella stand beneath it. Bathed in the fuzzy light, a dried grass mat marked a bedstead, and next to it there was a small table, and a comparatively big wardrobe, the sort that has a looking-glass on the door and was probably full of more moth-eaten fur coats.

Plainly evident, however, among all the other things, was an army of garden gnomes. They too had ganged up in this oddest of mountain dwellings, padding out most of the gaps between a bunch of rocky cones that ran along the southern section of the cavern. Maybe the pointy hats qualified them for their positions among the stalagmites. They stared back at the guests with their painted-on eyes, watching them draw one blank after another in their hunt for the squirrel jackpot.

"Quite the collector," Amjelle whispered to Sylthia, who was feeding Snowflake. The healer scratched the cub behind the ears as she leaned over.

"Who'd collect all those gnomes?" Sylthia whispered back.

"A gnome gone loopy in need of company?" Bormph hissed behind a cupped hand.

Whinewaeyn picked up the red-capped exemplar Tsynnslin had pulled out of his backpack and turned the figurine over and over in his hand. It was a little fellow leaning against an oversized toadstool, on top of which sat a lamp. One of the gnome's hands rested on the lamp, while the other held a tiny shovel, and a long white braided beard fell over his ample stomach.

"I trust there's a perfectly reasonable explanation for all of this," Whinewaeyn said politely to their host.

"There most certainly is. We only have to dig for it," the gnome replied, a little on the short side of revelatory.

"Dig?" repeated the wizard, rubbing his chin.

The campfire popped noisily.

Bormph peeked over the rim of his bowl to offer the ladies a disquieting look that said, "And that's why he brought garden gnomes with shovels... Any more questions?"

"Aye, dig. In a way…" Tsynnslin got up. He tucked a long-stemmed pipe between his lips and drew the moth-eaten bearskin tighter around his shoulders. "Mystic archaeology, one might call it. I've been trying to find connections, extrapolate, cross-reference, categorize, that sort of thing." Then he started pacing and puffing around the circle of his guests, watching them eat, mulling over something as he walked. "There are a couple more things left to experiment with, and then—"

"We'll save the world?" Thimble went for the shortcut. He hadn't given up on writing an epic about his adventures yet, and a world-ending scenario was just what he needed to score a bestseller.

"Perhaps, little one," Tsynnslin said, "and perhaps not."

Bormph blew on his spoon. All that pacing about made the dwarf anxious, and he had to turn this way and that to keep up with the gnome's whereabouts. He remembered hearing about lettered gnomes who enjoyed chasing rats through tiny labyrinths, recording their every move for whatever obscure reason, and he felt like one of those rats right now, sitting in a corner and gnawing on some cheese. Sooner or later the gnome would get his notebook out. He could puff on his pipe as much as he wished, but behind those thick eyebrows, he must have been thinking about his next entry.

"So what's with this end of the world talk, bear-wearer?" the dwarf challenged him.

"Let me explain first." The gnome came to a halt and picked up the glazed pottery figure Whinewaeyn had been looking at. "It all began with these…" He put the figurine before the slurping dwarf.

Bormph eyed it warily. "You stealing gnomes, gnome? Are you that secret DWUM agent everyone's looking for? They almost locked us up for that! Now, if these are your headquarters, and you don't count the clay gnomes, you're seriously understaffed."

Tsynnslin shook his head.

"What's so special about this one then?" Bormph reluctantly snatched up the figurine, drew his eyebrows together and studied it. He turned it upside down as if to reveal a secret button or a hidden compartment, but there wasn't one. It was a run-of-the-mill garden gnome for all he could tell. Not that he knew much about the clay thing anyway, only that people called it a gnome and it looked like a dwarf. But this offence against good taste applied to every garden gnome, without distinction; whether it stood leaning against a toadstool or tried a handstand was immaterial.

The object made its way around the group to Thimble, who – after a cursory glance – thrust it into the elf's hands with a long, rapt stare into her ocean-deep eyes.

"Cute," Sylthia said as she took it.

Thimble had a rethink. "Yeah, lovely, isn't it?"

The garden gnome finished the round, having been inspected by every mage, medic and mercenary under the cavern's spacious ceiling. Even Snowflake took a sniff.

"Now what?" Bormph urged. "What's with the gnome? And why are we surrounded by dozens more of them?"

"Other things too," Ramrok boomed like a foghorn. The barbarian had wolfed down his stew with abandon and, after getting up to stretch his legs, had made his own discoveries. Now he pointed his sword towards the section of the cavern separated from the gnome's mess by the welter of clay-based companions. "Ramrok see. Over there."

"Aye," Tsynnslin confirmed. He took the rusty oil lantern from its place on the rock and led the party behind the gnome perimeter where the light gradually revealed an outlandish collection of knick-knacks gathered in a huge pile. Among other things, there were flowerpots and fans riddled with holes and extravagant necklaces made for people like Prince Dymmling. There were plates and saucers, mortars and pestles, sextants and oars, two halves of a broken soup tureen, a cheesy plush pillow and, mounted on the cavern's tallest stalagmite, a cuckoo clock. Some of the stuff was dilapidated and dusty, while other pieces looked freshly painted and polished, as though they had been crafted just the other day. Farther back Thimble found a row of boots all lined up. Most of them weren't even the gnome's size. Nor were they in pairs. They were all left boots! If any of the party got the impression that the gnome was a hoarder of the worst kind, no one dared to say it aloud.

"Something's missing from all of these items," Tsynnslin told them. "Something nobody can see."

"Value?" Bormph snickered and threw the boot-inspecting Thimble an impish glance. In the dwarf's eyes the collection as a whole was nothing but trash.

Amjelle had already pushed past the two of them.

"Hold on..." She brought her rod of Novotroth forward and swayed it over one of the gnomes. The crystal flared, and the gem exuded a lime-green gleam. It wasn't to last, though. The shine turned jittery and expired. Amjelle tried one of the mysterious left boots next, and the same thing happened there, only with the initial gleam opting for a different colour.

Her eyes met the wizard's. "The gnome's right, Master Whinewaeyn. It's their natural aura. It's somehow…" She paused to pick the right word. "Tainted?"

While the gnome nodded, Whinewaeyn looked none the wiser. "Painted?"

"No, *tainted*, Archmagus."

Whinewaeyn's face remained as it was.

"Artifacts." Tsynnslin lifted one of his bird-nest eyebrows. "That's what *I* call them."

"So what?" Bormph grunted. "What's that aura thingy to anyone but wizards? Can't see it. Can't touch it." He declared this fact with an air of obstinacy the dwarves had cultivated for ages. "And why would you call any of this stuff an artifact on top of it? Nothing shiny, nothing precious. Not even these necklaces. Cheap fakes altogether. How could any of this be an artifact?"

"In as much as whatever you see here once went missing… somewhere, somehow… and I dug it up again, in a way. Well, I went looking for these things, and that's why I found them. Some turned up in different spots, some at different times, or both." Tsynnslin took the pipe out of his mouth and tugged hesitantly at his goatee with his other hand as he gauged each party member's reaction. "They're indicators, shall we say, of a cosmic aberration. That something has changed. Something ripped them from their proper places in the universe – and now they've wound up here."

The cuckoo clock struck the hour. As heads turned, a bird shot out and cuckooed before retreating again. The curious sound travelled through the cavern, echoing off the solid stone walls hidden somewhere in the gloom. When the sound returned, it had gained in eeriness.

"You see, this here," Tsynnslin continued, indicating the pile, "is just a selection of the things beyond counting that are getting yanked around these days. It happens with all sorts of objects." He jerked a thumb towards the strange device that had just struck the hour. "Cuckoo clocks." He nodded to Thimble examining the shoe collection. "Left boots. Brooms. Picture frames. Privies, even! I found one just around the corner, guarded by one of those gnomes. And that's only the beginning."

Amjelle took a wild guess. "The same thing must have happened with the tower."

Tsynnslin nodded. "A prominent example I would say, aye."

Bormph shifted uneasily. "The fireworks. The dune…"

"Never trust a wandering dune," Whinewaeyn mumbled.

"And these artifacts…" Amjelle let her fingers run over a figurine's pointy hat. Then her eyes locked with Tsynnslin's. "You didn't drag every single one of these fellows up here from all the way down there, did you? Just to have a tea party with them closer to the clouds?"

A smile flitted across the gnome's face. "No."

"That would just be dumb," Bormph grunted.

"Then you must have collected them up here," Amjelle concluded.

That idea, combined with the gnome's nod, wiped the smugness right from Bormph's face. "You've found the whole lot… up here?"

"Aye! *Around* here, in these mountains, at least. Let me show you… Come along!" The gnome, pipe in one hand, umbrella in the other, tapped his way across the cavern towards a pile of parchments. "Look. All my findings are marked on this map." Indeed, the parchment was bristling with Xs and Os, squares and exclamation marks; sometimes arrows pointed from one spot to another with dates written along the connecting lines.

Whinewaeyn studied the map. "You've gleaned a pattern then?"

"No doubt about it. There must be a vortex."

"Hmm…" said Bormph. "We're talking about a garden gnome–attracting disturbance?"

"In one way or another," answered the gnome. "There's something about these parts of the Silvery Sickle to which these artifacts, however large or small, important or insignificant, are drawn."

"Like iron to a lodestone?" Thimble brought up.

"Like iron to a lodestone, if you so want." The gnome took a last drag from his pipe, then knocked the ashes from it and buried it in a pocket hidden somewhere deep under his bearskin. "I've observed the phenomenon for weeks and weeks. It happens in waves, time and again. And it's been escalating. Looking at the whole picture, it's all falling into place."

"What place? It's still as murky as a mire from here," scoffed Bormph. "We know bugger all about *why* these gnomes and towers go on holiday. If there's a vortex, *why* is there a vortex?"

"Yeah," Ramrok boomed from someplace in the back, which pushed the number of words the barbarian had spoken in a day over his average output.

"And a valid point it is," Tsynnslin said. He looked about, then his eyes found Sylthia's. Not just, Thimble felt, because the gnome liked resting his eyes on elven beauties as he did. The gnome had a truth to share. "There's more…"

The elf's lips parted, though she held her tongue, as she was struck by a sudden realization – a thought that cleaved through her milky features like a butcher's knife splitting an untouched cheesecake, an image which Thimble, who had a penchant for both, the blonde elf and cheesecake, found particularly disturbing.

"Let me through. You're not insinuating that—" Amjelle pushed the dwarf to the side and pointed her crystal at Sylthia. Again, the stave flared into action, radiated, and picked up an aura: Sylthia's aura. The elf didn't dare breathe, but it made no difference either way. The crystal's flare stalled, broke into a violent sputter and went out. Sylthia emitted a shriek.

Goose pimples made their rounds over the group, from wizard to halfling to the intrepid barbarian who, bare-chested as he was, bore a sudden resemblance to a plucked chicken.

"Don't stop there," Tsynnslin encouraged the healer.

Amjelle's rod moved on.

Bormph, next in line, backed up a little, waving her away with both hands. "Whoa! You sure dwarves even have auras? I wouldn't—"

"Trust me, I can smell it from here." Sylthia shoved the smug dwarf back towards the healer.

Once more, the crystal flared; a tad darker this time. The blaze was ever so bright for a few heartbeats before the light faltered as if choked off by an unseen force.

Bormph, pale as a shroud now, let out a tormented grunt. Thimble, who'd probably be next, got a funny feeling in the pit of his stomach too, though he failed to see the humour in it. Especially as, at the same time, an icy shiver came racing down his spine. He pulled his cardigan tighter and hugged himself, for nobody else was offering.

Amjelle gasped, "What's this? Some kind of trick?" She confronted the gnome's prow nose with her rod. The crystal lit up... and stayed that way. She stood back, repeated the same thing, and arrived at the same result.

The gnome's goatee-covered chin lifted, and the small twinkling eyes observed each adventurer in turn, a knowing glimmer dancing in them. "It would seem like *you* are artifacts too. You... must have been affected." The way the gnome said it chilled the cockles of their hearts.

Silence ensued. The longer it lasted, the more tangible it became, measured by the cuckoo clock's nerve-wracking tick-tocks.

"What's that *really*?" Thimble demanded from the gnome. "The whole aura thingy?" The question had gained relevancy. Even Bormph softened his permanent scowl.

"Aura," said the gnome, "is here, there, and everywhere. Only to the eye, it isn't. And yet, aura is the world's tapestry. Without it, nothing is."

"So... are we here or not?" Thimble gave the gnome a confused look. "Are we less here than before if our auras aren't working right now?"

"Whether we're here or not, and what's there and what isn't and when and how is a matter for debate," the gnome said. "That's a mystic's conundrum. The sagest among the sages only agree that aura points away from us and, what's more, back at us too – all at the same time. Nothing stands by itself. There's no thing, living or non-living, that's not intertwined with others. Auras touch auras, and so lives touch lives. Which is also the troubling part. For if something's wrong with *your* auras..." He peered out from under the upper jaw of his bear skull, which protruded above his brow like a macabre canopy shading his words with a hint of menace... and left the rest unsaid.

"Spoooky." The barbarian shook his mane.

"But... how?" Amjelle stammered. "How could it happen that—"

"We ate something rancid?" Bormph let out.

Could be, however, that the dwarf had deficits grasping spiritual basics. That's what the party's healing department suggested anyway.

"Maybe it was the dune," Whinewaeyn offered, on a more sensible note. "The whole affair must have had something to do with it. Not that I'd know what." At any rate it seemed more likely than not that one mystery pointed to another, generating a whole mysterious messiness.

"So now what?" Bormph grunted impatiently. "I feel just fine. You want to put us in a museum, bear-wearer? We're nothing like those gnomes. I might look like one, but that's the gnomes' problem. What's the big d—"

"You plunged through a chasm in time." Tsynnslin's voice had an edge to it.

"And that's not so good, eh? Didn't feel a thing,"

Whinewaeyn stirred. "You think we might be drawn to that... What's the word?"

"Vortex," Amjelle filled in.

"It's a possibility," said the gnome. "The root of the disturbance must be around here someplace. I have a few leads to follow for your own sake, and the sake of—"

"Your garden gnomes?" Bormph gave a derisive snort.

"...everything that exists," Tsynnslin finished. "The universe, or this part of it, appears unhinged. It might be collapsing in on itself."

233

"So you say," Bormph grunted. "And if the world is unhinged, we set out on the off chance we can remount the whole thing and... oil it?"

"You've lost me there..." The images were a bit mixed up in Whinewaeyn's mind.

"But... how can the world as a whole be unhinged," Amjelle said, "if it works according to the Holy Quintity's eternal laws?"

"How can there be death and destruction if the gods are goodness epitomized?" Tsynnslin countered.

"Maybe it's just a temporary problem," Whinewaeyn said.

"With eternal laws?" The frown crossing Amjelle's face suggested otherwise.

"Maybe the Quintity thing's just in your head anyway," Bormph mumbled.

"Oh, yeah? So it's all your Stonefather's mess then? Well, congratulations! It's a dwarf yet *again*."

"Folks, folks. We have—" The gnome lapsed into sudden silence and raised a finger to his lips. "Listen..."

Up in the higher reaches of the cavern, a flurry of activity had kicked off. There was chirping and clicking, punctuated by occasional high-pitched shrieks. Shadows flitted and swooped about at breakneck speed, criss-crossing the ceiling. For a few moments, the frantic back and forth blotted out the sunlight pouring through the natural opening, then the turmoil faded back to morning blue.

"Just ba—" Thimble started, but that's where he left it.

It wasn't just bats. The bats had taken flight, but the noise that had jarred them remained. Actually, it grew. It came from the direction of the tunnel, like the babbling of a placid, faraway brook, which – before long – was more like a babbling, *approaching* brook – one that also had a few rapids thrown in. Already the clangour had turned into something closer to a strong current, perhaps a rivulet that opens up a bit as it goes along, and it echoed through the tunnel with rampant fierceness. The noise made much more sense when the distinct thumps of collective footfalls emerged from what had, at first, seemed like a riverish racket. The sounds were of scraping footwear, creaking leather, chinking chain mail. The sounds of trouble closing in.

"*Shmodork!*" Tsynnslin wheeled around. The gnome was caught off his stride for a moment, his mind racing. "Zarrafandans! They must have found us. Get your stuff and scram! *Quick!*" He gestured towards the back of the cavern. "There's a passage to another tunnel network underneath the mountain. Behind those stalagmites. Follow my lead." He pulled Whinewaeyn to his side. "Wizard? We might need some help to keep them off!"

"What's wrong with a proper conversation?" Whinewaeyn protested, crossing his arms. "It's all a misunderstanding, right?"

"They're not interested in a get-together, old man," the gnome hissed through gritted teeth. "They think you're set to destroy the world." His eyes gleamed.

"Am not! Somebody's got to tell them!"

Sylthia sided with the gnome. "From their perspective, you look pretty guilty, Archmagus. You blew up the Dimmerskeep Academy for one!"

"It was an *experiment*, for the gods' sake! Perfectly well prepared!"

"So it was premeditated, then," said the gnome. "And who blew up all that stuff in the middle of the desert if it wasn't you?"

"Why, that was the dwarf!"

Amjelle was already collecting her equipment. "I can see an angle where this line of defence looks problematic, Master Whinewaeyn. Can't plead occupational hazard for that one. You didn't have an occupation then."

"And, on top of all that," Tsynnslin said, "they're convinced by now that you stole their tower and whatnot. Now they're after you like the royal Dymmling after a purple blouse!"

The footfalls had picked up in volume.

"You were looking for an adventure, weren't you?" the gnome said. "Well, there you have it. Now, have you got something up your sleeve or not?"

"Not up my sleeve, to be honest," Whinewaeyn replied, "but I could do something with my staff, if that works too? I'd rather have my staff than my sleeves. Speaking of which, where is it?" He hustled back to the fireplace to look for it, as the rest of the party frantically packed up around him.

Right about then, three handfuls of men-at-arms poured into the cavern like a tide in a hurry. The crests on their breasts were resplendent with a gerbil on its hind paws, looking confused. One of the men barged straight ahead, issuing commands, while his subordinates spread out to form a semicircle around the haplessly crackling fire. Waving about their scimitars, bucklers shielding their chests, the intruders looked menacing enough to leave an impression one might prefer they didn't.

On the opposite side of the fire, the gnome and company took up positions.

"So we meet again, wizard!" Captain Klampf bellowed. "Got you! And your gnome friend too! You won't fool us twice!" Not that long ago, what with all that foul fish around and his nose pinched between finger and thumb, the captain hadn't sounded that intimidating. This time, the barking was more genuine, like a Great Northern Wayn hound's. The captain looked imperious now too, his long face framed by an iron helmet, his stringy flaxen hair peeking out at the sides, a bit like a tawny lion ready to leap at its prey.

"Left us a nice little trail with a bit of your clothing there, didn't you, eh?" He held out the evidence in the shape of a scorched piece of Whinewaeyn's robe. Some combative thistles had their moment of retribution.

No immediate reply came from the accused. Part of the reason was that the surprise didn't end there.

The trickling of feet into the cavern had long ceased when it suddenly started afresh following the captain's speech. In scampered more unbidden guests, lighter on their toes, nimbler, and in much greater numbers, putting the small collection of Zarrafandan men-at-arms to shame.

So when Whinewaeyn looked at Captain Klampf, tattered cloth and sword in hand, heading his troops, it wasn't *just* Captain Klampf, tattered cloth and sword in hand, heading his troops, that he was looking at. He was looking at all that plus the fifty or so goblins strategically deploying behind, grinning from ear to ear, their sharp teeth showing, fitting bolts in their crossbows and raising their weapons at everyone else.

"Time to surrender, conspirators!" squawked the head goblin in an uneven, combative screech. "In the name of Vensk the Vengeful, you are hereby taken prisoners! Hail to the Greedy... er... Grisly Goblins of Groo'cae'tran!"

In addition to the crossbow goblins, there were nasty-looking pike-wielders too, and axe-wielders, and some other wielders carrying odd goblin things no non-goblin had a name for. The goblin army fanned out, threatening to make all sorts of unbecoming dents in enemy armour if harassed.

Klampf turned, slowly but thoroughly.

"Now drop that sword," the head goblin clamoured. He was about half the captain's size, but twice as vile. "Or we'll make it drop, along with that beanpole body of yours! Let's see which of the two goes down first!"

Cackling spread through the goblin ranks.

Klampf's long face stretched even further. One could almost see him weighing his options behind his high forehead in conjunction with his eyeballs, which quickly covered all corners of the cavern looking for a way out of his predicament. And when they rolled up to the hole in the ceiling, they met an array of metal spikes flashing in the sun, even up there. One of his eyebrows twitched.

"Ghrimp-limp contingent at the ready!" cried a distant squawk from above. Tiny bat-eared heads emerged to line the lip of the hole. More and more arrowheads were pushed into position, picking targets further down. The cackling from below spread overhead too, until the whole cavern resounded with the cacklephony.

Klampf's fingers loosened from the sharp-edged steel he held, and his weapon clanked onto the stone floor. A series of distinct clatters followed, and soon every soldier in the cavern was swordless.

In the back, Whinewaeyn stood as inconspicuously as he could, giving his best impression of a frail old geezer holding fast to a gnarled staff to keep his bag of bones standing upright. He didn't mind the support of his staff, but mostly he was holding it like that so that the ground's earth aura could seep up into the wood too. The weapon was already throbbing with bottled-up energy and Whinewaeyn strained to hold it back.

"You too!" the head goblin snarled at everyone else who didn't look like a soldier. "Drop everything!"

And so they did. Mostly. Bormph and Ramrok dropped axe and two-hander, Sylthia let go of her bow. Thimble hadn't even got his dagger out, so he skipped dropping it and just gave a shrug instead. Amjelle did the same, having pushed her crystal-topped rod up her sleeve a while ago, and intending to keep it there a little while longer. And Whinewaeyn? Kept on leaning on his staff as old men do.

"Get that elf!" instructed the head goblin.

Little feet started scuttling across the cavern.

Now Whinewaeyn got the shakes. That's old men stuff. Old *wizard* stuff, in fact. Staffy stuff.

The wizard yanked the gnarled piece of wood, operating it like the pump of a water well. The rhythmic motion of the released energy shook the rocks out of the air in no time, like fruit from a limber apple tree. Heaps of stones as large as the goblins themselves exploded into being and did what the circumstances demanded, plunging down onto the floor to pile on top of each other, creating an awful racket. The cavern floor convulsed.

The goblin army froze for a moment, unsure how to handle this new development, but a shriek from their leader soon jolted them awake again. "At him! Shoot!"

Bolts whirred through the air. For a moment Thimble forgot to keep his head down. If it weren't for Ramrok, who shovelled him to safety, he'd almost certainly have had a taste of a projectile up his nose. Only a heartbeat later, he saw a volley of bolts bouncing off the rock they had chosen for cover accompanied by what felt like a gazillion light, hollow sounds as they spilled all over the floor. Some of the bolts cleared the obstacles but took unexpected turns – Amjelle's rod was out and glowing, busy with attracting and divesting any projectile intent on scoring a hit.

"Go, go, go!" she blared, and Tsynnslin led the way.

They seized their weapons and ran.

"This way!"

One by one they ducked away into the hole the gnome had uncovered: Sylthia first, then Amjelle, Thimble, Ramrok, Bormph and the polar bear cub.

"Over here!" Tsynnslin yelled at Whinewaeyn from the relative safety of the hole.

But the wizard was still adding the finishing touches to his pile of impenetrability, walling the party in and the others out. He was admiring his masterpiece when an inexplicable shift flashed through the cavern. A kind of veil slithered over his senses, his sight clouded, and a tingling sensation rippled through his body. The cavern developed a spin. Then it was his mind's turn to waver.

Whinewaeyn staggered. Maybe he had overdone his casting. He clutched his staff.

The sensations didn't let up. It was as if something impossible bled into existence, even if only for a lightheaded, chimerical, dreamlike moment. Everything seemed blurry, likely, indefinite. As though the equilibrium of the elements had ruptured and an unknown presence troubled the forces that held whatever there was together, shaking it through.

With a snap, reality returned. An almost frightening sense of sharpness, gravity and sobriety took hold of Whinewaeyn's senses, or his surroundings, or both; the world was once more made up of uncompromising matter.

When he got a grip on himself, a bitter taste of despair remained, an adamantine irreversibility. A sense of loss dropped on him – a curtain burying everything that wasn't, but could've been.

That was the moment he saw him.

The air bent, bloated, formed a bubble. It sputtered him out, on the other side of the rock wall. He could see it all through the only remaining gap when unreality receded. There he stood, in perfect focus, ringed by enemies: the gnome.

Not a garden gnome. A real gnome. A gnome of flesh and blood, like the only gnome he knew: the same bushy eyebrows, prow nose, goatee, everything. He even wore a bearskin. The gnome clutched something bulky, pulled it protectively to his chest like a shield. He seemed irritated.

Whinewaeyn swung around to face the very same gnome waving at him from his side of the wall, a harried look stamped on his prow-nosed face: "This way, wizard… Hurry up!" Tsynnslin and the other gnome were as alike as two peas in a pod, the one turning about confused, the other barking commands.

Whinewaeyn stepped back from the rock wall but couldn't help looking back once more through the gap.

"What on earth—" he heard the mysterious gnome say before uncompromising arguments in shape of crossbow bolts cut him off. They came at him from all directions, burrowing their needle-sharp tips into the bearskin. Between blinks, the gnome had turned into a hedgehog.

"Got him!" yelled a goblin's scratchy voice.

The hedgehog with the bear head fell over. Its short arms uncoiled from the item they had held fast, and a heavy leatherbound book thudded onto the ground.

"Don't just stand there looking like you've seen a ghost!" shouted an urgent voice behind Whinewaeyn.

There stood a Tsynnslin too, and he was gesturing towards a hole in the ground. "Get a move on! *Now!*"

Right. It was time. Time for Whinewaeyn to relegate further questions to the back of his mind and tear himself from his rock construction and whatever went on behind it.

"Yes, yes… Coming…" he mumbled and made a bolt for it before a bolt could make for him. Gathering his robe, he bustled after the gnome. He would get them out of here. After all, he was the Tsynnslin who was still alive… wasn't he?

Even as he fled, cloudlets of doubts drifted across the wizard's mind. At the same time, a rumbling issued from below. Which was puzzling, as he had ceased manipulating the elements for a while now. It didn't last long before the ground cracked open like an eggshell, and Whinewaeyn leapt away in panic.

A fraction of a second later, a chasm had replaced the once hair-thin crack. The rock wall swayed dangerously. The cavern quaked. Several stalactites abandoned their centuries-long impartiality and plunged into the fray.

Whinewaeyn took another step and trod on an even more recent crack. The next chasm was already in the making.

CHAPTER 14

Serious Soul-Saving

Sometime, someplace, somehow, among the nooks and crannies of the known and the unknown dimensions of the universal fabric, in an unnamed crease between existence and non-existence...

Something stirs.

"Dorm?" It's an ethereal voice, as in a dream. Female, melodious. "Dorm? You still around?"

"Uh-huh... Guess so." A reply drifts by, gruffer, manlier. Disembodied too. "Still dead as a doornail, I reckon. Otherwise, everything's tickety-boo."

"Just asking."

"Washed away by an iceberg in a lava sea... Gah!"

"That was weird. But let's make the best of it, shall we?"

"Ugh, you elves and your beliefs!" There's a ghost of a sneer. Or the sneer of a ghost. "You've been eradicated from the face of the earth, and all you can say is 'There must be a rosy side to it! Let's enjoy the experience!' Good grief! Did it ever occur to you that something's not right with your prick-eared attitude?"

"Grouse all you want, Dormy, but I know even dwarves as miserable as you have a heart... somewhere."

"Heh! Well, now that it's gone, I sort of miss it."

"A body isn't everything. You should know that by now. Once we shuffle off the mortal coil, only our spirit remains."

"Gah, Ilvith! Maybe you elves are more spirit than flesh, but with dwarves, it's the other way round. The stouter the dwarf, the more alive. It's troubling when you eat a healthy diet all your life and then find out that when you're a goner you turn all 'spirity' anyway."

For a while, silence hangs in the air – or wherever silence hangs in a place that isn't much of a place.

"At least we have us, you know?" says the voice that used to be Ilvith. "At least we can talk."

"Yeah? Is that all ghosts do? I'd have wagered there'd be some floating around, chain-rattling, you know, all that spooky stuff of the fireside tales? Well, nothing so far. Maybe we haven't got the hang of it yet. How do you get promoted from talking to haunting? Are we just supposed to mooch about in this nowhere until further notice?"

"Maybe it *means* something…"

"*What* means something?"

"The talking. Dwarf and elf. Matter and spirit."

"Don't be ridiculous, leafbiter. We'd have to listen to each other for eternity, like a married couple – only without a vow and no till-death-do-us-part to look forward to! Nah. No offense, Ilvith. You're okay. Really, I mean it. We've fought side by side, cleared out a couple of dungeons together, and it was the same iceberg that did us in. But all this talking for eternity sounds more like the Netherworlds to me."

"Ah, come on, Dorm."

"Feels like a big cop-out, doesn't it? Say I've banked on the wrong god. Fine. Then *that's* why I'm here. Or, say, I've got the god right, but the Stonefather doesn't deem me worthy enough to descend into his grand underground empire, well, so be it. If he'd rather have me roll stones uphill till the end of time or whatever instead of help him feed his forges or pump his bellows, then that's what I've to put up with, I suppose. But you know what? I haven't been told a thing!" Some table-pounding, finger-wagging, or eye-rolling wouldn't have gone amiss here, if Dormhelm wasn't completely immaterial. To compensate, his dour, bodiless voice rises to a passionate boom. "Anybody out there who can hear me?!"

The question wafts into nothingness, and oozes away.

"This is the thing, Ilvith. Nobody tells anyone in advance. You're in the dark all your life. You have to figure it out yourself. 'That's the journey,' the priests tell you. Well, they have to pretend for a profession. So you try and try, and then your number comes up. Hah!" A ghostly snort. "And the least you should expect when pegging out is that the powers that be tell us what it was all about."

Ilvith replies softer, calmer, warmer. "Elves don't see it like that at all. We believe in the Dream. Whatever spirit is out there in the world falls back into the Dreameress's illimitable mindscape, to reawaken – as an elf, a human, a dwarf, anything."

"Good for you, if you don't mind turning into a dwarf…"

"I could be a deer. Or a horse, a sheep. A leaf among hundreds of thousands on a centuries-old oak. I'd grow and thrive, to be torn from a branch by a gust at season's end. As soon as I wither away, the circle starts anew. Whatever dies gives birth too."

"Would you mind being a dung beetle?"

"I'd still be part of the whole."

"Well, good luck then with your Dream Mummy. Any idea when she'll show up? My Stonefather also seems delayed."

"Maybe it's a test?" Ilvith ventures.

"Ah, twaddle! First life's a test and now death's a test too? Do these trials and tribulations never end? What's next? The longer I'm dead, the more—"

There's a cough from somewhere... else.

"Um... Excuse me?" The new disembodied voice has a male tone to it, but still it sounds far removed from the depths of an ex-Dormhelm rumble. "I couldn't help but overhear, and wouldn't want to barge right in, but I—"

"Oh, *daín artanhé!*"

"Who're you?" Dormhelm skips a greeting. "That famous dweller on the threshold? A demon collecting lost souls? An angel conducting post-mortem examinations? Speak up, for either way I want to have a word about the proceedings!"

"Um... er... I'm so sorry, but from what I gather it appears I'm just the new guy."

"A visitor!" Ilvith declares excitedly. "This is getting fun! Isn't the afterlife full of surprises?"

Dormhelm is more reserved. "What was it for you then? Natural causes? Accident?"

"Got killed, it would seem."

"Would it now?"

"To be honest, it was all a bit confusing. No bright white light or anything, more like... But excuse me, maybe I should introduce myself first? I'm—"

A gentle correction floats by. "You *were*. Dying takes a bit to get used to."

"Ah yes, suppose so. Well, then, I *was* Tsynnslin. Tsynnslin T'shnolt. Once a gnome, now a spirit, I would assume?"

"That's what *she* says," mumbles Dormhelm.

"At any rate, welcome! Make yourself comfortable."

"And… this is it? This is *all* there is?" There's a contemplative pause. "A… support group?"

"Listen, buddy. Did I make the rules? You can bet I didn't. So just get on with it. Tell us about yourself and leave nothing out. Looks like we've got the rest of eternity to get through."

The massive portal swung open.

In tumbled a priest, squat and bald, huffing and puffing. Sticky sweet-and-sour marinade hung from the uneven sideburns, a stale ale aroma wafted around him, and a frenzied look danced in the eyes as if the man had just been coerced into cutting short a date with some late poultry. Wooden Quintity beads criss-crossed his chest like a Groo'cae'tran suicide goblin wears an explosive belt.

The Holy Quintity's Grand Cathedral was nigh bursting. Waves of sombre murmurs droned through the nave. A stirred-up beehive couldn't have been any buzzier than the clerics' chants of "Hail the Five". High priests manned the front, the not-so-high ones filled rows four to twelve, and monks and acolytes took up positions farther in the back. A bishop with a pointy hat marking him as the head of the operation was setting the rhythm from the pulpit in a booming monotone. The joint clerical forces were rounded out by select worshippers at the rear and to the sides – pious people who never missed a decent prayer for the world (this time in more ways than one). With everyone kneeling in the pews, heads bent, hands folded and pointing upwards, the congregation had something of the look of soldiers in their trenches raising their pikes against an advancing cavalry – in this case, the unseen horsemen of the apocalypse.

The squat priest tiptoed forward along the right aisle, scanning the rows, when he felt a penetrating gaze from the transept ahead that pinned him in place. Surrounded by a sea of candles, observing the concerted praise rising up to the vaulted arches, Archbishop Vynnfield loomed near the side altar. Bishop Wampramb stood next to him, and opposite them was Prince Dymmling, flanked by Princelings Klimbish and Rimfish, engaged in lively discussion. The archbishop's dignified hand beckoned to the newcomer, and the priest steered over.

"Reporting for prayer duty." He gave a brief bow to the dignitaries, both clerical and profane, dedicating a gasp extra to each.

"You're late, Quince." Vynnfield withered him with a look. "Again!" He unfolded a spreadsheet and consulted it. "It's pew four for you, second from the left, and make it snappy! Deacon Johnas had to extend his six-hour shift because of your impropriety. Add half an hour extra."

"Of course, Your Grace. At once, Your Grace." The priest pushed his plump figure past and scampered away to find his place.

Prince Dymmling's eyes followed him and his lips curled into a benevolent smile, appreciative of his subject's dedicated commitment to Prince and country. He had changed into a puffy blouse with frilly sleeves and a pair of baggy satin breeches – both purple, of course – and instead of his ridiculous hat he wore a more fashionable, but only a tad less ridiculous, sparkling headband. Peeking out from under his sleeve was Ruffles, his royal rodent, whose fur her master kept ruffling as he spoke.

"From what I hear, Your Grace," the Prince said, "things sound rather impressive, wouldn't you agree?"

As if to prove his point, the volume in the cathedral swelled. The spiritual combatants had reached a particularly heartwarming passage: the verse relating how the One and the Other met at the Dawn of Days, joined forces, and created another One – He who would become the One In-Between. From there, as the One and the Other grew to like the process, the world came to be. First, as an unplanned accident, and then as a family operation, full of unending love and compassion. So goes the Story of the Five, and sappy as it may be, it never fails to touch hearts.

"Well, acoustically, I concur, Your Majesty. Acoustically things are fine," the archbishop said initially, but then felt compelled to clarify that prayers weren't all about acoustics.

"As long as the approach is right, one can always improve efficiency," the Prince opined. "That's what you're here for, Archbishop, as we've established. Choice of prayers, mix of staff, shift rotation schedules and the rest of it."

"Yes, yes," the archbishop said hastily. "But wouldn't you agree that the approach predicates effectiveness? How effective might prayer be if decreed by royal order? How much heart can be wedged into timetables, I wonder?"

Prince Dymmling cocked an irritated eyebrow. Sometimes the words entering his ears almost sounded like criticism. Surely, he must have misheard. "Your priests have – how did you put it? – *heart* problems?"

A candle behind him sputtered as though picking up on the bad vibes.

"Your Highness," Bishop Wampramb interjected. He was a roundish fellow with a moon-face and a halo-like haircut to match. "All the archbishop is trying to say is that there's still… debate. There's always debate. Can faith *ever* be measured? Do a whole congregation's prayers have more worth than the same amount of dedication by a single person? How do three prayers on the long-winded side compare to a fourfold number of short ones? Do prayers stack up? What about devout prayers versus reeled-off ones?"

"It's more a mathematical question, then?"

"Mathematics of the heart, if you so desire."

Prince Dymmling resumed stroking his gerbil. "I'm curious about the gods' position on this."

"Well," Wampramb said, noncommittal, "so are we."

"The Holy Quintity doesn't speak," Archbishop Vynnfield informed the Prince, who seemed a little out of touch with anything religion-related. "Not in the regular way."

"The gods communicate with you in other ways?"

The bishop wrung his hands. "The Holy Quintity reaches out to us in… in miracles maybe, through signs. Little details. But in general, they leave it to the clergy to do the talking, and they just—"

"Any miracles so far in averting the apocalypse?"

"Er… no," Vynnfield admitted. "None that we know of. Which is not to say that—"

"So you *haven't* heard back."

"Not in particular. But how—" The end of the sentence didn't make it out of the archbishop's mouth. A chord had been struck somewhere, and everybody sensed it. A dissonant one. He'd got himself in deeper.

Prince Dymmling's hand became rigid on Ruffles's fur. A severe scowl crept over his features, and his eyes narrowed to a crack. Bereft of further fondling, Ruffles chittered and threw the archbishop her own version of an accusing stare. In a twinkling, in the time one might say it takes an icicle to drop from a roof and stab an unwitting bystander, the archbishop's features turned rigid too, right down to the lump in his throat.

"Klimby?" The Prince beckoned regally to his aide, ignoring the clergymen like a noble sidestepping an alms box. "Are we beginning to entertain the notion that His Royal Princeliness is wasting his precious time in these hallowed halls? Wouldn't we all agree that there's no such thing as an emergency theological debate in the face of looming doom?"

Klimbish inclined his head in confirmation. He was trained to.

"And would you, pray, convey this shared thought to all the parties involved?"

Klimbish informed the archbishop, using the exact same words the Prince had just said himself.

"Another thought that occurred to me," the Prince went on musing, "is that regardless of the world ending or not, certain careers may end either way. Which would be regrettable for some in the case that said end were to be postponed."

Klimbish repeated the words for the deaf and stubborn among them, and the archbishop made a muted gulping noise.

"You see, my dear Wampramb" – Prince Dymmling took a step towards the rotund man, not even gracing the archbishop with a look in passing – "it's the gods that got us into this pickle. If they created us, they also created this pickle."

"It's only fair to demand a serious word with them," Princeling Rimfish provided, getting on track with the Prince's thoughts.

"Only we can't seem to do that," Klimbish said, taking over from Rimfish. "For how can one have a word with someone who doesn't talk back?"

"And thus" – now it was Rimfish's turn again – "His Royal Highness takes the view: the louder the murmur, the better our chances."

"Indeed, indeed," concluded the Prince himself. "Cut the palaver. Now wouldn't that make things easier?"

"Ah, yes, Your Majesty. Of course, Your Majesty," Wampramb consented in the archbishop's stead. "Louder murmur. Easier." He looked out over the pews of worshippers that were already making the whole structure vibrate with the drone of devotion.

Even the archbishop finally seemed overwhelmed with enlightenment.

"W-w-would you please excuse me?" he stuttered, still twitchy – but with good reason, as though he felt the murmur inside him all of a sudden. "I notice a seat has just become vacant in pew three, and we wouldn't want to lose momentum, now would we, Your Most Valued Highness? I'd better add another voice. One never knows."

That said, the archbishop clamped his book of psalms under his arm, and hurtled off into the surge.

The crystal tip of Amjelle's Novotroth rod flared up.

With jittery movements, she scanned the hole at her feet. It yawned back at her like the dead of night. The light cone was hardly able to cut into whatever was down there. Nothing that was revealed looked particularly encouraging, but it would have to do. That it would have to do became very clear when Amjelle lost her footing. Her companions took the gesture for a display of the healer's brazen lead and jumped after.

"Get off me, morons!" Amjelle screaked when half of them landed on top of her. And from there things went from scary to outright crazy and then some.

The gnome's passage was as tight as a burrow. After a while they felt more like marbles tumbling about in a spinning pot as the ground tremored with fierce tenacity, threatening to run away with them. The tunnel zigzagged, slanted up and cut down again sharply, as though it kept changing its course every few seconds. In the nightmarish glow of Amjelle's rod, the stone walls looked very much alive, like the insides of a gargantuan beast – and like live entrails, their surroundings shifted, bent and bulged every which way. If it wasn't for the dirt and sand that came trickling down each time, one could've taken the ever-present thundering din for the monster's bowel movements.

Whinewaeyn rambled along far behind the rest. When he lost Amjelle's leading light, he had to summon one himself. A flick of the wrist, a little on the panicky side, and his own luminous floating globe made its entrance. The guidelight started forward, and he followed, squeezing himself through one cramped passage after another until the tunnel opened up into a more spacious area with several exits.

Whinewaeyn stood there for a bit, worrying about which was the right one when a shower of rubble came down from the ceiling. His orb escaped sideways and gave off a fitful blaze. The wizard, not so quick, got his share.

"Hey!" Whinewaeyn railed against the elements, earth in particular.

More rubble fell.

He stood back. The dust settled and the guidelight dutifully zoomed back to its master. After a moment of relative quiet, Whinewaeyn hitched up his patch-studded robe, and steered, agile as a weasel, between the piles of scattered debris – an aged weasel, but still a weasel. When he had successfully cleared the rubble, he tripped over his own feet and collapsed in a heap. At least this time the shower of rocks came down behind him. The orb skidded to an unsteady halt and treated its master to a pitying glow.

Well. There he lay, the wizard, reminded of the wisdom that it sometimes takes a fall to open up a fresh angle and look at things in a different light and all that. At other times, of course, a change of perspective is not so welcome, and this was one such occasion. A blazing torch flickered in the tunnel behind him. Two goblins emerged, made their way past the debris, spotted him – thanks to his guidelight now leading their way – and scurried closer, battle utensils glinting.

Something zinged past the wizard's head, and nothing good ever comes from things zinging at head height. Whinewaeyn rolled to the side.

Two more *zings* whistled past, this time from the opposite direction. Muffled screeches echoed through the tunnels, then the sound of two bodies hitting the ground. After that, things went quiet. The pursuing torchlight faltered.

A taut whisper reached the wizard. "Onwards, old man." Sylthia's hand extended and grabbed his. "Not the time yet for your afternoon nap."

Whinewaeyn picked up his staff, hat, robe, and finally himself. They changed places, and the wizard swished purposefully ahead into the half gloom, his exploratory guidelight hovering in front. The elf took the rear, bow at the ready.

KNNNNNR-rrrrkkNNN-k-k-k-k-CHRRRRRR, creaked the mountain.

A few steps further on, these primeval-sounding noises rattled Thimble to the bone. Bormph too, apparently, as all he had to say was, "That dratted gnome got us into all of this! That dratted gnome!"

Then the roaring went for a break.

"Hush!" Thimble breathed.

Unfamiliar sounds mixed with the discordant noise of shifting earth masses, a harmonic cadence of tones that had a certain rhythm to it. Very unmountain-like.

Bormph steadied himself on the tunnel walls. He arched his neck in all possible directions, trying to pinpoint what sounded like boulders playing a tune.

An eruption of energy pulled him out of it.

Somewhere in the obscurity ahead, a light had flared up, like lightning firing up a dark sky – a sight that quickly became a faint memory only a moment after its birth. Presently, the darkness snapped back, taking out Amjelle's rod and Whinewaeyn's spherical little assistant with a single blow.

A crackling sound burst out around them, like the mating calls of crickets on a warm summer evening. But the insides of the tunnel resembled anything but a summerly evening idyll, and instead of the smell of roasted suckling pig at a rollicking feast by the pier, the scent of brimstone surrounded them. And a whiff of… cinnamon?

Something sizzled. Spots danced about in their vision. Wispy threads broke from the shadows, luminous strands as straight and wafer-thin as spiders' webs. Line by line, they coated the tunnel walls.

There was a muffled *phut-uhmp* kind of noise, and the spots puffed out like fairy dust. The threads lining the walls, however, began to throb. And oh, how they throbbed! Like delicate veins of lava cutting their way through the stone, and in the weirdest of places: at the party's feet, overhead, along the walls – as if they made up the seams that wove everything together and yet threatened to rip them apart at any moment.

The mountain creaked and groaned.

KNNNNNNNNR-rrrrkkkkkNNN-k-k-k-k-k-CHRRRR-RRRRRRRRRR!

"Any other developments, Rimmy? Anything… groundbreaking?"

The Prince and his aides strolled through the cathedral's lofty arcades. A light breeze tugged at their clothes.

Rimfish's mouth twisted. "The general public hasn't caught on yet, but they're beginning to ask questions. Rumours spread fast, Your Magnificency. The public's getting restless."

"We're working on it, aren't we?"

Rimfish went through the latest missives. "The dwarven clan priests have come up with the idea of working on a sculpture. They recently started the project down in the Thourgethrum Halls. Two dozen stonebeaters have been assigned to the task."

"A sculpture, Rimfish? Interesting. Why's that?"

"It's how the dwarves express their faith, Your Highness. They aren't exactly the greatest spiritualists, as you might know. What they think and believe, they set in stone. That way they keep their heads free. They express an idea, and when they're done, they can simply look at it."

"Extraordinary concept," said the Prince. "Remind me, what are they sculpting?"

"They're honouring the Stonefather himself with an effigy in his likeness, Your Highness. A thirty-by-twenty-foot statue. Big idea, big sculpture."

"So… it's going to be a giant dwarf?"

"One could say so, yes." Rimfish nodded.

"Still a mite too small for a god, maybe?"

"That would depend on the size of the god," Rimfish countered. He had never seen a god, not to his knowledge, and in any case wouldn't know his own hat size.

"Let's hope it will turn out just right."

There was no point in denying a possibility, however unlikely its likelihood, thought Rimfish, and chose to forgo a reply. Instead, he permitted the murmur from inside the cathedral to cover the silence. The massive stone walls didn't allow actual words to pass through, but the swell and ebb of unison voices seemed to Rimfish to keep up with the wilfulness and energy the dwarves put into sculpting giant dwarf statues.

"What I find most compelling is that whole connection."

Rimfish turned to the Prince. He was a bit slow on the uptake, so he had to be helped along.

"The thing about the gnomes, Rimmy!"

Rimfish still wasn't there yet.

"The garden gnomes? Their striking resemblance to the dwarves? And that those gnomes are sculptures too?" He let it sink in.

Rimfish's lips moved, but he had nothing to say.

The Prince did. "Will they be moving this giant of a dwarf out into the open once it's finished? Into…" There was a long pregnant pause. "…a garden?"

Rimfish stared into space, tongue-tied. The Prince's mind was a mystery, even to himself. Sometimes, however, in its unique otherness and bottomless lunacy, in its thinking outside the box by never, ever, considering the existence of any boxes, his mind touched on thoughts others wouldn't even dare to prod with a stick from a safe mental distance. Once out in the open, such unfettered ideas often led to the perception that the product of the Prince's flaky intellect transcended the entangled webs of logic, nonchalantly bypassing the complex realm of thought with a fool's ignorance, thereby arriving at a solution that was surprising, simple and of striking soundness – if it wasn't downright rubbish.

Rimfish snapped out of his daze. "I'll… make a note."

Meanwhile, farther north, deep down in the bowels of the Thourgethrum Mountains, head sculptor Ulmor Gnumphrung perched on a piece of scaffolding. As commissioned, he was sculpting away at the features of a giant dwarf with a striking resemblance to a gnome. The statue reached all the way up to the Grand Worship Hall's ceiling, and he was up there too, about to add finishing touches to the nose when the structure beneath him scraped and grated. Ulmor held on to the guardrails. The block of stone he'd been dabbling with shuddered ominously. His mallet and chisel slipped from his jittery hands and banged onto the flagstones below.

Soon, the earth's movements became so vigorous that the dwarf lost his grip. He tumbled over and found himself latched onto the giant dwarf's nose, which – mercifully – was big enough for him to hold on to. A piece of the giant sneezer broke off, however, and plunged downwards, missing a colleague by a nose hair's breadth.

In a lucid moment, Ulmor understood.

"Yes, Great Dwarf." He sent a quick prayer Stonefatherwards (which was down, from where the tremors originated). "I hear you loud and clear," he grunted as he dangled, struggling and then finally clambering up again onto his rails. He re-examined the giant nose. "Way too large. Very ungainly. I'll chip some more off. Just give me a minute."

"Let me get this straight, Klimby… The elves *won't* pray for the cause?" Prince Dymmling wrinkled his nose in a way that curiously matched the royal gerbil's expression.

"How to explain it best, Your Magnificency…"

They brushed past the arboretum's overhanging weeping willows. Behind the canopy of lush tassels shaking in the wind, a handful of the fair creatures were sitting cross-legged – graceful in posture, humming to themselves, entirely untroubled it seemed.

"You see," Klimbish said, "elves don't have churches, nor temples, or clerics. They're all very spiritual as is. Some more, some less, but generally more than less. And some are spirits altogether, they say. Praying… is alien to them."

"Hmm…" made the Prince as he watched the cross-legged elves. "I've always been fond of elvenkind. Even the corporeal ones. No show of temperament whatsoever. Calm, reserved, never intrusive. These ones here especially."

"That's because they're wind elves," Klimbish informed his ruler. "They're not as moderate as your common wood elf. Their views, even to others of their kind, are sort of... extreme."

The Prince listened to the susurrus for a moment or two, and allowed himself to sway with the rhythm. The elven-tended pleasure gardens were a green sanctuary of tranquillity – except for the odd quacking duck or warbling songbird. Here, in the heart of Dimmerskeep and yet so far removed from everything else, it was tempting to believe that the rumours about the world ending were taking things a little too far.

Eyes closed, murmuring lowly, the sun rays that came peeking through the branches dancing on their noses, the elves appeared in perfect harmony with the world, unafraid that anything might disturb their serenity. From time to time, the humming turned into elvish words that floated through the arboretum: "*Ahm-gha-dham... Gha-dham-ahm... Dham-ahm-gha...*"

"*Looks* like they're praying, though," the Prince observed.

"They're meditating, Your Magnificency," Klimbish told him. "They aspire to become one with whatever there is, rather than to engender change. Their nature is... accepting. For the elves, the universe is a Dream, dreamed up by the Dreameress."

Prince Dymmling shrugged. A puff of wind rushed through the slits in the shoulders of his blouse and ballooned it for a moment. "What of it?" he said airily.

"They meditate to the Big Dreameress in the Sky then. Sounds good enough to me."

"It's not quite *praying*, though. You see, the Dreameress dreams the world into being. Without her, the Dream is *not*. Without her, nothing actually *is*, not even sky. But she herself is *not* part of the Dream."

Surprisingly, the Prince's face lightened at that. "Makes perfect sense."

"Huh? May I ask in what way, Your Highness?"

"How could one be part of something one creates anyway? See, that's the trouble with *our* gods, Klimby. We just assume they created themselves, and it's beyond ridiculous. This though... it's a chicken-free concept altogether."

The princelings looked at their ruler as though something essential had been lost in translation between the Prince's mind and his words.

"No eggs either," the Prince supplied, quick as a shot.

"Chickens and eggs, Your High Princeliness?" Rimfish probed the waters. For shallowness or depth. One never knew.

"The whole chicken-egg thing, Rimmy. Which comes first? And which after? Do they both pop into being all at once? Was it all just one big chicken-egg explosion at the Dawn of Days?" He threw his hands up, cackling, sending imaginary feathers flying. "Doesn't matter if it's all a dream, see?"

"Oh."

"Aaanyway..." Klimbish butted into the offing of possible further epiphanies. "As to why the elves won't help. With the Dreameress not being part of the world as the elves see it, she can't be reached. Not by prayers, meditation, whatever you may call it."

"But she could snap out of it," the Prince pronounced confidently.

Caught off guard, Klimbish looked over to Rimfish, where a pair of no less dumbfounded eyes stared back at him as if he were looking in a mirror.

"Ever had a nightmare?" asked the Prince.

"Your Magnificency is suggesting that a nightmare…" Klimbish produced with a tentative mutter, but didn't dare get to the rest.

"…could awaken the World's Dreameress?" Rimfish dared, and then wished he hadn't. The metaphysical heights they were exploring made him dizzy. "What… what… kind of dream could startle the Dreameress of the world?"

"Why, a dream about the world ending, I assume," the Prince returned cheerily, his lips twisted into a triumphant smile.

Rimfish cringed at the thought. "Um… Would that actually be… any better?" Rolled out into harsh daylight, his doubts glinted like a school of piranhas swimming close to the surface.

The Prince smoothed down his wind-beaten shirt as he strutted on. "Would you prefer to live in a prolonged nightmare, Rimmy?"

"No, no, of course not, but…" The princeling scratched his head. "What *then?*"

"Who knows, my dear Rimfish? I'm not an elf. I'm not one with the whole. But just because they think differently, doesn't mean they can't be right. I'm just being reasonable."

"Yes, Your Majesty. Reasonable. That's the word."

"If I may interpret freely," Klimbish inserted himself, "with Your Royal Highness's approval, we support the elves' endeavour to meditate *for* a swift apocalypse."

"Well put, Klimby. Well put." The Prince went back to stroking his gerbil. "Couldn't have said it any better."

Rimfish, for his part, looked on like an ox. Eyes wide, his mind tried to negotiate the idea of praying *against* and meditating *for* the apocalypse at the same time. The ultimate goal had somehow been shrouded in haziness. The more he thought about it, the stronger grew his suspicion that it had quietly slipped away, out the back door, and only a memory of it was still *ding-a-linging* like the hot sausage vendor's cart three streets away.

The odd thing was, a tinkling *did* erupt about then. But neither Hot Holly's Beefy Bun Cart or the court jester were in sight. The Prince checked if he was wearing his fancy hat. But he wasn't.

The jingling intensified. The draught that moments ago gently brushed against his cheek, had turned into a gust, as sharp as a sword stroke. His baggy trousers fluttered. Foliage, ripped from lush trees, swirled past; swaths of birds trundled over his head, their caws mixing with the rending howl.

A shudder coursed through the arboretum. In the distance, the outlines of roofs, rearing steeples, watchtowers and the otherwise trustworthy town wall battlements took to wobbling in the same disquieting rhythm as the ground under the Prince's feet. Behind everything, the horizon jerked just as much, then it tilted to one side as if ripped from its moorings.

Or maybe it was the Prince who staggered, leaning to one side, then to the other, to counterbalance the world's unexpected swerving. But wherever he turned, he failed to make a decisive impact. As his favourite rodent was of little support, they both hit the ground, clinging to each other.

Sprawled over the grass in the pleasure garden, the world juddering around him, Prince Dymmling looked up. Not a single elf in the circle under their willows had raised an eyelid. Lashed by the branches, they had joined the wind's sighs and screeches, mimicking the shifting pitch in perfect caterwauling disharmony.

Maybe they really understood, the Prince thought. Maybe they *knew* the wind and the willows and, through them, the world's wonderous whims. Maybe they had been expecting a whipping, and that's why they became one with it, absorbing it. The willows weren't deemed necessary anymore, and they… faded from sight. The Prince blinked as he got back on his feet. The trees were gone. Maybe the elves had dreamed them away. Or perhaps a chasm had swallowed them, since one had opened up right there, inches from the elves. Whatever had happened, only the elves remained, howling, soughing with the wind, riding the quake. Accepting.

Inside the Holy Quintity's Grand Cathedral a soft tremble rippled through the pews. The murmuring chorus floundered. One by one, the prayers tailed off, and for a moment a familiar church-like quiet took hold.

A low rumble swelled from ground level. Psalm books skipped around. Song sheets rained from the gallery. The myriad candles threatened to bring more light on the matter – in their own way. If nothing else, panic was sparked. Some of the worshippers would likely have made a dash for it if it wasn't for the fact that the clerical combatants at the ends of the benches couldn't make up their minds whether to stay or leave.

Amid the turmoil, it was the archbishop who proved the most steadfast. He rose, and with him the fervour in his voice: "Deliver us from evil…" he intoned. Belting out line after line, he held fast to his pew, like a helmsman at the wheel riding a storm-tossed sea. And in spite of the confusion and trepidation all around, row after row got up and joined the voice against the scourge of the End Times.

Whether this display of unity and defiance caused what followed or whether that was just the quake's inscrutable nature, nobody could say. But out of nowhere a bright ray of light came flooding through the stained-glass window and poured over the stone altar.

The altar moved.

Or rather it leapt – half a foot towards the congregation like a ram on the attack. When it landed again, its front legs burrowed into the ground as if the flagstones had morphed into quicksand. Thus at odds with the laws of nature, the massive body of stone toppled, and its full weight would have crashed onto the floor and made a racket if it hadn't suddenly disappeared. From the spot where the altar once stood, a sizeable crack wormed away noisily. It stopped short in front of the pews, and the tremors died.

Panicked dazzlement made its way across the benches. The murmur was unsure whether to rise or fall and sort of teetered. A few hands were quick to point up at the stained glass where the shaft of sunlight had come gushing in. Miraculously, there was a hole in the window, as if the light had burned right through it.

It *must* have been a sign. But… a sign of what?

Around the same time, a few miles away, head shaman H'roc-Noc'sh beheld what was left of his world with indifference. He sat on a pile of bricks with his ankles

265

shackled, his face sullen and his stare hollow. The chicken bone he gnawed on for lunch tasted bland. No wonder. There was no future in it.

By his orcen reasoning, things had already ended. The once revered shaman had seen the Great Darkness and, as prophesied by the ancients, it had harboured the Coming of Men. Now, days later, with the Last Battle fought and lost, disgrace had descended over the remainder of his tribe and race, and the ridiculous-looking Zarrafandans were bossing orcs around.

He didn't like any of it one bit – that the sky-high thing had ushered in the end, that the thing was human-made, or that an elf had betrayed them. H'roc-Noc'sh felt as though he had passed through the Gate of Roc'zok, the Portal of Dissolution, as foretold by the elders, and he attributed it to the blood gods' sense of irony that the place of damnation bore a strong resemblance to the world he'd been living in all along.

The head shaman found this post-apocalyptic world confusing. His bewilderment had begun when things hadn't quite ended with the End. No seer had seen any further than that. But how could they, considering the End had decided to cloak itself in the Great Darkness?

H'roc-Noc'sh groaned at his fellow workers along his chain, and they groaned back, equally low-spirited. How many moons would it take them to move the accursed tower back to where his human captors insisted the orcs had stolen it from? And then what? *Roc'zok fa-huck*, he thought.

And what about those little bearded fellows? The patrolling soldiers kept bringing them in from the-blood-gods-knew-where, insisting that the orcs must have stolen and spread them around the mountains on purpose in preparation for something vile. H'roc-Noc'sh knew not what to make of it. The bearded ones looked like boot-high dwarves to him, and as they stood lined up in front of the tower, with their suspiciously jolly expressions frozen on their faces, he was convinced someone had turned the little fellows into stone.

H'roc-Noc'sh shuddered at the perversion of it all. Vileness had a face, and it was human! The Zarrafandans had placed almost two dozen of those dwarves next to the tower by now, and H'roc-Noc'sh couldn't shake the feeling that they were meant as a deterrent. If they refused to comply, would he and his chain gang be turned into stone next?

Absent-mindedly he clawed a circle in the dirt. He tossed some of the chicken bones into a familiar position, broke an alligator tooth from his necklace and threw it into the mix. After sprinkling the construct with chicken blood, he spat into the circle to finish the process. Back in the day, this would have amounted to a curse. Old habit.

Whoag-wagh! He directed his thoughts at the tower, the root of all evils. His torso swayed back and forth to insist on the request. As if it were that simple. As if the blood gods were still listening. As if a curse after the Great Darkness would work no differently than before.

Well, one could try.

Yet, not long afterwards, when he was halfway through the rest of his chicken, he felt the manacles on his ankles shaking. H'roc-Noc'sh looked down and saw his feet were shaking too…

Tremors had seized the ground.

That was odd. Odder still, the sky had turned piggy pink. But – on top of the earth's quaking and the sky's sudden bizarre choice of colour – what really, *really* threw him was that he and his fellow orcs crashed and clattered to ground level. Chicken bones bounced in all directions.

When he heaved himself up a moment later, H'roc-Noc'sh found that the pile of bricks he and his fellow orcs had been eating on had disappeared. Also gone was the one conspicuous thing, visible from far and wide, that he had been staring at from dawn to dusk. Without a flash, without any fancy magic display, without the sound of bricks crumbling, the tower had vacated its spot. So had all the extracted stones. And the miniature dwarves had absconded with them.

"*Ksh-z-kh'tk!*" H'roc-Noc'sh fumed in orcish. "*Broo-arrrrrh!!*"

The rumbling resumed, undeterred. Humans ran hither and thither. Something was wrong with the End.

The shaman, now sitting on his sore backside a storey lower, craned his head. His massive body was rocking along with the ground's vibrations, the chain that bound him to his fellow suffering orcs jangling with it. Now that the tower had gone, the slopes of the Silvery Sickle lay in plain view before him, and on them, strange stirrings... For one, a rock slide came down the mountains, aroused by the forces of nature. And also, whatever it meant, lots and lots of... green-skins! Running from the moving rubble? About to take the occupied settlement by storm? Or both?

It was a moment in which H'roc-Noc'sh was pleased with being green. Had the gods resolved that he had completed his tribute, now that the tower, the symbol of the End, had been retracted? Was he to be given another chance? Was there a new dawn on the horizon? Was pink the new blue?

Above all pinkness, something sparkled.

Way up in the star-spangled sky beyond the sky – which some call "the Void" and others "space" because it's so full of nothing that there's room for everything up there – in the grand illimitable reaches of infinity, a wee little something dropped into view. It was only a wee little something as seen from way, way down below – from the flat, pie-like world known as Aenyros, and even then only if one looked very closely. To a cursory glance with the naked eye, the wee little something didn't even look like something wee. But from the Zarrafandan observatory, viewed through a skyglass – a spyglass with a difference in spelling, size and scope – whatever was up there looked anything but wee. And it could be seen sliding through the spheres, a panther on the prowl, on a trajectory towards…

"Disaster!" squealed Normi Stargazer, the one who had always seen it coming. "The comet! It's heading straight at us! Oh. Dear. Gods! And it's… HUUUGE!"

CHAPTER 15

Rumbles, Ripples, Ramifications

The threads lining the tunnel shimmered.

In the uncanny light there was a hurried shuffling of feet. Boots scraped backwards on the rubble-covered, fissure-lined ground. Bodies bumped into each other. A sword clanked, a halfling yelled, an elf squealed. The wizard made clear he was at odds with his overlong robe, and he told the robe so. Above all, from here and from there, for reasons impossible to fathom, grotesque sounds as of a crackling and chirping bounced around the rocky surfaces.

Wave after wave of tremors ploughed through, then gradually ebbed away. When the ground-shaking subsided, the bizarre strands edging the sides of the tunnel softened again and sank back into the shadows. The stench of mould replaced the combined brimstone and cinnamon scent, and the tunnel reverted back to the version it had started out as: dark and oppressive, with no fancy extras.

Amjelle's rod flared up. She cast around a glance, found everything mostly where it was before things went dark, and forged forward into the hole ahead. There was no turning back now. Splintered stones crunched underfoot.

A short distance farther, the passage forked, both options shut off by cave-ins.

"Great!" Amjelle chorused alongside Tsynnslin, each coming to a dead end in front of their respective branch.

"Now which—" Amjelle started, then faltered, eyes fixed on the tunnel on her side.

For the length of a long moment, a strange vision flashed before her eyes: the rubble she was looking at, the masses of earth and rock… had changed. In the centre of the heap, as if fiercely dug by hand, a hole had opened up. When she peered through it, she saw – even heard – figures, or the backs of them, arguing, pushing each other forward, and making off through whatever the other side of the tunnel concealed. At the figures' feet, a mostly-white fluffy something hobbled after.

The image swam away, replaced again by a wall of rubble.

She turned to Whinewaeyn. The wizard turned to Bormph, and the dwarf to the gnome.

"You saw that?" Bormph shouted over the tunnel-filling rumbling that was picking up again somewhere in the distance.

"What?" Tsynnslin barked back, busy exploring his own cave-in.

"The hole!" Whinewaeyn pointed. "On our side."

"Which hole?" There was no hole. Not now, anyway.

Meanwhile, Snowflake, eager to help make a decision, had a good snoop around. His nose dug through a narrow opening in the debris on Amjelle's side, and in a blink the bear had squeezed himself into it, his white fur shining through the gaps. The next moment, the rubble shifted, slid over the cub and buried him.

There was a sudden bout of shouting and gesturing.

Ramrok leapt forward. His giant fingers pulled out the largest boulders, and Amjelle and Sylthia raked through the dirt. Luckily, the furry little fellow was instantly freed and, as a bonus of the whole affair, a little further digging in the same direction exposed a passage wide enough for all of them to pass through.

"Move!" hissed Tsynnslin when everyone just stood and stared at the hole. "In there! What's the hold-up?" He pushed past the dwarf as more rubble ricocheted off his opened umbrella onto Bormph's helmet, and from there over Thimble's shoulder straight onto Whinewaeyn's toes.

"Move!" Whinewaeyn now hissed too, echoing the gnome, with the distinction that he sprinkled some pain over his instruction. By means of his staff he herded them forward, and one by one the party dove through the opening.

Safely arrived on the other side, Bormph and Thimble started grousing about the gnome's bulky umbrella, which was when Amjelle realized that this was the scene she'd seen before in her vision. She was tempted to turn and peer back through the hole, but then left it at that. The walls back there were wavering like a drunken horse, and who knew who might be looking back at her...

Further on, the tunnel broadened. It was infused with cracks, though, and the cracks turned into little rifts the longer one looked. Then, with a roar, they collapsed altogether only a short way back. A thick veil of dust came barrelling at them with the force of an avalanche as they ran, through coughing fits and with teary eyes, holding on to a streak of light that leaked into the mountain from what appeared to be an eternity away.

Luckily, it wasn't *that* far. One by one, half a dozen humanoid figures in various shapes and sizes – plus a speck of white fur – surged from the mountain's bowels, tumbling out like coal miners ending their shift in an uncoordinated hurry.

Freedom. At last.

Outside, a lot of puffing and blowing went on, and a proportionate amount of snorting and spluttering. Once everyone had coughed their guts out, heads were raised, though at the same time hearts came close to stopping. Something was very wrong. It was… the daylight.

"It's worse than I thought…" said the voice under the bear head.

"Is that… mauve?" Amjelle ventured. "The sky is… mauve? It's mauve, right?"

What was certain was that the colour of the sky wasn't playing by the rules.

"I'd say… it's more magenta-like," Sylthia said.

"AAAaaa—" began Ramrok.

"Indigo?" Whinewaeyn offered, turning towards the barbarian to hear him out.

"—TCHoooooo," Ramrok finished.

To Thimble, the sky had no particular colour at all. It seemed to shift, now growing darker, now getting lighter again with a hint of orange, and then it turned almost transparent, fragile, as if a blue background shone through whatever was veiling it.

"I'll tell you what it is," Bormph rasped. "Weird. Everything's weird. Like the hole back there that was and then wasn't, and then, once we'd made it, was again. For real. But if we *hadn't* made it, would it have been there at all?"

Weird. There was a reminder for the wizard.

Whinewaeyn's eyes swivelled sideways and locked on to the gnome. He sized him up from top to bottom, from the extra head to his regular one – bushy eyebrows, broad nose and goatee – all the way down to his worn-out, dust-covered shoes. There were all those multiple layers of apparel, the raddled fur coat, the shoddy umbrella he stood propped up on. The gnome looked and talked like the real deal.

As far as gnomes went, he was one of a kind, and yet the very same coat, umbrella, bear head and sturdy little fellow underneath – the whole set of bundled up peculiarities – had popped up a second time back in the cavern. That one too had looked very much alive. And then not so much.

Whinewaeyn raised his finger against the backdrop of the sky's incertitude, opened his lips, and—

As if on cue, there was yet another rumble.

This time it was a roll of thunder, right out of the blue… no, right out of the mauve-magenta-indigo ever-changing vastness above. The earth boomed just as much. In fact, the booming was everywhere as if the sky had found a way to do some thundering further down. Or a brazen earth-born tremor was aiming high, working its way up, up and away.

"Follow me!" Tsynnslin retook the lead. "I know the area."

Off he went, and everyone hurtled along the slope after him, away from the rocks that looked most likely to get fancy ideas in quaky times like these.

They had to stop after a quarter of a mile or so, though. Under different circumstances the spot certainly would have qualified for a panoramic vantage, but as it was now, the whole Silvery Sickle range lay in view below them, and with the ground below jittering, a phantom image peeled off the real thing. The translucent mountains wafted skywards reminiscent of hot steam off an apple pie, but steam with a mind of its own, as it settled farther off, hovering like the mountains' ghost.

Some extra rumbling later, the ghostly reflection shed yet another, and from it a further image wandered off northwards, and so it went on and on, in rapid succession, and every time the reflection of the reflection became a shade less substantial. Within half a minute, all the empty spots across the horizon were covered by what looked like a sea of frozen waves fading into infinity.

Whinewaeyn, aghast, reached for Amjelle's arm. "I swear, dear," he said in a low voice so only the healer could hear it, "I haven't had a shot of spirit for weeks. But as of late, I seem to be seeing things twice. And right now, even twice times twice, and then twice again. Is it just me…?"

Amjelle shook her head absently as she looked on. "By the One and the Other… and the One In-Between… and Those-Flanking-Them-All…"

This time, even the gnome saw it. "The world," gasped Tsynnslin, "is unravelling…"

It wasn't to last, though – the strange phenomenon, that is. The world did stick around for a while longer.

The haunting mountain sea washed away. Only a handful of peaks close by remained, the ones that were supposed to be there and, farther back, a more diverse, commonplace landscape re-emerged. The mountains sloped downwards and merged with rock-strewn hillocks; lush meadows came after, with flowing rivers and vast patches of trees, mostly wastelands across the east. Mist-shrouded morasses filled the gaps. The afternoon sun's presence did its part to provide a sense of normalcy. Only the sky still refused to reconsider. It had been teal for a bit, and now it gave ultramarine a shot, like a kid trying out a new paint palette. A strange calm had settled over the landscape, which in itself felt unsettling.

Thimble's short arm jabbed out. "Hey! Aren't these... gnomes?" He had spotted a ditch at the wayside and pounced forward to skid down to look at his discovery more closely.

At the lowest point, a handful of clay gnomes stood banded together as if engaged in a conspiratorial huddle. An immense piece of upended masonry was with them down there, a stone balustrade lined with vase-like shafts. Miscellaneous rubbish made up the rest of the ditch's contents, ranging from wooden spoons to candelabras and boots, none of which usually lived on the mountainside.

Thimble traced one of the figurines' faces with his fingers. It was pushing a wheelbarrow. "It's the exact same one! I saw that one back in there, in the cavern! He's got a broken nose, and one of the wheel's spokes is missing."

Tsynnslin peered down at the offerings, nodding sagely. "That might very well be, little one. Artifacts struggle to maintain their position in time and space. They skip around – towards a vortex in the end, I'm quite sure. But most of the time they only manage a certain distance. That's how I found them."

"They skip around?" Thimble cocked up his head. "And they all end up taking a break in places like this?"

"Aye. Nodes, I call them," Tsynnslin said gloomily. "I've seen it time and again. If there's one sure thing I've learned about artifacts, it's that they seek their like. Maybe they try to strengthen that way, I don't know. Tainted aura is drawn towards other tainted auras close by." He wiped a film of perspiration from his forehead. "Things would appear out of nowhere back at my place. Then I realized, the more tainted stuff I collected, the more I turned the place into a kind of vortex myself. More tainted auras in one place means more instability. And more instability means that tainted things taint other things. It's like an abyss reaching out." He watched Amjelle help Thimble climb out of the ditch by providing him with a hand. "An abyss reaches out towards another… and so it goes on and on. At some point there will be nothing left but abyss."

"Turnips with tassels, gnome!" Bormph grumped. "That's all just peachy. The end is nigh, and it all started with a gnome!"

"*Kh'ach n'avash,*" Sylthia breathed, as if talking to herself, but when Thimble met her gaze, she had to expound. "Ripples in the Dreamer's Pool. We elves… we have an old adage that says even the most insignificant, the most innocuous of things may change the whole world. Dip your pinkie toe into a pond, and it will make a circle, and the circle will grow." She heaved a sigh. "Who knows what the Dreameress is dreaming right now?"

"What you mean?" Thimble put on his most contemplative face as the sky flickered towards turquoise. "Your goddess chucked a garden gnome in a pond? In a dream?"

Plop!

Grand Empress Jesmarine of Great Caesh dropped another rock into the fountain and watched it sink. Circles spread softly over the water's surface, reflecting the sky's unblemished blue. Though "unblemished" was only seven-eighths true. Jesmarine leaned back from the fountain's edge where she was perched, and her eyes rolled up. A multicoloured tinge rimmed the sky's southern fringe and ever so slowly spilled northwards.

"Empress?"

A calm, lisping voice reached her ear.

"Everyone's ready. If you'd please…" Juvdor, the Empress's personal servant – who'd double today as master of ceremonies – stood waiting for Her Mercurial Gravel-Throwing Highness to get her royal behind in gear.

Jesmarine finally staggered up, her bell-shaped monster of a skirt rustling as she let the rest of the stones she held rain from her gloved hand. They hit the water in aggressive succession, like a barrage of cannons.

The nail-studded door leading back into the palace was already in the process of being opened. Which wasn't saying much. Opening doors in the palace took a while. The guards went about it so solemnly it was tempting to assume they had breakfasted on a special brownie fresh from the court alchemist. And it wasn't just the guards. Festivities put the whole staff under such a lethargic spell that the Empress let out a screech on occasion just to shake things up.

"Do I *have* to wear that abominable crown, Juffy?" the Empress snorted like a balky horse. "It's all itchy, and it's as heavy as a laundry iron. And should I stumble—"

"It's the symbol of your far-reaching powers, Your Imperial Majesty," Juvdor reminded her. "Each spike stands for one of the eight directions in which Your Highness's magnificent realm extends."

"Can't I wear it… symbolically?"

"Later, certainly. As for now, no. Rules are rules. Even for a ruler."

"No fair, Juffy." She stuck out her lower lip, first in a pout and then in thought. "Say if I married, only the king would have to wear that dratted thing, right? I'd be the decision-maker, but for crown wearing I'd just be the backup."

"We'll hold conference about that when we get there." Juvdor fortified his diplomatic lisp with a courteous smile.

"If only there were another empire around with a fetching guy on top, I'd be game. We could save on military expenses *and* solve the crown-wearing issue."

"Empress, please."

Needless to say, Empress Jesmarine of Great Caesh wasn't in the mood for representational duties including ceremonious pacing, obligatory speeches and prattle with dignitaries and underlings. She preferred plotting.

Plotting was a family tradition. In that sense, she followed in the footsteps of her devious mother, who had whipped the reins of power from her hypocrite husband and, subsequently, had gone on to conquer half the continent with a wave of her hand – which, paradoxically, had earned her the epithet "The Unwavering". Caesh had expanded and expanded into Great Caesh, and then there were Little Caesh and Wee Caesh too, and some other bits and pieces with as-of-yet very un-Caesh-y names.

Jesmarine, as the only child and heir, felt that she still had some imperious waving to do.

However, the Empress's mind was elsewhere. Her hair looked a mess. Her vassals besieged her to talk taxes. Wee Caesh demanded the same privileges as Little Caesh, and Little Caesh had a problem with being belittled by Great Caesh. What's more, a dispatch had arrived from Zarrafanda earlier in the morning – the negligible lot of land along the southern border, only spared from her mother's conquests out of pity. Apparently, that laughing stock of a prince down south had requested her assistance against forces unknown to save "garden gnomes and everyone who owns one." If anyone needed proof that the simpleton was more than a ton simple, this was it.

"Shall we?" Juvdor inclined his head towards the now open double door, where the guards had assumed grave expressions.

She let Juvdor lead the way. He almost floated through the side entrance of the throne room with his smooth, scuttling movements, while the Empress pushed after him with the charm of a milkmaid wedged into a corsage. Ruby-encrusted crown sparkling, jet-black curls flying, she rushed into position at the centre of the dais. The whole royal household and an audience of select courtiers and townsfolk rose to their feet. Dignified looks everywhere. A little cough or two entered into the stolid silence to make the awkwardness official.

"Let's get this over with quickly, shall we?" Jesmarine squeezed out of her thin, pallid lips into Juvdor's ear. "I have an appointment with the royal hairdresser."

Three knocks with the ceremonial staff later, the main entrance doors at the end of the aisle swung open, or started to. "Ladies and gentlemen, please welcome... the candidate!"

What felt like a quarter of an hour later, a young man in a green doublet with baggy sleeves and fitted brown breeches stepped in. He crossed the hall in measured steps, following the red carpet laid out on the aisle, his strut accompanied by the polite clapping of hands. At the dais, he took a deep bow, and the Empress nodded in greeting.

"Just one?" she inquired from Juvdor under her breath, and got a nod back.

The candidate got down on one knee. He didn't dare look up as some protocol or other dictated – either that, or he was studying the carpet patterns, carefully.

"He appears so… clean, Juffy," Jesmarine went on whispering. "Almost beyond recognition. Has he shaved? I seem to remember him differently. Is this the same one who found that prize cow? The cow some rival farmer had hidden away in a manure pit?"

"Aye, this would be the one, Majesty. Also, more importantly perhaps, he exposed a conspiracy against Your Imperial Serenity."

"Ah yes. With a headquarters down in the sewers," Empress Jesmarine recalled. "I still have that picture in my head of him barging in at the council, reeking like a vile rat, spreading the news… and" – she wrinkled her nose – "that… that odour. He has a gift for this kind of dramatics."

"And that's why he had his ritual bath yestereve," Juvdor confided. "It's been made a mandatory part of the procedure for all candidates." Then, with a bow, as the audience already showed some signs of restlessness, he presented her with a rolled piece of parchment.

The Empress unrolled it dutifully. "Today," she recited, "we've all come together to honour the numerous deeds of a truly sterling man, a character whom we are fortunate to welcome in our midst. A valiant, prime example of the grandest of virtues: loyalty, generosity and compassion." It was her standard speech, and it was punctuated by uninspired cheers every now and again. "What we have here is a man of resolve, rectitude and unequalled moral fibre, racing from quest to quest…"

She could've snoozed off right there, having read the thing as often as some changed their unmentionables. As always on these occasions, Empress Jesmarine had started off the tedious speech with a vestige of enthusiasm, but her energy waned with every succeeding line. The whole litany went on and on and on, and all it ever boiled down to was "Blahdy-bloody-blah…"

Irritating throat-clearing drowned out her droning delivery.

"Crap! I said that aloud," she hissed to the side with a start, slanting Juvdor a furtive glance. "*Did* I say that aloud?"

Juvdor neither denied nor confirmed any flaws in the Grand Empress's rhetoric performance.

"Anyway, and that's why we're here." She whipped the next piece of parchment from Juvdor's hand. "Oaths now."

Mild applause. If there'd been a slip-up, everyone seemed to agree to ignore it.

"Pray answer after each pronouncement 'I swear,' Mr…"

"…Swinger," was all she picked up from Juvdor's whisper.

"Mr Swinger," the Empress tried again, but once the word was out of her mouth, it seemed to belie all seemliness. It was a far cry from, say, a Mr Baker. She saw Juvdor mouth the full name again.

"Ah, excuse me, Mr *Sting*swinger," she finally produced, which was supposed to make more sense. "I will be loyal to my Empress," she then recited, face impassive, voice toneless.

"I swear," pledged Valerius Frilbo Stingswinger.

"I'll be devoted to the church."

"I swear."

"I will be charitable, defend the poor and helpless, and walk the path of the righteous, whatever comes my way."

He swore on that too.

"Never will I shirk danger out of fear."

Ditto.

"And whenever I see a lady in distress, I will volunteer to rush to her defence."

Sworn.

It went on for half a page more, a long fussy talk about chivalry, faith, and all-around goodness. The piling-up of morality sickened the Empress. It stank to high heaven. Should she ever tie the knot, she'd sort all those spineless flakes out first.

"And," she resumed in a stately, funereal voice as seemed to fit the tedious ceremony, "I swear to this last bit of nonsense too – for that's how mindless I am, just saying my two words."

"I swear," swore Valerius Frilbo Stingswinger.

A hint of a quiver had come through in that virtuous voice after all, Jesmarine noticed, an unexpected display of emotion providing some extra amusement. Her Majesty was thrilled. She sniggered in Juvdor's direction, and the old man's scowl at the deliberate deviation from protocol completed her mid-morning entertainment.

Next, the squires fitted the candidate with plate armour from head to toe. When the attaching of the steelware was done, the ceremonial sword was brought in. The Empress preferred not to fool around with this part: blade on the right shoulder, half circle over the candidate's head, blade on the left shoulder. Done. Accidental beheading avoided.

"Arise, Sir Stingswinger," she intoned, her voice grave and sombre for effect. Though, however she tried, she couldn't stop her ears from blushing. Still, arise he did, the knight in shining armour, and the audience with him, offering compulsory claps and cheers.

A post-accolade brunch was held, but Empress Jesmarine only paid it a short visit – mainly because the fresh knight was quite the show-off, and the babbling about his inflated ego's oh-so-chivalrous deeds soon became trite. She had better things to do. Time for the hairdresser. Also, some serious realm-related decisions were pending. And as it so happened, just then, as she was walking the corridors, her eye caught a glimpse of the skies through one of the windows. The odd kind of storm seemed to have crept further Caesh-wards from the south, and that was incentive enough for Empress Jesmarine to make her decision. Waiting for the weather to change was a peasant's approach. An empress had to *be* the weather.

"Pray, Juffy," she said, "see to it that the Lord High Steward makes room for the War Council to convene. I sense myself in the mood."

Juvdor's face lengthened.

"As soon as my curls have been brought in order," she clarified. "You see, it occurred to me that ever since my unwavering mother occupied the Southern Isles, we haven't had a proper show of force. And we should have one, as a matter of principle. A bit of ravaging, plundering, conquering, that sort of thing. That's how empires work. That's what men-at-arms are here for. That's what Mummy would have wanted. Lands won't fall into our hands by themselves. They need to be pushed in the right direction."

"Pushed…" Juvdor lisped. "Of course."

"This Zarrafanda-thing is only a formality anyway, right? And now that the Dymmling has declared it's hunting season for garden gnomes or whatever, we wouldn't want to stand idle, right? Time to lend him a hand and push…"

Juvdor bowed from the waist. "As you please, Your Excellency."

"Up here!" Tsynnslin hollered.

The gnome had crested a grassy knoll and now drove his umbrella into the earth as a general would ram his two-hander into the soil when surveying enemy positions on the battlefield below. Hands on the wooden pommel, leaning forward, the gnome's hawkish gaze swept over the green open range.

A picturesque mountain pasture lay before him, dreamily embedded in the Silvery Sickle's higher reaches, dotted with colourful blotches: blooming flowers made up half of them, the caps of garden gnomes peeking out of the grasses the rest. A rivulet ran through the meadow, nestling up against moss-covered mounds as it meandered its way across, and yet, according to the gnome, there had never been any such creek up here, ever. Even this seeming idyll was proof that the world was out of whack.

"Like a wheel, aye, wobbling all over the place." The gnome put on a grim face. "Or…" He thought some more. "…like a whole lot of wheels, actually. Like one of those big tick-tocking things that's missed a beat and can't catch up anymore and starts tick-tocking all over the place."

"Like the Weaverring clock?" Thimble ventured, because he knew a thing or two about that one. "At the top of the big tower?"

He had been at the grand opening about a year ago or so. *Clockwork is all about cogs.* That's what the master gnome had said. And in his mind he saw the gnome pointing at a whole collection of spiky, intermeshing wheels of various sizes at the heart of his marvellous machine. Some wheels were even stacked onto each other, some were linked by way of strange shafts and mechanical contraptions, and only because they were put together the way they were, the whole thing was able to turn here and there and just about everywhere. But first, someone had to push it into gear. Without a push, it was just there, like a piece of art.

"A volunteer!" a voice called. "Hmm? Anyone?"

The head engineer, an ancient gnome with hairy tufts peeking out of his ears, had looked through the gathering of onlookers. His hand reached out and picked some curious kid from the masses. "How about… you? Yes, *you!*"

And a little girl, despite herself, stepped forward.

"Grip this!" The gnome pointed at a part of the contraption. "Just give it a little push, as hard as you can, and observe. Anyone can do it. Even the smallest person."

"Just… push?" The little girl gave the gnome, and then the part he was pointing at, an incredulous look. She stared back at the wheels upon wheels. "What about all the rest?"

The gnome raised his fingers and tickled the air with them. "The rest… is magic!"

"Magic?"

"Don't you worry, little one. Now and again, it might need some extra help. When the time comes, we'll find another one, just like you." The gnome winked at her. "Now push!"

"Maybe just like that, aye," Thimble heard Tsynnslin say, drawing him from his reverie. "Clocks are works of precision. As is the world. One thing leads to another, to make it all work. Conversely, if one thing leads to something else, then the other thing leads to something else too, and so it goes on and on. In the end, you've got a lot of things that go how they're supposed to go. Or they don't."

The gnome had a further look around. He looked irresolute and a hint baffled too when he saw a bunch of initials carved into bark of a maple tree on the mound next to him, enclosed by hearts of varying degrees of craftsmanship, as though a whole hamlet's relationship history had been documented on it. There was no trace of a hamlet, though.

Everyone was glad about the creek, however, regardless of its dubious journeying habits, and rushed to wash up and take a long drink. As they rested, more questions came up. Like, what a vortex might look like, why there was a vortex in the first place, and what to do about it.

"Let me tell you something you might be unaware of," Tsynnslin began. "Ancient scriptures are full of lore for this region. It's been a well-kept mystic secret for centuries. And I'll be damned if it isn't the very same site we're looking for. It has to be. What else could it be?"

Amjelle gave him a sidelong glance. "What kind of site would that be?"

"Braargh." Bormph was less excited. "Sure enough, it's a place nobody has ever found for only-the-gods-know-how-long, and now we've got about five minutes tops before the world ends."

"The place has many names," Tsynnslin said. "The native mountain folk that lived in the caves of the Sickle millennia ago called it the Rifts of Ram. Or, in a more poetical turn of phrase, the Edge of the World."

"They must have been confused then," Thimble piped up. "The Sickle's nowhere even near the Edge."

"It's not *that* kind of edge, halfling, if we give credence to the tales. They speak about a holy place, a gateway pointing into the Beyond. Some call it the Eye into the Void, the Spark in the Dark, the World's Cradle or the Forge of Fate. Elves might tell you the mountain harbours the entrance to All Souls Keep, and the Dreameress is bedded there in a place before the world."

Amjelle and Whinewaeyn exchanged glances. Her clerical misgivings were traded for the mage's informed scholarly perplexity.

"The Dreamkeep itself? Why, that's just a legend!" Sylthia flapped a dismissive hand. "And there's no way a mortal could ever enter it." As any elf, she thought it to be a bedtime story for little elflings. Something for the heart and the mind.

"I trust, none of the accounts match any other," Amjelle said.

"Naturally," Tsynnslin conceded. "Make of it what you will. No scholar would put these tales above myth, true. The rumours about a lost continent of Adphrantis are more to the sages' taste. Aye, and why not? People make up their own tales. People want to believe in something."

"Spark in the Dark..." Bormph muttered. "Sounds like treasure to me. A rare vein perhaps. Unattended stuff like that can't be good for the world. It makes some sense! Must be someplace inside these mountains then." His spirits lifted as he talked on. "We should get cracking! 'Talk gathers no gems,' as my great-gravelgramps used to say."

Snowflake had headed off already, exploring on his own. The gnome bustled along after him.

"Hey!" Bormph yelled after bear and bear head. "Where do you think you're going, gnome? Nowhere and fast? For someone who claims not to know exactly what you're looking for, you make off at a smart pace. How would you even recognize the place?"

"I'll know a vortex when I see one," Tsynnslin shouted back over his shoulder, scampering on, keeping his pace. "I'm a mystic. And we must be close."

Impatience grumbling out of him, Bormph trudged after, and the party after Bormph.

The vortex's whereabouts, however, remained elusive. The farther they got, the more stuff popped up between the wealth of boulders and natural rock formations littering the place, as if an explosion had hurled things in all available directions. A cluster of objects lay scattered on one side, almost trail-like, and an archway made up of stray balconies reared up in the opposite direction. It looked as though the pieces of masonry had bundled together to climb a steep hillside.

"How can you think of resting now?" Tsynnslin growled when Bormph suggested a break. "Haven't you seen the skies? Felt the earth shake and the landscape go wild?" He fidgeted with his umbrella. "How can you call yourself a dwarf and not see the gravity of the situation?"

"I'm hungry," Bormph put up as a defence. "What's the worst that could happen to us in a few minutes anyway? The vortex would send us through time again? I'll take it. Didn't hurt the first time. Wouldn't mind at all if it saves us part of our journey up there."

Tsynnslin tapped on a gnome hidden in the grass with his umbrella. "A chasm in time might work both ways. You went *forward*. You could've just been lucky, but who knows? What if it happens again, but this time you go… backwards?"

Thimble didn't see the problem either. He'd have second breakfast twice, but he'd manage.

"Just think about it for a minute…" the gnome went on. "It would be a paradox. You might be drawn towards your own time-tainted past selves, just like each of those gnomes ends up next to another displaced gnome somewhere else, only you'd end up some *time* else. If you were to turn up in the past, would you exist twice? Is the universe prepared for that to happen?"

Thimble tried to wrap his tiny head around this but didn't get very far. This was much more complicated than a second second-breakfast. Some concepts just weren't made for halfling-sized heads, nor for more robustly built dwarven equivalents, as Bormph's frown attested.

"Or," Tsynnslin said, "let's assume, for the sake of argument, that the universe gets rid of your past selves when you travel back. Because, due to whatever laws of nature there might be, you can only exist once. So your present selves would be undone by your new future selves – and then you couldn't possibly have travelled into the past, precisely *because* you did." Tsynnslin looked around, and the most apprehensive expression he could find was from Ramrok. But looks can be deceiving. Preoccupied with watching the sky's buffoonery, the barbarian hadn't been listening.

Whinewaeyn had. "Yes, yes, of course." He nodded, not quite registering what he was nodding for. His face had clouded over, though, and he was thinking about something rather similar to the gnome's talk that he was sure he ought to remember, but then didn't. The shadowy presence of a thought – shapeless, hazy, indistinct – slipped across his mind, wafted from one hideout to another before arriving in a secluded nook of his brain, the place where his dream of the perfect explosion and irrational fear of opossums had pitched camp side by side. Whatever it was, the phantom of a thought slunk past like a thief in the night, whispering something… something—

"If that happens… it might be the beginning of the end," the gnome concluded.

"You mean the sky would turn a garish green or something?" Bormph sneered. "Now wouldn't that be something?"

"It would be more than that, dwarf. With everything connected to everything else, *everything* would change. In the past. But if the past were to change, what would be left of… the present?"

"Wait, *what?*" The wizard suddenly snapped out of his thoughts. Something wasn't quite right about all the gnome's talk. Then it occurred to him: it was what he'd said!

He felt trapped all of a sudden, and not only in a robe twice his size. Trapped in a universe gone mad. His eyes soaked up the olive-greenness of the sky, flicked over the pasture sprinkled with gnomes and balconies, and eventually came to rest on the other gnome in the centre of it all: the live one with the bearskin, the ridiculous umbrella, and his disquieting ideas – the one he had seen one time too many back in the cavern. He was about to say something, but then his tongue went numb.

"We… had better move on, no?" he finally produced. He re-buckled his loosely hanging belt and checked whether all the pouches dangling from it were accounted for.

"Let's try this way then." Resolve glistened in the gnome's eyes. Already he was heading towards an archway formed by a cluster of stone slabs, pointing in the direction of an incline.

"*Up* the mountain?" Bormph protested, panting. "Why not the other way? There's lots of stuff over there too. Looks more like it's heading towards a cave or something, *into* the mountain. That would make a whole lot more sense to a dwarf!"

"Non-dwarves would build temples higher up, closer to the skies," said the gnome.

"Rocks and rigmarole!" Bormph pouted. "What's the world coming to, indeed? Whose apocalypse is this anyway?"

CHAPTER 16

Gone Gods Gambit

Bormph let out a grunt. Guttural, gruff, irked. He meant it this time. His teeth tore into a chunk of flesh on the bone lodged between his greasy hands, and he crunched and groaned along as he ate. At least there was food.

Other than that, let's face it, the expedition had been a washout so far. The motherlode of washouts, as a dwarf would put it. The self-declared band of world-savers had failed to find anything even vaguely resembling a vortex, a temple, a forge, a path, or a clue. No spark in the dark. What they *had* come across was more junk: at the bottom of hillsides, at the top of a crest, hidden in the gloom of a tiny cave and glittering from the shallow banks of a mountain brook. Wherever they ventured, the garden gnomes were there waiting for them, as were spinning wheels, brass kettles, and other gaudy rubbish. Apparently, the gnomes' fancy artifacts were attracting the heck out of one another. Rather than leading them to a single definite source, the junk formed nodes of pieces of trash enjoying each other's company.

Bormph's eyes rolled towards Tsynnslin. "'I'll know a vortex when I see one...'" He stuffed more wyvern inside of him. "Pah!"

The irony in the whole affair was that their only ray of light had come with the emergence of a shadow...

Around an hour ago Whinewaeyn had suddenly snapped to attention. He whirled around. His head leapt up. The shadow around him broadened and deepened at breakneck speed. A wave of his hand, and tiny sparks danced across his fingertips.

His eye caught the creature stabbing earthwards. It had a horn-covered head, feathered wings and long spindly legs, which it held cocked for the attack. Its sickle-like talons glinted as the beast came down like a streak of lightning – a little too fast for the wizard, who was still busy focusing his energies.

Fo-cus... FO-CUS! He breathed in and out, in, out, in and—

A screech.

Maybe a blink before the collision, Ramrok yanked his two-hander from his side and slashed at the attacker, all in one smooth movement. The beast's shriek had ended in a burble.

A body the size of two full-grown cows whooshed past between wizard and barbarian, wings still thrashing and flailing, the barb-edged tail whipping the air. A couple of steps farther, it crashed to the ground with a hefty bump, rolled some more, careened down the next decline and – judging by the muddle of off-view noise – admitted defeat.

"And that was... what?" Bormph commented, now that he'd got his heavy axe ready.

"Wyvern," Ramrok said, in a level monotone. "Young one. No get old now."

Sylthia glanced up at him, then down the slope at the felled creature, and lowered her bow. "Can't be. Feathered wyverns only live in the Amcalladams."

"Elf tell wyvern," Ramrok deadpanned, scanning the sky overhead for further predators. No more drakes were to be seen, but the scattered piping of errant gulls filled the colour-insecure sky.

"The world's going haywire." Tsynnslin sounded disenchanted. "Time is shortening."

A howl came from Whinewaeyn's direction.

The wizard held up his quivering hands. A stray flare was still buzzing around his fingertips, the last of its kind. It flickered and fizzled before it zapped back into his wrinkly palm, wresting one more tortured yelp from Whinewaeyn's lungs. His hands looked as though they had dug through a bucketful of coal dust as he frantically blew at his fingertips.

Amjelle tutted. "Master Whinewaeyn! Might you perchance happen to know the third law of magical energy preservation?"

Whinewaeyn paused his puffing. "Never let building energies go unsupervised?" Fingers steaming, he turned to his fellow campaigners, beaming with pride. "See? *My* student!"

The episode had secured the party its dinner and Whinewaeyn a manicure. While the others ate, Amjelle stuffed cotton balls between the wizard's charred fingers and applied lotion to his fingertips to cool them down.

"Don't forget the nail polish," Bormph quipped. "For a certain magic touch."

They had scavenged the cotton wool from a drawer, a drawer they had found in a dresser, next to a bedstead, in part of a house – a tiny abode built from logs, complete with a stone chimney stack, sitting a tad askew on an outcrop of rock. This wasn't your common wayside inn, more like a how-the-heck-did-it-get-there uninhabited cottage up in the mountains, but the party was happy enough to take what they could get. Certainly, chancing across a whole home was an improvement over scattered cuckoo clocks.

Garden gnomes guarded the log house as if it were a fortress, but nobody seemed to be home. Since the door was locked and there had been no key under the mat, Thimble's tools had a little persuading to do.

The inside was neatly furnished and comfy. A prominent fireplace, a large table and a sideboard with kitchen utensils occupied one corner. On the wall opposite, a bedstead now held all the equipment the party had brought with them. Black oak rafters stretched overhead. The threadbare hearthrug and the knitting needles on the mantelpiece, with a half-finished stocking still attached, indicated that either the place had once been lived in, or that the gnomes outside were more crafty than they let on.

Yet, despite the crackling fire in the hearth, the smell of roasted wyvern hanging in the air and its meat warming their stomachs, the overall mood was in dire need of improvement. While Amjelle treated the wizard, throwing in a snippy word every now and again, Tsynnslin wallowed in self-pity and quaffed the evening away by depleting the wine reserves. Ramrok had conked out early on, snoring over the day's events, and Bormph ate for comfort. Nothing, absolutely nothing, can take away a dwarf's healthy appetite. He had his complaints, though. Mainly about the seasoning, and that he'd have preferred something on the side, like pork. But, all in all, a fed dwarf is a happy enough dwarf.

When the conversation had reached its lowest point – and only silence was speaking volumes – Sylthia stepped outside. "Come on, Snowflake! Let's see the sunset," she said, cradling the polar bear cub in her arms. Maybe this would be the last sunset she'd see, ever.

Thimble snuck out after her a little while later. Maybe it was the last time he'd see Sylthia enjoying the sunset, ever.

"Cheers!" Tsynnslin hollered from the high-backed armchair he had made his own. It had the look of a throne, but the gnome slouching on it certainly lacked a royal demeanour at this point in the evening. His feet resting on the pulled-up footstool, he looked weary and irritable. He leaned forward and raised his flask, then sank back again to watch the hearth fire spurt and splutter and cast ominous shadows.

Whinewaeyn looked up from his rocking chair and his manicure. Alongside the half-drunk gnome, snoring barbarian, munching dwarf, and fingernail-polishing healer, there was also the elephant in the room, and it took up whatever space was still available.

"So you say nobody ever found this secret place of yours before?"

The wizard's question hung about for some time. Right before it got away, the gnome barked a bitter laugh.

"Told y'already, old man." Tsynnslin stared vacantly ahead, sloshing the flask about. "Wouldn't be much of a s-*hic!*-cret otherwise, would it? But no, nobody's ever found it. Not even zat crazed Zarothaster back in ze day. And roaming around up here, I gots an idea why zat is."

Bormph perked up. "Who's that Zaro-something? Name sounds familiar." The dwarf smacked his lips as he peeked over his gnawed-off bone. He certainly got more affable with a fuller stomach. "Zaro... the Toaster, was it? Or is the one I'm thinking of Zaro the Taster?"

"Zarothaster, dwarf! He was one of us m-*hic!*-sticks. One of ze first. Dinn't end well for him, zough."

Bormph brought his sleeve up to wipe some grease from his beard. "What did he get up to then?"

"Zerching for enlightenment? Immortality? Ze usual."

"And the Toaster-guy sought your fabled temple too?"

"Aye, aye. Went questing up theze very same mounz-things." Tsynnslin's head bobbed multi-directionally in confirmation. "Tha's notta say he believed in ever finding a shrine, or whatever. People say he was r-*hac!*-zer trying to prove... ze opposite."

"The opposite? And what would that be?"

"That ze gods are dead."

"Which ones?" Whinewaeyn inserted himself, staring at the gnome, confused. "The One and the Other?"

"Oh, he didn't mean any in part-*hic!*-lar. More like *all* of zem. Whatever looked like one." The gnome's flat hand, palm down, cut the air. "Dead."

"*All* of them?" Whinewaeyn sat up. "That's so much worse! Did you know about this?" The wizard's eyes turned to Amjelle and her puzzled expression and then back to the drunken gnome. "When? How did this happen? In that temple, you say? In a temple that's not a temple? Either way, how awful! Who knew that gods were even mortal! Um... are they? I mean... were they?"

Tsynnslin took another swig. "He meant it more... in a mezer... metah... Whassaword? Metamphorical kinda way. Said zey couldn't ever have ex-*hics!*-ted in ze first place. Oh, well. Zey never bozzered showin' up anyway."

"What!?" Whinewaeyn sat up, eyes glinting in the firelight. "First, you tell us the gods might have died, and then that they never existed at all? This is getting worse and worse, gnome!"

"Hold still!" Amjelle pulled the wizard back down and stuck a cotton ball back in place. "So what did he find?" she then asked herself. An unconvinced grin played over her lips.

"Whoooo knows?" Tsynnslin moaned, his face lighting up with a sudden blaze of the fire. "Man wents up... neeeever came down. Cler-*hic!*-s say ze gods took him out for h-hear... hearsay?" The gnome looked stumped for a moment.

"Heresy?" Amjelle made an informed guess.

"Tha's the one!"

Bormph snuffled. "So much for the misadventures of Zaro the Toaster. With a name like that, no wonder he ended up as toast." He belched a little, then reached over to balance one of his gnawed-off bones on the ridge of the sleeping barbarian's nose. It slid off a few times before the bone finally stayed put. A hush had fallen over the room again, save for the crackling of the fire, Ramrok's snoring, and the occasional *glug-glug-glug* of the flask at Tsynnslin's lips.

"Now consider this," Whinewaeyn began after a time, steepling his fingers in thought. "We don't know what we're looking for, or where, or how to go about it..."

"Hear, hear!" hollered Bormph.

Whinewaeyn let it pass. "But do we know *why* we're here at all?"

"Wents up ze mounz-things," Tsynnslin informed him. "Tha's why."

"True, true. Impeccable logic, gnome," the wizard admitted, "if a little narrow in scope. We went up the mountains because you led us here, and you led us here because we fled from the orcs, and we fled from the orcs because we rescued the elf, and we just *had* to rescue the elf because, well, she disappeared. Right after that dune fancied going for a stroll."

"So?"

"So the whole thing started there, that very night. With the dune. With the elf getting whisked away into that tower. Just her." The pepperminty scent of Amjelle's lotion on his fingers appeared to have awakened the wizard's investigative spirits. "Ever seen anything like it before?"

Tsynnslin shrugged. "Seen lots of things poppin' up elsewhere si-*hic!*-ince it all started," he slurred, "but never *someone*. Not until you lot showed up and di-*hic!*-sappeared ze next minute. Days later, zere you are. So you tell me." The gnome put the flask to his lips again, sucked on it, and wondered about the sudden blandness of the drink. Then he realized that the bottle was short of a key ingredient: liquid.

"So you say it's unusual for a *person* to get spirited away?"

Tsynnslin regarded the wizard with expressionless eyes. "Would have said so back zen. But not anymore. Now's diff'rent. Things 'ave changed, old man. You see? Everyzings getting tainted, 's like a disease. Just look round…" He brought up his short arm and waved at the room. "Zis place must 'ave been nessled in some granny's garden at some point. You know ze ones I'm talking about. Got everyzing li-hittered wiz gnomes… jus' for the heck of it! Suppose ze gnomes are tainted. Ze vortex affects the gnomes, and ze gnomes pull ze home wiz 'em. An army of gno-homes… Tha's like opening a rent in ze fabric of ex-*hic!*-stence. Only a matter of time until everyzing ends up being dragged into the vortex. Wa-woooosh!" He lolled over the armrest, fumbling for another flagon.

"But back then, when it all started," Whinewaeyn said calmly, rolling about a thought around in his head. "There were no gnomes anywhere nearby when our elf disappeared. We were in the middle of the desert."

"See how unlikely zat is?!" Tsynnslin got hold of another flagon and popped it open. "You'd need a whooooole army of artsifags to pull a person zrough space. Even mag-*hic!*-ians should know zat people have potent auras. Zey're *creatures!* Zey're like many, many smaller zings put togezzer. People's aura 's like… like…" He ran out of words.

"Like an entire house, shall we say?" Whinewaeyn raised an inquisitive semi-blackened forefinger.

"If you want. Like zis one here. Whassever."

"Or like an east wing tower?"

The gnome heaved himself forward and gave the wizard a blank stare. "What're you getting at, wizzer?" he garbled. "All's I'm saying's, without lots and lots of artsifacts, *hic!*, you couldn't draw no single person."

"Nor a tower."

"Did you see any gno-homes around ze tower when it showed up at ze orcs' place?"

"No."

"So zere. How d'you explain that?"

"What about just *one* artifact then?" Amjelle brought up. "If it's something super powerful?"

The gnome hesitated for a moment. "Even so… Might pull eizer a tower *or* a person. You'd need to 'ave *two* powerful artsifacts to bring ze tower and ze elf togezer. It's unlikely zat even *one* ex-*hic!*-s, never mind two of 'em!"

"But something made the unlikely likely," Whinewaeyn declared. "And isn't it so that artifacts attract each other? You said so yourself. If a tainted garden gnome is drawn to another gnome, wouldn't two potent artifacts attract each other?"

"There's not even *one* such artsifact!" Tsynnslin slurred with impatience. "Anyone l-*hic!*-stenin'?"

"Come to think of it," muttered Bormph from his table, "actually, we found something back there in the desert. Just a piece of junk in my book, but maybe that's your thing."

Tsynnslin crooked his head in the dwarf's direction, then his eyes shifted back to the wizard, a question dancing in his dilated pupils.

"Ah, yes, yes…" Whinewaeyn gave a curt nod. "What was it? A pin? Women pin down their hair with it. I guess they call it a hairpin. Maybe it's nothing, but we dug it up close to the dune, so—"

Amjelle froze. "Sylthia… By the One and all the Others! *Sylthia* put it on!"

The gnome bounded to his feet – a sudden motion that sent the bear head reeling back on his head. His tiny hand pawed for the umbrella leaning next to the armchair. At his feet, a collection of emptied flagons clinked and clanked as the gnome tottered towards the door, even startling Ramrok from his peaceful snooze.

The mighty barbarian jerked forward. His drowsy eyes tilted open, and the first thing he became aware of was a greasy bone sliding off his nose. Propelled by the sudden jolt, it skidded along the whole length of the table, and sailed on past the bear-wearing gnome barging out the front door.

Minutes earlier. Outside.

Thimble squared his small shoulders, groomed his hair and sucked in his cheeks. Everything in place, he strode purposefully towards the slender figure steeped in the soft dying sunlight. She sat perched on the ledge only a few feet in front of the doorstep. With Snowflake snuggled in her lap, Sylthia let her gaze sweep over the lands below.

Thimble shooed away a seagull arguing with its pal a bit further down the ledge.

"So…" he started as he slumped nonchalantly down beside the elf. "Sooo-oh-oh-oh!" he ended up yowling, not quite as planned. His backside had landed hard on the unyielding stone.

Sylthia smirked back at him. She pulled the blanket from underneath her to spread it out for two.

Thimble's pained face turned into a valiant grin. When he flopped down again, he did it with more grace. He tugged his cardigan tightly over his knees, wrapped the short arms around his legs, and joined the elf in peering down into the mostly tree-clad valley that lay before them.

The land rolled away like a map, a welter of wooded patches and gentle hills, enclosed by precipitous ravines and gullies. The little light there was glinted off a few bodies of water peeking through the pines beneath, fed by a multitude of rivulets cascading from the rocky walls. A sublime spectacle was alive in the sky, but more and more darkness snuck in – subtle, unobtrusive, laying out its gloomy veil. Unlike the day, the night seemed to have no issues sticking to its established black-is-beautiful pattern, with the usual suspects – sparkling stars and a waning moon – contributing to its majesty.

It was a perfect, magical moment for Thimble to pluck up his courage.

"S-say," he began, his fingers turning one of the buttons on his cardigan. "After… the whole thing… Do you have any plans?"

The elf's shining hair uncoiled as she tilted her head. "After the apocalypse I probably won't do very much, Thimble, to be honest," she said. "And neither will you, considering…"

"We could do that together then, hmm?"

Sylthia caught the halfling's innocent gaze for a second before she burst out laughing, almost tipping Snowflake off her lap. She grabbed the cub tighter and scratched him behind the ears to make up for it. "Oh… You're sweet, Thimble, you know that? Even as a thief supposed to operate in the shadows, you always look on the bright side."

"Sure do." Thimble's tiny chest swelled half an inch. He broke into an impish gap-toothed smile. "That's what being a halfling is all about. For the grouchy stuff, we've got the dwarf."

Sylthia giggled. "How would you imagine your life afterwards anyway, Thimble? When you no longer have to rescue damsels in distress from orcs and such?"

"Well…" Thimble's heart was racing. His cheeks – bracketing his dimples – were burning. Could it be that Sylthia was actually interested in his tiny post-apocalyptic halfling self? Assuming, of course, that the apocalypse wasn't half as bad as everyone said it was, and there would still *be* a tiny post-apocalyptic self. This was the time to make his case, to say something glib, scintillating and suave… If only there was something to make a case for, rather than stating the obvious – that he was a mildly roguish rogue, a purse-returning cutpurse, and other than that, well, he was gifted with the ability to eat five slices of apple crumble in one go if necessary. He was also not half bad with his slingshot, and a decent teller of untruths at the weekly pub challenges in Willwold-on-Glee. Plus, he was the undisputed shire-wide champion at marble casting. Last but not least, on good days, when the wind was favourable, he could spit over the breadth of the Glee!

"I'm a writer." It erupted out of him, because it probably was in him, somewhere. When Thimble heard himself speak, he was surprised by his own audacity. *Yes!* he thought. *A writer!* He'd make a lasting impression with that angle.

"A writer?" Sylthia glanced down, charmed indeed by the looks of it. "You don't say!"

"Oh, I say!" Thimble flung back his thatch of curly hair. "I'm a weaver of words, a dreamer of letters, a poet. A… friend of the quill, if you will."

"You even did a rhyme there!" Sylthia chuckled.

He had her right there. No doubt, he was a natural talent – at least in remembering that little rhyming bit from Dringle Rumlunger's *Verse with Verve.* If he'd only read further than the first three pages in the privy where he once found it; it seemed romantic headway was to be made on a rhyme-by-rhyme basis.

"Who would have thought that you had such dormant skills?" Sylthia's hazel eyes were alight. She was caressing him with those eyes!

"Uh…" Thimble said, wringing his hands, but then stopped. He felt Sylthia pulling his wrist closer, and then her slender fingers locked into his clammy counterparts. The warmth of her palm made him sweat even more.

"Th-that's nothing," he stammered. "It's just what I am. I make up rhymes all the time." Which was a lie. But it had gone well so far. "You see, I'm not just spry… I'm also… um… as handsome as I am sly." He wanted to rhyme more, so in his head he went on with, *All good reasons why… I'm meant to be your guy!* It sounded perfect. It rhymed. It had a message. And he had come up with it on the spot. Too bad that his tongue wouldn't follow through. He was too shy to give the rhyme a try.

Sylthia laughed nonetheless. "Sounds like the beginning of a poem."

"Erm… You know, I could write you one," Thimble offered, with feeling. "A proper one." His heart was pumping faster than ever.

"Oh, I'm sure you could… And, by the way, speaking of the pleasures of literature…" She turned around and rifled through the backpack she had brought, pulling out a leatherbound tome. "I've been dumb enough to lug this heavy thing around ever since I hit you over the head with it, remember?"

Thimble recalled a perfect jaw descending upon him and a kiss, but little beyond that. He wouldn't mind taking another hit for a good cause.

"Look…" The elf cracked the volume open. "It's a peculiar one. Written in runes or something. See?"

The pages were brimming with strange handwritten symbols, which to Thimble looked like hen-scratching. Every so often, the occasional abstract picture had been inserted, and there was an irritating cow's head at the front with a muzzle that was drawn all wrong.

"Something's the matter with it," Sylthia said. "It disappeared when I threw it against the wall, at least part of it did."

"Really? How odd. How can that be?"

"I bet some magician's apprentice got a spell wrong, and there you have it."

"If it was an orc… it must have been a dork," Thimble rhymed cheerily, now in full poetic swing. Then he got to hear the whole story about the orcs, an uncalled-for ten-foot fall and the prickliest hay under the sun. The book played the role of the villain in it.

"How about I toss it down the cliff to avenge your honour?" Thimble proposed. He clambered to his feet, grabbed the tome and, with Snowflake's nose following his every movement, scurried over to the cliff's edge. "There's enough artifact-rubbish down there already anyway. How high do you think I'd be able to count before we heard a bump?" He grinned as he held the book aloft over the nothingness looming beneath.

"Don't…" slurred a voice from behind him. "Don't… mooove!"

Thimble swung round. The silhouette of a shaggy bear filled the cottage's doorframe, wreathed in the red glow of firelight gushing out into the deepening night. For some unfathomable reason, an airborne piece of bone overtook the bear and clacked onto a rock, making the whole weird picture complete.

Tsynnslin lurched forward… and immediately missed a step – the only one there was, right in front of the door. As he slumped over, his umbrella rammed itself into the ground, and the gnome found himself in an awkward position suspended over the mud. "Whoops!" he let out, just hanging there for a moment. He heaved himself up again and drunkenly zigzagged onwards, fighting a constant battle for balance. A few feet farther on, he lost, and landed for real in the dirt. Regardless, the gnome crawled on.

"A *hic!* hairpin. You got a *hic!* hairpin?" he yelled at the elf, flourishing his umbrella like a weapon.

After a moment of hesitation, Sylthia lifted her hands up over her head and unfastened the scarab pin. Who knew what mud-covered gnomes in bearskins reeking of booze might do if they didn't get the hairpins they asked for?

"What are you looking at?" he barked at Thimble, who stared back at him a trifle intimidated.

But before the halfling could answer, the gnome cocked his head, as if he recognized something. The tip of his umbrella shot up again, and travelled past the stumped halfling's expression… to the book he was still swinging back and forth between two of his tiny fingers, dangling over the precipice.

"Stop r-*hic!*-ght there!"

Not too far away, in the eastern Silvery Sickle. Two hundred and eight years, seven months and twenty-three days earlier. Half-past two in the afternoon, give or take a few minutes…

A chunk of rock, repeatedly prodded by hours of torrential rain and local flurries, finally succumbed to nature's pestering. It loosened from the little wayside pyramidal stone structure it had been sitting on and hit the trail beneath with a splash. The path it dropped onto was a mushy affair, ankle-deep mud winding upwards alongside a steep cliff towards the pyramid on top. Above the cliff, the sky wore its most glowering grey, and while the worst of the storm was over now, it was still drizzling. A small rivulet had formed alongside the mushy mess skirting the rock wall, seeking its way into the valley, gargling with excitement.

Moving in the opposite direction, human whining rose from below.

"How much further?" came floating upwards.

"It's all slippery," whimpered another voice. "We could fall off!"

"How about a rest? I've got blisters all over!"

"Just a short lunch?"

"Maaaster!"

"Pleeeeaaase!"

"Move, louts!" thundered a penetrating voice over the whining, spitting and sputtering. "The time is ripe. Only a couple of cairns left."

"If the time is ripe already, it will be even riper later—"

"Quiet, you bumbling fools!" The deep voice got louder the closer it neared the top. "You're not worth the mud you're walking on with your petty chatter about mundane things like lunch… and feet… and falling off! We're almost there. Today's the day. The hour is *the* hour."

"How many minutes until it's the minute?"

The question went unanswered. Instead, the master emerged from the valley, reaching the stone pyramid that only moments ago had lost its peak.

Zarothaster was gaunt and wiry, with a white beard that came down to his waist. He had a heavy brown rough-spun cowl wrapped around him, which had picked up an extra layer of dirt at the lower end. With each step, the mystic's man-sized staff dug forcefully into the soil as if to drive home the point that the inconveniences reality imposed on him were negligible.

Also, he was of a capricious nature. Very much so.

"Begone, lazy mass of matter, make way!" he barked as he came across the fist-sized piece of slate that occupied the space he was set to tread on. Impatience coloured his voice, and his blue eyes sparkled with resolve. A swift kick, and the stone plunged into the chasm. The master sloshed onward, sure-footed and brisk, ignorant of the battering sheets of water or the gusts tearing at his cowl and beard.

With a significant delay two more cowl-wearing shapes passed the same spot, both considerably shorter than the gaunt man. One was lanky, the other more on the pudgy side, each in his own way teetering a bit like a wind-up doll from a Weaverring toy store.

"There… The Ram's Horns!" Zarothaster exulted.

They had arrived at the ridge that marked the end of the serpentine mud path. Two oddly shaped rocks jutted out of the ground at this point, bent outwards. If anything, they looked like a bull's headgear, certainly not like a ram's. The pathetic shapes trailing behind swapped glances, but neither of them dared to contradict the master. And he was moving on already.

The trail now transitioned into a more open, rocky affair without a cliff on one side to steady themselves, and with two downsides instead: a steep gorge to the left and another one to the right. In between them stretched a four-foot-wide travesty of a path. More strangely shaped pillars, boulders and cairns made up of smaller stones were dotted along the way. A raging gale, roaming free on top of the mountain, pitched the passing troop from one miniature pyramid to the next.

About half a mile farther, the ridge sloped downwards into a gloomy valley tucked away between rugged mountainsides that led up to soaring peaks. It was still drizzling, and lightning skewered down from the faraway sky as the group dipped into what they hoped was the final stretch of their journey. The wind, whipping and howling up on the ridge, didn't bother to chase after the travellers once they entered the sheltered valley.

At long last, Zarothaster's frenzied pace let up. It was getting darker by the minute now – not because the sky was ratcheting up its dreariness, but rather because the mountains on either side closed in. Also, something enormous was already blocking out the light ahead.

Eventually, the mystic jerked to a halt.

A giant cliff of age-worn stone reared up in front of him. The place was bounded by rock on all sides, and now only a sliver of greyness cut down to the ground from above.

The lanky youth was first to catch up to his master and stop dragging his feet.

"That it?" Flix puffed, breathing hard under the weight of his backpack.

The more sluggish Nobburt hadn't even got close enough yet to recognize anything that would qualify for an "it". All he saw was an odd rock formation looming before and above them, a craggy, overhanging cliff face, a few hundred feet in height. The structure as a whole leaned forward like a drunkard on the verge of tipping over.

"Hanging Rock," announced Zarothaster. "We're here." He peered up in awe.

Flix and Nobburt didn't share the excitement. For all they could tell, it was just a rock hanging around, aptly named. Neither of them had expected much, but when their master had raved about an occult sanctuary up in the mountains, both of them had more or less anticipated a temple of sorts. Temples evoked images of columns, braziers, altars, a priest and – if things went well – a vestal same-aged acolyte or two. This, however, in no way matched up to the mental image. It wasn't even close.

"Stay back!"

Their master need not have bothered with the warning. Neither of the muddy-to-the-ankles mystics-in-training had planned to inspect the rock up close anyway. They stayed where they were, snuffling and sneezing from a distance.

The old man shoved his cowl back, revealing a long, thin face with sallow cheeks, a pointed chin and thin eyebrows that curved down onto the upper end of his nose like a vulture's talons zeroing in on their prey. He took a step forward, let his hand glide over the granite as if to absorb any lingering ancient essence, but if any essence was up for it, it wasn't immediately apparent.

Nobburt sighed. The sprinkling of adventurous spirit he had started out with was long gone. "Now what?" he whispered under his cowl, his face moist and clammy.

"There's... nothing," Flix muttered through gnashed teeth, so that his master got the hint too. Things must have gone pear-shaped a landmark back.

Zarothaster bent down. A dirt-caked boot was hurled back at the boys. "The ointment!" he barked, and there went the other boot.

"Ointment... ointment..." Nervous hands unfastened one of the backpacks and produced a small flagon.

"Uncork it," Zarothaster instructed. "Smell anything?"

Nobburt did as ordered, but try as he might, he couldn't smell a thing. There was something in the flagon, but whatever it was gave off nothing fragrant, nothing rank, no hint of odour whatsoever. He shook his head.

"Good, good." At least the master was satisfied. "Now toss it over!"

The young fellow almost dropped the vessel when he looked up. The old man now stood there stark naked in the drizzle, save for a loincloth. His cowl had joined the boots on the rocky ground.

"Uh-oh..." Nobburt backed up a step and bumped into his fellow sufferer.

"What are you waiting for?" snapped their master, reduced to skin and bone and the bare minimum amount of decency. "We haven't got all day!"

Nobburt swallowed his trepidation, shoved a foot forward and held out the vial.

"You deaf? I said *stay away*, and *throw* it!"

"Throw it, yes…" Relief spilled across the apprentice's face. He backed away and hurled the damn thing over to his master.

"Now the bell!"

This time, Flix had a rummage in his backpack. He uncovered a hand-sized bell-shaped item and pulled it out, a neat little thing made of solid polished brass with all kinds of incised squiggly ornaments and a beautifully carved wooden handle. Curious as he was, he turned it over in his hand, and was surprised to find it didn't make a sound. Flix held it up to investigate whether the little clapper that made it ring had fallen off, but it was still intact. He gave it a slight jiggle. Nothing. He shook it some more. Same thing.

Watching him, Nobburt raised a brow.

"Don't play around, numbskulls. Get it over here! I'm freezing!" Most of Zarothaster's naked flesh was greased up by now, owing to the ointment he was spreading all over his body. The mystic looked sleek and shiny like a fish.

The bell travelled through the air and the master's greasy fingers almost fumbled the catch. But even then, the bell gave off not the faintest of sounds.

"Now hand me over one of those apples, and you" – he waved at Nobburt – "get me the pail."

Flix did as he was told, retrieving three apples and throwing one to his master. In joyful anticipation he rubbed the other two against his cowl. Whatever the mystic was up to with his apple, the rest were going to find their way into an empty stomach.

Nobburt, however, had trouble freeing the requested pail from his bundle. When he loosened the cord and opened the cloth, he found nothing in it, nothing at all, and yet there had been a bulky shape before the bundle was untied – and a weight to it, as he could attest to, after having lugged it up a whole mountain.

"It's see-through, dolt!" The glistening mystic cackled. "Can't you see that?"

Nobburt threw the old codger a sheepish look, then stuck out his hand to grab whatever it was and, after all, there *was* something. He felt around it. The invisible thing had a flat bottom and sides, an opening at the top and even a curved handle, very much the definition of... a bucket. Chances were, it *was* a bucket, only that it didn't look like one.

"Well?" demanded Zarothaster, impatience driving a wedge into his ruffled brow.

"Er... coming!" Nobburt quickly realized that it was going to be difficult to throw an invisible pail, and so he mounted the pail-shaped piece of nothing on the mystic's staff and held it out to him.

"There we go." The mystic accepted the load and unfastened it. Then he stood for a moment in his nakedness with his collection of objects as if to launch into a big speech, but it turned out to be a short one.

"And thus," spoke Zarothaster, "I declare that pigs can fly."

That said, he pivoted on his heel to face the looming cliff. The rock face, for its part, received the scrawny geezer unfazed.

The oiled mystic slipped the bucket with the visibility issue over his head and raised his arms – the inoperable bell in one hand and the apple in the other – presenting the items to the mountain as one might hold out an offering. However, no offering was taken, and when the figure in front of the cliff went on to awkwardly hug the stone-cold surface, the show of affection remained unrequited. From a few steps farther back, it all looked like a solid nutcase on display.

"Don't wait for me," the master's muffled voice rang from behind the invisible bucket. "I might be away for a bit. Should I miss dinner, consult my journal. May it be signpost and pathway for generations to come." Which was about as vague as it could get.

Zarothaster stood perfectly still for a time, and then a little while longer, and after that he stood for some extra time doing the same thing: nothing much.

Flix leaned over to Nobburt. "He's waiting for the stars," he muttered unctuously in his ear. "They're not aligned with his delusions yet."

"Hmm…" Under his odd headgear the mystic raised his chin against the overhanging monolith. "Maybe… just maybe I was—"

A blaring racket crashed through the mystic's musings. *KNNNNNR-rrrrkkNNN-k-k-k-k-CHRRRRR*

It was a peculiar kind of noise, something between a crunch and a groan, both of massive proportions. It was twisted and haunting, as though the elements themselves were grinding against each other.

A blinding light burst from the foot of the cliff.

The two apprentices stood hypnotized, straight as yardsticks. The world juddered, and a moment later they found themselves riveted to the ground.

A whooshing of waves amid a rooster's cock-a-doodle-dooing joined the din. Colourful lights danced around them.

Wisps of smoke curled up and evaporated. Even the sky, as if inspired by all the sudden excitement, decided to transmogrify its bleakness into a happy-go-lucky light blue with a couple of fleecy clouds sprinkled in. Bereft of the opportune conditions to work under, the drizzle ceased. The crunching and groaning peaked, then ebbed away into a spectral silence, taking the lights, the smoke, the juddering and whatever other strange sounds were left with them.

The great Zarothaster was nowhere to be seen.

His two apprentices, pale as milk, remained. They stood there for some time, like statues on a day out, not budging an inch. Strangled noises struggled up their throats. Birds began to chirp. Wind whistled. A ray of sun crept over their features. Flowers bloomed within seconds on the wayside. Or it looked like it, now that the sun was out again. It was all mighty irregular.

"What was *that* all about?" Nobburt found his voice after all. He pushed his hood back.

"Search me." The other one did the same. One eye still fixed at the foot of the cliff, Flix risked a furtive side glance at his colleague with the other. A thousand and one questions fired through their minds.

"Strange, huh?" Nobburt finally produced in a low voice. "No druid circle, no pentagram, no fairy ring. Just a stupid piece of granite." For a moment, a feeling stole over him as if the stone had wavered and wobbled, just a tiny wee bit. But then he pulled himself together, and once he stood up straight, the rock stood straight too – as straight as was to be expected from a leaning rock. After a pause, he said: "Did you hear some cock-a-doodle-dooing too?"

"People do the strangest things in the face of death," Flix replied, not missing a beat.

"You think…? I mean… could it be that—"

"Spontaneous human combustion."

Nobburt made a face. "Didn't *look* like combustion to me."

"Ever *seen* spontaneous human combustion, Nobby?"

"N-no. Never seen an animal combust either. Or—"

"It's a thing," Flix said confidently. "People combust. It happens. I've read about it. Nobody knows why." He leaned a bit forward from where he stood, careful not to step inside the perimeter where his master had copped out of existence. His gaze swept the area. There was no mystic anymore, no bell, no apple. Probably no invisible bucket either – but really, who could say?

"Don't see no ashes," Nobburt argued.

"*Magical* combustion then."

"But… a mystic is no mage," Nobburt pointed out. If there was one thing he had learned in his apprenticeship, it was that mystics didn't do any spellcasting. He knew that for a fact now. His "career" as a mage-in-the-making had started off with an embarrassing mix-up.

"Well, call it *mystic* combustion then." Flix scratched his cheeks.

"But… but… why would a mystic combust? Why any human?"

"Happens to big thinkers." Flix clicked his tongue. "Because they… *over*think."

"I don't know. The master had lots of madcap ideas, but—"

"Here's a question. Can you *see* a thought?"

"Er… No. Why?"

"Has to be gaseous, then, a thought. It's none of the other elements, for sure. It's not earth, not fire, not water. Has to be wind."

"Hmm… Maybe. What of it?"

"I'll tell you what I think. Rather than going the way of nature through the other end, clearing the system, crazy wise men hoard their ideas. They dwell on them. For ages." A knowing smile spread over Flix's face. "Big mistake. Makes them more susceptible to combustion, that's what I say. One spark of an idea, and… *boom!* It ends up spontaneous, but it's been a long time in the making."

"Wow," said Nobburt. "That's… that's deep."

They stood for a bit longer in solemn memory, after which they ate the remaining apples. None of them had any taste.

Nobburt blinked. "The old codger couldn't even buy decent fruit!"

Zarothaster was a no-show at dinner too. When, as instructed, Flix and Nobburt had resorted to consulting his journal, the runes filling the page proved indecipherable to them. Maybe it was their master's way of telling his apprentices that they should have done their homework.

After a month or two had passed, Flix and Nobburt gave up hope altogether. By then, their master had missed more dinners than was good for him, and his behaviour didn't bear well on his profession in his apprentices' minds. Which is why they arrived at the decision that mysticism wasn't for them. It did away with people. So they sold the old man's unusual bequest to the highest bidder and looked for work elsewhere. Flix became a wainwright, and Nobburt went into carpentry. They always made sure to let their ideas out, one way or another.

In the centuries that followed, Zarothaster's notes changed hands numerous times – from mystics to sages, to wizards and witches, to curiosity dealers and even the odd commoner oblivious to the bundle's contents. Among other things, the leatherbound journal got drenched in the Feynoost Floods of 841, almost burned in the Great Calamity of Cape Colt in 902 and at some point was locked away by a concerned cleric, who suspected a Netherworldly origin. He claimed that was suggested already by that horned strange-eyed creature drawn on page one, followed up by a three-legged rooster. The writings were also declared heretic, deceptive, dangerous, banned and confiscated and locked in a vault. The book was stolen, though more by accident than intent, and sold at a junk sale to a taxidermist looking for inspiration to make a change work-wise. However, the three-legged rooster he put together following the template didn't sell.

Eventually, however, the tome's value was recognized again, and the book wound up in the halls of the Zarrafandan royal library, where – many years later – a prince who for all intents and purposes was a king, once dug it out when looking for a goodnight story with a difference. And this was definitely that. It was weird all around, with strange pictures and odd runes. As he could read none of it, he mostly used it as a paperweight.

It was last seen in the bed chamber of a certain east wing tower.

CHAPTER 17

Fate for Fellowship

B ormph peeked over the gnome's shoulder.

"So they found each other, the Toaster's memoirs and that fancy pin? Who would have thought?" An undercurrent of scepticism ran through the dwarf's grumbling. He rummaged in his beard, found a chin, and scratched it for emphasis. "Like, what's their names? Romiet and Huelio? Artifact romance, huh?"

"Shhhh…"

A snarl issued from the armchair, in whose sanctity the gnome was poring over the book. His head had cleared almost instantly with the discoveries they'd made. Though he had also become more irritable.

Thimble poked his head over the armrest and after about two seconds of patience, started badgering: "What's it say? What's it say? Does it say anything? It's got to say *some*thing."

The book didn't say anything out loud, and Tsynnslin said just as much. All the gnome did was chew on the stem of his pipe and ogle the yellow pages from top to bottom. He turned one rustling leaf after another, smoke billowing overhead as if his brain was smouldering under the pressures imposed by the book's contents.

It was fascinating enough for Thimble just to watch though. Because when the gnome shifted, and the book with him, and the angle was just about right, all he saw was Tsynnslin staring into his empty lap. Wherever it was that the book hid, it did it thoroughly. And then he'd tilt his head, and the edges of the thing would come back into view as if rising from an unseen pool, and there would be the gnome reading the book again. Or trying to.

"*Shmodork!*" Tsynnslin snapped the tome shut and it slipped from his hand onto the carpet with a hollow *thomp*. Dust plumes swirled about. "And here I was, thinking an artifact as powerful as the fabled *O'neyricon* would hold a clue. Any clue. Signpost and pathway..." He flapped his hand dismissively. "Whatever."

Bormph peered at him. "What was that you mumbled there? And why's the memoir thing got its own name?"

"Signpost and pathway," the gnome repeated, as listlessly as before. "Zarothaster's oh-so-famous last words. For whatever it's worth. And never mind the book's name. Guess any artifact has to sound like something, or the mystery would go away." He heaved a sigh. "The great, all-mysterious *O'neyricon!* All those stories I've heard about it, and the thing just drops into my lap. And what treasure does it hold? Nothing but the scribblings of a madman!"

"A madman! You can say that again," Whinewaeyn agreed, creaking back and forth on his rocking chair, a glance away. "But don't bother, I just did." He had joined the gnome looking at the pages for a bit, and now he flashed him a commiserative smile. "If only your mystic friend had written his gobbledygook in the Common Tongue like anybody else. But no, he had to do it in ancient runes and crabbed script for the heck of it. The way it is, you get a headache deciphering it, and then find out it's *still* gobbledygook. And what about that hideous looking cow at the front? The guy sure wasn't much of an artist either."

Tsynnslin cocked up both of his heads, gnome and bear. "The *runes*, wizard? What do you know about them?" A glint broke into his empty-eyed stare. "Don't tell me you can actually read any of it?"

"Why, it's the tongue of the Forgotten, to be sure. You must have figured *that* one out. No? Not in the mystic curriculum?" Whinewaeyn seemed surprised himself that he, who regularly drew a blank when it came to remembering things, recalled the tongue of the Forgotten. "A while back all the scholars used to write that way. Well, the archmages did. The ones with more secrets than the rest. They wrote in Forgotten, so that no ordinary man, mage or minor mortal, would get a whiff of it. T'was a thing. Until the thing became too much of a hassle, 'specially for students and such. But before the hassle it was a thing. Forgotten is ancient, you know. Arcane. Altogether alien compared to today's Common Tongue." He paused for a moment as if he had hit on something profound. "Forgotten's a whole lot of things starting with 'A', come to think of it…" And there went that train of thought. The wizard looked about, bemused for a moment, until Thimble tugged at his sleeve.

"So… what's the deal with them?"

"With whom?" Whinewaeyn's brow puckered.

"With these… Forgotten?"

"Ah, yes. Well, little one, nobody knows what their deal is, that's just it. Nobody can say who they were. Or when. Hence, they're called the Forgotten, because there's not much around to remember them by." His eyes narrowed.

"Tell you what, these days their runes are only good for answering a question or two at the Archmagus exam. If you haven't forgotten to study them."

Tsynnslin dragged the mage's rocking chair closer. "How about we work this out together then, wizard?"

"The gobbledygook?"

"What else?"

"But it's abstruse!" Whinewaeyn insisted. "Heady stuff. Crusted like Feynoost spirit. Written by a man who's as mad as a box of frogs! You said so yourself."

"Well, yes, but that was before I knew this *could* be read."

"And I told you after I'd read some of it. On balance, box of frogs."

"It's all we've got." The gnome dusted the tome off and flipped it open again. Then he tamped tobacco into the bowl of his pipe, clamped it between his teeth and relit it. "Nothing regular going on these days," he said. "Maybe a little madness is precisely what we need."

While Whinewaeyn and Tsynnslin muttered to themselves – the one translating, the other trying to make some sense of it – Bormph clomped over to the sleepy-eyed barbarian. The big fellow was still under the impression that "Toaster runes" meant "toasted prunes" and was wondering why there was so much fuss about a cookbook.

Bormph filled him in. "Nah, it's one of them gnome artifacts. It pretends not to be what it looks like."

Ramrok cocked his head at the book, which was sitting upright in the gnome's lap.

"The prick-eared one says she saw it disappear once. Partway. And then it came back."

"No way," boomed Ramrok.

"Shhh!" came from behind the book.

Bormph hunched his shoulders and lowered his voice. "But *right now,* it doesn't want to. It only disappears when it likes."

"You have to look at it the right way," Thimble whispered. "Like so." He leaned back, forward, sideways, aiming for the sweet spot, but couldn't find it.

"You sure it's not the *wrong* way?" Bormph imitated Thimble's contortions, with less elegance, and about the same success.

"Shhhhhhh!"

The three of them stood quiet for a moment.

"Do that thing with... that thing of yours," Bormph rasped at Amjelle, who stood watching.

She gave him a look, but brought out her rod of Novotroth nevertheless. She held it against the back of the book first, discreetly, so as not to disturb the gnome, then against the scarab pin. Each time the light in the gem didn't bother even to flicker before capitulating – it was ripped away immediately. Once removed from their adverse influence, the jewel's pristine whiteness returned.

"See? And this one" – Bormph held up the hairpin – "is even loopier. Look, big one. It can do tricks!"

Ramrok pushed up his helmet, drew up his chin and squinted at it. He watched as Bormph flung the pin straight down at the floor and the scarab-shaped piece bounced off it like a rubber ball, somersaulting wildly before Bormph reclaimed it. Next, he threw it against the wall, and from there it arced back into the dwarf's hands without so much as a clack, a clink or a tinkle.

Bormph looked up at the barbarian triumphantly. "*Looks* like a pin. But... it isn't."

Bewilderment drew some funny lines in the big one's features. "No?"

"No. It jumps around like a grasshopper."

"And when it's supposed to make sounds, it doesn't," Thimble chipped in.

"What it be?"

"Weird."

"Weird?" Ramrok turned the thing over in his extra-large fingers.

"Oh," Bormph added, "and it has a thing for the book, would you believe that? The story goes that they took a tower and our elf and went on their honeymoon – or something like that."

A snigger emerged from the mighty warrior, developed into a chortle and then swelled into a force of its own that shook the barbarian from helmet to toe. He threw back his head, roaring. Bormph and Thimble were quick to back off from the thigh-slapping guffawing beast, mindful of the sharp sword dangling from the big fellow's convulsing side.

"Elf!" Tsynnslin's gritty voice cut through the smoke cloud. "Take that thing away from these scallywags!"

The gnome's face, surfacing from under the bear head looked so serious that Sylthia reached out immediately to snatch the bouncing hairpin mid-spin from the fascinated barbarian.

"It's a unique artifact," the gnome said in a tone that demanded attention. "Powerful like no other. Chances are that this is the reason your aura is tainted, just because you touched it. Keep it safe and, most importantly, keep it away from me – or it might affect me too. We know too little about it yet, but we're learning a thing or two from the journal. Like that Zarothaster was a collector too."

"Of what?" Bormph said. "Disappearing books? Hopping pins? What's it with you mystics squirreling away all the strange stuff?"

The gnome tapped at a rune-laden paragraph with one of his claws. "Zarothaster wanted to connect the dots. Isn't it so, wizard?" As Tsynnslin turned a page, Whinewaeyn gave a languid shrug in sagely ignorance and sat back for a rock in his chair. "Zarothaster sought all kinds of things that were, for lack of a better word, *faulty*."

Whinewaeyn stopped rocking and brought down a shaky finger to retrace a few runes. "Faulty *as such*," he stressed.

"Faulty as such?" Bormph gave the wizard a sidelong glance.

"Faulty as such." Whinewaeyn restated.

"That's what the nutcase writes?"

Tsynnslin nodded. "That's what the wizard translates."

"Oh, I'm just the middleman here." Whinewaeyn drew his head back and turned his palms. "From nutcase to gnome."

"How can pins and books be faulty… as such?" asked Thimble.

"In that they're pins and books, and yet somehow they aren't," Tsynnslin said enigmatically, peeking over the book's frame.

"The pin's plain wrong," Bormph said. "That's what's not right with it." He gave it a wary eye. "By old Stroppy Shumgulth's Swiftslammer! And the Toaster must have jinxed that book!"

"Just let's suppose he hasn't," Tsynnslin said. "Nor that anyone else has. That's where things get interesting."

Glances turned towards the gnome, expecting further support for his assertion, but none came. He only brought the pages of the tome together, this time with a slow, solemn gesture of finality that kept the century-old dust at bay.

"Time to move on," he declared and slid from his seat, stowing the tome under his arm.

Bormph watched the gnome's resolve with suspicion. "Where are we going? Are we any wiser on that vortex-temple-forge-nobody-has-any-idea big mystery place of yours? Any word on it in the Toaster's memoirs?"

"Aye. He mentions not only a path, but also an important detail relating to the place itself. Isn't that so, wizard?"

Whinewaeyn's head bobbed vaguely.

"What detail's that?" urged Bormph.

"Says it's faulty as such, too."

"What? The whole place? My foot!"

Tsynnslin turned to the mage for clarification.

"A 'dent in creation'. According to this, er, Zaro…roaster guy," Whinewaeyn declared in a diplomatic monotone.

"A dent in creation?" Amjelle, in the back, was preparing more bandages for Whinewaeyn, just in case. But she couldn't let that one go. "Haven't you skipped a few lines or something? How could it be that the gods…?"

"Well," the gnome said, "nobody's perfect. If the gods abide by their own principles they can't be perfect either."

Amjelle glared at him.

"Here's an idea…" Bormph said, rubbing his forehead as if to wring an all-explanatory thought from his mind. "Say, does your journal mention the Toaster having a penchant for smoking weed? Rather strong stuff? And… a lot of it?"

Not long afterwards, the party slipped out into the night.

Aside from their torches, they also brought with them a glimmer of hope – in an anthill of unknowns. Maybe, with a little luck, they'd find it after all, that elusive site, and what was wrong with it and the world in general. Maybe the apocalypse would be averted by breakfast. That's how Thimble's mind worked anyway.

The hour was early, or late, depending on how one looked at it, the journey eerie. The probing chilly fingers of a predawn breeze tugged at their shapes as they picked their path around the mountain. What scant moonlight there was silvered the hillsides and the peaks rearing up above them, but merely hinted at travel options through the craggy labyrinth shrouded with gloom and fraught with dangers. Where the darkness weighed less heavily on the stone, swaths of fog crept about like sluggish ghosts sprawled out for a post-midnight moon bath. Even the few lights they held up to choke back the eeriness rather added to it. From afar they must have made a curious sight, like will-o'-the-wisps on a family trip.

Huge boulders drifted by. Obscure stone formations. A grandfather clock leaning against a rock face. A balcony turned upside down. The usual suspects. Once in a while, a lonesome garden gnome sat perched on a precipice or peered from behind a tree trunk at the wayside, lost in secret garden gnome thoughts.

"Are we looking for something like… this?" Amjelle gestured at what her rod had picked up. In the outer fringes of the light beam it cast, a triangular stone structure had taken shape. It was a bit uneven in places, but still recognizable as a man-made pyramid. The party crowded around it.

"Aye…" Tsynnslin stooped to inspect it. "A cairn! A waymarker. This must signify the ancient trail Zarothaster followed."

He scanned the surrounding area with his torch, scampered away, scampered back, consulted the journal and listened to the mage's translation to find his bearings. Then he was off again, in another direction.

"This way!" he called out after a time.

Some distance later, they passed another cairn and steered their way towards a path that wound alongside a steep drop-off. It was a narrow trail, and the blackness at their side grew by the minute the higher they climbed, until it reached frightening proportions.

About halfway through the ascent, Whinewaeyn called out for the gnome, who was way ahead.

Tsynnslin stopped for a breather when called, but his impatience was showing. "What is it, wizard?"

"You hasten as though you have a date with destiny," Whinewaeyn said. "Perhaps that's what your mystic thought as well, and then he was never heard of again."

The gnome's bear-clawed hand drummed on the pommel of his umbrella as he waited for the others to catch up. His goateed chin lifted and he looked down the path at the mage. "We all must be here in this world for a reason, no? Why are you asking, wizard?"

"Just so. Big things ahead and everything."

"We mystics *know* our place." The gnome never so much as blinked. "We're not privy to eternal knowledge. Our thoughts can merely scratch the surface. And yet, I'm certain there are no accidents. Too many things point towards the same conclusion. We have to play the role we've been assigned, Zarothaster his, and I mine."

"Mystics, eh?" Whinewaeyn gave him a queer look.

"There are rules behind everything. Unseen laws." Tsynnslin's voice rose and fell, battered by the wind. He got moving again to escape the chill, and Whinewaeyn started after him. "But are we aware of all the rules? *All* of them? No. How could we?" the gnome continued as he ascended, from time to time turning back to the wizard. "It's as the halfling said. Like with the gears operating the Grand Weaverring Clock Tower. If you knew all the rules, and I mean *all* of them, how everything fits together, you could predict the way of the world, couldn't you? And what's the way of the world if it's not... fate?"

"But," Whinewaeyn interjected vociferously, "wouldn't that make us mere playthings of the gods? Pieces in a game? Like that one with a king and a queen, and all those rooks, bishops, horses and peasants? It would be the gods playing, not us."

"Ah, I envy you spellweavers, clerics and the like. You never see the whole."

The wind howled around their ears.

"What hole?" Whinewaeyn puffed.

Tsynnslin stood for a moment. "Well. Maybe the time has come. Maybe I ought to share something with you, before it's too late."

The gnome took the final footsteps towards the clifftop, where a gathering of bizarrely shaped rocks marked the beginning of a trail leading over a ridge. Dawn was already spilling over the rim of the world by then, even if it was the strangest sunup any of them had ever seen; the breaking day wasn't sure yet what colour to wear and was still going through its recently acquired wardrobe.

"The world… it's a strange thing, friends," Tsynnslin began when the rest arrived and clustered around him. "So very little do we know. But now that the world is unravelling, the truth about its make-up must come out. The world…" Everybody's gaze drifted with him over the patchwork of heaths, copses, marshlands and mountains spread out toward the horizon. "*This* world… is not what it appears to be."

"Looks like a mess to me," Bormph said hotly. "How's it looking to you?"

The gnome ignored him. "Let me tell you the story of the first mystic word." A long dramatic pause followed, but its impact was lost on the non-mystics, at least for now. "You see, the word was discovered centuries ago, according to legend, by someone as simple as a swineherd. It wasn't a sage who stumbled across it, no person of import, nor anyone gifted. It happened to a swineherd… by accident, in a fevered dream, they say."

"So a swineherd sniffled and snorted," Bormph grunted, "and ever since all mystics have worshipped sniffling and snorting? Do I get this right?"

"Not quite. You should know that the swineherd came upon a word of creation."

"Ha! That makes you a wizard!" Whinewaeyn cried out. "I *knew* it!"

"A mystic word is no magic word," the gnome reminded him.

"Mystic, magic, potato, tomato, cucumber, turnip…" The wizard's argument had started out fine, but veered a bit off-track.

"Mark the difference…" The gnome held a hand up in the air, fingers spread out. He uttered a loose mumble of consonants that sounded distinctly unlike anything an Academy-trained mage would say. But it sure had an effect. There was a *ding*, quickly buried by a crashing sound on the stone nearby, just a couple of feet away.

Everybody flinched; only the gnome remained perfectly still. Bits and pieces of shattered porcelain flew outward in all directions, including a tiny ornate handle.

Thimble eyes had widened to button size. "What was *that?*"

Ramrok cautiously tapped one of the pieces with his toe.

"The first mystic word. Also the word that was the troll's demise," the gnome said. "*K-rn-tk-prt,*" he repeated, and as he did, there was a *ding* again.

This time they all saw it: an entire teapot, suspended in mid-air. Briefly, at least. It popped out of nowhere and when it found no support, came plummeting down. Unattended plummeting teapots have a habit of hitting the ground and bursting, and the freshly conjured teapot demonstrated the process. Fragments spilled out in a star-like pattern around it.

"*K-rn-tk-prt*, eh?" Whinewaeyn said, as if it wasn't a big deal. "So what? You can make teapots out of thin air with fancy words!"

That's what he wanted to say anyway. But as soon as the bizarre word left his mouth, he was interrupted by a *ding!* Another teapot crashed onto the stone floor next to him.

Tsynnslin's eyes connected with the wizard's. "You have just witnessed one of the world's most well-kept secrets."

Several jaws hung open. Brains were visibly struggling. Whinewaeyn's face twisted. He stared at the porcelain carnage.

"*K-rn-tk-prt?*" It was Thimble's turn now. He held out his arm, though, just in case… And sure enough, another teapot slipped into existence and dropped right into his open hand. He caught it, stared at it, let his thumb brush over the smooth surface. Then he wrapped his fingers around the handle and knocked on it. It gave off a light, hollow, teapot-ish sound. It was a teapot, alright. For an absurd instant, Thimble envisaged himself on stage, performing. With a trick like this, he could pretend to be a mage. Or a mystic, whatever. A mini-mystic. But… would it still be a trick if just anyone could do it? Why *could* just anyone do it?

At his side, Bormph shifted his weight, but whatever position he tried, the dwarf was no more comfortable with a universe full of surprises. Dwarves and magic don't go together, and mysticism wasn't his cup of tea either. Nor was it his teapot.

"What other silly schemes are you mystics hatching in the backs of your caves, gnome?" Bormph growled through his beard. "Flying saucers? You one of those roundworlders? Speak!"

"Don't be daft, dwarf." Tsynnslin made a swatting motion. "How on earth could the world be round? You'd slip right off! It's a slab, floating in the spheres."

"Who says it's not a pancake?" Bormph contested. "With a crust? To keep the oceans in."

Meanwhile, Sylthia had squatted down to examine the mess. "How's this possible? This cannot be." She was looking at the individual pieces from all sides.

"The swineherd must have hit upon a name behind names," the gnome said. "A name that's not of our own making. Speak it, and you will create. The Creators must have devised it."

Sylthia brushed a wayward strand of hair behind her ear and glanced up at Amjelle, who was turning Thimble's still unscathed mystic creation in her hand. Judging from the healer's tense face, she was busy reconciling pop-up crockery with her faith in the One and the Other and all those Other Ones, and neither the One or any of the Others had mentioned anything about teapots in the scriptures.

The elf got up again. "Elves are no strangers to true names. And some of our tribes believe in nothing but them – *elven*-crafted names, that is – for people and things too, names they settle on after years and years, names into which they weave their elven magic, to find the spirit within. It's a sacred process. But this" – she looked about – "is like a true name from the outset."

"Yeah, from the time before vowels were invented," Bormph chipped in.

"The world… it's a strange thing," the gnome repeated, the way he had set out. "Ever since the incident, mystics from all over have sought to uncover more of these words – and while they had only limited success, there was some. I guess what we can all agree upon is that everything there is must have begun somewhere…" Tsynnslin looked more like a sage all of a sudden, although a sage who had run out of clothing options. "Creation, aura, the spirit of life…. fate, even… It must all draw from the same well." His gaze shifted from face to face. "A well that lies somewhere ahead."

There was something memorable about a bear-wearing gnome on a mountaintop silhouetted against a greenish sky unpacking something profound. More so, when it involved crockery.

"But… but…" Amjelle stammered, her head swimming.

"You've got to have trust," Tsynnslin said. "The answers are out there. You're a woman of faith, aren't you?"

"Trust in what?" Amjelle reacted somewhat indignant. "In erring gods? In fate working us like a machine? In the world's flatness? What is it now?"

Tsynnslin pressed his lips together and said nothing further. His eyes were already lingering on the ridge ahead. In the distance he'd spotted a gnome, and next to it another one, and then one more.

"If you're looking for a word," Bormph quipped, "try *shmodork*."

Back in Dimmerskeep.

The notoriously unshakable Shady Shoo for once seemed a shade shaken. His grip on the wrinkled hand he was holding tightened, for fear that the woman it belonged to might not be around much longer. She was ancient, blind, weak, confused – and also his last hope to complete his mission.

"Bertha," he croaked. "Let's try again. One last time."

Shady Shoo was at his wit's end. He had called on every professional clairvoyant and self-proclaimed soothsayer in town, and not one of them had been able to get a glance behind the end. In fact, there was agreement among any number of prophets that after the end of ends, things were over. That was the bad news. The good news was that no seer saw that particular end coming. The caveat: the good news wasn't worth much. The idea of an ultimate end wasn't compatible with the scrying business, and that's what it was, after all: a business.

He had already come to his own conclusion before the ground started shaking, before the clefts had opened up all over the place and trees split in half and caught aflame. Among other things, Shoo had seen a woman bolt down the streets, tearing her hair out, shrilling that her husband had vanished before her very eyes! Gone! All his clothes too, right off the washing line! And the closet he had made with his own hands, and the roof too![*]

He almost couldn't believe how life-changing all this puzzlement had turned out to be for those who should have had seen it coming. One prophet was found in his attic, dangling from a noose. Talk about life-changing! Another, Trustworthy Trudy, recanted all her prior predictions and at the last minute embraced elven Dreamerism, putting her hopes in the possibilities the Big Dream offered. And then there was Know-It-All Cybill who, once faced with the prospect of Judgment Day, confessed that she used to "borrow" all her accurate divinations from Blind Bertha.

Blind and frail, but always reliable, Bertha.

"Bertha!" Shady Shoo shook her by the shoulders.

She answered with a groan. "What is it? You think I'm deaf? I can hear you whisp'ring loud 'n clear!"

"What d'ya see, woman? Ya see sumthin' *after?*"

"All I can see is… the way things were." Bertha's words were wrapped in rattles. "That's all. That's all there is to see."

"Nothing else?"

"Haven't you washed your ears?"

"But… Normi says he sees the comet comin'. Ya see the comet? Comin'?"

---

[*] It's not altogether unheard of for husbands to disappear. It's called "moving out." Now, a husband moving out and taking his clothes with him is one thing. If the roof feels compelled to join him, something's probably afoot.

"The comet, aye," Bertha wheezed. "Of course I see it." She writhed in her bed, then lay quiet for a while, as if receiving a vision. "There it goes… big, big explosion… and now it's gone. As is… everything else."

Shady Shoo gulped. He had no doubt that she'd seen it. "And then?"

"I see old Snoggle's house…" Bertha's shallow breath grew even fainter. "You remember old Snoggle's house, Shoo?"

"Yeh? The one what crumbled, eh?"

"Big, big house… And there's Snoggle too, Shoo!"

Well, so much for that. They had buried the old man last week when his dilapidated home had collapsed on him. Nothing left for a seer to see, thought Shoo. Nothing but the past. This is it. This *was* it. In an upside-down world, even the seers were getting it backwards.

"Will you take me with you now?"

Something changed within the blackness of Shady Shoo's cowl, where rumour has it that he harboured an expression. "Bertha! Don't ya recognize me anymore?" He was used to these kinds of mix-ups. People often took him for the Grim Reaper – not an entirely unfounded assumption, considering his line of work. But right now, a tear welled up in his eye.

"Who do *you* think you are?" Bertha threw back at him. "You're Shoo, Shoo! Who else would you be? I've known you since you were soiling your diapers! And you're still a featherhead if ever there was one!" She coughed for a while then heaved a wretched sigh. "I was talking about my morning stroll. Now, will you take me out or what?"

Apprehension glinted in Shoo's cowl-sheltered eyes. He wiped away that tear. "C'mon then," he grunted and scrambled to help the seer up. "Now where've ya put yer slippers?"

A strange stillness lay over Hanging Rock.

The place hadn't seen visitors for ages now. Not proper ones like little men chanting, invoking spirits, sacrificing animals and offering choice gifts, that sort of thing. Little men were funny that way. There was no end to their inventiveness.

Quite a few had tried to climb the cliff and then fallen to their deaths. Once, a few pentagram-drawing greyrobes had summoned a ten-foot demon to give the stone a sound thrashing. Alas, to their detriment, the stone couldn't be bothered to react, and so the creature had to vent its frustrations on its summoners instead. It had been a riot! Blood sacrifice with added entertainment value. And every few years, fresh visitors used to call on the oversized stone for variations of such untimely demises, which they – one way or another – inflicted upon themselves.

As of late, however, things had been quiet. Until very recently, in fact, when the first tiny clay fellow put in an appearance. Although he looked like a little man – a very little little man with a pointy hat – he made no signs of acting like one. Because he was such a quiet lad and didn't do much aside from keeping the rock company, none of the usual irritation ensued: no chanting, no demons, no bloodshed. Then friends of the little fellow arrived, and his friends brought their friends, and the friends brought things with them, and if they hadn't all been so hushed and dawdling, one might have called it a party.

Now, a lump of rock, whatever the size, has no frame of reference for garden parties. Let alone garden gnome parties.

Hanging Rock wouldn't have known if the gnomes had contacts in higher places. Or low ones. And it could've gone either way, for at the same time the gnomes began appearing the sky opted to drape itself in the weirdest of colours, and the rock's home turf occasionally roared from below. That seemed to get things really started. Over time, shiploads more of the little clay visitors arrived, with all kinds of stuff in tow.

Throughout all that, Hanging Rock remained composed. More leaning forward than laid back, as was its nature. Stone-stiff.

But when nobody was looking, it flickered. Just once every couple of years.

Da-cling! Da-clong!

The sounds of a halfling shuffling through a sea of shards echoed off the mountainsides. Thimble was dead on his feet, and the fact that he had to thread his way through a huddle of rickety figurines didn't make walking any easier. More and more, he also felt the knot in his stomach tighten and his heartbeat thump in his ears. Who knew what they would find up here?

Ahead, he heard Snowflake and Tsynnslin make their own set of sounds, the cub traipsing in front with the boldness of a polar bear who had survived a desert adventure, the nosy gnome following shortly after. Farther back, much less subtle noises announced wizard, dwarf and barbarian, drowning out more delicate female feet that brought up the rear.

Cling-ding. Da-clang-cling.

Maybe there was a trail buried somewhere deep down beneath the junk they were treading on, but if there was, it now lay submerged under thousands and thousands of figurines – or pieces of them. Apparently, early retirement for garden gnomes was nothing to look forward to. Instead of enjoying their mountain resort, they lay higgledy-piggledy in bits and pieces and got trampled on. Only a few pointy hats in blazing colours jutted up in the right direction.

Clong-dong, cling-da-clong. Cling-a-ding, ding-a-cling.

A few stray sun rays reached over from the horizon, glistening off the piles, shining through swaths of listless mist that curled around gnomes and travellers alike. Quietly, imperceptibly, dawn slipped in a pinkish twilight gown, with hints of bilious green woven in – a firm reminder that the past day's colourful escapades were not yet out of fashion. No silver lining showed through, only a prominent grey that entered the picture at long last in the shape of a cliff.

It reared up against the breaking day, marking the end of the clay road. Droves of gnomes undulated from it back into the shard sea, as if the tiny fellows had tried to scale the obstacle but failed in the attempt.

As the noise of footfalls on clay fragments petered out, Thimble cobbled together a quick diary entry in his mind. *Dear diary,* it went. *This is it, I guess. If you don't here from me anymore, then thats what it was. If you here from me again, I'll tell you all about it later.* He ended with, *Be S. Wish me luck!* He didn't hear back, but expected as much, especially because he was too flustered to actually write any of it down.

"Now why am I not surprised?" Bormph jibed from about two feet away. "Another dead end. You doing this on purpose, gnome?"

Sylthia stepped forward and took the measure of the cliff with her eyes. "*Néash ác avín, cárpa ác naí.* What's an end to some, is a beginning to others. Maybe this is a beginning. One never knows in advance. If this is where our path leads us…"

"How about the beginning of a picnic, blondie? Roasted wyvern, anyone? We've still got some left, and we certainly aren't getting up there, are we? Dwarves don't do rock climbing." Bormph began scouring his backpack for food, but Tsynnslin pulled him to the side and put a finger to his lips.

"You hear that?" The gnome's hand cupped round his ear, pushing back a thick tuft of ear hair.

Everyone stood stock still to listen. A low, monotonous hum peeled off from the soft whistle of the morning breeze. A thrummy kind of hum. It came from everywhere and nowhere, lingering on the cusp of their hearing, as if the world was purring like an oversized snoozing pussycat. Other sounds mixed in the more they listened. Much closer, much more urgent. When their heads turned, they saw that Amjelle's rod had lit up of its own accord, spraying sparks and guttering like a flame braving an aggressive gust. At her side, the wizard's staff shuddered just as much. It shook notably more than it did usually when the geezer was on the move, which was especially suspect because the geezer holding it wasn't on the move at all.

Sylthia raised a cautious finger. "Look at that!"

Thick snowflakes mingled with the breeze and landed on hair, noses and cheeks.

"Careful…" Amjelle's eyes were alert and sweeping. A standard cleric's blessing broke from her lips, just in case. Maybe it had an effect, for her stave returned to a bright whiteness, and Whinewaeyn's staff steadied itself. It continued snowing, though. The pottery at their feet did nothing out of the ordinary, and no surprise attack was launched by the giant piece of rock either. Only the humming and thrumming went on, the shards of clay dancing with it. Necks cranked, blades glinted.

"Oi dee doi!" The gnome's voice sounded over the rubbing of his hands. "I'll have a poke around then, if you don't mind, lads. Cover my back in case anything happens, but stay where you are, *all* of you. We wouldn't want your artifact" – here he eyed Sylthia and especially her hairpin – "to interfere with whatever's going on up there. Not yet, at least."

The elf nodded, and the clay figurines ground and clinked against each other again as he made his way up the most prominent pile of gnomey mess. It became more of a struggle the higher up he went, with figurines rolling about under his feet and whatnot, but he scaled his way through, and went on to haul himself onto the safety of an upended balcony. Snowflake, always the adventurer, went scuttling after him on his own, although much slower, navigating the uncertain terrain with hesitant paws.

At the lower end of the gnome pile, the mood had tensed. Sylthia nocked an arrow, just in case. "You sure we shouldn't go up too, Am? He hasn't a single weapon on him!"

"You heard what he said. Stay put. He's got an umbrella and my blessing."

"And he has his fancy words," Thimble said, rocking on his toes. "He took on a troll with that."

"Sure, Curly…" Bormph's eyes didn't leave the gnome. "He'll probably talk the mountain out of whatever it's up to. Just you watch."

Thimble squinted up with bated breath. All that talk made him fumble for a weapon too, but it took him only a moment of sober reflection to recognize that brandishing a tiny dagger would do very little to protect him against a cliff. A slightly larger slingshot would be no great help either. But in the halfling's mind pulling out a slingshot was a start, and a start is half of the way, as his mummins always used to say. What worried Thimble was the bit after the start.

The gnome had inched closer to the rock face and was now studying it. No telltale dented outlines of a hidden doorway became apparent, no breach of any kind. Tsynnslin prodded the stone with his umbrella, knocked here and there as if to check the plumbing. Nothing happened. His pawed palm reached out, connected with the crude stone, felt its way along the rock's surface, when… more nothing went on happening. The stone wouldn't yield.

Getting more desperate, Tsynnslin jammed his hands into its cracks and attempted to climb, but soon gave up on the idea. He threw several vowel-lacking mystic words at the rock too, none of which impressed the granite wall so much that it divulged its secrets.

"Blargh! An axe is what he needs," Bormph rasped from further down. "Beats playing nice."

"Need any help?" Sylthia shouted up.

Tsynnslin didn't respond. He staggered back and, eyes still upturned, scoured the rest of the cliff for anything that might be a clue, when the monotonous droning deepened and grew in volume. Jitters rippled across the shard sea. The gnome looked around, but the only difference to a moment prior was that the cub had now joined him on his upturned balcony… and that the elf was waving at him from below. Also, the *O'neyricon*, the diary of the famous Zarothaster, was skipping about in his arms like a fresh-caught fish fighting for its life. Tsynnslin tried to grab the book tighter, with little success.

"It's the gnome!" it spouted out of Whinewaeyn all of a sudden from the foot of the gnome pile. "It must be him! *Him!*"

Bormph's eyes slid off Tsynnslin and his skipping book for a moment to check for signs of lapsing sanity in the wizard. It couldn't have been sunstroke with all those snowflakes dancing around. But the mage looked more focused than crazed, albeit a trifle uncoordinated, as he stared up fixedly and waved his arms about.

"I can sense it!" Whinewaeyn was squawking again, and fidgeting. "I sensed it back then, and I saw it, and now it *will* happen... Why, it must!"

Bormph's raised eyebrow found its equivalent in Amjelle's face on the other side of the old man.

"What are you yakking about, wizzer? You alright?"

Whinewaeyn swung round. "No, it's not *going* to happen! It happened *already!*"

"Huh?"

"Two sides of the same coin!" The wizard stammered some more, then his staff dug into the clay mountain and he pounced after the gnome like a scalded cat.

"Back!" he clamoured up, his voice cracking. "Baaack!"

The gnome didn't listen.

"Wizzer!" Bormph now called after Whinewaeyn himself. "What the—" He motioned to Thimble and Ramrok, and, befuddled as they were, the three of them advanced abreast, hot on the mage's heels. The old geezer had to have his reasons, so they'd better face the music together, whatever was playing.

The hum was still playing. Not exactly music, but now that it was intensifying, the vibrations pounded on their eardrums. A protracted scraping blended into the noise, and it kept returning in a weird steady rhythm, like the creaking of a giant invisible wheel.

KNNR-rrkNN-k-k-k-k-CHRR...

The overhang! It's tilting! Thimble thought as he was approaching the cliff, uneasily shifting his backpack from one shoulder to the other. *Nah!* he calmed himself down the next moment. *A lump of rock that size shouldn't... wouldn't... it just couldn't... move.* He decided that, if anything, it had to be a perspective thing.

KNNNNR-rrrkNNN-k-k-k-k-k-CHRRRR...

A few steps further Thimble's feet refused service. Rooted to the spot, he just kept staring: at the rock face, at the still scrambling Whinewaeyn, at Tsynnslin... The gnome now stood as stunned as he in the wake of the eruption of that awful noise. Beneath the gnome and the panicky polar bear on their balcony, the sea of shards was all a-jitter now, whirring and throbbing. The gnome crouched and held on to his platform.

"Get back!" Whinewaeyn's desperate shout mixed with the noise. "It's you! The end of the world! It must be... YOU! Can't you see?"

The rock face glistened, flickered, transformed.

The stone's sturdiness waned, and what once had been rock started to billow in parts, to rise and fall, ripple and roll like a mountain-wide sail battered by a gale. A mere giant ghost remained – a smooth, translucent canvas – and through the spooky, mystifying fabric shone...

Tsynnslin. Still crouching and holding on to his platform, the gnome blinked. It took him a moment to recognize that he was looking at... Tsynnslin.

His own reflection wobbled into life in front of him. The ever-shifting stony surface of the rock had morphed into a giant mirror, casting back what was thrown at it. In the contorting image, the gnome in a bearskin staring at the whole marvel was surrounded by a graveyard of garden gnomes piled up in heaps alongside large pieces of masonry and whatever further junk had chosen to undertake this unlikely journey. It was all there was. And yet, it couldn't be.

Still on his knees, Tsynnslin twisted around… and there they all were, plain as day, his companions – each one of them making their own way up the gnome mountain.

When he confronted the mirrored image again, there was… nothing. No wizard, no dwarf, no barbarian, no halfling, no healer, no elf. No cub either, and the bear was right next to him.

The gnome leaned in closer towards his own billowing reflection. What he saw was wrapped in a whitish haze roughly his shape and size, bearskin included. When he moved, the mirrored image moved with him, and the glow around the image wafted along with it. When he stood motionless, the image stuck closer to his side, swaying in and out of his frame, only little by little settling within the shape. And all that swaying and wafting, it wasn't just him; every single gnome at his feet was in on the reflection just as much as he was, figurine-shaped shreds of mist swirling about the rock face, merging into a vast vapoury gnome-soup.

"Could it be, Am?" Sylthia gasped at the foot of the gnome pile, eyes fixed on the spectacle. Were they seeing the same thing? The elf let her bow sink, and her thin lips moved on in wonder, speaking so low no actual words came out. "*Sá val'áy*," the elf repeated more loudly, holding on to the healer's arm. She shared a sidelong glance with her. "A… soul mirror?" The elf's eyes grew wider. Her fingers tightened around Amjelle's wrist. "There's an ancient elven myth about places hidden away in the Dream, places to catch a glimpse of one's true self and look behind the veil that clouds our senses. Places to see… *sá vál…*" Her eyes flicked back and met Amjelle's. "The soul…"

"The soul?" Amjelle squirmed. "How could it be? Whatever this is, it only shows a load of gnomes – and Tsynnslin!"

"It only proves that the gnome is right, Am! That we're… tainted somehow. We aren't there! Our souls…"

The thought sank in, and terror gripped them both. Holding on to each other, they fixed their gazes back on the spot where Tsynnslin had picked up probing the rock wall again – even if the wall currently seemed in serious denial about being one at all. But while it might have become more malleable, it was just as impenetrable as before.

A commotion erupted on the balcony.

The bear had spotted the gnome inside the mountain too. There was another one wearing a bear head! He turned tail, but found his path blocked by the real bear-wearing gnome, on account of which he backpedalled some more, this time in the other direction – towards the wall.

"Oi!" Tsynnslin yelled. The cub's back had half vanished into what had seemed an impassable mass only moments ago. "Oiiiiiiiii!" The gnome reached out to pull the cub back.

Something happened then.

An odd sensation coursed through him when he touched the bear. Something menacing. Something huge. Something impossible to place. His mind swirled. Elation bubbled up in him, and memories he thought long forgotten, shaded by a melancholy of sorts. His senses picked up the glimmer of a prospect, the bleakness of a shattered dream, all at once, and it came down on him like the weight of the world.

The air crackled. The gnome felt an odd kind of pull, as if the ethereal rock curtain was tugging on everything that had come to explore it. The cub slipped from his hands. It bowled over, rolled into the curtain… and disappeared.

The throbbing and thrumming grew ever more urgent and the shard sea's clatter gained in vehemence. A forceful tremor seized the ground, knocking Tsynnslin off his feet. Pinned to the platform, he only dared lift his head. His reflection looked back at him from the overhanging rock-like fabric, aghast, jittering, but not for long; the image wavered and fluttered away. For a few blinks, he was looking at a gnome-shaped haze, then the haze waned too.

Things picked up from there. Things picked *themselves* up, and of their own accord. Garden gnome by garden gnome rose up, zombie-like. Propelled by an invisible force, dragging their boots and shovels and wheelbarrows with a wild jingle-jangle over the clay shards, the figurines tore towards the rocky canvas and burst into bits.

CLAAAAASH! DA-DING! KA-BLAMM!

Almost instantaneously, more tiny bearded fellows popped out of nowhere, replenishing the depleted rows of suicidal gnomes.

DA-DING! KA-BLAMM!

"Get away from it – now!" Half a pile down, Whinewaeyn held on to a piece of rock, shouting his throat sore. His staff flashed briefly, but the magical energies it attempted to bundle fizzled away. "Leave!"

The gnome, however, to the contrary, pointed his claw at the sail-like rock, the cub-devourer and gnome-shatterer, and scrambled up *towards* it…

"…!" Whinewaeyn shouted after him, his words buried by the fresh racket ripping through the bedlam behind him. A roar of a racket. The wizard swirled about.

Like a titan from the depths of the Endless Ocean, a monstrous mass surfaced from the shard sea. Gnomes came pouring down from it. The creature rammed its claws into the closest piles left and right and heaved itself up, freeing its galley-sized body. Its eyes glowed a toxic yellow as it grappled for support on the slippery potteryscape, shrieking with a vengeance. Pungent steam oozed from inky nostrils. A maw full of razor-sharp teeth allowed for a moment for appreciation, before it hinged open. As the creature reared its horned head and jerked left and right in search of challengers, it revealed a host of spikes running down its back, leading up to a pair of wings. Right in front of them, at the end of its elongated neck, sat the dragon's skeletal master – a staff topped with a deformed skull in his bony clutches and a gem-studded amulet dangling before his open ribcage.

The lich peered down. The glow from its hollow eye sockets appeared a tad flummoxed, as if unsure where it was and why. But a lich has got to do what a lich has got to do – if it wasn't in his blood, it must have been in his bones. Wherever it was, the undead issued a vicious hiss because of it, and its pet answered dutifully with a snarl. Talons glinted, nostrils fumed. The earth quaked. The air droned. The rock face was adrift.

KNNNNNNNNNR-rrrrrrrkkkkNNNNN-k-k-k-k-k-k-k-CHRRRRRRR

"Oi!" The gnome's shout mixed with all-around pandemonium. Then he lost his foothold. "Oiiiiiiiiii!"

Whinewaeyn scrambled away. A balled-up bearskin was barrelling right at him. No. Somehow, miraculously, without changing direction, it somersaulted right *past* him, in a way he hadn't quite anticipated.

The gnome took a detour…

through space…

…and time.

CHAPTER 18

Doomsday Dawning

Little is known about how apocalypses go about their business. Speculation abounds. If one were to believe scholarly opinion, as laid out in the centenary edition of *Wiff Zack's Encyclopaedia on Everything and More*, it all begins with...

Apocalypse Hour. Also known as the Ultimate Point of No Return. Basic time unit of Doomsday. Singular in occurrence per universe. Apocalypse Hour is distantly related to the more commonly known Happy Hour, the key differences being:

1) They are located on the respective extremes of the fun spectrum.

2) Happy Hour provides only a limited relief from everyday life, Apocalypse Hour a permanent one. Indeed, with Apocalypse Hour any specific need for relief is eliminated along with all life as we know it.

3) Happy Hour lasts an hour. Apocalypse Hour begins and never ends. That is, because with it, time ends too.

4) Unlike Happy Hour, Apocalypse Hour is not tied to any specific location or event. Rather ALL locations and events are tied to it, as to a millstone heading doomwards.

It's all pretty hypothetical, though.

Apocalypse Hour. Doomsday.

Tsynnslin lost focus. He trundled along, body and mind. Unless it was the world that was revolving around him.

Either way, for an indeterminable amount of time, somewhere between a fraction of a second and the stretch of eternity, he felt surrounded by gaudy chewing gum – pulpy, doughy, as if everything had turned into a wheel of fortune at the funfair, spinning in slow motion. A hurdy-gurdy kind of noise howled alongside him, unsteady and protracted. But it wasn't just colours and noises journeying past; somehow *he* was part of the carousel too, coalescing with the swirling, shifting, swerving – at some point even whirling away from the one who thought or felt it all. So much so that whatever was left of Tsynnslin the gnome got lost in the ballyhoo like a particle in a treacle-filled kaleidoscope of things and thoughts and feelings.

Was he but driftwood in an ocean of unfathomable enormity? Driftwood, dipping away into the far reaches of the unknown? Was that the reason why he smelled fish and heard seagulls squabbling? The oddest thing about it was the existence of *someone* who had those strange thoughts, that there was that single piece of driftwood enveloped by enormity. And as there was driftwood, therefore he was.

The universe coughed its thinker up.

Tsynnslin felt for his limbs, sensed his lower half connect to something for a moment, until his knees folded of their own accord. He careened sideways, toppled. When he groped about to reassure himself, an object close by offered itself to his hand, and he held on to it. Dazed, he dragged himself up and planted two feet firmly on the ground to keep the world from turning.

The mists parted. Through the veil peeped a pointy hat. The gnome was looking at… a gnome! A garden gnome. And it wasn't the only one. It was a gnome ringed by a whole family of gnomes! There was also the odour of onion broth with surprise extras, and the more he took stock of his whereabouts, the deeper the striking feeling of déjà vu.

Tsynnslin swung round. A wall of boulders loomed on one side, Zarrafandan men-at-arms spread out on the other, and an army of goblins lined up behind him. A feeling of impending calamity filled the space.

"What on earth—" Tsynnslin clutched Zarothaster's tome to his chest, but – *tack, pthock, thang!* – took an array of bolts in the back.

"Got him!" A goblin cackled.

Tsynnslin, with a choked shriek, slumped to the ground.

For a moment or so, the felled bear-skinned gnome lay still, then the stone floor was overtaken by a shudder, jostling his body with it. Cracks snaked towards the human soldiers and the goblins holding them in check. Terror-stricken, the fighters on both sides scattered.

Pottery figurines began to vanish. Replacements popped up almost instantly. The new ones populated the gaps, tinkled against each other, bowled over, rolled about. Three gnomes, seven, a dozen, twenty—

WhooooooooooooooooooOOOOOMMMP!

A roar exploded amid it all: deep, hollow, weighty.

The racket echoed off the walls and slithered away through every opening, leaving churning dust behind. The dust mushroomed, chasing after the sound in its own majestic way by ponderously rolling up and sauntering off. By the time most of it had settled, the outlines of a structure filtered through the curtain of greyness like a pencil sketch with potential, jittery but recognizable. An east wing tower had materialized. Four-fifths of it, at least. The rest looked like it had been forcibly dismantled.

Now a cavern isn't an east wing tower's natural habitat. That's why the structure stood, in part, on stalagmites and reared up in a lopsided, hunched kind of way against the rim of the aperture above, just to fit in at all. Cave-dwelling took a bit of getting used to, and with all the quaking going on, there was little future in it for an already partly demolished building. Loose bricks danced on the rampaged top. No other opportunities presented themselves high up, so the bricks opted to rain down on the poor bear-wearing gnome at the tower's feet. After the first pioneers had tumbled earthwards, the rest of the tower felt inspired to come crashing down to join them, and it was mushrooming cloud time all over again.

Some of the bricks hit the ground. Others would have buried the gnome, if they hadn't slipped right through him, heading instead through space...

...and time.

Sixteen days before Apocalypse Hour. On the corner of Weaverring's Thinglefang Street.

Lady Bryanna of Pickeringstrim snorted. She ripped the pendant from her neck and shoved it into her purse. Her thirty-nine-coppers' worth of footgear slapped the cobbles in fretful despondency as she made for Grand Rimm-Zing's Magical Emporium – for the very last time in her life, for all she cared.

How, she chided herself, could she have been so dewy-eyed as to buy a luck charm from an obvious fraud? For the price she had paid, it smacked of a scam. And she had proof! After a whole week where everything that could possibly go wrong *had* gone wrong, she was set to cut Grand Rimm-Zing down to size, demanding a) an apology, b) a refund, and c) a charm that worked like one.

Lady Bryanna's suspicions as to her failing luck charm took on greater significance when she spotted one... two... three strange little somethings in the blue overhead. Unless she was very much mistaken, the specks weren't just suspended there. They were getting closer.

She held up her handbag, shading her eyes.

Moments later, a couple of massive bricks with an airborne garden gnome for company ploughed into the spot Lady Bryanna had been occupying – and left a chasm as wide as an ox cart.[*]

The bricks vanished almost as instantaneously as they appeared – but not into the hole they had torn in the street. They banded together with a bunch of cobbles they'd bumped into and took them along on a ride...

...through space and time...

Sixteen days later. Apocalypse Hour. Same spot.

Thinglefang Street had existed in a complacent, cleft-less state for years, with no plans to change any time soon.

Until history caught up with it, reminded the street about a certain past incident, and promptly reinstated the

---

[*] Tough, gruesome business, that. But an apocalypse has to start somewhere. Why not take advantage of someone with a flawed luck charm?

chasm. An ox-cart driver passing by disappeared right into it. After him, it was the rag-and-bone man's turn, and with him all smiles left Weaverring.

Two hundred and fifty-six days before Apocalypse Hour. The Grand Cathedral, Dimmerskeep.

An array of cobbles and bricks surfaced in the moonless sky, disturbing the serene midnight quiet. The batch travelled earthwards for some time, picking up speed, and reached the ground by smashing full tilt through one of the Grand Cathedral's stained-glass windows. For an instant, the night was anything but quiet.

The morning after, in addition to the broken window, the altar was reported missing from the locked premises, and a gaping star-shaped hole had opened up in the sanctuary floor. There was no trace of a perpetrator, or of any cobbles. Authorities immediately dubbed the incident an "act of Netherworldly machination". Who else, so the reasoning, but some Netherworldly demon would rise from the depths and make off with a whole altar by bursting through a church window?

Besides, this wasn't just any altar. This particular one had been hewn from the Miracle Mountain of Morrow, the place where according to legend the One had first met the Other and begotten the One-In-Between. It was said that the weight of the coming ages had seeped into the mountain as a sign of their union. Lugging the piece of rock to Dimmerskeep had taken months, and likewise had chiselling it into something vaguely altar-shaped. And yet, minions of the Darkness Beneath seemed to have found a way to snatch it overnight...

Apocalypse Hour. Same place.

Ironically, when the cathedral was awash with prayers two hundred and fifty-six days later, and the very same altar disappeared before everyone's eyes, the congregation present chose to see the affair more as an act of a god. As it was, the memory of the so-called "Netherworldly incident" was all but a haze to them, lingering in their minds like a hard-to-remember nightmare, which by no means could've been true, could it?

The altar had no opinion, and continued its time travels before going for a dip in the sea.

Eleven years and eighty-one days before Apocalypse Hour. Somewhere near Cape Colt.

One could say the altar did an unholy thing by taking a bath. But it didn't know any better. It could also have been more subtle when it sought out a treasure chest on the ocean floor. As it was, a fish cutter happened to be in the way when the altar fell out of the skies.

The Altar of Morrow crashed through the deck and the hold. Luckily, this time, it didn't score a direct hit on a crew member. Too bad that the enormous hole in the keel ended things on an unsatisfactory note for everyone on board, regardless.

Also buried at sea that day: the dream of a picture-perfect farm up a hilltop near the Wending Woods, which was how deckhand Dick had imagined his life to be. "One day," Dick used to say when reeling in the nets, "I'll buy meself me own piece of land, you'll see, an' I'll be done with all this. Aye, I'll settle down, marry me lassie, an' we'll 'ave a couple a sprogs 'n' stuff."

And indeed, without the altar's interference, that's exactly what he did. Seven years later, and four years before Apocalypse Hour, his fairy tale had finally become reality. Until, well…

Apocalypse Hour.

One of the unpleasantries of an altar hurtling through time and space and plummeting onto fish cutters in the past was that it put a swift end to deckhand Dick *before* he got chickens and all the rest of it. Consequently, reality retracted the picture-perfect farm from the present, since it couldn't possibly be there. Revocation of progeny was implied, and executed. The universe had gotten a little smaller.

A precedent had been created. The apocalypse had something to work with, and chaos got going for real. It took as many fish as it could get for provisions and stretched its fateful world-undoing tentacles southward.

Hanging Rock. Still Apocalypse Hour.

"*Oouhm-goooorosh! Woosh-grou-posh! KHOOM-AK-DROSH!*"

The lich's oversized pet bobbed its head up and down as if drunk on its master's sepulchral voice. The incantations sounded as though they welled up from a Netherworldly pit, dripping with dark power. The dragon answered the call, fire rained down, and everybody got a taste of it.

Whinewaeyn rolled sideways. Droplets of flame sizzled all over his robe. He fumbled for his staff.

"*Groumagn-gn-gn-gn-gnnnn?*" he heard the lich stammer, and then the undead's skull-headed staff spun through the air. An arrow, stuck in one of the eye sockets, was swirling with it. The corpse snarled and thrust its withered head to the side. The shine in its undead eyes turned blood red when it spotted the fleet-footed elf climbing over the boulders like a goat.

Sylthia, leaping, ducking, weaving, reached the wizard, her bow still fixed on the now unarmed lich.

"Got any magic of your own, old man?" she urged, nocking another arrow. "I'll keep the lich at bay!" She took a glance at the mage only out of the corner of one eye. He appeared not to be moving. but perhaps he was plotting a particularly devious spell.

"Wizard?" When she looked again, the wizard was gone.

"*Oouhm-grooom!*" the lich roared again, dodging the shot coming at it. In the same motion, he wheezed in the ear of his horned mount: "*Kr'ukh cam-KAAAAH!*"

The dragon's neck swooped down. Its maw hovered for a bit in front of the weapon-flourishing Bormph and Ramrok, then gaped open like a drawbridge, revealing foul-reeking storm clouds brewing inside its cavernous throat. So transfixed was Bormph with the fuming beast that he almost missed the claw swiping past him. From the other side, Ramrok's two-hander whistled through the air, merely diffusing some of the smoke.

With the view clearing, a pressing urge to abandon position suggested itself. Bormph pushed away a second round of thoughts submitting more valiant ideas, and decided to make a dash for it. Ramrok had no such thoughts to begin with. His barbarian's instincts simply yelled "Out! Out! OUT!" which is why the big one had swivelled around already while the dwarf was still having his think, and pelted away. Their paths crossed.

Ba-DANG!

A hefty collision later, Bormph dropped left, Ramrok right, and a jet of fiery dragon's breath roared through the space that presented itself.

The wind knocked out of them, the mighty warriors shook the soot from their shoulders and dug their heels into the shards again, this time hobbling off alongside one another. After some distance, the pottery ahead formed into a bulge, and the rear of a tousle-haired mop cropped up, unannounced and in the way. The rest of Thimble emerged shortly after, gasping for air and flailing – in short, celebrating the fact that he had just escaped a premature burial by gnomes. What gave him pause was that his fighter friends were crawling past him on all fours, and… fast!

Thimble swung around to get the full picture.

The full picture involved smouldering gloom, framed at the top and bottom by sword-like spikes. A no less enormous greasy tongue lolled out of the darkness, adding certainty to what had started out as suspicion. Fire flashed, Thimble's stomach lurched, and he squealed his little heart out.

For what it was worth, he also clamped a pebble into his slingshot and released it. It disappeared without even making a sound, as if the dragon's throat couldn't be bothered to take notice of it. A fresh idea hit him.

"*K-RN-TK-PRT!*" he croaked. "*K-RN-TK-PRT!*"

The words were almost drowned out by the beast's roar, the shard sea's jingling and the savage droning that rattled everything and everyone and reverberated from the mountainsides.

But suddenly Amjelle was with him too.

"*K-RN-TK-PRT!*"

If ever there was a battle where a teapot could be a decisive factor, this was it. A piece of crockery popped up in the midst of the brewing tempest, and it was quickly succeeded by another.

The dragon choked. Just a little. He was a dragon: an armoured, fifteen-foot-tall steaming mass of pure annihilation. Whereas a teapot was, well, altogether a very different entity: a couple of inches high and wide, porcelain-made, floral patterned, unable to whistle without the aid of a stove.

"*K-rn-tk-prt!*" came at the dragon from halfling-height.

"*K-rn-tk-prt! K-RN-TK-PRT!*" Bormph and Ramrok shouted as one now too.

The mighty monster gagged and retched. It twitched and reeled, and its master had a hard time staying on its back. His *oouhm-groooming* dithered out of rhythm.

Further off, Sylthia, perched on the highest boulder she could find, fired again. This time the arrow zipped past the head of the convulsing beast.

"Wizard?" Her eyes went searching again. What in the Dreameress's name was the old codger *still* waiting for? Where the heck was he anyway?

"There!" Amjelle pointed, ducking behind a boulder, and Sylthia spotted the windbag of a wizard clambering up the main gnome pile, up and up… This wasn't the time to take a hike. "Wiiiiizaaaa—"

At the same moment, Whinewaeyn was, as gracelessly as he possibly could, hauling himself onto the final upturned balcony. Succeeding in that, he turned to face the fight. Holding out his staff in approximate dragon direction, he began mumbling something wizardly.

At last! Sylthia's shoulders sagged with relief. *This will show them!*

She wasn't really expecting Whinewaeyn to cast a spell that would sweep her off her feet. Or sweep anyone else off their feet. But he did! He scooped *Amjelle* off her feet as a whip-like jet of energy leapt from the wizard's staff, streaked past the elf and curled around the healer's waist. She was yanked upwards and, in seconds, despite all protests, Amjelle found herself on the balcony with the wizard, bruised and fuming.

"What's got into you, Archmagus?" she erupted, struggling to her feet. She seized the wizard's scrawny wrist. "You can't just— We're in the middle of a fight!"

"You *were*." The wizard, eyes frantic, wrested himself free and got his magical whip working again. It lashed out like a fishing rod, and the energies he was channelling zapped past the healer and a flabbergasted elf a short distance away, back into the fray below.

"If you don't tell me at once—" Amjelle screamed at him.

"No time for explanations, dear. Conjure more teapots. I'm just putting two and two together."

"K-k-k... r-r-r-..." As Amjelle debated with herself whether wizards were to be trusted with arithmetic, she felt her body shake and her voice tremble when she tried to raise it. Now that she stood closer to what had once been a rock face, the thrumming had intensified. It shook her to the bone. The source must be close by. She glared up at the reflections in the billowing wall, but the undead and its dragon were all she could make out in the milky mist.

One by one, the other party members arrived on the platform, dragged up by Whinewaeyn's energy-wrought whip. Thimble and Bormph, tied into a bundle, came first, then Ramrok – and each brought their own cussing. In the meantime, Sylthia did her best to create more of a distraction for the lich and its beast, before climbing over to Whinewaeyn. Whatever he was up to, it had better be good.

At the foot of the gnome mountain, the monster's head reared up. Its opponents were farther away now, but conveniently crowded in one place. A vicious glow entered the behemoth's eyes. It unfurled its wings, ready to strike.

Amjelle stared down in sheer terror.

"What. Is. Happening?!" she yelled.

The shard sea heaved. One of the gnomes levitated as if drawn by an invisible string and hurled itself at them. Amjelle dodged the assault, but more gnomes rose to their clay feet and tried their luck. "What have you brought us all up here for?" She grabbed the wizard and shook him. "To be killed by rampant gnomes?"

Surrounded by irritated looks, Whinewaeyn's eyes glinted. "No. The exercise I have in mind is more a leap of faith, dear. If anyone should know about that, it's a cleric. All it takes, whatever you do, is a leap of faith."

The thrumming had reached painful levels, underpinned by more forceful rumbling rolling beneath the mountainside as if the rock face was about to come down on them any moment now.

KNNNNNNNNNR-rrrrrrrkkkkNNNNN-k-k-k-k-k-k-CHRRRRRRR.

"Well, 'leap' is more a figure of speech," Whinewaeyn specified, unblinking. "A step might do as well. Follow me."

He faced the rock wall, stuck out one leg, wobbled a bit, and, with a lurch, the rest of his body followed, merging into the stone. The wizard's shape briefly remained discernible, then that slipped away too.

Amjelle was panicking. "Archmagus? ARCHMAGUS!"

More threatening droning was the only answer she got.

Bormph rubbed his bearded cheek. "Um… So… Faithfuls first, eh?" An extra noisy clatter below reminded him that a Netherworldly creature was about to have its revenge. "Or was it ladies?"

Amjelle gave the dwarf a revolted look. "You—"

A heart-stopping bang so close that it tore through Amjelle like lightning stopped their argument short. Splinters sprayed all over the place. Her stave's shaft hung from her blackened hand like a withered bouquet, and the way her hand was throbbing, who knew what was going to explode next?

"Well then, here's to adventure!" she proclaimed, to Sylthia mostly. Then she took a deep breath, clenched her jaw and, without looking back, dove into the rock wall.

Moments later, Sylthia slipped in behind her.

"Wizzy say go!" Ramrok boomed at the half-sized remainders of the party. "So we go… No?"

"Do we though?" Bormph looked at Thimble, and Thimble at Bormph. Even the sturdy dwarf was quaking in his boots, which were quaking with the platform. It was an altogether quite shaky affair. A garden gnome projectile crashed against Ramrok's helmet. The giant didn't even blink.

"Erm…" Bormph still wouldn't budge. "Give a Shumgulth dwarf some time to collect himself." Apparently, collecting a three-hundred-pound-plus dwarf took its time. He kept staring at the mirror-like wall that had eaten gnomes, a wizard and two women. The dragon reflected in its surface. The beast was hoisting its enormous body uphill, navigating the treacherous shard sea terrain. It had some trouble, but it was getting there.

"He's coming!" squealed Thimble, looking back and forth between dwarf and dragon, curls flying. "We have to—"

"Go!" There was that booming, monotonous voice again, imparting practical advice in one-word chunks. "Monster." Two immense hands extended. "In."

"Hey… *Hey!*" Bormph yelled. "You're pushing! Heeeeeyyyyyyyyyyy!"

Thimble closed his eyes.

It was only about a second after the party was gone in its entirety that Hanging Rock reverted to simply being a hanging rock. Its looking-glass fancies yielded and the malleable wall became stone again, freezing in mid-billow. For the dragon homing in on the remaining barbarian, such timing was… inopportune. The creature didn't exactly glide into the rock as it had intuited. It *slammed* into it. Full force and headlong, its massive body concertinaing after. A grating shriek burst from the lich when the dragon impacted and catapulted its rider skywards. Skywards, of course, also meant rockwards, on account of Hanging Rock's newly restored imposing outcrop. A snap concluded the short flight. Bone fragments showered into the sea of clay below.

And Hanging Rock? Exposed to all this quaking, droning, ramming by a dragon and a barrage of garden gnomes, it pitched forward. The precarious angle went over its limits, way above an optical illusion, and the cliff tipped over. With a drawn-out crescendo its bulk crashed into the ground, tore the turf asunder, and away it plummeted, the massive, age-old clump of rock.

Underneath, in the cleft it had opened up, the absence of light was absolute. Depth was in there too, but even the dark couldn't tell that it had such company. Hanging Rock dropped unhindered into both, the dark and the depth, flashing one last time like a falling star on the wrong side of the earth's surface. And as it fell, it shrank until it was a pale shimmering dot, merging with an illimitable saturnine void, smoothly, soundlessly.

On the surface, the chasm widened rapidly. Eating away the rest of the mountain. Treating the gathered gnomes as a side dish. What started as a hesitant trickle of clay figurines diving after the giant rock gained momentum and developed into a furious maelstrom. Soon, an army of gnomes was spiralling downwards into the bottomless pit like grains of sands sucked through the neck of a giant hourglass – only faster. Much, much faster.

KrrrrrrrrrrrrrrrrssssssssssssSSSSSDSSSSSSHHHHHHHH!

The chasm reached out westward, broadening into a canyon.

The Zarrafandan observatory. Dimmerskeep.

"A dot? That's it?"

The wrath of the gods seemed negligible from afar.

"Well, it's a dot *now*, Your Highness…" Normi Stargazer's wall-eyed gaze aimed at the Prince, but covered his whole entourage – including Xoormrax the Elder, Archmagus Emeritus, who had joined them to talk about all things apocalypse.

"It was half a dot only hours ago," Normi expounded, "but it's going to be a monster-sized dot soon. And before you know it, it will be fully monstrous and not a dot at all anymore."

Prince Dymmling felt surrounded by Normi's gaze. He ventured another peek into the eyepiece of the skyglass, the pride of the observatory. He didn't like what he saw through the tube. *Had the dot just grown to dot-and-a-half size as the gnome had insinuated?* He rubbed his eyes. *Was this the cataclysmic comet in its infancy? The particle of perdition?*

"Have you ruled out, say, a speck of grease? Fly droppings?"

Normi's eyes drifted even further apart as his brain attempted to work through the perplexing query.

"On your thing!" The Prince's delicate hand turned one of the wheels on the enormous instrument. The apparatus pivoted somewhat, and the comet slipped out of view.

"No, no, Your Magnificent Majesticalness. The lens is quite spotless, I'm afraid. It's not that—" He broke off as Princeling Klimbish beckoned his master to join him for a look at something closer, something out in the street, through the round window set into the observatory's dome. The commotion was impossible not to overhear.

"The word is out," the princeling announced, pointing. And sweating.

The stargazing gnome just *had* to blare out his discovery over the rooftops of the whole town, and now the fat was in the fire. The streets were thronged, on the brink of riotous. The crowds brandished placards saying things like "*Comet go home!*" The main chant ringing through the alleyways was "Not with us! Not with us!", closely followed by the more sinister "Burn the Harbinger of Doom!" Some banners by believers in the Holy Quintity were more forgiving. "*Hail to the One!*" they read, or "*Our time has come!*", or "*We're ready! Take us with you!*" How the whole transaction from comet to selective salvation would work, who knew, but quite a few out there were willing to make a bet on it.

The Prince gingerly craned his head out. More noise spilled over from the other side of town – merrymaking noise. The first End of Days parties were underway, and everyone ate, drank, sang, kissed around and smoked prohibited weed as if there was no tomorrow. And maybe there wouldn't be. People even danced to the rhythm of the off and on quaking earth, and whenever fresh tremors came rippling through the lanes, the revellers broke into yowls and cheers and started a wave. From the neutral zone between the protesters and the merrymakers, the city guard pushed into the scrum to keep the groups apart – though it didn't really seem to matter much at this point.

Prince Dymmling stood for a time with his head tilted skywards, cupping his cheeks as he wistfully observed the pastel-coloured immensity above. It made the Prince think, *How about a tinge of purple towards the edges to match his blouse?*

"So… it's to be the comet then," he said with the passion of a death row inmate learning that it would be the axe's call, not the noose's. "The comet will be our end. But… what about the tower? The gnomes? The quakes? People and houses disappearing? Surely the comet couldn't—"

"It's uncanny, Majesty, isn't it?" Xoormrax interrupted politely. "One might almost assume the apocalypse bears down on us from all sides at once." With his hunched posture, the archmage more closely resembled an age-worn vulture than a wizard, the shoulder pads of his aquamarine storm cloak jutting up like folded wings. "But see, the world is suffused with magic, albeit not all of us are aware of this very fact. One way or another, magic's everywhere, beyond, beneath and in between, only different people have different words for it. How else would the stars move if they were not propelled by arcane laws operating from within, I ask? There's a universal harmony at work."

"Until…" Prince Dymmling tilted his head. "Until there… isn't?"

"Indeed, Your Magnificence. I would say the matter then becomes abundantly clear. When a celestial orb veers off its destined orbit, it turns into a comet, and the orb's inherent magic must affect the skies it travels through, for one. Hence, the changing colours we perceive."

The Prince was now pacing back and forth along the length of the room, his princelings scurrying to get out of his way.

Normi nodded eagerly after him. "And down here, it must be like weather pains, Your Fanciness."

The Prince threw him a puzzled glance over his shoulder.

"It's like with those people who get headaches and strange sensations in their limbs *before* there's thunder and lightning…" The gnome's eyes glinted, two polished gems complementing an equally sparkling bald head.

"Quite so," Xoormrax said, picking up the thought. "An off-course celestial body could be seen as a headache for our world. Magic's going wild down here too because the comet casts its shadow ahead, metaphorically speaking."

"And our gnomes…?" the Prince asked. "They don't appreciate a comet's metaphorical shadow?"

"Possibly. A detailed study on the subject establishing the links between gnomes, towers and quakes would certainly be of paramount scholarly interest. Alas… time is pressing."

"Ah." The Prince came to a standstill. "And how would all that explain Vensk? According to our sources, he's about to attack any minute now. Coincidence? I think not!

Far from a gnome disappearing from our backyards, he's more like a rogue, planting goblins in our forecourts."

Normi made an unsuccessful attempt to look the Prince straight in the eye. "Destiny is tied to the stars... Think about the zodiac signs, Your Highness. Those who are born in the Days of the Lion are said to become strong-willed and stout-hearted. The Chameleons can adjust better. The Monkeys—" One of the gnome's eyes locked with the Prince's, and froze in position. Normi's high forehead developed an instant extra coating of sweat.

"In times of a cosmic imbalance," Xoormrax rushed to continue, "men inclined to acts of folly... How to put it? Well, they get *ideas*. Hence Vensk."

"Hmm..." Prince Dymmling's feet got going again. "And you are sure of the soundness of your theorizing, wizard?"

"It's the best we could come up with on such short notice." Leaning forward, Xoormrax added with a hint of a pride in his voice, "Speaking about ideas in light of our situation, Your Magnificence..."

"Yes? You see any chance of altering the comet's course?"

"More than that." The archmage's vulture-like neck bobbed a nod. "But credit where credit is due. We might as well call it *your* idea."

The Prince raised an interested brow.

"For as per your forward-looking suggestion, we've been dusting off our arcane vaults and scouring their contents. With little luck at first, admittedly. No explicit actions suggest themselves against vanishing gnomes and towers. But in light of the cosmic overall picture, we were able to narrow our options down to concrete measures.

Like grand-scale projectiles capable of inflicting harm of epic proportions. With that in mind we left no stone unturned and, indeed, our search has borne fruit."

The Prince cocked his arm and let his hand roll over his frill-sleeved wrist. "Please do carry on."

"You see, Your Highness, in the past few hours, with the help of the Princedom's most revered sages and mages, we've unearthed, unsealed and decrypted little hints scattered through a collection of grimoires. Put together they point to various parts of a powerful multicaster invocation we thought was never meant to see the light of day again. But maybe the notion was premature." Xoormrax's voice trembled with pride, and his wrinkled face split into a smile. He held up a stack of scriptures. "Its ancient name suggests that this utterly unique spell dates back beyond the Warlock Wars, and the devastation it promises makes the things we've been dabbling with for ages at the Academy look like child's play. No wonder it was kept a well-guarded secret until now, for fear that it might fall into the hands of a madman. But under the current circumstances, under our supervision, directed with the utmost precision, focused at the comet..." The archmage's and the Prince's eyes locked amid a pregnant pause.

"And you'd be ready to try... when?"

"Any time now. All we need is your explicit order to go ahead and unleash..." Xoormrax rifled through his papers. "Ah, here we are: *Ar-ma-ged-don*."

The Prince inclined his head approvingly. "Whatever ancient language this is – it has a certain, shall we say, ring to it. And I like things... that ring."

Beyond Hanging Rock.

"Hu-hullo?" A feeble squeak with a breathy finish rose against a bulwark of shadows.

The darkness met it with grim silence and a musty chill. Not even an echo picked the disturbance up to play with, and the squeak was left where it was, as it was: irrelevance in noise form, buried deeper in the past's ever growing reaches with each passing second.

"Huullooooo?" A louder, more desperate attempt threw itself against ongoing burial procedures. This time with some effect. Lured from their recesses, vague echoes bounced through the unknown. Once, twice, thrice the yell was repeated, however faintly, dwindling in volume with each iteration.

Wait! What was that? A word? A cough? A coughed word?

"...umble?" It sounded small, distant. But it promised something big.

"Ramrok?"

"...umble... umble..."

"Ramrok ...ok ...ok!"

"Thumble ...umble!"

"Shhhh!" A hiss. Far away, brisk and sullen.

"Hmmph?"

"...ssshhhhhhhh!"

"You shhh!"

"...mph?"

Silence.

Moments later gravelly muffled words tumbled over from a spot maybe a shade darker than the rest. "Wizzer! Was that you?"

"Bormph!" A squeak again, from the other direction.

"Hush! Keep it down you two!" Now the voice sounded distinctly Whinewaeyny. "Of course it's me, dwarf! Whom did you expect?"

"You tell me what I'm supposed to expect, gramps. *You* got us into this mess! Where the heck are we? It's not the realm of everlasting sunshine, I can tell you that."

"Archmagus!" There was another voice, breaking in relief. It sounded farther away, also soft, female, faint and floating. "I'm here, and I have Sylthia right with me!"

"Wherever you are, whatever you have or haven't," the Whinewaeyny voice cautioned, "stay put before you drop into a pit or something. Give me a minute. I'll summon something up."

"You do that, Archmagus. We're not going anywhere," Amjelle's voice said. "And I already thought, Syl, this would be the end of us."

"Not yet, Am. Still alive, apparently!"

"Unless," a grumble cut in, "we aren't. I for one am not so sure."

"Twiddletricks! If we were dead, could I do this?" There was a rummaging noise. "Now where was that…? Without any light, how am I supposed to make one?"

Then there was nothing. Not even rummaging.

"Archmagus?"

Utter silence.

"Wiiiiiiiizard!"

Finally – *finally* a glimmer broke through the perfect black.

The spark flickered as though intimidated by its oppressive surroundings, then fought back, and grew into a luminous orb. In the soft, amber glow, the wizard's features surfaced, followed by his bristling beard and patched robe. A chequerboard of flagged stones unrolled underneath and around him, subjected to the orb's unsteady quiver. With a gesture of the wizard's hand, the guidelight hovered farther up, its shine spilling over... even more tiles. They seemed to stretch on in all directions, smooth and shiny, each large enough for a person to stand on comfortably. If they ever reached an end, that point was well lost outside of the glowing sphere's limits. Little else was revealed in the sparse light, aside from the occasional pile of gnome shards scattered about.

The clay pieces crunched underfoot here and there, until all the trusted faces dipped into the light pool's radiance and the party was back together again.

"What's going on with those?" Amjelle pointed at a shard pile. Smoke curled off the bits and pieces, or lingered around them, thickening. Amjelle squatted down and reached for one of the fragments, but as soon as she held it aloft, it only remained a shard for so long.

Maybe it was the air, maybe the place. Maybe the shard itself. Or perhaps all of it together. A presence of some sort, unseen to the naked eye, seemed to tug at the piece as soon as it was lifted, and its edges started to glow, smearing the solid lines between object and air. What at first looked like a trick of the light turned even more peculiar when the item was turned over. The now glimmering outlines, lending the piece shape and form, took their time to follow the motion imposed on them, and eventually – one by one – they detached themselves from whatever they contained. Now the once solid shard was anything but. Like the flame of a candle, its upper half broke loose altogether and the escaping luminous strands curled themselves aloft, wafting away, and drawing the lower, still solid half in their wake. Within moments, the piece of gnome was no more. Amjelle rubbed her empty fingers together.

Baffled glances were traded.

"Where's Tsynnslin?" Thimble piped up, looking about. "Maybe he can tell us what's—" He felt a sudden chill pass through him. "Is he…?"

"Gone, little one." The wizard's eyes delved into the darkness. "Gone perhaps to fulfil his destiny." As he talked on, his breath grew ragged. "But he saved us too. He showed us the way."

"Did he now? And *where* has he gone?" Bormph kicked a shard aside as he poked his head into the light's crackling shine. "Have I missed something, wizzer? Straight into the fangs of a dragon is where he led us! And what was all that you were rambling about back there anyway? With the world ending and everything?"

The world ending and everything… Scenes of quaking earth, of mountain chains drifting like surges on the high sea, of Tsynnslin appearing twice at the same time whirled through Whinewaeyn's muddled mind. There was also a wizard screaming at a gnome, and as no other wizards were present during the making of this particular memory, it must have been him. It was time to face whatever needed to be faced.

"The world is ending," he muttered, "it's just as the gnome said. All that ending… it must have begun somewhere. And now I know where. It must have begun in that cavern of his. It began with the gnome."

"Were you hit on the head or something, geezer?" Bormph snorted, and then looked to Amjelle.

"My head is perfectly fine," Whinewaeyn retorted, adamant, fending off Amjelle, who had stepped closer to take a look. "At least, I didn't get hit or something. I saw it all happen with my own eyes. But my mind needed to catch up... I saw where the gnome turned up after he disappeared from the cliff."

"Where?" several whispers asked at once.

"You might as well ask *'when?'*" And then he told them all how he had seen the gnome in two places at the same time.

"You saw the gnome twice? *Our* Tsynnslin?" Amjelle whisper-shrieked, goosebumps crawling all over her skin. "Why are you only telling us now, Archmagus? And, by the gods, what does it mean?"

Whinewaeyn hesitated. "At first, I-I thought *Mongolf's Stonewalling* must have drained me. Made me see things. Because, you know, it's a tier-three spell. And I *saw* things. Once, I walled myself into my study over the weekend. Smelled potatoes everywhere and had visions of sausages dressed up in cheese. It was horrible! Horrible!"

"Hungry?" Amjelle speculated.

Whinewaeyn cocked his head. "Hmm. Never thought of it that way."

A grunt from Bormph contributed something incomprehensible. Could've been a snide remark, a swear word, or perhaps it was just the dwarf's grumpiness due for an airing.

"But there was more to it than that back in the cavern," Whinewaeyn rushed to continue. "More than me being hungry, I mean. We had onion broth, remember?"

A shared memory swam up, bland with surprise extras.

"No, no. There was a strange energy in the air when the second gnome showed up. And I remember it clearly now, much more clearly than I'd like: how he stood there, how he slipped out of nowhere, how he held the Toaster's journal, looking about like he didn't know what was what."

"The journal?" Sylthia perked up. "Tsynnslin didn't even *know* about the journal when we were with him in the cavern!"

"Neither did I," said Whinewaeyn. "That's why there can't be any doubt. He went up to the cliff with the journal in his hands, and *then* it happened. What he feared would happen to us… It happened to *him*." The wizard threw his hands up. "*He* got yanked back in time. *He* must have gotten too close to this… rock-mirror-warfax kind of thing…"

"Vortex," Amjelle corrected him. "But… why?"

"Something to do with the journal," Whinewaeyn said almost apologetically. "It's a powerful artifact, is it not?"

"Why the past? Why the cavern?"

"It must have served as a focal point," Sylthia suggested. "The gnome said so himself, and he had quite the collection of artifacts there. What if they attracted unstable forces present in the universe? With the quakes, the collection almost certainly got destroyed. But it was still intact and larger than ever right before that." Her lips thinned. "Paradoxically, the gnome's passionate investigation into these occurrences must have caused what he feared the most."

"That's… weird," said Thimble.

"It's almost like one of those romantic bridging-the-rifts-of-time stories from the *Perilous Passion* tales you used to read during class," Whinewaeyn said with an eye on Amjelle. He gave the healer a wry smile, and she flushed in response. "Only with time-travelling gnomes." The wizard rubbed his nose. "It all sounds very strange, and yet strangely sound."

"And where… *when*… is he now?" Thimble wanted to know. "Our gnome? The one that got yanked back? The… *right*… one?"

"Well…" Whinewaeyn's voice dropped to an undertone. "He got struck down."

"He got *what?*" Amjelle screeched for real this time, summoning quite a few distant echoes.

"Ah, it was awful! But I'm afraid it's true. The arrows of the goblins did him in. There and then. He's gone. He managed to travel through time and space in one piece and then—"

"Gone?" Amjelle snapped. "And you didn't *tell* him?"

"Well, he was very much alive too!" Whinewaeyn shot back. "If what I saw… what I *thought* I saw… was no illusion, then it had already happened, and if it had already happened, there was nothing I could do about it, no?" The wizard shook his head. "I-I wasn't even sure I hadn't dreamed it up… He just stood there, and the bolts came at him from everywhere."

An aching silence draped around them.

Then, on top of that, a sound like the tinkling of a wind chime came drifting by – gentle, dissonant, as one might imagine a premonition cruising in the gloom. It lasted but a moment and a half before it faded back into the conglomerate of shadows and stillness, just long enough for everybody to doubt their hearing.

"Excuse me."

"Archmagus?" Amjelle watched the wizard sweep purposefully past her.

"Shh!" Hand on his staff, Whinewaeyn edged forwards, trance-like, one half step at a time, with his conjured light-casting companion floating overhead. His gaze was glued to a point some twenty feet above the floor, and he jerked towards it with his chin.

A pair of tiny, gem-like orbs glimmered down from the spot, weaving in and out of the shadows in perfect synchronicity. The urgent clatter of weapons being drawn echoed across the tiles. Which seemed not to have a deterring effect on the unknown presence in the least, because the glittering gems bounded forward despite that and, in a matter of seconds, swooped down, right at them.

"Snowflake!"

The polar bear's paws pitter-pattered into the light.

"Snowflake! Thank the gods you made it too!" Amjelle sobbed through misty eyes. She crouched down to receive the cub in her outstretched arms and treated the little rascal to a cuddle. The cub yelped, nuzzled at her ear and pawed at her cheek in return.

Whinewaeyn's reaction was more reserved. While he registered the reunion with one eye, he and his orb kept forging ahead. A broad stairway had emerged from the darkness, stretching along the whole amber perimeter of the guidelight's glow. Like the flagstones, the white-veined marble steps leading up were pristine, with shallow, rounded edges. Thimble let out a low whistle as he came closer, climbing the stairs with his eyes until the reach of the light dwindled.

Whinewaeyn looked over his shoulder at Amjelle, with a stern eye on the bear too. "Any of you have an idea what this little fellow is?"

"What? The cub? A bloody nuisance," was Bormph's judgment.

"Nah, he's not. He's as cute as a button. *That's* what he is." Amjelle rubbed her nose against Snowflake's wet snout. "Aren't you, my little furball? Aren't you, hmm?"

"And…" Whinewaeyn said hoarsely, "he's what the gnome called 'an artifact.'"

CHAPTER 19

Cataclysmic Conclusion

Amjelle stared at the wizard, her hand frozen on the bear's fur.

"Is the sky blue, my dear?" Not a sliver of a doubt showed in the wizard's features, but then his face started to cloud with uncertainty about his choice of words. The party's questionable whereabouts considered, it was impossible to tell where the sky was hiding and what colour it presently preferred. "Erm…" Whinewaeyn cocked an arm and cupped his chin while he rearranged the thought. "I guess what I'm trying to say is that the cub's like us. Just like us. And we are like him."

"How?" Amjelle sputtered.

"Remember that the gnome was the only one with a reflection in Hanging Rock? And then suddenly that reflection wasn't there anymore?"

"Yeah?"

"Something changed when he touched this little fellow." Whinewaeyn let the thought float between them for a moment, squinting up the looming stairway where more suspicious quiet was lurking, doing what it was best at: spreading unease with its sheer presence. Two fingers lifted ponderously from his chin as the wizard cast a sidelong glance back at Amjelle. "I would assume the gnome hadn't touched the bear before."

"You're saying the gnome picked up the cub's aura? Like the flu? Up there?"

"Sounds strange when you put it like that but, yes... it would appear that way."

"And we have too? Picked up something? Because we've... petted a pet?"

"Maybe so, and maybe not." Whinewaeyn's gaze shifted to Sylthia. "What's more likely, is that powerful artifact of yours had something to do with it. Maybe it affected the cub too. And so, when the gnome stumbled into the cub, well, his aura touched the gnome's, and there you have it. The gnome got tainted."

"...which is why his reflection vanished?"

"Quite so. And because he was tainted and close to the source – and holding a powerful artifact on top of it – well, you know the rest. Therefore, considering our own... daintiness..." The wizard had raised a finger, but now broke off, searching for something in the mysteries of his mind.

"*Tainted*ness?" Amjelle suggested.

"Taintedness, right. Considering that, *we* might have been next."

"Going back in time and everything?"

"Probably."

"But we weren't."

"No. Because, as the cub showed us, if you're dainty enough, it seems you can slip behind the warfax kind-of-thing."

"So you got us behind the rock."

"Right."

"And what kind of place is this exactly?" Thimble still didn't know whether being here beat a fire-breathing dragon.

"Sylthia mentioned elven lore," Amjelle said. "About mirrors."

"Soul mirrors," Sylthia provided. "But… it can't be true. If it were—"

"We'd have no souls anymore!" screeched Thimble. His head was spinning. Hairpins hopped through his boggled mind, where it was raining teapots and gnomes. Had his favourite polar bear cub really sent someone through time?

"Curious," Whinewaeyn said.

"Yeah, right," Bormph groused from two heads further down. "This is getting better and better. Either it's a hairpin or a cub that stole our souls!" His hand coiled into a fist, despite the fact that spiritual stuff wasn't a dwarf's strong suit. Still, a soul-stealing cub took the biscuit! "Pole-a-bears!" he cursed. "Said it the first time round. Those mages down south should be locked up! Animal experiments with poles!" He picked on Amjelle to complain further. "Why didn't you check on that cub with your what-d'ya-call-it, anyway, healer?"

Amjelle stammered something, but Whinewaeyn interrupted her. "Speaking of which…" He looked her up and down. "Where *is* your what-d'ya-call-it when we need it?"

"It exploded on me, Archmagus…" Amjelle raised her blackened forearm, half-burnt sleeve included. "Back there. All these forces around me tore at it, and then it just went *bang!*"

Whinewaeyn winced. "Aye. And why shouldn't it? Has every right to. A warfax is supposed to be a bit showy. It's in the name, I guess." The wizard looked about. "Anyone else got a spare weapon? We can't let her explore this place unprotected."

"Don't look at me, gramps," Bormph growled. "Dwarves have principles. We found each other, my axe and I, and I could never cheat on it with an extra cleaver tucked in my boot. Wouldn't be right."

To everyone's surprise it was Ramrok, who stepped forward. He grabbed the shaft of something bulky sticking out of his backpack and thrust it into Amjelle's hands. "Here."

At first, she looked a tad bewildered at what was clearly a grubby frying pan with limited battlefield experience. But better an armed chef than an empty-handed healer. She put Snowflake down, weighed the pan in her hand and attempted a few swipes at an invisible opponent, the rush of air sending robes and hair flying. It was all a bit too much action for the cub, who sought shelter between Bormph's and Thimble's feet – which, in turn, earned him a glare from the dwarf.

"Be as cute as you want." Bormph gave the furry refugee a shove with the blunt side of his axe. "You can't hide that you're the spawn of the Netherworlds and gave us soul-stealer's flu."

At that point Thimble thought he picked up that strange noise again, somewhere distant, somewhat eerie, as if out of this world... He strained his ears, but what filtered through was so soft, it could've just been his overwrought imagination with the volume turned up. The only sounds he could really hear were Amjelle practising her swing, and Mr Guidelight spitting out a crackle every now and again.

"On another note..." Whinewaeyn said, his voice reestablishing some familiarity in the soundscape. "Now that we're here, let's not waste the trip. Shall we?"

"Alright," Amjelle said. "We'd better find out what place this is that needs a tainted soul to get in."

"Heaven?" Thimble hazarded.

Bormph's take was more on the snide side. "How about the Netherworlds? Word to the wise, guys. If you run across a god, be polite. If you smell a demon, don't bother with the courtesy."

Whinewaeyn's robe swept up the first steps, the butt of his staff tapping on the stone. The guidelight's soft glow glided upwards with the wizard in a slow, gentle motion, and as darkness pushed in after him, everyone quickly flocked into the light so as not to be left behind.

The stairs ended at a railless landing. The checkered flagstone floor went on for a distance, leading up to three oblong frames looming side by side, several feet apart. They looked like portals, but nothing wall-like surrounded them. Above each of the rectangles a stone tablet in the shape of an overturned trapezium was mounted, engraved with strange symbols: a single figure per portal, followed by two vertically aligned dots as if to present what lay below. Each symbol was different.

"What's this?" Bormph grunted. "Choose your own adventure?"

"Most unusual," observed Whinewaeyn. Whether he meant the missing walls or the puzzling symbols remained anyone's guess.

Thimble peered up at the leftmost portal, almost breaking his neck in the process, so enormous was it – about twice the barbarian's size! He could barely make out the rune all the way up there, but it looked like two sticks – or maybe two doting, limbless, headless stick*men* – leaning against each other, pierced in the middle with a spear-like implement. The two-winged massive stone door underneath stood wide open. That, however, was of little use, as a pile of massive rocks poured out of it, blocking the passage. *Maybe it's better that way,* Thimble thought, considering the gruesome rune, which was a far cry from the curlicued letters of the Common Tongue that he was used to.

"Hmm," Bormph let out, investigating the rocks.

Amjelle, perched on her frying pan, watched him. "It's no use. We won't get anywhere with that one."

Bormph turned. "Wizzer? You summoned rocks before. You think you could do it the other way round?"

"Well…" Whinewaeyn's mouth twisted. "*Summoning* is easy, relatively speaking. *Un*summoning…"

Bormph held up a hand. He sensed already where this was heading. "What about turning those rocks into, say, cabbage?"

From the wizard's expression, he didn't seem to chime with the idea.

"*Quorfex's Equation,*" Amjelle replied before the wizard could. "Transformation basics. Also known as the *Law of Mass Maintenance.*"

Bormph still looked puzzled, but Whinewaeyn approved the educational lecture with a nod and added that turning rocks into cabbages *could* be done, if one wanted to, but no one would, as the result would be boulder-sized cabbages, retaining the original weight of the rocks – and where would be the point in that?

As the dwarf groaned, the guidelight swung further along and Thimble got the chance to contemplate the rune above the second portal. It showed another stick (or stickman?) with two belly-shaped bulges attached on the right-hand side; a smaller one at the top, and a larger one at the bottom. If the upper bulge signified a head, it was definitely crooked and far too big in comparison to the stick, and by the same token, any healer would warn against a belly as large as the bottom bulge. This portal again had two wings, each equipped with a large iron ring to pull them to the side – which Bormph and Ramrok promptly did. The wings swung open without resistance, but then—

"You've got to be kidding me!"

Behind, now framed by the door casing, was a solid marble wall – as if what was missing on the left and right had somehow gathered in the centre.

"Particularly unusual," Whinewaeyn commented, scratching his head.

"An illusion?" Sylthia speculated.

Bormph rapped on whatever it was or wasn't. The sound was reminiscent of what it looked like: a wall. "Sounds like a wall." He knocked some more in different places. "Could someone make a sound illusion on top of a wall illusion, wizzer?"

Whinewaeyn considered the idea. "Possibly. But permanently? Questionable. If it makes the right sounds… How does it feel?"

According to Bormph, it felt… like a wall.

"And smell?"

Not being a big smeller of walls and hence ignorant of their normal aroma, Bormph noted that it was pretty much as expected. "Let's just say it's a wall," he summed up, and so everyone moved on to try their luck at portal number three.

The rune on the tablet above this one was more refined. Romantic, even. *It's the shape of a crescent moon,* Thimble thought. *Maybe it stands for the Silvery Sickle? Or it's a lot more sinister than that – a depiction of the instrument preferred by the Grim Reaper and his ratty bride...?*

If this one *was* indeed a portal, it hid it very well. Thimble noticed that no strip ran down the middle to separate the wings. It was all one single enormous wooden plank, hewn from what must have been a hell of a tree! No scratches tarnished the grey-painted surface. There was no handle to be found, no knob, no latch, no keyhole, no suggestion of any mechanism to operate it, and yet there were iron-wrought hinges on both sides.

Sylthia fished for opinions. "You don't think we're supposed to just knock, do you?"

Bormph's fists thumped against the wood. "Politeness gets you everywhere!"

But... apparently not.

"Could be some kind of puzzle," Thimble cautioned, taking one, two, three, four steps back to get a good look at the line-up of rectangles in its entirety. The only additional thing he registered was that everything – portals, frames, plaques, the piece of wall behind door number two, and the boulders, of course – was in shades of grey, as if all the colours had been sucked out of the place. Or the decorators had lacked imagination.

"If we can get through either one, the wooden portal is our best option," Sylthia said, committing herself to option three. She inspected the wood further. "Have you seen these?" Strange etchings ran down the sides of the rectangular slab. They came together at the bottom and the top, framing the unblemished smoothness in between.

"Runes..." Whinewaeyn followed the course of the markings with his eyes. "And numbers. None of it makes any sense."

"We've heard that before," Sylthia said. "Translate, wizard!"

"But these runes aren't even words. And the numbers neither."

"Reeks of some sort of protection," Amjelle ventured. "Make way!" She pushed the elf and wizard gently aside and held her hand up to perform an in-depth check, but then noticed her frying pan's deficiencies in the magical department. "Oh…"

"Don't worry, dear. Let me see what I can do…" Whinewaeyn started browsing mentally through his repertoire. "How about *Trinstrail's Universal Trap Trimmer*? Only works if it's a trap, of course. If it's not, it might… backfire, I guess. Which could make it worse. Better we try *Trinstrail's Trap Trier* first. That's a common spell often used to determine whether arcane mages have protected their spell books." He hesitated. "Though we're not talking about a spell book here. Hmm… Now, one could also make a case for *Murph's Wide Wide Wood*. Opens temporary rifts, if the material's right. One can slip right through, trap or no trap. But if I'm the one holding the hole open, how then would I pass through?"

Eventually, they tried the *Trap Trier*… with no effect whatsoever.

Whinewaeyn gave the portal an accusing look. "Should have turned dark blue if there was a trap. Or a lighter shade, if there isn't. I'm sure there's a good reason why it didn't do either." He wiggled his eyebrows, as if to shake a thought loose. "Could be the material," he hypothesized. "Maybe wood isn't *Trap Trier's* forte? Maybe it really only works with spell books. But aren't books made of wood too?" He thought some more. "A pity that we're out in the open. Give me a laboratory in a mage-tower and I could—"

"Wizzy?" An unexpected voice broke into his musings. It rumbled from the most unlikely of places: up. "Is head problem, yeah?"

Taken by surprise, Whinewaeyn turned in the direction of the rumble, and found Ramrok's sharp features looking back at him. The giant stood with his thumb pressed against his chin, as if thinking – a most unusual sight. "A… head problem," Whinewaeyn agreed. "Yes, yes. Quite right."

The barbarian stepped out of the shadows, and the thunder in his voice grew in volume: "Old barbarian ancestor say use shoulder for head problem. Always work. Or not."

"Er…" Whinewaeyn's thoughts knotted together.

"Is this: think less, hit hard. Ramrok show."

The giant left his deliberations at that, cracked his knuckles and then vaulted forward, launching his frame against the obstacle. The door protested with an irked groan, but refrained from retaliation, magical or otherwise. Before anyone could get a word in, the barbarian's steely body slammed once more into the wood, and then again and, yes, again, with no further objections raised. Finally the portal bent, splintered and burst open with a resounding crash.

"Done," Ramrok announced from the other side of the giant-sized hole. He lay sprawled over the floor behind the so-called portal, but was already collecting himself, as though this was a completely normal turn of events for a giant with too many muscles on his hands, and feet, and… just about everywhere. "This no trap, wizzy," he declared, rubbing his shoulder as he peeked back through the hole he had torn.

"Th-thank you," Whinewaeyn stammered, baffled. Then his mind came forward to have its say on the matter, and what it said was, *But… but… how could that ever have worked?* Only that Bormph said it first.

"With a door *that* size" – the dwarf's arms reached out to take its measure – "and *that* thick, with *that* kind of wood… It *shouldn't* have worked. It's outright *impossible*."

The hole refuted the argument by being there.

Ramrok paused from tearing away some loose splinters from the passage to look up. "Eh?" The barbarian's enthusiastic face eased back into its default state of bovine blankness.

Bormph poked his head through the hole and then crawled in. One by one, the rest came after and assured the confused barbarian that his ancestors' approach had been just fine, even if the details were still a bit muddied.

When Whinewaeyn's orb caught up with them, it unveiled yet more checkered flagstones. At first this was all there was to make out – nothing but a straight strip of stone floor marching away into uncertainty, wrapped in velvety night. No walls on either side. Bormph attempted to peek over the ledge into the looming abyss. That taught him two things: one, not everything is what it seems, and two, bumping your head on an invisible wall hurts just as much as the regular version. More so, if you take your headgear off first so as not to lose it to the depths.

"Ouch!" Bormph howled. "Damn it!"

"Allow me." Whinewaeyn kept his own head out of it, and tested the edge of the path with the lower end of his staff instead. Something sturdy and unbroken was established, which – when the wizard pressed his hand against it – was cold to the touch. Same on the other side. That made the strip more like a walled passage, maybe even a hallway: boundless in appearance, but limited in practice.

With a wave of the wizard's hand, the guidelight swooshed upward. No ceiling impeded its journey. High above, in the night sky–like infinity, streaks glinted in the orb's amber glow: dozens of pathways honeycombed the gloom up there, running along and across the curious hallway below.

Has something of a web, Thimble thought, and Sylthia nodded in agreement when she heard him whisper to that effect. Bormph's dwarven mind saw mineral veins in a translucent mine. *It's like the luminous Wheel of the Five with the stronger streaks serving as spikes,* thought Amjelle – even though, admittedly, the "wheel" was hung seriously askew. To Whinewaeyn the display resembled a level seven searing spell that had gotten a bit out of hand, where the strands had frozen in mid-sear and then someone had tiled over them.

"…" thought Ramrok. "…"

"Archmagus?"

Whinewaeyn felt a nudge at his side while he was still busy looking up, contemplating what it would take to freeze searing streaks and then tile over them. True wizardry, probably.

"I just remembered something. Those runes back there…" Amjelle's voice dropped to a hush as she noticed that everything she said bounced between the invisible walls long after she had spoken. "When you told us you couldn't translate them… You said the runes didn't form any *words…*"

"Yes, dear?"

"But you recognized them, right? We've seen the runes before."

"Why, of course," Whinewaeyn mumbled, as low as she. "The Forgotten."

"The Forgotten!" Thimble echoed. "Uh-oh."

Three days after Apocalypse Hour. Dimmerskeep.

The sky was alight. Actually, it was *a* light. One huge flash of white: bright, blazing and everywhere.

And yet, as sky-wide and sky-high as it was, the sky's light it was not. Instead, this extraordinary display of the incandescent kind had detonated into existence close to ground level with what can only be described as a din almighty. Which was very fitting. Nothing could've been more suitable for the launch of *Operation Big Bang*. What a racket it was! And what a light!

In time, the ringing in the ears of thousands of onlookers slackened into a tinkle. Eyes and ears adjusted, and by and by actual shapes resurfaced from the whiteness, confirming that – yes, indeed – Dimmerskeep was still around.

"There!" Shouts bubbled up. "There it is! Look!" Fingers pointed. Necks stretched and twisted. Small people stood on tiptoes. The tall ones just stood, rolling their eyes up. And everybody, tall or small, was in awe. Shrouded by a revolving cage of lightning bolts, a giant fiery object had just skyrocketed into... well, the sky. And it was still travelling. The magical monstrosity was on its way into the spheres, conveying defiance... and vowing destruction.

"It is… done!" Not too far away from the crowds on Main Lane, at the Studyarium of All Things Magical, Archmage Xoormrax yelled after his creation. "Done, *done, DONE!*"

Body aching, mind awhirl, energies spent and eyes fixed on a point high, high up, he collapsed. His slump was softened by a pool of three dozen fellow mages littering the inner courtyard. The scene was comparable to a battlefield. A whole hierarchy of wizardkind lay sprawled about in layers of arcane proficiency: apprentices at the bottom, elemental mages a level higher, with master magicians above, who were in turn cushioning the archmages on top. Everywhere around them, stray energy fields were still sputtering. Smoke slunk through the yard carrying a sulphurous miasma. A cough here, a moan there, and other less subtle noises of mages being sick filled the courtyard.

Xoormrax's tortured nose tilted up, and his eyes, weary as they were, followed the voyage of their deadly creation. *Armageddon* had been cast. Now everything else lay in the gods' hands… For the first time in his life, Xoormrax wished there were some.

Over at Mission Control in the Zarrafandan observatory, Normi Stargazer gazed at the stars. Also at a falling comet, and the magic missile heading towards it.

"Well?" Prince Dymmling petted his favourite gerbil with slow, strained strokes. "What do you make of it?"

"It's…" Normi's googly eyes checked and rechecked, then checked again. He jotted down some figures, pushed a few beads around on his abacus and scanned two columns in his notes simultaneously with one eye each. Then he went back to peering once more through the lens for final confirmation, and turned to report that "Yes, Your Highness, it's spot on! The trajectory is… *spot on!*"

"So we *will* hit it?"

"I've never been more certain about anything in my whole life!" Normi declared, producing his calculations. "See here, Your Majesty. The diameter of the missile is supposed to be close to seven times seven yards, give or take some yards, which should amount to an approximate mass of—"

"Spare me the details." The Prince waved him off. "Jolly good, then."

To tell the truth, Prince Dymmling wasn't certain about the gnome's certainty, but he didn't particularly care whether he multiplied or potentiated aiming for a seven. This would have to do. He ambled over to have another glance out of the window, under which exuberance was now sweeping the streets. Even his princelings at long last crawled from their hideout under the desk and joined him. They came to notice that in the wake of *Operation Big Bang's* launch, the protesters had switched sides. Once the tide turned against a common enemy, everybody flocked behind the best option, more so if it was the only viable one. For the first time since the disappearance of the first garden gnome, Klimbish and Rimfish tasted the scent of hope, and they didn't mind its awful smell. They could even admire the crimson sky now that it wouldn't last much longer.

"Makes you think, though, doesn't it?" the Prince mused.

"What does, Your Majesty?" Klimbish gave him a polite smile.

"That it would work. If the comet is to blame for whatever transpires down here, casting such a potent spell should have brought nothing but out-and-out disaster upon us."

"Well, it hasn't," Klimbish replied, wrapping the idea up.

"And that's that." Rimfish put a bow on it.

"Unless…" the Prince unwrapped it again, "it's the other way round. Has anyone thought of that? What if something's not right *here*, and it brought the comet down? If the universe is in perfect harmony, going about its universal business, then why is this happening? Maybe we're missing something."

More hoots and cheers from outside washed over the awkward silence manifesting itself in the observatory's dome.

"Besides…" The Prince's eyes narrowed. "Didn't you predict the end of the world only recently, Normi? Because it's… in the stars?"

"Oh, yes. Yes!"

"So what of it? Can't be both, now, can it?"

"Ah, there's still plenty that could make *that* happen, Your Majesty," Normi supplied cheerfully. "Even if we shoot the thing down, the stars still aren't aligned properly. An apocalypse has many faces. If it's not one thing, then it's another."

Plonk!

Without handing in prior notice, a curious, out-of-place jingle-jangle issued from deep inside the bowels of the skyglass. There was a stunned silence long enough to attract hard, inquisitive stares. Then it quickly became apparent, even for non-tech savvy observers, which part of the intricate mechanism had a problem: the part that held it all together. [*]

---

[*] That particular part had once been put in place by a budding youth not keen on tilling the family fields, which is why he set out to become an

Plonk-a-donk!

The skyglass creaked sideways, one of its joints unfastened. Bits and bolts spilled all over the place. At one point, the main tube had had enough of losing components and pooled some weighty parts somewhere inside itself, causing the whole apparatus to tilt streetwards. To shrieks of terror, the instrument tore from its mounting and ripped half the wall with it as it came – *ka-ba-da-booossssh!* – crashing down. The building jittered and swayed, masonry raining after, as revellers emptied the place in a jiffy.

The dust settled. From inside the remains of the observatory's dome, several pairs of eyes gaped through the apparatus-sized cleft. The sight on the street below spelled disaster, and yet the gazes locked on to something even more alarming: a dark shape in the now clearly visible sky. It grew rapidly like a hole with an appetite, zooming towards the brilliant magical light rocketing up at it from below.

Finally! Normi thought as he gawked. The pinnacle of his stargazing life had come into plain view. No need for a skyglass anymore.

What a marvellous black, mused Prince Dymmling. *And how it's glittering! Goes so well with the sky's crimson…*

A few streets away, Archmage Xoormrax – bedded peacefully on his pile of fellow mages – was also watching.

---

engineer in the Dimmerskeep observatory. Or so had been the case until an apocalyptic chain of events began fraying the universe in reverse. In the process, it occurred to the universe that the lad's father never had a second son. Long story short, a screw got loose somewhere.

A half-smirk lingered on his lips, a blissful reminder of a job well done. Magic would save the world once more. Magic always did the trick. Magic, and pitch-perfect precision. Though the more he looked at the fiery missile and the celestial body it would – with utmost certainty – collide with, the more his eyes became apprehensive, and his smile melted away.

He jolted up, oblivious to the aching pain in his limbs. A thought stabbed through his head, riding a surging sense of doom. The comet's make-up was… what? He could see it clearly now. Really?

"Obsidian?" he stormed. "OBSIDIAN!?" Of every bloody material in the whole universe, it had to be magic-repellent obsidian… "The gods must be KIDDING!"

At the same time. On the fringes of the Peet Fields.

Valiant Defender of the Realm and Bear of a Man, Commander General Royt Montrakhán, didn't concern himself with comets, nor with magic missiles. He was a man of the sword. Which is not to say that he wasn't aware of the white flash that had flared up from the direction of Dimmerskeep – something that would give anyone pause – but whatever had been launched into the spheres was on its way now, and there was little to be done about the remainder of its course from down here. So that was that.

The sky flickered a little while longer, then reverted to its former crimson. If anything, the blood-red skies made it easier to get in the mood for battle, Montrakhán found. Though he didn't expect anything of the sort, of course. Vensk wouldn't dare. The whale-sized harebrain and his bat-eared friends might have ambushed the hapless Klampf while tower hunting, but a wimp like Klampf was only good enough for heading the Mish-Clash parade anyway. The commander general considered himself cut from a different cloth. Besides, he had everything but the kitchen sink behind him. Heavy cavalry was deployed in strategic places. Dotted over the Peet Hills, foot soldiers, pikemen and archers lay in wait, and reinforcements from allied Aermerlyn were about to arrive any minute. If the enemy tried to get through the Fields – and there was no other way to move a massive number of troops – he'd be there, waiting. The ground was open, flat and firm, perfect for ploughing right through enemy lines. Truth be told, Montrakhán kind of regretted that there would be no attack. He would have loved to teach the clown a lesson.

Suddenly the camp stirred. Hushed voices scattered. Several mailed hands extended in the direction where an attack *could* possibly happen but certainly *wouldn't*.

Commander General Montrakhán drew himself up in his saddle and edged his horse forward. It was hard not to notice that the south-eastern side of the Peet Fields had turned hazy with movement. Also, that the haze was getting greener by the minute… and it had grown heads! On top of that, his own outriders had come galloping back! That was the point at which Montrakhán realized that the Fields were teeming with enemy forces.

"They're advancing! Fast!" His lieutenants sounded the official alarm. "Goblins! Orcs! Thick as flies! Take positions!"

Goblins? Orcs? On the advance? The commander general kicked his destrier forward and surged up a nearby elevation to see the unlikely alliance in its fullness. And there it was. Everything green, big or small, was… charging. The gruntlings must have been about a mile away, maybe two, but not for long. They were quick. *Why* were they so quick? This was an exercise worthy of one of the Prince's fancy medals, for distinguished silliness perhaps. If they kept moving at a rate like that, the bat-ears and their oversized cousins would be too exhausted to do battle even before they reached the other side! Montrakhán was a man who honoured a proper fight, and if they wanted to have one…

He signalled, and a whole regiment arrayed behind him. A throng of lances jolted up. A minute or so passed.

"GOOO!" The force of Montrakhán's voice carried over the field. And with that, horses thundered eastwards, the ranks fanning out to engage the enemy.

There was a twist, though, that the battle-trained commander hadn't seen coming. Halfway through the charge, it became apparent that the gruntlings weren't attacking after all. They were fleeing. Fleeing like mad!

Farther back, where the Joghavri was supposed to waste away in the numbing sun, the desert looked more deserted than ever. That's because the sand had deserted the desert, and a pitch-black hole – a yawning, wasteland-sized void – had replaced it. Now, the Joghavri was without a doubt among the least exciting places in existence, but Montrakhán began to miss it dearly when he and his troops realized they were storming full speed towards hordes of orcs and goblins being chased by what seemed to be aggressively expanding nothingness.

"Whoa! WHOA!" Montrakhán tore on his reins as hard as he could. The hole was even closer than he thought.

Yells spread across the battlefield, mixed with whinnying and snorting as further mounts balked, reared, broke rank and swerved about. Lances dug into the turf, heaving riders out of their saddles. The most overzealous soldiers close to the frontline got hurled over the brink of the advancing abyss screaming, screaming and… screaming no more. The blackness widened, pushed nearer. In the confusion, gruntlings ducked and weaved through what had once been a tight formation.

"Back!" Montrakhán blared into the mayhem, yanking his destrier around. "REGROUP!"

He was facing the Peet Hills again, the direction from which he'd set out, and somehow the enemy forces were in front of him still. Who was after whom here wasn't as clear cut anymore. The commander general decided to let goblins be goblins and orcs be orcs, and shot past a band of scampering snout-noses to collect his troops and thoughts someplace northwards.

If the battling parties had paid any attention, they would have seen banners emblazoned with the Aermerlyn weasel and its three-spiked crown lining up in the west; the Zarrafandan ally's vanguard had arrived. Seeing all hell break loose, the fresh troops dug in their spurs and rushed into the fray to save the day. At this point Montrakhán's heavy cavalry was already in a state of dissolution, chased by a handful of goblins here and the odd club-waving orc there, and together they all made for the hills. Halfway into their advance, the newcomers too realized there was a lack of landscape looming farther back and joined the merry scattering across the Fields.

Just when they thought things had turned weird, they got even weirder still.

Moments apart, without so much as a sound, hill by hill wavered, shifted, tilted and slipped away, and when all of them were through, the once verdant Peet Hills were naught but an unbroken line of horizon.

Montrakhán stared back at the emptiness gaining ground behind them. His face buckled even more when – due to the lack of landscape – his gaze travelled further northwards than it should have been able to, and he saw that the stretch of hill-less bleakness was also swarming with a host of people. Literally. A host. Of people. On foot, mounted, operating heavy war machinery. He pulled his reins yet again, more vigorously.

For a fraction of a second, the commander general wondered why Aermerlyn's forces were advancing from the north as well, why they were thrice the size of the western contingent, why they had been hiding behind the now non-existent Peet Hills, and why on earth they were pushing Caeshian catapults. Then he realized the forces actually had something very Caeshian about them, including their banners. The Empress's sigil – the spiked crown – flapped in the wind on all of them. Suddenly Montrakhán got a sense of what a pebble on the shore must feel when waiting for the tide. A war horn blared, and the hordes came flooding southwards.

The Valiant Defender of the Realm's insides churned. The end of his tether had been officially reached. An army was storming in his direction, his ally's defence line had started off half-hearted and was breaking further, and his own soldiers and hundreds of snout-noses were circling each other like startled chickens chased by an abyss that was still closing in. Just as he considered all this, the earth underneath him went for a serious rumble.

Amid the roar, a series of lightning bolts lashed out at what was unfolding below. Their garish brightness flooded the battlefield, torching the commander general's incredulous eyes.

He cocked his head skywards. "What the..." – *KA-BOOOOOOOOOOOOOM!* – "...IS GOING ON?"

Never before had the crack of dawn sounded so intense. Peals piled upon peals came cascading down like a class reunion of thunders remembering the good times.

When Montrakhán's squint finally broke through the unreal light, the scene seemed to change blink by blink. Though one common thread ran through it all: the battlefield was emptying out... Rows of soldiers, regardless of fealty, dwindled left and right, going the same uncanny path as the Peet Hills: wavering, shifting and slipping away into some unknown pocket of existence, leaving no trace behind. When the commander general finally managed to pry his eyes fully open, all that was left was but a handful of his own men, the odd orc or goblin, and less than half of the allied and enemy forces.

The thunder kept rumbling, but the eye-hurting light was gone, replaced by a dark mass that blotted out a sizeable portion of the crimson sky and stabbed earthwards. The giant rock, unblemished, shiny and fatal, hadn't deviated an inch from its course. And the field of magical energy it had now picked up and was dragging behind it only continued to expand...

Miles away, Prince Dymmling watched the phenomenon through the recent hole ripped in the observatory wall.

"Isn't it utterly...? Unspeakably...?" He stood wonderstruck, screwing up his eyes to make the most of it. "Rimmy, would your care to enlighten me? What's the word I'm thinking of?"

"Um..."

"The word, Rimmy!"

"P-portentous?" stammered Rimfish. "Ill-boding? C-catastrophic?"

"Grisly?" Klimbish offered crisply by comparison. "Grim?"

"No, no, none of those. It's more like—"

Rimfish made a princelier guess. "B-beautiful?"

"Beautiful!"

Princeling Rimfish blinked. He was choking on the sensations coming and going inside of him. "B-but, if I may... Beauty aside, the plan didn't quite..." How else to put it? "It didn't quite p-p-pan out, so..."

"Sooo beautiful..." breathed the Prince.

The spectacle offered more colours and sparks than any fireworks he could've envisioned, reminiscent of a butterfly spreading its rainbow-coloured wings. A rather humongous butterfly circled by an army of fireflies, growing larger by the second as it hurtled towards them. Utterly unique.

In the Holy Quintity's Grand Cathedral, Archbishop Vynnfield peered out of his own version of a hole, in his case a stained-glass window with a sizeable lack of stained glass. Behind him, at the far end of the nave, the voices in the pews were still murmuring, more desperately and out of rhythm than ever.

Might this be... the Advent of the One? the archbishop pondered, his thoughts spurred by the abandon professed by the anti-apocalyptic praying unit. He felt a rare flush of anticipation course through his mortal flesh. Could it be that the Grand Revelation, the Time of Reckoning, was here? What was it he was looking at through his hole? Was the One riding the comet with... angelic wings? Even if he squinted, he didn't quite see it yet. Perhaps the One had turned into a giant butterfly? Certainly whatever was coming down looked like one. Divinity could take all sorts of shapes, he knew. Legends on these matters were all over the place. Why, when he was but a squirt, he'd been convinced that his teddy bear had been something divine too.

The prophets' verses were vague on the minutiae of the final hours, he realized now – very vague indeed. But suggestive. Maybe deliberately so. Archbishop Vynnfield strained his eyes in an odd mixture of hope and fear to get a glimpse of the god through the swaths of incense slinking around the sanctuary. Then another thought struck him: if this was the One… then where was the Other? Not to speak of the whole holy rest…

From a nearby alley, Shady Shoo's view was coloured a little differently.

"It's a strange beast, so it is. Like a black hole with wings. Bit tentacle-ish," he told Blind Bertha, cocking his head this way and that, and then that way and this. "Kinda like an inflated insect, ya know? Big, big bugger about to eat us all! Is that what ya saw? Ya seen the big, big bugger eat us all?"

Blind Bertha said nothing. She only pushed her toes into her slippers. She was ready. Warm and ready.

In the palace gardens, something big awaited the comet's descent. It was a pointed nightcap-wearing giant of a dwarf – that is to say, a rock-hewn version of one. From the comet's perspective, the fellow probably looked more like a garden gnome, which was part design and part coincidence.

The sculpture was ringed by a bunch of dwarves – actual dwarves – who had first chiselled and then lugged the whole thing through half the town to comply with the Prince's latest stroke of genius. Now all of them, statue included, were staring the apocalypse straight in the eye. It was only common sense to a dwarf that said eye looked like a piece of black rock, so there was some confidence among them that the oversized stone fellow in their midst would have some effect salvation-wise. In the end, faith was all that mattered.

"Stonefather," the head stonemason's gravelly voice declared, "we've done our part." A slight quiver slipped in, despite his conviction, adding a few pebbles of doubt. "Erm… Your turn, Great One!"

But if salvation was going to arrive at all, it was delayed.

The obsidian menace continued to rumble along. Its titanic sun-eclipsing shadow crept like the darkest of nights over the goings-on below. Around its edges, the sky glimmered and shimmered with scores of tiny flashes, soon stretching from one end of the horizon to the other, a web of magical discharge trailing behind. The air trembled, thunder roared and a growing thrum underpinned it all from below.

At some point the earth was so a-jitter that everything on it seemed to exist in two places at once. And maybe it was the burden of picking one spot over another that did it for everything, because whatever there was, little by little, became less of something and more of nothing, until there wasn't much of anything anymore at all. A little bit here, then a little bit there jittered away. The bigger things went first. The landscape. Then livestock. People.

The apocalypse worked its way down its list. Among the more prominent victims was Commander General Royt Montrakhán. Gone with a shake and a flicker. The Valiant Defender of the Realm and Bear of a Man was reaped from the battlefield without having suffered even a single blow. Archbishop Vynnfield dove into a cloud of incense and never came out again. Head Shaman H'roc-Noc'sh found that despite life after the Great Darkness having some promising twists, one of them was that the aftermath would do away with him after all. Shake, flicker, gone. Next, the apocalypse had an appetite for a gerbil.

"O-o-oh…" his Royal Princeliness stammered as the rhythm of his stroking fingers broke. "Ruffles?" he spluttered. "R-r-ruffles!"

The Prince twisted his head to look around, but got more than he bargained for. His whole body was sent for a spin, courtesy of a universe breaking apart. He landed facedown.

Trying to get up again, the Prince found that he lacked a helping hand, which – as he realized – was because there were no assistants around to lend him one. Inconceivable under different circumstances. But there was no bald gnome astrologer keeping him company either, and no skyglass (or pieces of one for that matter). And – more puzzling still – there was a distinct shortage of furniture and decorative items, why, even walls! Most inscrutable of all, the floor he had just hit also lacked a handful of basic qualities, among them colour, texture, and, most glaringly… presence. How could he have hit it then? he wondered.

Maybe he hadn't, because he wasn't there either, like everyone else. And thus, as Prince Dymmling weighed this as the most plausible of all potential explanations, he potentially eliminated his own plausibility too.

Plop!

The End of Days was mostly ignored in Dimmerskeep's elven-tended arboretum. The elves brushed aside the rocking and booming, the panicking on the streets, the fact that bits and pieces of what others called "the world" were dwindling away by the minute. They didn't even mind that the soil next to them was showing signs of caving in. Turmoil was met with calm and singsong, and to keep their focus, they had even bought blindfolds and earmuffs – at only 4.99 in a set from Bargaining Bert's Big End Times Sale.

"*Ahm-gha-dham... Gha-dham-ahm... Dham-ahm-gha...*"

But the blindfolds and the earmuffs quickly disappeared.

So be it, thought the elves. The Dreameress dreams beginnings and endings, even for stuff from the bargain bin.

Little by little, the elven chants thinned out.

Things moved fast from there. Phenomenally fast.

Shortly before the grand collision, there was nothing much world-like left anymore for a comet to collide with. Landmarks that once loomed large, picturesque stretches of land, dormant hamlets or thriving cities, whole mountain chains – they were all notably absent. The world had shrunk to a bare, lifeless expanse, and even that had already been nibbled away in great measure by an abyss's brazen voracity.

Then it was curtains for that last bit too. The abyss ran out of anything to gnaw on and made itself obsolete.

Which left nothing at all. Except maybe the stench of betrayal; the comet's rendezvous with another kind of rock had fallen through, and maybe that's why, as though ashamed or cross or both, the obsidian menace and the rags of magic dancing around it slipped out of time and space as well, leaving nothing but nothingness itself.

And yet, a throbbing and a thrumming pervaded the Void, crescendoed even. It turned into a screech that howled and howled on... and on... and on, until it grew into a choppy, unrecognizable, otherworldly kind of shriek – violent and urgent, a travesty of a shrill – cutting through what was left of eternity.

Eeeek-k-k-k-k-k-k-k-eeee-k-k-k-k-k-eeee-k-k-k-k-k...

CHAPTER 20

Worldwide Weavings

Thimble turned the object in his hand. It was a book, for what it was worth, identical in shape, size and thickness to all the others they had found: square, slate-coloured, leathery, a handspan wide and high, and altogether untouched by the looks of it. Not so much as a single dog-ear. Only the titles etched into the bindings varied, abound with pierced or big-bellied stickmen and all kinds of other twisted runes, characters once devised by the Forgotten.

The party had arrived in an octagonal chamber, one of many they'd met since the end of the strange hallway. And like the corridor this chamber, as the others, had no ceiling. Darkness reigned above, punctured by far-away twinkling dots a bit like indoor versions of stars – but in open-ceilinged labyrinths one never knows what's in and out, beneath or beyond. Otherwise, the tiny rooms were sparsely furnished. Uncluttered, to give it a positive spin. At most, the odd alcove accommodated pedestals holding alabaster cubes, glassy orbs, crystals and pyramids, or vases without flowers – all glued on.

Nobody had bothered to put doors onto any of the chambers they were poking through either; the only things on the walls were book-lined shelves, and there were more books than could be read in a lifetime. The rooms were connected by corridors with invisible walls and tile-less spirals that substituted for stairwells, which made everyone woozy the higher they climbed, stout warriors included. Ramrok, for his part, had found refuge in some corner and was snivelling like the little girl he had uncovered deep down within. He couldn't even rest on a chair, because there were none. The place was like one giant library without a single seat. Whoever it was that had built the place, must have had no rear-ends. The sight of someone like that would at least have livened the place up a bit, but there were no traces of anyone, with or without rears, and so neither were there any librarians snarling "Shhh!"

Amjelle held a tome under Whinewaeyn's nose. "What's this one about?"

"*On Back…*" he translated, "*…and Forth. On Back and Forth.*"

Amjelle put it back where she had pulled it from. "Why, it must be the sequel to that other one… What was it? *On Beyond and Beneath*? Gripping stuff, I'm sure."

"Patience," Whinewaeyn said slowly, letting his fingertips run over the spines. "Haven't found you a romance yet, but I'll keep looking."

He bustled over to the next shelf, tingling with anticipation that some thousand-year-old suspense novel was only waiting for its great discovery.

"Ah, here we go, dear! *Longing,*" he read aloud, going through the next stack, but then shook his head. "No, false alarm. Certainly not a romance." He looked at some more titles. "*Lengthening…* hmm… *Loathing, Lodging, Lathering.*" None of it looked like bestseller material, let alone sultry erotic adventures. The next shelf changed theme. "*Daylight. Debris. Dirt. Dust.* Odd assortment, I'd say."

"Speaking of which, here's what *I'd* like to know," Bormph grunted from a corner, where he was chewing on a piece of wyvern meat and a deep thought. "Dust." He swallowed as only a dwarf could, skipping most of the chewing. "Where are the dust bunnies? You see any around here?"

Whinewaeyn clutched his robe, giving it a vigorous shake. As he did so, the air around him came alive, swirling with a myriad of particles as if a miniature universe had been born. All and sundry were invited to the dance, not just good old dust, but all its relations too: sandy reminders of their days in the Joghavri, campfire ashes, morsels from the past couple of meals and chunks of dirt kept as souvenirs from non-retraceable mud road journeys. The dust plumes prompted immediate evacuation.

"Wizzer!" Bormph bellowed through a cough from a wall-less corridor he had just escaped to. "What are you *doing?*"

"Dust," Whinewaeyn coughed back. "You wanted dust, and there it *is… cough, cough.* Dust."

"But that's *your* dust! It wasn't here, gramps! Would you listen?" The dwarf fanned away most of what was still swirling around him. "I'm talking about *this* place," he snorted. "Why do these Forgotten have books on dirt and dust, when there's not a single mote of the stuff here?"

It was a strange thing to complain about. Nobody, starting with chamber maids, was keen on having dust around in the first place.

"Who knows how ancient this place is and what's been going on all this time if it wasn't gathering dust?" Bormph lumbered over to an identical-looking chamber on the other side of the corridor, where he let his thumb run over a random row of books. "See?" He held his finger in the wizard's face as soon as he joined him. It was greasy from the dwarf's wyvern snack, and so were the books now, but no dust blemished its greasiness.

Whinewaeyn eyed him. "So you're saying there wouldn't be any dust without us?" Somewhere under the wizard's floppy hat his brain must have begun working. "Same as we wouldn't be here if we hadn't brought us?"

Bormph tried the thought, but couldn't hack it. "Wizzer, think straight! Strange things are going on here. Open your eyes!"

"To see what isn't there?" Whinewaeyn scrutinized the room in even more detail than before, focusing on the bookless part of it. "Hmm… What else should be here that isn't?"

"Chairs, tables, lamps…" Amjelle listed. "Almost anything one can think of. It's as if the builders just made off this morning… As if…" She stopped short of a thought. Her eyes rose to trace the top of the room, looking for any signs of cobwebs – but as there was no visible ceiling, there weren't any corners either, let alone cobwebs occupying traditional cobweb space. She shouldered her frying pan and drew in a long shuddering breath, trading glances with Sylthia and Whinewaeyn. "As if… the passage of time itself has come to a standstill around here."

Thimble stuck up his nose, eyes glinting with excitement. "What if it's like that place the gnome told us about? What if it hasn't aged, like, ever?"

The wizard's bony hands quickly waved the idea away. "Why, that can't be, little one. Someone *made* this. It's just

412

not been lived in. Also, we did something *before* in here, and we'll do some more *later*, I'm sure. And whatever we've done since a moment prior is now a thing of the past. There wouldn't be a current moment, if all this wasn't so."

"Here's a thought," Sylthia said. "What if all these moments… are like the dust?" Hovering behind Thimble, she looked the wizard square in the eye. "This is certainly no ordinary place. Time must have something to do with it. What if we—"

"…brought the notion with us? What a peculiarly curious thought…" It took the wizard a few more moments. "Why, threep-throlly-thrum-throb! You've touched on something, elf. Time… it's at the centre of everything we've been through. We skipped ahead in time. The gnome went back it. Now we enter this fancy place, and it might not have any time at all. Not by itself, anyway. Huh…" Another thought arrived. "That rock… Could it have been a sort of a time portal?"

Thimble had never imagined a time portal before. He tried to cobble the thing together. "What, with all the time in the world on the outside, and none in here?"

Whinewaeyn stooped forward and peered around the spotless, cobweb-free chamber. "If only the gnome were still here. He might have had some ideas."

"What about that word?" Thimble asked.

"What word?" Sylthia rubbed her milky chin in thought.

"The gnome's word! The only one he told us. We fought the dragon with it."

"Oh, that." The elf's tone was all but hopeful. "That's not much of an answer. More like another question."

"*K-rn-tk-prt.*" Thimble tried it nevertheless. It was the only magic – no, mystic – word he knew, and it wasn't much. But it reached somewhere deep he couldn't understand, into a mystic *somewhere*, and it had saved his life once. Besides, he hadn't heard any china smashing for a bit.

No sooner had he uttered it, than the shape of a teapot slid out of thin air.

Presently, the ghostly image began to flicker, as if reconsidering its appearance. Instead of creating a solid teapot, however, the image fell away into nothingness, then came back and, while still shaky, drifted across the room like pipe fumes on a mission. The teapotty fog started towards a non-existing corner of the non-existing ceiling – but en route it gave up and wafted away.

Thimble looked after it, perplexed. "Is it supposed to do that?"

"After me!" Whinewaeyn swished purposefully out of the room, his robe billowing behind. "Out here." He set such a brisk pace that it was too much even for his magical light, which came swerving behind, bouncing against the doorless doorframe and sputtering sparks of disapproval.

"*K-rn-tk-prt?*" the wizard now croaked from the corridor. He cocked his head in anticipation.

A fresh image of a teapot swam up, and the whole spectacle repeated itself. The apparition formed, curled upwards... and vanished.

Whinewaeyn's observant eyes beamed from their sockets. "It's being drawn!" he said with conviction. "It points someplace. To something... high up."

Already he was on his way towards the next spiral connecting them to the floor above, the rest of the party close on his heels. He bustled up and unleashed the mystic word yet again, thus conjuring up fresh bearings. Then he chased after it along wall-less paths, past book-filled chambers, up a whole series of vertiginous ramps. He climbed and climbed and climbed still, until their ever-so-fleeting ghostly guides no longer soared any higher when called upon, and just darted straight as an arrow into the passage ahead.

Keeping their steps cautious, they followed until an archway surged from the darkness. A huge one, important looking. It spanned a gate-sized opening underneath, behind which the gloom thinned down somewhat.

Bormph hefted his axe. "Draw your sword, big fellow," he muttered to Ramrok. "Big nasty teapot boss coming up or something." He peeked over his shoulder to make out his large-framed colleague-in-arms, but it took the barbarian some time to take shape amid the shadows. When he emerged, his muscled bulk staggered forwards, then backwards, then careened sideways, almost knocking the wizard off his feet. Bormph leapt between the two of them at the last moment before the wizard was squashed, and parked the barbarian's massive body against one of the corridor's invisible walls.

"Bleurgh…" The mighty warrior's face was pickle-green. The party members cleared the throwing-up perimeter.

"No head for heights," Amjelle diagnosed from a distance. "And Snowflake isn't any better off," she supplied, seeing Sylthia pick up the tottering cub. He was more colour-resistant than the barbarian, but just as dizzy. "They need a little rest."

"Well then. Keep an eye on the cub, big one…" Whinewaeyn hesitated. "Or let the cub keep an eye on you. I'd say, just guard each other, somewhere around… here. We'll holler when we need, um, a shoulder or something."

A thankful groan later, the barbarian plopped onto the floor and pulled the cub close.

"After you?" Whinewaeyn suggested to his guidelight. It was still hanging in the air in front of the threshold underneath the arc, hissing mildly.

The orb heeded the command, gave its version of a huff – a mix of a low buzz and a prolonged flicker – then trundled off into the void.

Speaking of voids…

Meanwhile, out there in the post-apocalyptic Void, the grandmother of all emptiness, nothing much was going on.

And that's no exaggeration. Nothingness is what voids stand for. The post-apocalyptic Void naturally had a higher degree of emptiness than any common void, which one might colloquially term a "hole", "gap", or "pit", any of the kind encountered in the wild when looking down a chasm or into a cave mouth. Your everyday middle-of-the-road hole, invariably has something that enfolds it, something that thus makes it what it is: a contained bit of nothing, or – put another way – a lack of something else.

The big thing, *the* Void (with a capital 'V'), is a whole different hole. It comes in two varieties. One – the *pre*-apocalyptic version – is an inside-out kind of hole, so empty and vast that it swaddles everything else there is in it, rendering it infinitesimally small in comparison. Quite a clever concept for something that isn't much to begin with.

The *post*-apocalyptic Void for its part has nothing to engulf. As a total absence of anything, it's illimitable nothingness, honed to perfection. The crux: being a paragon of everything empty defeats the grand Void's self-esteem. It cannot stand out against anything, as there's nothing to compare itself to. Even if you're the greatest Void in the universe, there's no one to brag to. The post-apocalyptic Void has no friends, no enemies. In fact, being a post-apocalyptic Void is no fun at all.

So who could blame the Void for shrieking incessantly?

Eeeek-k-k-k-k-k-k-k-eeee-k-k-k-k-k-k-k-eeee-k-k-k-k-k...

Wizard and company passed through the archway into a kind of antechamber. Pallid light filled it, though its source remained undeterminable.

While as octagonal as the rest of the rooms, the chamber turned out to be far more spacious; the orb had to ascend a great deal to capture the entirety of it. A stone lectern dominated the centre. Grouped around it, four marble columns grew ceilingward, equidistant from the stand and whatever made up the room's confines. Only the lower parts of the columns were actually visible, of course, for the higher they reached, the more the darkness ate them up. Likewise, the gloom had half feasted on the "walls", or rather the wall-sized tapestries that covered them. On the far side yawned another exit the size of a gate, leading into yet more gloom, with which the place seemed well equipped. A chilly draught wafted through like a bad omen.

They checked the wall-substituting tapestries. A common motif ran through them. They formed a patchwork of...

"Maps?" Amjelle's eyes drank it all in. "This is..." she started, but then fell silent, muted by the overwhelming level of detail woven into each of the hangings – the precision of the embroidery, the lush, lively colours surrounding her. She stepped closer to study one of the pieces in particular, her hand reaching out to trace the mountain chains and rolling hills sprawling across the fabric. Her fingers travelled across forests and fens and wolds, over rivers, lakes, waterfalls, and even a whirlpool working on wrecking a ship. Sprinkled in between were symbols marking settlements, strongholds, places of worship and the like.

A hand touched her shoulder. "Look at this one, Am…"

She turned and followed Sylthia's eyes to another spot on the same chart.

"See that forest? The one next to what must be an ocean?" The elf nodded at the canvas. "Isn't it shaped like… like our Thyael'ka'lar?" She bit her lip. "Almost… *precisely?*"

Amjelle mouthed something inaudible as she locked on to the tree symbols Sylthia had pointed out, the ones hugging a sea. Her gaze lowered and came across a wriggling line wending its way towards the great blue expanse directly south of the forest, emptying out into it. The thread it was woven from shimmered like an actual river touched by the sun. When she traced its course backwards, her finger ended up at the far side of the tapestry, at a body of water fed by two tributaries, a lake next to a major settlement. "And this river's like…"

"…the Voldrinar," Whinewaeyn filled in with a rasp like sandpaper working away on a piece of hardwood. He cleared his throat. "Says so here." The end of his staff dabbed on the Forgotten runes snaking along the thick blue line in lighter blue shades. "And over here we have" – his staff found the spot Amjelle had started out with – "the Grand Lake. And all around it…"

"Dimmerskeep!" Thimble hooted from below.

The wizard finished with a sweeping gesture covering a large part of the map and the runes that ran across it. "*Zar-ra-fan-da*," he spelled out.

Thimble couldn't believe it. "Dimmerskeep? Zarrafanda? In those exact words?"

A helmeted head popped up at hip height between the wizard and the healer. Its wearer elbowed Thimble out of the way to see things with his own eyes, and after some roving back and forth over the canvas, Bormph had identified items that very much looked like the Peet Fields, the Silvery Sickle and his declared nightmare of a landscape, the Joghavri.

"Words of the Forgotten?" he muttered in doubt as well.

"Words of the Forgotten," Whinewaeyn confirmed.

"But… this cannot be!" It was all foggy for Thimble. "Zarrafanda wasn't even there half a century ago! And it's only been Dimmerskeep since the Prince named it so! The Forgotten couldn't have—"

"*Dim-mers-keep*," Whinewaeyn read again, bringing his nose so close to the canvas that it almost touched it. "No two ways of writing it. Or reading it."

"How old *is* this map?" Thimble made out what must have been Willwold-on-Glee. Then he stood on tiptoes to gauge the tapestry's upper parts. It just went on and on and on.

"How old can maps be, little one, if this is a timeless place?"

Thimble simply goggled back up at the wizard, who was tugging at his beard.

"We must have entered the gods' sanctuary," Amjelle dared to say out loud, if only in a half whisper.

"The… gods?" Thimble said slowly, checking for divine eavesdroppers. "You sure?"

"Would explain a couple of things, wouldn't it?"

"That the gods are… the Forgotten?" Sylthia ventured.

"Any better ideas?"

"How about seers?" came from Amjelle's left.

Arms crossed, the healer gave Whinewaeyn a one-eyed glance. "With a magic loom behind the world, Archmagus? Forgotten seers making future maps? Well, I doubt it."

"Or…" Bormph inserted himself in the conversation from below, "whoever owns this place is still around, and has kept up with developments."

"And who'd that be?"

"Otherworldlings."

"Otherworldlings?"

"Otherworldlings. Hailing from who-knows. A different dimension or some such. Whatever's out there."

Lost in thought, Thimble pursed his lips and a mystery-laden whistle came out.

"You tell me what's out there," Bormph said. "Could be anything. Anything that's not *in here.*"

"Why would they have a place like this, your otherworldlings?" Amjelle's hand raked through her hair. "It's not like they ever launched an invasion. Not that we know of…"

"Well, not yet perhaps," Bormph maintained. "So far they have just invaded this particular space behind the magic mountain."

Thimble still had his questions. Like, "And where are they now?"

"Hiding?" Bormph hovered about uncomfortably. "Might be spying on us right… now." However, no spy, alien or otherwise, leapt out of the shadows to congratulate them for having found them out.

"Hmm… Then what about the Forgotten?" Amjelle tilted her head quizzically. "There are Forgotten runes all over the place. They must have been here first."

Bormph shrugged his broad shoulders. "Obliterated?"

"And the otherworldlings stole the Forgotten runes? To put them in their weavings? Sure. Because they liked them so much, your space invaders!"

"What do I know, healer? That gnome's word… that '*k-rn-tk-prt*'… It's not Forgotten, is it? Then what *is* it?"

Thimble watched another teapot draw itself into the air the moment the dwarf uttered the word. Once more, the strands that made it up were pulled away into the blackness gathered at the other side of the chamber with such force that they almost twisted into a thicker rope before coming apart again. *They must be tea drinkers too*, he reasoned, *those space invaders.*

"What do you make of this one anyway, wizzer?" Bormph had jabbed his thumb at another piece of tapestry. "It's a map too, right?" Instead of landmasses and landmarks, the lines the dwarf pointed at snaked around symbols of gems and coins. In midst of it all, a dragon's head added a lizardly component to the composition.

Whinewaeyn translated the runes, if a little slowly. "*Sa…pho…teph's Lair.*"

"*The* Saphoteph?" Bormph eyes bulged. "Saphoteph the Eternal from the Age of Dawn? The dragon with the legendary millennia-old treasure hoard? Star of countless tales under the mountain?"

"Says here, his home address would be '*Shan'car'daar Mountains, Third Peak from Sunup. Level four.*' No postbox mentioned or anything. Want to write him a fan letter?"

"No, you silly old geezer," Bormph grunted slyly. "More like relieve him of his treasure. If the map's not a hoax, that is, and if we ever get out of here again."

Whinewaeyn, seized by a sudden impulse, paced briskly to the stone lectern they had ignored to investigate so far. Stooping over it, he found another one of the square, wheat-coloured leathery books. Lettering in sparkling gold adorned the binding.

"*Read Me,*" he announced, drawing some incredulous looks. "That's what it says here. Just that. *Read Me.*"

It sounded like the oddest title ever. The most pompous too. Upon reflection, Whinewaeyn decided to be non-judgmental about it. Sometimes titles tried too hard. A colleague had once titled his treatise, *The Flair of Hot Air.* The text dealt with ways of extracting elemental fire from your everyday breeze, a smashing topic for thaumaturgical academia, if done right. Only that this particular piece of vanity publishing proved a rehash of wind magic basics living up to its unintended titular promise: empty and flatulent.

Sylthia leaned over Amjelle's shoulder to catch a glimpse at the challenging cover too. "What kind of book would be called *Read Me?*"

"A lonely one?" Thimble ventured, looking up at her with a broad smile. He got two arched eyebrows in return, evenly distributed between the female party members looking back down at him.

"If you were looking for a trap," Bormph chipped in, "look no further. They lure you deep in here, you're all curious and open the thing up, and..." Here, he looked wild-eyed at the wizard and his raised hand, which was poised to do exactly that. "*Bam!* A piece of advice: stay back, gramps, or it's instant incineration for you!"

Everyone backed up. The wizard stayed put.

"Incineration?" he mumbled. "You think? What gives you that idea?"

"Just a hunch. Does it matter if you're turned into a pillar of salt, or a cone of ice shoots up, or it's a fiery inferno? Take your pick. My money's on a classic."

Whinewaeyn slowly withdrew his hand.

A lively discussion got going. Amjelle advocated casting a range of protective spells and, following that, flipping the cover open from a distance by way of telekinesis. Bormph opted for a hack-it-in-two approach, no spells required. Sylthia thought it wisest to just let the bone of contention sit where it was in all its smugness and explore further before taking any rash actions.

"Well," Whinewaeyn said after a minute or so of listening to all the arguments. "There's no harm in giving *Trap Trier* a shot this time. It's a book. Plus, I can do it by standing way, way back. Perfectly safe."

It sounded reasonable enough. So Amjelle administered an extra blessing, the wizard stood way, way back, and everyone else stood way, way, way back.

Staff brandished, Whinewaeyn got to his wizardly mumblings.

The air wobbled. A little, then a lot. The end of the wizard's staff sizzled, fumed and started to glow fiercely. A blinding flash broke from it, then a white tongue lashed out, aiming for the lectern.

Instantly, a fiery roar engulfed the stone. Everything on it went up in flames. Charred pages peeled away and crumbled onto the tiled floor. In a few heartbeats, the contents of the lectern were soundly reduced to a clump of ashes.

"Called it!" Bormph rumbled, clenching a fist.

It took a moment to sink in. What other perils might the place yet hold if even harmless-looking books were that dangerous? That aside, the affair, for once, had been an exemplary party moment, complete with proper discussion, agreement on a strategy, perfect execution, and – last but not least – lives saved. Whinewaeyn got a few claps on the shoulder.

"Well done," he heard, and, "Imagine if we'd just opened it!"

"Yeah..." Whinewaeyn nodded slowly, skipping the actual imagining. Something kept him thinking, though. To be honest, he remembered *Trap Trier* a little differently. More bluish, less red. More *in*structive and less *de*structive. Less like, well, whatever had come out. All the burning had looked suspiciously similar to a fire-based spell. Unless other uncalled-for factors had injected themselves into the process, this outcome was...

It dawned on him, then. *Fizzlecheese!* He must have taken a wrong turn in the transmutation department! Why, with all the talk about hot air and incineration, he'd tapped fire instead of wind, and cast... *Incineration*! Not the most elegant version of it, but good enough for bad results. He had just scorched a helpless book lying innocently on its spine!

Whinewaeyn looked around. Everybody else seemed to be treating the mishap as a good thing, relatively speaking. It surely wasn't right to dissent and dampen the regained community spirit.

Better to change the subject.

"So... that teapot..." His gaze flicked Thimble's way. "Where did it go? There?" He tilted his staff at the gate-wide opening between two tapestries at the room's far end.

"Uh-huh." Thimble nodded at the spot and its gaping blackness, perhaps a shade more intimidated, given recent events.

"Fine, then. Amjelle, Sylthia, how about you two stay back here for a bit? Check on the big one, would you? And we three will go and have a look-see, shall we?"

Not too far away, the gloom shifted.

Rising to the noise, a thick midnight-blue blur broke loose from the black currents around it. It surged from ground level like a seriously low-hanging cloud about to do some exercise. Once up, it reshaped, grew a towering posture and slithered forward with a probing purpose to its movements. An ever-so-slight chiming sprang up around it, sounds that rode the cool air for brief moments then trickled away again, as though only briefly nudged out of their slumber.

Muffled mumbles reached it. The blur froze in place, then slipped back into the guise of a shadow among shadows. A dull glow shimmered from the same place where the voices originated, bobbing in and out of view. Now the light soared... and soared... and spread... and spread... like a sun piercing the night. The agitated babble dropped off, as if overwhelmed by what the light revealed.

Still not too far away, but a bit closer this time, the inky currents parted once more for the murky midnight-blue blur to gingerly forge onward...

The orb flickered. It tried its best, but the ocean of blackness that pushed against it from either side was a constant reminder of its limits. Open space stretched away all around Whinewaeyn, Bormph and Thimble, and for some time nothing broke the monotony of their journey across the black and white flagstones. At times, the air felt heavy, as if they were wading through mush.

The three of them half saw something in the half dark, and their footfalls slowed. A looming presence ahead emanated an ancient air, as though it had been waiting for eons for someone like them – an unbidden guest, who just happened to stumble upon its lair.

It was a rack.

A big rack. A *really* big one.

As racks do, it held items. Neither the sides nor the back were enclosed, giving the thing the look of a supersized ladder. Huge, granted, but still only a piece of furniture, and so the overall threat level didn't rise to match its size. Slightly more impressive than the rack itself was the fact that another stood at its side, an aisle away. And next to it was yet one more, and all three together weren't even the half of it. Rows of racks lined up in the extent of the guidelight's reach, to the left, right and much further ahead. Dozens of scraggy laddery columns reached into the illimitable beyond, as if tasked with holding an unseen, unknowable weight.

"Stay back!" Whinewaeyn hissed, extending his arms to keep Bormph and Thimble from wandering off. "Let's observe first."

In their stead, the orb scouted the shelf giants and the wealth of items they held. The innumerable objects appeared to rock back and forth, mimicking or mocking the orb's inability to hold still.

Whinewaeyn's eyes followed the guidelight's path. "Now would you look at that…"

"Looking at it," Bormph mumbled. He tutted. "Whoever lives behind the magic mountain sure does hoard a load of junk."

"The gnome was right," the wizard said. "This... *is*... bigger than us."

"Yeah, gramps. Question is, by how much?"

Thimble's eyes roamed around until curiosity won out over his anxiety. There had to be more than just junk hidden away here, he was sure of it. And there was only one way to find out. His short legs made off. But when he reached the closest rack and tried to grab one of the items on it, his outstretched hand drew back, almost by itself.

"Uh... gh... pht." Thimble's throat had gone dry.

He stood squinting at a quill and a broom, an ashtray and a comb. A mason's spatula. A... ploughshare, maybe? The shelf above held a five-stringed lute, a tiny stool and a ball of wool. In short, a merry convention of unrelated stuff populated the boards. Some of it he recognized, and some he didn't. As far as he could tell, nothing was there twice, and every single item, large or small, had the same amount of space dedicated to it, which it occupied with a certain orderly pride. But what had really startled him was that the things, as much as they looked like things, weren't... actual... things. They were mere hints of things: hollow, see-through, insubstantial, woven from ghostly strands. Despite all that, they cast real shadows that swayed hauntingly as if spectres came to life in them, dressed up in black for some otherworldly carnival.

"By the Stonefather's shiniest glimmerlings!" Bormph joined Thimble to marvel at what appeared to be a carafe but, sure enough, wasn't. "A collection of all things... ghost!" The dwarf scuttled along the stretch of shelf and glimpsed tiny runes on tiny brass plaques affixed underneath each item. An inquiring look at Whinewaeyn was answered with a nod. Forgotten runes. Bormph hurried to investigate the next rack.

Thimble's mouth had hung open for a while now. He tried to form a thought, but his voice didn't comply, and his lips just moved. He blinked. He was uncertain whether a ghostly ball of wool and its colleagues were meant to chill the marrow in his bones, but then a cold hand fell on his shoulder and took care of that.

A shiver slid down his spine… Thimble froze in place for a heartbeat. The moment to jump out of his skin had slipped by. Instead, he went for a yell. Had his voice not faltered, the silence would have been shattered by his outcry.

The ghost at his back was Whinewaeyn. Not that the wizard had turned into one, just that Whinewaeyn's fingers were cold as ice. One of them was now on the wizard's own lips. "Shh…"

A soft tinkling reached across the hall from a distance away. After a pause, there was another, but from a different direction.

"*K-rn-tk-prt!*" Whinewaeyn put to the room.

Once more, the obligatory teapot drew itself into the air and lingered for a heartbeat before it got going. When it did, it snaked its way between the racky regiment stretching into the night.

Without missing a beat, Whinewaeyn swept after it, the orb after Whinewaeyn, and Bormph and Thimble in pursuit of them all – teapot, wizard and orb. An assortment of weaponry that wasn't quite there passed by: the spectral forms of swords, maces and staves, arranged in descending order by length, followed by pieces of ghostly armour, with the occasional see-through trinket or fruit bowl thrown in.

The chase ended at a ghostly teapot. It sat there in row seven or eight, swaying at halfling height, between a kettle and what might have been a tea cosy. Their shadowy companions painted magnified if broken silhouettes onto the rungs of yet another giant rack-ladder in the back. Whinewaeyn stooped to the teapot's level to inspect it.

"*KRNTKPRT*," he read from the plaque attached underneath.

As if in reply, the teapot's ghost flared up in bright vivid colours, fanned into being. For a second or so, the wafting strands pooled together, tightening into a sharp-edged shape whose surface clouded over and thickened fast. What once had been a swaying mass of mist almost resembled porcelain now, delicate and dainty, but then – in yet another blink of an eye – the almost-teapot sank back into translucency, once again cloaking itself in a spectral shell.

Whinewaeyn stood captivated. Like a slingshot-wielding urchin cornering a squirrel in some backyard, he edged closer and whipped up his staff, an incantation on his lips. This time he stepped up his focus. And yet, he broke off, mid-mumbling. The staff snapped forward and remained stuck in mid-air, juddering, whereas Whinewaeyn lost his grip and tumbled back. The wood gave off a full-on aggressive purr.

Bormph, apprehensive, bounded forward to grab it and wrestled invisible forces with all his might, in a tug of war without a rope and no apparent opponent. And how he tugged! The wood bent and groaned. It was a tie for about half a minute, after which, with a reluctant *twang!* whatever held sway over the staff gave in. Both staff and dwarf were catapulted several feet back.

"Potent," Whinewaeyn commented.

"Ah, that was nothing," Bormph muttered, feigning modesty and failing. "You should have seen me back at the Shumgulth Dig-a-ton. I earned three—"

"Er… what I meant was" – Whinewaeyn clutched the petulant implement to his chest – "the *place*. It's filled with energies, the like of which…" He felt an urgent tug at his sleeve.

"Over there!" Thimble pointed down the aisle. "Something's—" He was staring through the gaps between the racks, transfixed, his hand still tugging away. An ashen glimmer spilt across the gloom.

Whinewaeyn's gaze slid from the teapot ghost towards the warped, shuddering kind of shine. Chime-like sounds danced about it, a *ching-a-linging* as fragile as it was faint, as though a pixie was sprinkling fairy dust in a very considerate way, so as not to pour it out all at once.

They sidled up to the goings-on. No doubt, it all hailed from one of the ghosts sitting at the far end of the rack, and this one seemed to be the odd one out. The complex contours made it more difficult to recognize what it stood for, especially as the wispy threads kept stuttering in and out of the darkness. Still, it was easy enough to see what the shape resembled more than what it didn't.

"What in the world…?" Bormph blurted out.

"It's the ghost of a gnome," Whinewaeyn observed, keeping emotions out of it. He held fast to his staff now as he watched the strange spectacle before him, this time keeping his distance. "Didn't the gnome say something like… all threads must lead somewhere? Well, it's not exactly as I imagined it, but I guess we're here."

"Like flies in a spider's web," Bormph said slowly.

Thimble turned anxiously, wondering what kind of spiders might have been holed up in the recesses of this place and what threads they wove, apart from the decorative tapestries.

Tinkles came from all kinds of directions now.

"There's another one!" Thimble cried out. "And another…" All of a sudden, they seemed to be everywhere – phantoms drawing their attention with gentle *dings* and *rings* floating about them. Their spectral threads wafted, flickered, quivered and blinked.

The nearest of them was only half a shelf away. This particular ghost was round and larger than a human hand. An ashen glimmer was hovering over it too, a shine that grew brighter, dimmer, brighter again. As its threads twisted and turned, Thimble noticed that gems were embedded in it, or the ghosts of gems at least – tiny, delicate strands that kept weaving into the shapes of insubstantial jewellery without ever finishing the process. The overall frame of the thing, right down to the gems in it, somehow looked familiar, and when he studied the ghost a little while longer, it came to him that he was looking at an amulet. Stranger still was that this was the same one he had seen not too long ago, dangling from the bony neck of the dragon-riding lich, in a time and place that seemed utterly unreal.

"It's like a music box gone bonkers around here!" Bormph rasped somewhere behind him. The dwarf's voice trickled away into a murmur, only to burst forth again a little later, spluttering in shock. "Fire and thunder! Look at this! They're *all* here!"

Thimble edged after, picking up the gleam of more out-of-place ghosts. Each stirred something in him: a cuckoo clock, a left shoe and…

"It's our pinhopper!" Bormph pointed.

Then Thimble saw it too: the ghostly scarab with its wings spread wide. It put on a show of the brightest flickers and the loudest tinkles of them all, as if it was its own music box. Thimble stared at it, spellbound.

He was startled from his thoughts when a babble of voices welled up somewhere in the distance behind them. Agitated voices. The sounds of a scuffle. Then a shriek! After that a *thud* and a resonant *clonk*, followed up by its acoustic cousin *clang*.

"Quick!" Whinewaeyn pivoted on his heels. The guidelight lurched past him towards their starting point, and a rush of feet stormed back down the aisle.

The orb's glow spilled across an upturned frying pan. Further on, it unveiled two hunched female shapes and a body sprawled facedown on the marble floor between them. At first, Thimble thought it could only be Ramrok, but then the barbarian's face disentangled itself from the shadows next to him, still half green, but looking a good deal more alert too. Whoever it was that lay on the floor was wrapped in a blue silk robe with gold-hemmed sleeves.

With joint effort, the body was rolled over, and Amjelle and Sylthia found themselves staring at a face as fair as could be, framed with a shock of blond hair. The man was in his prime, tall and lithe, almost a youth. Barring the serious bruise forming on his forehead, the stranger's skin was smooth and pure; not a hint of stubble blemished his jaw.

Amjelle's grim expression met the wizard's surprised eyes. "B-b-banged him over the head, Archmagus…" she stuttered. "What else was I supposed to do? He was sneaking around in the dark! What if…?" A nervous breath shuddered out of her.

"…it's a stalker with a dirty mind?" Bormph said grimly. "Well, I'll—"

Amjelle shook her head. "No, no. What if… it's a god?"

CHAPTER 21

Beyond Big Bang

The party crouched around the fallen.

For a divine being, he groaned and writhed very much like the guy next door. If the stranger didn't quite look the part, it was only because he had something of a town beau about him, and town beaus – for some odd cosmic reason – very rarely happen to live next door. His robe, dyed midnight blue, was swathed around him, with exotic-looking ornaments bedecking its sleeves and hems, and from his neck dangled a heavy gold chain, adding a little extra preciousness.

They sat him up. He seemed seriously dazed.

"How would you know if it's a god?" Thimble ventured over the man's groans, keeping his voice low and dignified, to be on the safe side, as one would in a church.

"Yeah... how, healer?" Bormph was with him, and they both searched the circle of faces. "Ever *seen* a god?"

Ramrok grunted something to the same effect.

"Just look at him!" Amjelle brushed back a few strands of silken hair. Traces of a recent battering aside, his angelic appearance was hard to ignore. Maybe he bore some relation to the One or the Other? "He looks like life itself," she declared, "and he's *here*. Who else but a god would roam these dustless, timeless halls?"

"But… a god wouldn't—" Thimble stopped right there.

With a rustle and a moan the divine candidate shifted. His lids peeled halfway back. The pupils behind the narrow slits slid left and right. Then, with a start, his eyes flicked wide open, staring ahead, unfocused. His lips twitched a couple of times before parting for real.

"Are you the one?" came out in a rusty voice.

At the other end of the stranger's glare Bormph made a face.

"The one from my dreams?"

"I certainly am not!" the dwarf shot back, livid. "You walk into a gay bar – *once!* – and everyone just assumes you're—"

"You entered this place through… a *gay bar*?" The stranger seemed confused.

"O' course not, stalker! Through a piece of rock, or maybe it wasn't. What do I know? And, what's more, what do *you* know, eh?"

The stranger suddenly twisted about, erratic, as if looking for something. "It's gone now, right?" His voice sounded creaky. "Gone. Just like in my dreams." The eyes settled on the dwarf again.

"What's gone? The rock? The magic squirrel? Your mind?"

"All of it?" The filmy eyes grew wider.

"Rock, squirrel *and* mind?"

"The *world*, bearded one!" The stranger shook like a birch in the wind. "The *world*… is gone!"

"It did sort of *look* like the sky was falling back there, I'll give you that. What's it to you?" Bormph came back at him.

"Everything... and nothing at all." Whatever else the stranger muttered remained with him. He leaned back again, resigned. "Threads untangling, souls crossing. Eternity knotting into itself. Ha!" He produced a bark of a laugh, dripping with sarcasm, gripped his head with one hand and struggled into a slouch with the help of the other, the gold chain jangling around his neck. "Brought any dice, dwarf? A Knucklebuck deck? No worries if not, I'm sure I'll find one. Takes at least five to buck the knuckle and we're a handful now."

For once, Bormph was fresh out of snide remarks.

"Or do dwarves not buck the knuckle?"

Bormph opened his mouth, but Whinewaeyn, snapping out of his owl-eyed stare, beat him to it. "So, what are *you* then? A legitimate knucklebucker? Does that make you a human then?"

The stranger stirred as if to try to collect his limbs before his thoughts.

"But... how *could* he be?" Amjelle whispered into Whinewaeyn's ear, one eye on the professed knucklebucker. "In a place like this?"

"Well, *we're* human too, my dear," the wizard reminded her, "and we brought ourselves, remember? We're like... the dust. If *we* can be here, anyone can."

Even Thimble saw the logic in that. A halfling had made it too.

The wizard stuck his nose in the stranger's face. "Whether you're a human, a goblin with questionable roots, or a god who's forgotten about it, it doesn't make sneaking up on ladies in the dark any better. So what's your business here?"

Bormph closed in on his other side. "Were you following the gnomes too?"

"Gnomes…" the stranger drawled at last, as if it rang a bell in him somewhere. "Gnomes, of course. Gnomes lead the way. Gnomes first. Women and children next, and after that… just about everything else."

"Speak sense!" Bormph rumbled like a rockslide. His fiery beard braids swung forward. "You on your own, card shark? And what odd corner of the world is this? The whole story!"

The stranger absorbed these demands like a sponge, slowly and thoroughly. And, like a sponge, he didn't reply right away.

"Ah, no, it's just me over here," he said at last, rather airily, but then a glint entered his dreamy eyes. "And you now. Maybe that's all we'll ever be, now that there's nothing left of what you'd call a world. See, this isn't a corner of that world at all. No, no corners here. It's more like the far side, as opposed to what lies someplace over there" – he jerked a thumb to his right – "or there…" – then to his left – "or wherever anything's supposed to be, anything with… corners. Who knows? Who can say?" He shrugged as both his thumbs tilted downwards. "Anyway, here would be… the *other* side? The back side, maybe?" He cackled. "But it's tricky, all that talk of sides. One might as well call it the Beyond, or the Beneath. Take your pick." His thin lips formed a grin. "As for me, I'm first fool around here. Whee-heee! Who else but a fool could've made it thus far?"

"Did he just call us all fools?" Bormph turned an evil eye on the wizard. What might have looked like a god at first glance seemed to babble more like a nutcase spouting insults on second listening, and Bormph wasn't having it.

For a moment, a violent altercation was in the air, but Amjelle quickly intervened. All it took to throw off the dwarf was a soft whisper and the light touch of a female hand on his bearded cheek – plus an extra pair of fists, Ramrok's, gripping him for backup.

"Let me have a look at you!" Amjelle drew closer to the presumed nutcase and reached out to cup his battered forehead in her palm. Had she picked up a deafening scream for medical attention amid all the rambling? Where the patient's roof damage began, no one could say, but the frying pan might have had no small part in it. Sylthia rushed to assist by propping up the man's drooping head from the other side, whispering soothing mantras.

And it's not that the stranger resisted. He simply brushed Amjelle's hand away, with a gentle, composed motion, along with a mumbled plea not to worry on his behalf.

"See?" he breathed. "Nothing there…" His blue eyes rolled up towards his bruised forehead and, before Amjelle was able to utter a word, the marks melted away like fresh snow in the midday sun.

"Just a little trick." A half-smirk lit up his now unmarred face. "Like conjuring an apple" – the stranger's hand plucked a fruit out of thin air – "or getting rid of one." A wiggle of his fingers, and the apple somehow got lost between them. The healing team sank back, stunned.

"Now who are you *really?*" Whinewaeyn resumed his interrogation. "A god in human guise? The other way round? A half-god? A Forgotten, or a warlock, involved in some divine misconduct, banished to this abandoned, riddle-infested ghosthold at the edge of the universe?" He poked the stranger with his staff as he would a venomous viper.

"Who says he's not a trickster?" Bormph added. "A Netherworldly demon of the applemuncher ilk, plotting devilry and collecting ghosties like others do stamps, for his sordid purposes?"

The stranger rolled his head back, glanced over his nose at Whinewaeyn's staff and then into the dwarf's beard-wreathed face before he screwed a crooked finger up into the air. "Fun fact. Did you know… there's a hole in the sky?"

Judging by the group's expressions, the insight fell a little short of being revelatory.

"Ah, but there's sky," the rambling went on anyway, "and then there isn't, in places. Like… down south. Sometimes you can smell them. See them. Eat 'em, if you want. *Fish…*" The stranger's voice thickened. "*Fish!* Deep down south… raining from above. In the middle of the Joghavri!"

No one spoke, and yet everyone heard more than the mystic's words ringing in their ears. Out of nowhere, the incoherent talk had struck close to home, like a galley's prow ramming the dockside. Something large and ominous had come in bumping and screeching along the metaphorical quay.

"That's how it all started." The stranger pulled himself up. "A long, long time ago. With me, asking questions. Like, what about… fish… in the Joghavri?"

Whinewaeyn withdrew his staff, at least a little. "So what about fish in the Joghavri?"

"Wouldn't we all like to know now, oh, inquisitive ones? Well, first, there were the fish, aye. Then came the loophole. The rip in the fabric, see? Fooled the universe! And how was it done, you ask?" The stranger's eyes shone like cut diamonds. When he answered his own question, he did so with relish. "Made the crack… my size!"

In the front row seats to this madness, Bormph and Whinewaeyn simultaneously checked on each other.

"Couldn't go through the hole in the sky up in the desert, now, could I? No, no. Not I. Not as the little earth-walking creature that I was... Thus, instead, I sought out the mountain. People used to say things weren't right up there. The world's veil's thin in a place like that, they said, and maybe there was something to it. Well, I would find out. So I brought with me everything that no archmage had ever been able to explain, not even the great ones. Got myself quite the collection. For each sense I had in me, I brought a piece, thorough as I am. And if the veil was thin already, who knew what might happen...? Once up that mountain, I put myself smack in the middle of it, and that's how I became one with it... with the crack... how I *became* the crack, how I slipped behind the veil... How I..." – his eyes glazed over – "crossed the gulf of space and time... How I turned into the first pig... that flew. Me, Zarothaster, the flying pig!"

There was a collective unrest.

"Nah!" Bormph grumbled eventually. "No chance you're that Zaro the Toaster guy. My foot!"

"They called me Zarothaster back then," the stranger said airily. "Lore might remember my name differently now. Not that I care."

"But he was ancient, and he got toasted ages ago. Now, the cuckoo part fits, knucklebucker, but that aside—"

A hand suddenly shot up, clutched Bormph's thick wrist and yanked him closer. "Look at me! *Look* at me, redbeard!"

Gazes locked, frowns met, minds clashed. So arresting was the adamant stare put on him, so insistent the command, that Bormph found himself unable to tear himself away. The deeper he dug into the blueness of the eyes before him, the more something unthinkable seeped through that stare – until, for a fraction of a second, the probability of the improbable washed to the fore, bright and clear.

As if on cue, everything was taken by a tremble: the stranger, the mix of party members, the axe Bormph held in front of him and the guidelight illuminating it all – or trying to, given the guttering going on. The stranger, though, slipped from view for longer periods of time than anybody else, as if he was only halfway with them.

"Lamps on lard!" Bormph swore, and shrank back.

Now the flickering was one thing. A steadfast dwarf shrinking back unannounced was another. Put together, it led to a whole chain of adventurers backing into each other and tumbling like dominoes.

At length, the guidelight steadied, but the figure before them wasn't quite the same anymore. No one had ever seen a beard the length of an arm grow in the timespan of a gasp, or watched wrinkles sprout across a man's temples into crow's feet like rampant ivy. Amjelle had tried another hair colour once, but her blondeness was short-lived. The stranger, however, didn't seem to mind his hair whitening one bit, nor his skin withering into an old geezer's, and all of it together took but a few blinks of an eye. The passage of time swept over him like a racehorse.

There was a sudden snap, as of the cracking of a whip.

Things went dark.

In the guidelight's stead, only an orb-shaped afterglow held position overhead, at least for a short while. After the afterglow, only black came after.

Abruptly, a firm, commanding voice broke through the chaos of the agitated clamour: "Let there be light!"

And there *was* light. With a deep-pitched, bone-rattling hum that flared up like a swarm of bumblebees, the gloom drained from the heights down to floor level as if a plug had been pulled from a giant bathtub. One by one, the rack giants reared from their dusky hideouts; a few rows lined up, then a few more behind the first ones, and then more than more, unveiling legions of humongous guardians holding ominous ghostly shapes as far as the eye could travel. Towering canyon-sized gaps cleaved in between, with faint misty tentacles prowling the upper racky regions.

"Dimmed!"

This one word chased away most of the humming, and the endless hall shrouded itself in its most presentable twilight. The stranger's now age-spotted face was thrown into relief as the old man rose to full height. Thus exposed, his features merely hinted at the youthfulness they had exhibited just moments ago, and yet his posture and facial traits left no doubt that he was still the same person.

"Come," Zarothaster told the collection of travellers spilled across the floor. "Now that you're here, you might as well take the tour."

Beyond Hanging Rock. Two hundred and eight years, seven months and the whole rest of it earlier.[*]

Zarothaster ventured a peek through his fingers.

The explosion of brightness that had hit him like a blow to the head was on the retreat now, and he felt his vision slowly adjust. At the same time, he was wondering, why it had happened at all. For hours and hours, he'd been

---

[*] To be taken with a cartload of salt. After Apocalypse Hour, dates become malleable.

stumbling through these otherworldly premises in thick-as-oil darkness, with nothing but the odd glimmer and guesswork to go by. Not a thing had he been able to make out, and then, the moment he pled to some invisible entity to grant him something, *any*thing, the light had hit him like a cudgel. Now he saw nothing *but* things, or spectres of things anyway, bathed in utter brilliance, as if the shadows had made off to party elsewhere.

He rubbed his eyes. Nobody had yet put in an appearance to greet or confront him. Which made the ghosts galore all he had for company – them, and the muted droning that suffused the air. Strangely enough, it sounded less threatening the longer he walked and more like an obscure, unaccountable tenant asserting its presence. The vibrations tickled his naked skin, and he felt silly because of it. Loinclothed as he was, he longed for a coat. But all he could do was hug himself to battle the chill, craning his neck about, looking, listening and freezing.

His thoughts kept circling back to that sudden eruption of light. As if he had somehow willed it into being... Ha! If he could only do the same with some clothes! He'd have brocade, or ermine... *No, no, too regal*, that other voice inside of him advised. He started arguing with it. If he was going to meet the master of this outlandish domain, the livery had to spell official, yet subtle. He recalled once meeting a foreigner who visited the king's court from distant Paen'oul'ocea, an ambassador. *Such* finery would fit the bill. Exotic, stately—

"Well, I'll be damned!"

He looked down at himself, and there it was: the blue silk robe in all its splendour, complete with playful swirls of embroidery, satin lining, sparkling buttons and wide, laced sleeves, topped off with a high collar that reached well over the ears. He touched the fabric in fascination. A sash was knotted about his waist and a gold chain dangled from his neck. None of Paen'oul'ocea's most famous tailors could've woven him a better fit, let alone in just a heartbeat. It was as if an unknown arcane force had latched onto his innermost desire and, for reasons beyond his grasp, granted it. Which indeed made him something of an emissary on an official visit to this… other world.

But was it? Another world? How could something… someone… whatever it was… clothe him in a robe from *his* world then? And where was this wish-granting fairy to have a chat with? How many wishes had he left? Zarothaster peered down the aisle between the racks, ready to meet his benefactor. But a dark red carpet was all there was, stretching into the unknown, inviting him for a stroll.

Straightening his collar, he forged ahead, flip-flopping in the most splendid sandals a mystic had ever worn.

Fresh wooden giants sprouted up and melted away again. Eerie mist rolled everywhere, steamier than the hot springs of Hothrogh, and yet, as much as the shelf phantoms billowed, slackened or drifted, never did they falter. Earlier on, he had stepped closer to observe their curious dance; the ghostly strands, as if afraid, had appeared to unravel, but when he stood still for a bit, they came circling back, cording into a tight shape – whether it was an insubstantial lute, a sugar tong or a horseshoe. Every now and again flashes leapt up in the steamy brew, to his left, right, ahead and behind him, sometimes several at a time, banding together into ripples that travelled through whole rows, tingeing the spectres in all kinds of colours. Thread by thread, a new hue was introduced and taken for a spin – red, blue, green, a steely silver. Whatever was happening, each flash picked another colour for the ghosts, and so, clad in such merry dyes, their gyrations went on for a time until they faded back into their default greyness.

Zarothaster reached for the misty shapes, but to no avail. Coloured or not, the phantoms only gave off a faint glimmer and continued with their swirling. When he ran his fingers over the strings of a ghostly harp, a soft rustle was all he could elicit; he plucked nothing but air. Pulling back his hand, the strings straightened of their own accord. Fair enough, he figured. There's no way one can just play a ghost, or seize one, take it home and put it on the mantelpiece like a trophy. Nonetheless, here they were, right down to a spectral cupcake. Never before had the mystic considered means of spiritual storage, or a ghost's diet for that matter. What was it that a ghost would carry around in a ghostly jar anyway? Spiritual stuff? And where were the spectres that all this stuff belonged to? Where was the ghostly harpist? Or the confectioner?

"You can come out now!"

The mystic's holler petered out among the shelves.

"Seen you!" he tried again, sly humour baked in.

Several breathless moments went by. No ghosts took the bait. Was the ever-present hum all he'd get in return? Was that hum the sum of all the ghostly whisperings? All he knew was that it swelled and waned with the rhythm of the flashes and ripples as they skipped through the rows of insubstantial items, but was that all there was? And what was it that there was?

"Anybody home?" The words drifted off towards a point where the light dwindled into impenetrable infinity.

Infinity didn't reply. Maybe it wasn't used to visitors.

"Toaster, wait!"

Bormph groped about for his axe. Once he got ahold of it, he struggled to his feet and set off, Thimble following a close second. Behind them, the knot of longer-limbed party members was still untangling itself.

"What you think he's up to?" Thimble panted as he and Bormph chased the mystic down the ghost-filled alley.

"What do *I* know? Looks recent enough to me for the hundred-odd years he claims he's got on his back, and that's not a healthy age for *any* human, not by my great-gravelgramp's granite-crusher. Maybe the fumes in here have turned this funny guy funnier than what's good for him, and now…" He snorted. "Now he thinks he's not just a mystic, but a magician too, and a Medusa-thing… or whatever's the word for those who live long past their expiration date."

"Or he's a shapeshifter!" Thimble whispered anxiously.

"Exactly. Next thing you know he'll turn you into a pink rhinoceros or something! Better stay on your toes."

Looking down at his hairy feet, Thimble almost bumped into their dubious guide who, rather abruptly, had come to a halt among the rows and rows of shelves. One by one, the stragglers caught up.

"You know what I was seeking when I went up the Sickle many, many years ago?" the mystic asked over his shoulder.

"Enlightenment?" "Immortality?" Amjelle and Sylthia recalled the gnome's words when he had told them the story.

The mystic turned and his sunken eyes narrowed on the healer and her elven friend. A hint of a smile cut into his hollow cheeks. "Ha! And who would have guessed I'd find them both, neatly bundled up, back here? Who'd have thought I'd exchange the sight of morrows for eternity?" The mystic's tone had sobered up somewhat. "But what good is any of what I'd aspired to on *this* side of things, where there are no… things? Here, all there is, is everything *else*."

Zarothaster's words hung in the air on their own. If they were sage, then they were sage on the sketchy side, enjoying a figurative hammock.

"Erm… we hear you," Whinewaeyn tried for a reply, "but what are you… um… *saying* exactly?"

"That we're at the place *before* all things. A possible place."

Bormph looked about. "Where's it hiding, your possibility?"

A gnarly hand swept across the ghost-studded space, and their glances followed it, looking for anything matching the description. But there was nothing beyond whitish smoky tendrils, twisting and turning without rest. Dead silence fell and thickened.

"It's all ghosties!" Bormph grunted, underwhelmed.

"Even possibility must have something to choose from." With Zarothaster's words, the buzz that had been lingering in the shadows rekindled, only to die away moments later as though out of breath. "You may call them ghosts. Moulds, I say. Frames. Images before all images. Threads to weave the world's yarn with. If you'd only seen it before the end" – a sparkle entered his age-worn eyes – "when the Grand Pool was stirring, when it ebbed and flowed and the world still drew from the font, you'd have seen the brilliance of it. That's how the Weavers must have wrought their Forgotten magic: by twining the two parts together, that which could be from here, and that which comes of it from over there."

Bormph coughed noisily and threw a wary glance Whinewaeyn's way. When he got the wizard's attention, he shoved his headgear up a handbreadth to make room for a stubby forefinger to tap furtively on his brow. "You know what *I* see, wizzer?" he mumbled out of the corner of his mouth, low but emphatic. "Another loopy one. The world's full of them, and – surprise, surprise – there's one more hiding behind it as well! There's no end to it!"

Whinewaeyn's eyes shifted between the dwarf and the mystic, and he made a noise halfway between a pensive "hmm" and a doubtful moan. It came out a little vague in judgment.

"At times," the mystic continued, pacing on past the shelves now, with the party following in train, "all was quiet back here. Like a drowsy noonday pond, hidden away in the remotest of groves, unvisited for ages. Now and again, the idyll came alive as if stoked by an unseen force. A crackling entered, and colours began glimmering everywhere. I saw the unseen spindle spin."

"There are tales about a place like this," Amjelle said, but her voice faltered even as she spoke. "Tales about a site harking back to the outset of time, but I never…" She stole a glance at Sylthia and found the elf's eyes roaming reverently around the space.

"Might this be… the Goddess's Dream?" the elf asked in a thin voice. But whatever else was on Sylthia's mind, or Amjelle's, slunk away unuttered.

"Hold on." Whinewaeyn waved the mystic to another halt and scurried over to one of the racks. "If this place is what you say it is, mystic – and let's say, for the sake of argument, that it is – then we still have a few more questions that need answering." He reared his head to admire some of the ghostly content with fresh interest. "Stands to reason that these... Weavers you called them? They would have had a plan ahead of all creation. And why not? Without a plan, creation would be mere folly. So they might have set it all up first, just about here, and then proceeded to walk the earth at the Dawn of Days – when the whole thing was still unformed and in need of, shall we say, basic decoration – and armed themselves with these names behind all names, I would wager."

He pointed at a lean, branchy, gently swaying ghost. "Take this one here. A creator ambling along might be on the lookout for a nice cosy spot to place a bit of shrubbery. And when they find it, they simply..." He bent forward, squinted at the letters written on the plaque underneath the object, then pushed a few consonants through his teeth, which made a bushy ghost bloom into existence right in front of him. The fibres twisted and curled as if touched by a breath of air, lingered a moment or two, and then – once they had demonstrated their potential – merged back into the shelf-ghost. A faint lilac-like impression was left behind, along with a hint of a matching scent.

"However," Whinewaeyn added, "I'm a bit in the dark on, say, the concept of teapots, and all that other stuff this place seems to have stored in abundance. What use have your Weaver gods for... teapots?"

"Taking a break?" Thimble offered.

"Well, yes, little one. Er, um... But is a teapot...?"

"A basic world-creating necessity?" Amjelle suggested.

"As you say, dear. I guess where I'm heading, Zaro-er-roaster, is that I've always been under the impression that someone other than the gods must have come up with an idea as mundane as a kitchen utensil, no?"

"And yet," Zarothaster maintained, "how would a teapot-maker know a teapot from something else? How would one know a teapot to be possible at all?"

"Oh. *Possible.*" The wizard's mouth fell shut with a clack as though the full meaning of the word had just hit him. The presence of millions upon millions of ghosts had all of a sudden become argumentative. "This place must go way beyond basic decoration, then!" A more informed look at the matter was in order, so Whinewaeyn got to it.

"Doubts, redbeard?" Zarothaster glanced down at Bormph, interpreting an unspecific grunt. He then stepped aside with a bow, clearing the view down the aisle like the ringmaster of a carnival show. "Well, then, why don't *you* think of whatever strikes your fancy, and see for yourself what this place can do. Or is your mind limited by your size?"

"What are you getting at?" Bormph huffed. But the offer was tempting. "Just think of... anything?"

"Anything."

Bormph plodded forward. His gaze made a few rounds and his thick fingers plucked at his dangling beard braids. Something went on behind the dwarf's helmet-covered cranium. "And now what—"

A low, energetic judder gripped the air.

It lasted about a second before dropping into an obscure tinkle, which in turn was smothered by a roaring rumble issuing from a dozen or so racks ahead. There – lo and behold! – emerged a horn-nosed, flesh-coloured colossus, which by all accounts was... a pink rhinoceros! The majestic beast clomped from one side of the aisle to the other, not unlike a ship making its way across the horizon, only accompanying its journey with considerably more of a racket. The flagstones trembled. The shelves shook. The fleshy colour hurt their eyes.

Quite a spectacle, Thimble thought, as he ducked away behind the mystic. *As unreal as spotting a unicorn!* But then it occurred to him that a rhinoceros – whether pink, checkered or plain rhino-grey – was actually sort of a unicorn too.

"Wands and wonders!" Whinewaeyn swore, and thrust his staff forward, ready to fend off an attack. None came. They all watched, watched, and watched some more, until Exhibit A slipped behind the shelves again, where it stole away into the same thin air it must have dropped out of. By the time the beast was out of sight, the quakes it sent down the aisle had gone with it, like a fleeting memory.

"Where horny come? Where horny gone?" Ramrok swirled left, right, and all the way round, holding on to the hilt of his sword like a skipper to the tiller.

Light as a breeze, the mystic's voice re-entered the confusion. "Back…" it said, "to being possible."

"Yeah?" Bormph shook off his stupor but – being the dwarf that he was – not his disbelief. He squinted up challengingly at Zarothaster. "That was an illusion, right? Saw right through it! Now you might be a shapeshifter and a mind-reader on top of it, but it takes a little more to fool a Shumgulth, more than just… smoke and mirrors!"

Zarothaster's gaunt face broadened into a hearty laugh. "You give me too much credit, dwarf. I'm an observer, as are you. Many an idea lies dormant in this vault of wonders, and you summoned just one." His gaze wandered from one dumbfounded face to another, until the old eyes locked on Amjelle. "As did you, pan-wielding priestess. You expected a god behind the world, well, so you saw one. And yet, I'm just an old fool stumbling about same as you."

"But… what about the gods?" said Amjelle, startled. "If this is the place of creation, why is it deserted?"

"I suppose we can't just have the gods sitting around," Whinewaeyn opined matter-of-factly. "Gods are more subtle than that, no?"

"Suuuper-subtle, apparently," groused Bormph.

Zarothaster only motioned for them to move on. "If there's one thing I've learned for certain, it's that everything inside these halls is not at all. And even these halls… aren't halls at all."

Bormph snorted. "Now that you mention it… Noticed a wall problem. And up there…" He threw his head back to look into the darkness above as he was walking. "What's going on? We're lucky we've got a floor."

Once more Zarothaster ceased his steps. "But have we?"

The party had stopped with him. Gazes dropped to floor level, where they found… a floor, flat and functional.

Ramrok *tock-tock-tock*ed on the flagstones with the pommel of his sword. "Floor."

But with a little delay, the time it took for the thuds to subside, a soft scraping issued from the knocked-on slab, and its outlines grew more pronounced. With a sudden jolt, the square fell away. It spun out of view, its former spot replaced with a hole of perfectly framed blackness.

Feet staggered back in horror.

A cackle drifted across the glaring lack of ground. "Can't you see, oh so valiant travellers? That this is the way it's supposed to be? How else would one be able to walk through the other side of things? How else could anyone step behind what is, across the reaches of space and time, without imagining… taking that step? Our eyes and ears and what other senses we have – with our minds gluing it together – are all we can go by. We may only glimpse into what lies beyond if we help the glimpse along. *You* are helping that glimpse along."

Nobody moved. Only Whinewaeyn, closest to the gaping chasm, now that the barbarian had backed off, dared to lean over the edge. Nothing but shadows lingered underneath, and a whole lot of questions filled his mind. Like, what if the mystic spoke the truth? And, if so, what if someone, even just one, were to utter a doubt? Would they all join the flagstone's fickle fate? Somehow asking those kinds of questions made a believer out of him – and a firm one too. The solidity of his footing attested to that.

Amjelle gave a sudden yelp. "The portals, the spirals, the corridors turning back on themselves, all those libraries… a-and books attacking us? Would our minds make all that up too? It *cannot* be true!"

"Ah, what's in a mind?" Zarothaster returned as he ambled back towards them. With a swipe of his arm the missing tile regrew, and he treaded on it walking on, as though it was the most natural thing in the world – or outside of it. "Why do we see things that fool us? And who can tell where the Weavers' thoughts begin and ours end? When we enter a place like this… aren't we supposed to bring our sense of wonder with us too? And with wonder come illusions, fears, uncertainties… We wouldn't be what we are without them."

"But there must be *more* behind the world!" Amjelle protested stubbornly.

"Oh, I agree," Zarothaster said. "There must be something the eye can't see. But who can say what it is when we aren't looking? It's just that we're… *always*… looking."

Amjelle and Sylthia swapped glances.

"So this is *all* this place is? Just that?" Amjelle choked out. "The grand enigma?"

The elf's lips parted, but nothing came out.

The grand enigma.

The words tumbled down the hum-filled aisle. All eyes were on the ghosts. All minds too. *Or was it their own minds everybody was looking at?* Thimble wondered, unable to wrest his gaze away from the shelves. What *was* he looking at, and what *wasn't* he looking at, and what was he only imagining looking at? Would the Toaster turn into, say, an aardvark, if he only… only…

His breath stopped. He had fixed the mystic in his sight, and while doing so had witnessed the old man's features twist and reshape into something else, something with a nose way too long for its own good! Short forearms with clunky claws had replaced the limbs protruding from the now oversized sleeves of his blue robe; the mystic – no, the aardvark – was waving them about as he spoke. *Bells and whistles!*

But… Was he the only one who saw what he had just engendered with his silly thoughts? Nobody else seemed to have noticed.

Thimble's head swivelled back aardvarkwards. The thing was still speaking, but he couldn't make out any meaning from its squelchy grunts. Not a moment after his doubts had begun to set in, the creature's arched back straightened, its elongated head shortened and the funny snout bent back into a distinctly human nose. Once the nose had taken shape, it was only a matter of time until it surrounded itself with what Thimble thought must have been there all along: a whole mystic. *Bells and whistles!*

"Tell me this then, mystic," Thimble heard Amjelle. Zarothaster had started walking again and she was still arguing with him as she followed. Thimble scurried after them. "If it's us who make all this up... the floor, the ghosts, this whole keep or whatever this is, *everything*... how come we all make up the exact *same* things?"

Thimble's eyes anxiously flicked between Amjelle and the mystic, but he kept his little aardvark experiment to himself.

"How come, mystic?" the healer insisted.

For a while, only the subdued sounds of their footfalls merged with the ever-present hum, as subtle on the carpet as raindrops tapping gingerly on the pavement of an empty street.

"I guess we must all have something in common then, pan-wielder," the mystic said eventually. He snapped his fingers, and the ghost sea melted into the gloom. What little light still lingered began to twist into fresh shapes. "Something that lifts us beyond being mere... question marks."

CHAPTER 22

Forlorn. Forsaken. Forgotten.

Beyond Hanging Rock. Two hundred and eight years, seven months and the whole rest of it earlier. Sort of.

Beard tucked into his sash, Zarothaster lengthened his strides. He vowed to get to the bottom of all this – which, he surmised, must lie right ahead. So that's where he went.

And yet he felt that he was walking on the spot when he passed one silent wooden companion after another. In fact, so determined was he to get somewhere, that he missed the subtle shifts that entered the floor's checkered pattern altogether. Neither did he notice the racks tilting out of view one by one and the airy load they held slinking away, back into obscurity's embrace. Ever so gently, the gloom encroached on him. What light was left to fend against the amassing black grew paler and paler still, tightening into a diffuse plume. Until something went bump in the night.

Actually, it went *Ba-doooomp!*

Startled from his daze, the mystic lurched to a halt. A blur of movement a few paces away smudged different places in the dark, and a draught brushed over his features, sending a vibrant tingle through every fibre of his body. His senses sharpened. The ghost racks were gone. He breathed in and out, then sidled forward, alert.

He saw lines. A kind of frame. Straight and square, next to and on top of each other. With a start they pulled away from him when he pushed closer, clattering, as if frightened. Close to the ground, higher up, and higher still, frame by frame withdrew, all the while coinciding with a staccato of clacks – a *roll-clack-bang, roll-clack-bang* – until whatever was behind it all locked into place. *Roll-clack-BANG.*

One single large square remained.

He inched one more step towards it.

A set of five-by-five panels, handles included, emerged.

The drawer-monster – was that what it was? – stood quiet now. Stacked on top of one another, each about a foot high and wide, the fine-grained front pieces seemed to await his next move. The whole collection made up a perfect cube that reached shoulder height and extended about half that distance back. There was, as he now came to realize, another cube of drawers, a little offset, to the left of the one before him, and one to its right as well. And each of those was flanked by yet another, almost as if the giant shelves from before had shrunk down to something more manageable. The cubes stretched from left to right, forming a semicircle and continued two or three rows further in, like an archipelago of islands anchored in luminous pools, braving the dead of night in a long-abandoned storeroom.

Zarothaster eyed the handles. Above them, tucked inside tiny metal frames, labels boasted between one and three Forgotten runes.

Another puzzle? He prowled around the gathering of new furniture on offer and, eventually, decided upon one. It opened without protest.

He might have expected a filing cabinet to be crammed with, well, binders. And indeed it was. Lots and lots of them – parchment tied together with cord, aged in varying degrees, but mostly well preserved. Some bundles were voluminous, others flimsy, a handful close to tatters. What he hadn't foreseen was that they concerned themselves with odd topics like *paintbrushes, pastries*, and *pawnshops, pears* and *piers* and *pipes* and – his fingers slowly scuttled back to the front of the index cards – *pendulums*. Even – and this is when he flinched and his beard whipped from his sash – *Paen'oul'ocean Robes!*

No matter how often he read the words before him, every single time, as plainly as the twilight would let him, they spelled the same thing: *Paen'oul'ocean Robe.*

He fished for the whole binder.

It was a register of sorts. An itemized list on yellowed paper, spread over two columns. Forgotten words ran down one side, measurements for all he knew, or specifications on patterns and styles, colours, sizes, fabric used and embellishments suggested, the like of which a tailor would find useful to fashion the garment. In the other column, the right-hand one, the items were answered – at least, the Forgotten characters were there but, for reasons of their own, steadfastly refused to make sense. In place of actual words, the runes stood huddled together in jumbles of eight, often interspersed with figures, or the other way round, as if written in some otherworldly code. Some lines had just a single pack of letters or numbers in them, some were populated with whole clusters, and a few lines remained empty altogether. The pattern repeated over pages and pages.

A choked sound left the mystic. His gaze slid down the cryptic list, and then off it.

"Well, well, well," he said, rather lamely, just because something had to be said and he had no idea what. "Well."

He looked at the binder from all sides, when something slipped from its side and flopped onto the flagstones with a hollow papery sound.

He picked up a scroll, a very tiny one. Quickly he unrolled the length of it, only to find more rune hotchpotch. As different as it was from the other papers, he couldn't make heads or tails of that one either. The scroll contained just one neatly spaced row of runes, aligned in four sets of jumbles; however, underneath, as if commenting on the cryptic row or mocking its observer, four eight-letter sized packages of question marks stared back at him.

Now, Zarothaster was no stranger to silly riddles and genuinely arcane puzzles, and if anyone knew how to separate the one from the other, it was him. But this one, this jigsaw of cosmic proportions, hit the jackpot. He could almost hear it sniggering.

He fixed his gaze on the runes.

Was his mind beginning to fade? Or had one of the numbers just changed?

There it was again! He waited, then witnessed a number somewhere in the middle take on the shape of a letter and, conversely, a letter turn into a figure.

Zarothaster's head lifted; his gaze went roving. He strained his eyes, scouring the dark for yet another hint, and when he turned and turned some more, he indeed recognized a shape right behind him, as if it had slipped in when he wasn't looking.

As he approached, he made out a stony lectern on a small dais. Like a guardian, it appeared to oversee the cabinets at its feet. A tome rested on top of it, fastened to the stone by a piece of chain. It was, by all means, massive. Ancient too, he was sure. Tangles of embossed ornamental knots crowded one corner of its front cover, and likewise the corner diagonally across. Eagerly the mystic's hand reached out for it.

No treasures were buried within. Only more columns and rows. More rampant rune sets. And yet it wasn't just that. The more he rifled through the ledger-like pages, the more he recognized it as a queer kind of index. All the binder names he had seen were there, populating one column, ordered meticulously, and the other column translated the names into... something else: a Forgotten name into a jumble of letters. It was, no doubt, a catalogue of things, from *abbey* to *zebra* and back, with a *Paen'oul'ocean Robe* tucked somewhere in between.

He returned to the binders.

The writing was in various hands, elegant, crude or unassuming, and sometimes sprawling or lopsided. Each folder was as inscrutable as the first, and all of them had an extra scroll in a pocket at the side; the scroll was sometimes brimming with rows and rows of runes, others contained just a few lines, and almost all of them shifted, changed, reinvented themselves upon his gaze as if they had a life on their own. Only when he went back to where he had started off, to the binder on the robe, something occurred to him. It was *that* one, the very first he had looked at, that was the odd one out. Or rather the scroll it harboured was the odd one out. It was the only one with question marks.

A thought flickered through the mystic's mind. It cruised and cruised, and at the same time a dark hunch crept up his spine – a hunch so troubling that he clutched the fabric of his robe until his knuckles grew white.

Sleeves streaming behind him, he bounded back to the cabinets once more and wrenched a drawer open. With a twinge of panic, he flicked through the faded index cards. Flicked, flicked, flicked… until his nervous browsing eased into listless taps. Nothing. For a time, he stared out into the shadows folding in around his little island of light, then he shuffled back up the two steps of the dais to once more rifle through the tome. All he found were entries on *snuff boxes*, *rolling pins* and *cotton candy*.

Acid laughter rumbled out of him. Why, this was a joke! Behind the world awaited nothing but… a *joke!*

His shaking hands seized the bookrest and, with the grace of a learned man mishandling a heavy crate, he hefted the tome up, about to slam it full force whereverwards. Only he couldn't. The massive chain attached to the monstrosity of a book strained and clattered violently as it reached its limit, ripped the tome away from him, and it bumped back onto the lectern with a resounding bang. As if to insist on its place. As if to show the sage *his* place. Only the ornamental knots had changed corners. The tome lay back to front now, upside down. And not a nail's breadth askew.

Call it curiosity, a hunch or a premonition, but something led the mystic to open it yet again.

The runes inside were the right way up. Even when he pushed hundreds and hundreds of pages back, he found the runes were still the right way up! Now, however – and he clawed through the remainder of the tome like a maniac, going back, back, back until the end – they weren't cataloguing *things* anymore.

"Impossible!" he hissed.

He scowled at the outer darkness beyond the lectern, and only then did he see them. More rectangles came out of their hideouts, as if being drawn once he started wondering whether they really were there.

He wheeled about until he came full circle. The dais was now ringed with cabinets.

"No!" Like a swordsman who'd just decapitated a dragon only to witness a backup head sprouting from the defeated beast's shoulders, he lunged back to the tome. He tore a page from it, extracted another bundle from a drawer, one bulging with content, and let it flop onto the cabinet's top, as though he'd pulled a glowing lump of ember from a live fire.

For a time, he just stood with it propped against one of his silent companions, listening hard to his own breathing as it wheezed in and out of him in short, aching bursts.

Eventually, he crammed the bundle and the page under his arm and stormed back the way he had come. This time, the cabinet rows folded away like a magic napkin, and in their stead the racks grew back to monumental heights.

His eyes darted about. Now that he was looking for them, the Forgotten runes etched into the plaques beneath the ghostly items on the shelves were impossible to miss. He checked a few, then a few more. Some matched the ones on the page he held, others didn't, but he vowed to find the remaining matches too, and so – now endowed with purpose – he swept through the aisles, checking and rechecking, threading his way deeper and deeper into the racky labyrinth.

He broke into trot. Around him, the ghosts kept morphing – in shape, in size, in bizarreness. His head tilted upwards to the more spacious higher levels. Anxiety flickered in his eyes. Phantoms of what must have been rocks drifted past, whole trees – ash, sycamore and elm – and what looked like a ghostly waterfall cascading from the top shelf levels before dropping down into a spray of unreal mist. Thrice he floundered, and thrice he stumbled on. The final time he careened so violently to the side that his grappling hands scattered a ghost all over the place, but the threads were quick to realign themselves into the image of a wheelbarrow and resume their incessant spinning.

He spied it, then, high above him, doing its own spectral dance: a shape among shapes, a ghost among ghosts. The figure stared down at him, and he back up at it, out of breath, but otherwise stock still.

The binder slipped from his grasp. Parchment tumbled out, fluttering away like flushed birds and coming down again in graceful seesawing motions, gently sliding over the folder… and the all too familiar name written on it.

"Threep-throlly-thrum-throb!" Whinewaeyn sat forward. "*Names!*"

"Names, Archmagus?" Amjelle stood stooped over one of the drawers. She rose a pre-emptive eyebrow at the wizard.

"Dozens, no, hundreds of them, I say!" Pages flew left and right from the perch Whinewaeyn had made out of binders. He was sitting with his back against the cabinets, studying their contents with keen interest.

Amjelle drew closer, not quite getting it. "What kind of names?"

"Names as in… names!" Whinewaeyn specified.

Two more pairs of eyes watched the exchange from the sidelines, swivelling back and forth at different heights. Up there was Ramrok, leaning on the pommel of his sword with the grace and dimness of an unlit lamppost. The more earthbound of the two was Bormph, with an expression not much brighter than the barbarian's. He might have been mistaken for the bigger one's brother, except that he had grown in the wrong direction and been dipped into a paint bucket along the way. Height difference aside, they locked gazes.

Whinewaeyn tapped a finger on the binder spread over his lap. "Names, Amjelle dear, with first parts and then second ones, so the first ones aren't all by themselves. Put together, it's the whole thing. You know, a *full* name." Without waiting to gauge a further reaction, he burrowed straight through another pile. "There are Tjillmers, Bryannas and Cordrolias, Minclings and Thromps, H'rocs and Kn'hocs and whatnot. All sorts."

"Names as in *names?*" Bormph mimicked, always the sceptic. He leaned close and, raising himself on tiptoes, glared at the runes he couldn't read anyway. But a dwarf has to see.

"Human, goblish, orcen…" Whinewaeyn rummaged around. "And the whole rest of them, I would say."

"Who *are* all these people?" Amjelle demanded from the mystic. "Why are there records of them here?"

"Why, indeed?" Zarothaster's spindly fingers fanned out like a peacock's feathers. Which was all he did for a while. When he finally spoke again, his words came out slow and deliberate. "Why indeed is… anyone… here, travellers? Aren't we all but *ideas?* Unique, yes, every single one of us. But ideas, nevertheless. Then again, what else are we looking at in a place like this but the Weavers' minds, and then only through the trappings of the minds we call our own? Maybe we'd better ask ourselves why *we* put names on everything?" He seemed to wait for suggestions, but then answered himself when nobody offered. "Names tell us what things are. They give everything its place. By the same token, we give every*one* a place too. As the Weavers must have done."

"You're saying the Weavers... gave *us* names?" Sylthia struggled visibly. "*Our* names?"

"Isn't it so that you elves believe, among other things, in the concept of naming?"

Sylthia fixed him with a stare. "We believe in true names, yes. Names *behind* all names, but these are—"

"*Actual* names!" Amjelle hissed. "These are—"

"Aren't actual names true enough for you? Everyone knows everyone else by an actual name." The mystic's eyes grazed Sylthia, then drifted past Amjelle, past the giant barbarian, beyond Whinewaeyn and the miraculous cabinets that merged with the haze further off. "To be..." he intoned as if talking to the inky beyond, "or not to be..."

Expectant silence.

"Um... What was the question?" Pulled from his own thicket of thoughts, Whinewaeyn had cocked his head up.

Then there was an awful clang, a noise as of a hundred plates shattering and spilling across the floor in merry anarchy.

"Sooorry." The voice sounded deep and resonant. Ramrok stepped forward, reached down and picked up his two-hander. "Ramrok try... er... think. Ramrok no good with... er... think." He resumed his lamppost stance. "Ramrok stop now."

Thimble whipped around.

What was that?

The clang had made his heart flounder for a moment. He tried to snatch a glance of what was going on back there. All he could make out were blurry shapes motioning in a pool of grey, but he just about heard the barbarian rumbling his muffled excuse. *Bonehead of a barbarian*, he thought to

465

himself and forged on. That pea-brain! Wasn't he supposed to be looking after the cub? And now the bear had absconded. Whatever this place was up to, it owed him a polar bear.

Inventive as he was, Thimble had tried to wish him back. If only. What worked for an imagined rhino clearly didn't for a live cub, and so he'd had to go about it the old-fashioned way – by looking for him. At least it didn't take long to spot a white, fluffy something roaming around in the dark. It only needed picking up.

"Snowflake!"

Saturnine darkness grew around him. The further away he inched from the light pool, the less there was to discern ahead. If only he had brought his—

An intense smell of pine and sulphur crept into his nostrils. With an abrupt sizzle, something bright and hot burst to life close by.

"Ha!" Thimble stared at the stick in his right hand, a little intimidated. Then a smile stretched over his face. A flame was writhing about the piece of wood he held, feeding on an oil-drenched rag covering its top. It bathed his face in warmth, but before it could do too much of that, Thimble shoved the torch an arm's length away. The flame reached further now too, revealing a stirring in the shadows – and, sure enough, a white wedge-shaped head at the end of an extra-long neck swung back at him. He held his torch aloft. The white thing flicked an ear.

"Snowflake! Here, Snowy!" Thimble coaxed and threw in a whistle. "Here! Got you some fish!"

The lie caught the bear's attention. Thimble tiptoed closer, holding out a piece of invisible food. Still, the polar bear was no lapdog, or his eyesight was considerably better, for the cub saw through the ruse, turned tail and padded onwards. Thimble raised his torch even higher. The bear was a mere bowshot away, negotiating his way over pieces of flagstone.

Wait... What? Thimble looked again, transfixed. Indeed, pieces of white flagstone were all there was to see. Two to be exact. Just a bear and two stony squares, and nothing – absolutely nothing – covering the space between the escapee and his pursuer, unless one were to count absolute nothingness as something, which Thimble didn't.

A sensation hit him. A joggle.

In the red gleam of his torchlight, Thimble looked down. To his horror, he caught only a negligible selection of flagstones there too. Just two brittle slabs that held him afloat – and one of them, right now, was tilting to the side.

"Nooo!" he cried out and centred himself on what he'd got.

His blood ran cold. All around, including – weirdly – the way he had come, an abyss of unimaginable magnitude yawned back at him. Despite the torch he held, the gloom seemed closer now. So heavy was it that one could've cut it with a knife. Or a dagger. Like the one at Thimble's side, to which he held on to right now. But then he gripped the weapon so hard that it slipped through his sweaty fingers and leapt from his belt to join the abyss.

Bormph rubbed his nose.

"Well, I'm not sure I'm okay with... this creation thing." He had his beady eyes fixed on the cabinets. "I'll say it as it is: I'm sort of... uncomfortable... with all this archiving of people behind the world without their prior consent, whoever's responsible for it. And I don't care whether it's the Stonefather Himself, or a Weaver or a Toaster. What about the protection of privacy?"

Zarothaster gave the bunch of them a mild smile. "The order we see back here might just be the order we *seek*. The eye of the beholder never rests." As if to prove his point, the lines making up the cabinets appeared to blur for a moment, only to straighten the very next.

Bormph's mulish expression made clear he still couldn't see a consoling factor. "Well. A strange operation altogether, I say. If that's how the Stonefather—"

"So it's your Stonefather now, is it?" Sylthia interrupted heatedly. "How come you're getting pious all of a sudden, dwarf? Here, at the beginning and end of all things? Since when does your Stonefather deal in ghosts? Answer me that!"

"Not saying he does," Bormph jabbed back. "I'm just saying that with all these world-creating secrets tucked behind a mountain, it smacks of dwarf."

"But this is a place like no other. It might just as well be the Dreameress's abode."

"Maybe it's the Five who weaved all these ghosts." Amjelle felt professionally challenged. "The Five from *our* scriptures. We have the One too, but also the Other, and the rest. We've got them all, the dwarven Forgelord and the elven Dreameress. They're part of the Hyleian pantheon, only different in name."

"Any looms mentioned in your scriptures?" Bormph goaded.

"Where are all the anvils from yours?" Amjelle swiped back. "I bet your Stonelord's diaries are full of them. And yet, I see none."

"Advanced forging." Bormph clicked his tongue. "Someone must have started it. Someone must have forged the first anvil, sledge and all. The Toaster guy may call it weaving, but he's just being poetic about it. Forging's the proper word, and any dwarf knows it."

Sylthia rolled her eyes. "Now that figures. There's nothing in the least bit material about this place, and a dwarf thinks he can talk right past it."

"So? *Matter* is what matters," Bormph said. "It's in the name. Just think about it. Why is there no rock-solid stuff here? Easy. Because everything that counts is on the other side. As the Toaster said. I'm not a cleric, but it may just be that the Stonelord needed a place to *make* what matters. And he hid it away behind the mountain, so as not to embarrass himself. The more I think about it, the more it sounds about right."

"And then he hid himself too for good measure? Hid away from his own hideout?"

Arguments flew left and right. A debate was struck up, and it swept back and forth and round and round. Until the mystic raised a hand.

"Would it help," he said abruptly, "if I'd told you that your gods are recorded in here too? *All* of them?"

Everyone talked over each other. The cabinets? Seat of the divine?

A rustling filled the air. Whinewaeyn shoved several pieces of parchment back into their respective folders. He faced the mystic. "Are you implying that someone... created... the gods?" He slid from his pile of binders, prodded his hat back and scratched his head. "But... who would have created *them*? And, speaking of which," – he weighed another thought – "would those creators have been created too? If so, by whom?" The scratching slowed and his hand moved on to tugging at his earlobe, as if it helped to marshal his thoughts. "Are we to assume that – as every race and tribe, and even kings and madmen, have their own gods – everyone's right to believe, because that's how it was supposed to be in the first place?"

"Sometimes I do wonder," Zarothaster replied, but it was as though something else spoke through him. "I wonder whether the Weavers created the gods and left them to their own devices, just as the gods left us to our own. Maybe there are other universes to attend to, and everyone was left alone for a reason. Maybe that's why things aren't perfect." He paused. "What would be the point of a perfect universe? Who would we be if there was nothing to aspire to?" The ensuing silence had no answer. "At times, I wonder if maybe it's just us. Because that's all we may ever discover back here. Us. What if it's *all*... us?"

"Us?" Whinewaeyn paused too now, from tugging at his earlobe. "What's us?" Then he tugged some more.

"The Weavers. The Forgotten." Zarothaster's gaze shifted from one far-away place to another. "The ultimate paradox. The insoluble circle. The question and answer to the enigma of existence. The dragon eating its own tail, and the knot that ties it all together. *We* weave our world. All the things that are of import to us, *we* create them. *We* destroy them. *We're* our salvation and our doom, and even make up our gods as we see fit. And all the while we forget, forget that we're in the middle of this, that we're our own beginning... and end." His voice grew fainter. "Sometimes, we take a whole world with us."

"What was that?" Whinewaeyn's face turned from contemplative to inquisitive. He looked about and saw the same look in other faces too. "Could you perhaps expound a smidge on that last bit? That... end thing? Did you have anything to do with—"

"Haven't you figured it out yet?" The mystic let out a throaty, mirthless laugh. "How the world's demise came to pass?"

All he got in return were blank stares.

"I was tempted." Zarothaster's hand dropped onto the stack of binders, where it landed with a weighty thud. "I fiddled with them."

CHAPTER 23

Art Among Ants

Thimble's head shot up.

The bear was gone. So were the floating flagstones his furry friend had occupied only a moment ago. Now he was just a defenceless, ashen-faced halfling against the abyss, with only some very questionable support in between. A chilly rush of air eddied about him, and his belly knotted up tight.

He half turned on the little scrap of floor he'd been given. The eerie breeze carried a strange welling of noise. Whispers. Whispers that had lifted from the untiring susurration and drifted unintelligibly past him, as if of a dozen different tongues. For a moment, he took them for Bormph's, Amjelle's and Sylthia's, but they clearly weren't, and the only one he thought he actually recognized among them was... But no, that couldn't be. Thimble strained his ears, yet the whispers had woven back into the underlying hum again already, to a point where he dissuaded himself that he'd heard anything beyond a low rumble in the first place.

Breath shuddering, limbs quivering, he stalked about on his two flagstones. He inched closer to the edge, leaned forward… Nothing. Not a thing to hold on to. Not for hands, feet or eyes. And all the looking got him exactly nowhere. So he drew back again, only to realize that he was now a flagstone shorter. He had lifted a foot in leaning forward, and that particular piece had slipped into the shadows.

A squeal of mortal fear leapt from his lungs. The darkness absorbed it like a meal.

He swivelled, hopped quickly to the side on one foot so as to make room for the other. That brought most of his weight too close to the edge for its own good. The tile tilted. Flailing his arms, Thimble caught his balance. He shimmied back to the centre.

Then his only standing leg buckled. The rest of him folded like a jackknife. Arching his remaining leg forward to find purchase elsewhere, it quickly became apparent that there wasn't anything around to make a deal, apart from the pitch-black gorge, open for business 24/7. Thimble fell.

And yet, not quite.

Well, he fell alright, just not abyss-deep.

About a blink later, Thimble found himself sprawled over the length of two flagstones, holding on to his torch as much as to his life. Somehow, he had gained a flagstone. Everything considered, it was a sizeable improvement.

Thimble collected his wits. He drew himself back up. Carefully, very carefully, he spread his weight, placing one foot on the first slab and the other on the second, when he was startled by something moving within the stones. His instinct was to leap somewhere else, but as he couldn't, he stayed in place and, hesitantly, looked again. It was just the windings of the flame he held reflecting in the stone's surface. But after a bit of swaying the torch back and forth, he saw fragile threads dancing in the marble, wispy strands that contorted on their own, sometimes following, sometimes countering the flickers of the light he held. What he was looking at was its own kind of fire, a fire that hugged his reflecting features, a fire blazing around a... ghostly... face. *His* face.

He yelped. And yet he kept staring down at the ghostly strands, the slabs, his bare feet, all the while thinking – about feet, slabs and strands, about how the slabs must be supporting his feet, and therefore him, a live halfling. But what was there to support the slabs if not the ghostly strands? And they somehow owed themselves to... him, a live halfling.

His fist clenched around the torch. He held it out low and leaned forward, into the void. The hair on the back of his neck pricked up. One of his feet followed the torch's lead, lifted and angled forward, then dipped down.

There. His big toe met resistance, and a wispy thread flourished from it. More toes followed his first. Then his heel. His whole foot. And attached to his foot... the weight of the whole halfling. Ghostly strands danced across the freshly birthed flagstone.

A darkness away.

"I tried to... understand things."

"Oh, you tried to *understand* things." When Bormph repeated the mystic's words, sullen-eyed and in a mocking voice, much less understanding came across.

"Stranded behind the world, I hungered for figuring it all out: the reams of runes, the names, the ghosts, the hums they seemed to feed. I was like you, looking for answers." A long moment passed. "Then again, looking at numbers among numbers… it's like staring at a wall for hours. However bland and grey, the longer the eye dwells upon the intangible, the more one is bound to make something out. *Anything.* A pattern, and another one on top of the first, and then patterns within patterns." The mystic's voice had almost dwindled to a lament. "As if I was *meant* to. I thought that whatever was out there, however it did what it did and for whatever reason, it must have *wanted* me here, must have… called upon me."

"Yeah?" Bormph bristled. "Are you the same guy who had his doubts about the gods? Why would anyone have called you back here then, fiddler?"

"Why, to fix things. Something was wrong with the universe."

"Like the rock that reflects ghosts like a glass darkly?" Amjelle whispered apprehensively. "The one through which we crossed over?"

The mystic nodded. He tapped on the pile of folders Whinewaeyn had left on the cabinets. "And, to be sure, if you go looking for that rock, you'll find its binder too, among all the others. So I studied it, for the place was patient with me, and I took the soft sounds that live here as being in agreement with my efforts." His robe flapped for a moment as a chilly draught swept past them.

"But the rock…" Amjelle began. She gave him a hard look.

"I failed." The mystic's own verdict came down like an executioner's axe. "All I managed was… re-arranging numbers and runes. I lined figures up to give them a symmetry they lacked, as to restore an order, and yet" – more and more spirit drained from his already feeble voice – "I'd not a clue how the world worked. When the visions came, I knew that I was wrong."

"Visions?"

"Aye. They're like dreams in reverse. On the other side… from whence we all hail… you dream of what *might* be, what *could* be, of what *never will* be. Here, one dreams only of what's real, what *you* made real. That's why my mind was haunted by the sight of the rock when sleep wouldn't come to me. Again and again, I saw the rock slip from existence in my mind's eye, and as these images kept recurring, I sensed the truth behind it all, which I so dreaded. The truth about that loophole, the one I tried to mend so desperately. Yet I still didn't understand. Not then."

"…?" Bormph asked, forgetting words.

"*I* opened that loophole. *I* made the very flaw that got me here."

Bormph glared back at the mystic, hands on his braids. He had been listening with both ears, and neither of them had picked out a part his mind could cope with.

"*I* am at the heart of that circle. *I* broke the world."

"Why, that's just ridiculous!" Bormph burst out at last. "Curd with a cape! There's no such thing! How could anyone waltz through a loophole and create it from the other side afterwards? It's like… like…" – his thick fingers groped about helplessly – "like mining gems without a mine, Toaster. You can't mine gems with no mine. How in the world—"

"Is *this* the world?" Zarothaster fired back. His hand jerked up to describe a circle as if to capture the essence suffusing the miraculous halls, and his eyes rolled with the motion of his outstretched fingers. "All this is just what keeps the world in place. It holds no judgement. But mess with it, and…" He struggled to finish the sentence. "I… I put my mortal hand in things eternal. I altered the rock.

Unglued it. Bereaved it of its ordained role. And from there, it all started. A long, long time ago, long before my time even... That's when the Eye-lander came in."

"The Eye-lander? Who the heck is the Eye-lander?"

Back then. A long, long time ago. Sort of.

Art O'neyri's gaze travelled upward slowly, ever so slowly – to get the most out of it, to savour what he was seeing, to drink it like sweet mead on a star-studded evening at a campfire. The view was... breathtaking. Daunting. August. "Mental" as the kids of the Eye-land would say! Mon-u-mental. Even just standing there, right underneath it and gaping at that inconceivable mass reaching forward already made him queasy. If it came down on him, he'd be squashed like an ant. It would grind him to dust.

His long journey had paid off. This was the subject he'd been looking for. He fished some loosely bound pages from his satchel along with a bundle of charcoals, picked a stump, and raised his chin. That rock... it could stand for all kinds of things. It was only a matter of how he chose to approach it. Ah, the artist's dilemma. Sometimes it worked, and sometimes it didn't.

He skimmed through a few of his previous sketches. Among them was one from his animal phase: two cow heads opposite each other, with all the eyes on one side of the heads as to indicate a bovine one-sidedness. These cows would never see another side of each other, which, admittedly, was a bit on the nose – both, the eyes *and* the intention. A bit too Quinchy-ish. The other sketch coloured his ears violently lavender. A three-legged cock strutting on a muckheap? What was he thinking? Well, he had learned. He flipped to a fresh page.

Eyes not leaving the outcrop above, he turned around and let his back rest against the granite. This had to be the way to do it. The ant's view upwards, with the everlasting rock bearing down on the viewer in detached, weightless, timeless suspension. Ambitious? Sure. Offbeat? Check. Food for thought? You betcha. And, in all likelihood, an artistic failure. *Bugger that*, he thought. *Here I come.*

He leaned back, starting to trace the jagged line between the heavens and the earth. Once the zigzagging edge was committed to paper in its velvety intensity, he smudged it upwards to suggest a couple of crags, upside down, the way he saw it, and as his eye flicked back and forth between reference and copy, the off-kilter nature of the forming picture began to grow on him. *Yes, that's it!* he enthused. He settled back further, smudging and smearing, surprised at how smooth and forgiving the rock he was resting on felt to him, almost like a cushion. As he thought that thought, a shadow dropped over his hand. Quickly it reached further, blotting out the sky, the cliff and the line separating them.

A dark veil had enshrouded him.

He hadn't been aware of the birds chirping guardedly in the distance, nor of the wind caressing the blades of the high grasses at the wayside, sometimes making them sough and sometimes swoosh, and sometimes both at once. He hadn't noticed the sunlight itself guiding his hand into shaping light and shadow. But when it all suddenly ceased and he was falling... falling... into a stifling pureness of void and a silence so much more complete than anything he had ever known, when he was falling into an otherness, he became acutely aware of everything that wasn't there anymore. With a jolt and a gargling scream, he thrust his arms out, lunged forward through the veil, and—

The world returned.

It came at him fast. Like a rock attracted to a gravitational pull.

He looked about. His nose was bleeding. But it wasn't stone that had hit him. It was plain, dry dirt, and he had dug his hands into it. Dust had swirled up around him and now was showering down. Other than that, the dirt was firm and flat seen from eye level, and it smelled of soil baked in the midday sun. His breath came and went, came and went. A train of ants scuttled past. Lying there like that on his stomach, watching the blood from his nose form a little brook and listening to his heart beating, he cocked his head. The rock was still there. As was the sky beneath its looming presence. And everything else was still there too. Birds twittering. A breath of a breeze on his cheek. Sunlight slanting down.

He chanced a peek over his shoulder. The rock face behind him appeared solid, unbending – a single massive chunk of granite with no suggestion to the contrary. He narrowed his gaze. At the very bottom, where the stone connected to the dusty ground, lay his sketchbook, part of it at least, peeking out as if tucked under a door. Shadowy tendrils oozed from the crack.

Without thinking, Art pounced, seized his work from the smoke's grasp and backed away immediately. The shadows retreated. Other than that, nothing happened for a moment.

A moment after that moment, the rock twitched.

And Art… made a dash for it.

"Few believed the Eye-lander's tale, whimsical as it was, and even fewer knew what to make of it." Zarothaster buried his head in his high collar, as if the memories were weighing him down. "Yet many sought it out, that place he spoke of so vividly, steeped in so much mystery, high up in the Silvery Sickle. Who knew what they hoped to find? Some claim they saw things. Others didn't. Some never even returned. Most lacked the patience for waiting. A trail was marked leading up to the rock, as to guide the pilgrims, but over time, with the passing of the centuries, even those most devoted to the tale moved on to more promising distractions to busy their searching minds."

"And the Eye-lander?" Sylthia asked. "What happened to the O'neyri fellow?"

"Who knows. He got rid of his sketchbook, though, which he was convinced was possessed. He sold it to the Magical Emporium, along with his fancy story, and that's how I stumbled upon it. And what a strange collection it turned out to be! An odd choice of drawings, sure, but the pages went beyond the artist's meagre talent. I acquired it… and investigated."

Bormph jerked his chin up at him. "Let me have a guess, Toaster. The thing has trouble remaining what it looks like. Like the rock."

"Why, yes, dwarf, that's one way of putting it. The pages… they appeared out of place, out of time – in part at least. A most unusual case. And why else would that be, I reckoned, if not for their brush with that fabled spot the artist mentioned? I vowed to find out more, not knowing that at my journey's end, I would be the one to set things in motion too, and from that very place I was so eager to find – the place beyond all places, at a time predating all times… *Here*." He paused for a moment, gaze narrowed, in thoughtful silence.

"I see," Whinewaeyn said, breaking into it, fingers drumming away on his staff. "And as you were studying this peculiar item, I assume you used those very same pages to document your progress."

Zarothaster perked up at that.

"'Signpost and pathway'," Whinewaeyn quoted from memory. "I remember, mystic. I translated your odd turn of phrase. Sticks in your mind like a Khapashian honey-nut between your teeth. But I never figured out what that weird-eyed cow and his three-legged rooster friend had to do with anything."

"My journal… led you here?" Zarothaster stared at him, and then at Sylthia, who nodded back at him.

"We followed its bearings, cairn by cairn—"

"Show me!"

Whinewaeyn ceased the drumming on his staff. "I wish we could."

"It vanished," Sylthia said.

"*Pfff!*" Bormph added a flourish with his short arms.

"Vanished?" The mystic's eyes shifted wildly. "You say it's been… claimed?" His head turned owlishly around his shoulders. "I've considered this for years and years, or whatever a year may amount to back here. That I was supposed to return it in the first place, and to leave it at that. That *that* would have been my true purpose. But *you*—" The gaunt man's eyes lit up, but for no longer than a flicker. "Ah, it's no use."

The shoulders in the splendid clothes sagged. "You see, it didn't end there… with the rock. My mind wouldn't surrender. For if I couldn't understand the rock, maybe something else would do the trick, you know? Something simple and insignificant, a small, unspectacular, wayside kind of thing… If only I was able to grasp the nature of just that and how it relates to everything else in this oddest of places... maybe then, just maybe... I could learn about the rock, and from there—"

"*Gnomes!*" Whinewaeyn's staff banged on the floor. The wizard's long arm swung forward, an accusing finger at its end. "Why, you must have experimented on gnomes, mystic! Behind the world!"

"Aye." Zarothaster's voice was but a thin whisper. "Gnomes. It was gnomes... among other things. But it started with gnomes."

"But of course," Bormph grumbled, deeper than usual. "Gnomes. You couldn't help but fiddle with gnome ghosts. And now the world is ending. Bit of a stretch, Toasty."

"Are you as unseeing as I was?" Zarothaster snapped back at him. "A gnome back here is not just any gnome."

Bormph found his thoughts lagging.

"Remember Tsynnslin?" Amjelle said suddenly, and the dwarf turned. Her eyes were fixed so intensely on him that his mind went seriously gnome-sorting. "Nothing in the world is by itself. The gnome's words. And if everything is connected to everything else, one way or another, then everything must be connected by six degrees or thereabouts..."

Bormph's brow lengthened.

"...to a gnome too," Sylthia did the maths.

Elf and healer looked at each other for a moment, their faces frozen somewhere between epiphany and horror. Bormph shook himself like a wet mutt. But the weird thoughts about gnomes wouldn't go away.

"Ever since," Zarothaster picked up from there, "the gnomes were lost to the world. I'd ripped them out of it, in part. They didn't know their place anymore, nor their time to be in it. Hence, detached from whatever is, they were drawn back to their before-the-world origins. All that I've seen in my visions. They were aiming for where the fabric of the world was broken, for—"

"Hanging Rock!" Amjelle and Sylthia cried out as one.

"And now your fancy rock eats gnomes but doesn't swallow?" Bormph stared into the round, and the round stared back at Bormph. And because the only one that rose above it all was Ramrok – literally – everybody ended up staring up at him, as though enlightenment must come from somewhere higher up.

The big one looked down on everyone and let out a grunt.

Thimble's attention snapped back. The tile he had just lifted his foot from was no more. Not to the naked eye, anyway.

He dared another step. The same thing happened. His foot found a flagstone that wasn't there, and the one he left behind faded away as if its day's work had been done. He was… walking. And as it had gone so well, he did some more of it. Without looking down he soldiered on, picking his way flagstone by flagstone along a path that paved itself right under his feet.

"Snowflake!" He cupped his hands around his mouth. "Snowflake!"

A dull glimmer answered from across the abyss.

Thimble pointed his torch in its direction. As if summoned by his flickering flame, a round, jagged something stood out against the realm of shadows. It was an odd thing to behold in this oddest of places, something he couldn't quite connect with anything else – until the round, jagged something did the job for him and connected itself to something else. It connected itself to more round, jagged somethings.

Whatever he was looking at stretched far and wide out in front of him, to his sides, and, yes, even behind him! More and more glints from wheely things flashed back when his questing torchlight brushed past them, and soon he recognized he was inside an entire dome made out of wheels, which bent from here to there, arranged at unlikely angles.

Some wheels were rusty and speckled, some shiny, and some were mere streaks in their oily environs. While most were simple at first glance, none looked exactly the same. A few were amazingly tiny, delicate and wafer-thin, others large-scale and sprawling with spear-like spikes, or thick and vast, sturdy as wagon wheels with broad spokes splitting them up, secured with nuts and bolts. Their chunky teeth meshed with their broad-teethed kin. The really giant ones, exceeding the size of the halfling, perhaps a halfling and a half even, were iron-cast pieces with only a couple of holes punched into them, their jaded golden shine reminiscent of flattened cheese loaves.

Thimble fixed the first wheel in his sight, and drew closer. As the tiles had done, the wheels right ahead cast back a distorted reflection in their shiny surfaces, almost like in a hall of mirrors. One moment Thimble saw himself in it puffed up like a blowfish, then he'd move, and he turned needle-slim. The wide eyes staring back were all over the place – only with some contortion could he find a regular-sized halfling to go with them. Cogs, Thimble realized. That's what the wheels were. Cogs.

Like the ones in the Grand Weaverring Clock Tower.

But unlike the cogs back in Weaverring, none of these ones were moving. They weren't working their magic... or mystic, or whatever. Cogs made the hands of the Weaverring Clock Tower move, he knew. Not much, mind you – the hands on the dial appeared to be frozen like signposts on the first look, and yet they were good enough to announce the exact middle of the day. Or Sundrown when it came to that. If you kept your eye fixed on the hands, you could see that they did indeed shift in tiny wee increments. The whole apparatus worked without a sundial, and thank the gods, because it rained buckets all the time. It ticked and tocked away in the shadows, hidden from view, and clicked and clacked the whole day through. Thimble remembered a couple of drizzly afternoons when he had stared at those hands for hours on end while waiting for the sun and customers, marvelling at how the thing did what it did. Once or twice he'd got up at the ungodliest of hours, just to see if the hands were still moving. And they were! Even in the deadest of night!

It was the dead of night here too. But the wheely wall peeking out of the gloom's icy silence stood stock-still. Like a painting.

CHAPTER 24

Destined to Dream

"We shouldn't be here." The mystic's bleak words trickled into the silence. The longer they lingered, the harsher they grew. "Not here, not *behind* the veil. This is not place."

Bormph cast a searing glance at him. "Shouldn't you have thought about that *before* you broke the world, Mysty?"

"Is it just me who has to see before he believes?"

"Actually, you two could be related," Amjelle observed.

"Strictly speaking," Whinewaeyn inserted himself, "tampering with gnomes and stuff, that's one thing. At least you didn't try to—"

"And what do *you* know?" The snarl buried the wizard's words. As if fanned by a dark memory, a wild light flared up in the mystic's eyes, and he started pacing about. "What makes you think I'd stop at tinkering with lousy gnomes, wizard?" His swelling voice was taken by a tremble, and as he walked in circles the gnarled fingers curled into a fist that pounded on the mystic's chest, again and again and once again. "The rock... the gnomes... all these other things. Whatever I tried my hand at to uncover the mystery that is the world… it all availed to naught. I made things worse. And why? Because everything I tampered with had already been made. I told myself that until I actually believed it. But what if I started with a clean slate? Would I be able to forge… *things*… *life* even… afresh? And if I could, what would that make me? With the world at my fingertips, was I destined to become one of the Chosen? Meant to replace the forgers, now that they had moved on?"

"But that's just… preposterous!" Amjelle blurted out.

"You cannot just *create* life," Sylthia said. "Like that."

"Skips the procreation bit!" Bormph saw the practical aspects. "That's… cheating!"

"Aye." The mystic spat at his own words, rank with hubris. His eyes hardened, and the fist he had clenched came apart. Finally, he ceased his pacing. "I made a shambles of it. I marred the eternal circle. Corrupted what it was by usurping it, trying to make it my own. But as soon as the dreams returned, I knew. I saw it, that great, first creation of mine, tumbling out of the skies, only to end up stillborn" – his gaze dropped with his voice – "in its sandy grave."

Silence fell between them as if it owned the place.

"It was a bug, wasn't it?" Sylthia said after a while.

The words rode the semi-darkness only a hint above a hush. Loud enough, though, to make Zarothaster twist around as if stung by a hornet. Or bitten by a beetle. As the clanking chain around his neck settled, he was facing the elf. The puzzled eyes searched her composed features.

"A scarab," she said. "That's what you tried to concoct in your unending arrogance, mystic. Here, behind the world, however you went about it, like a god that you aren't. A creature as simple as a bug... and yet as wondrous as the whole universe."

The mystic's eyes flashed, shifted. His brittle lips twitched. "How would you know, elf?"

"Because we brought it with us."

The great mystic stood petrified for a moment. Then he leapt forward. "Where is it?"

Sylthia reached back behind her head, but when her hair unrolled her delicate fingers came up empty. Instead, a sound fluttered past, a rattle too fast to chase with eye or ear, and from the pin's former place a thin, ghostly thread uncurled to steal off into the distance. Zarothaster's hand slipped from the elf's shoulders, and now he swayed sideways, gabbling in half sentences and slumping into the barbarian. The giant caught the flailing bundle by the collar before he collapsed altogether.

"I'll be damned!" Bormph rumbled. His helmeted head swivelled back at the elf, wreathed by her now loose and tousled hair. "So the old codger dreamed it up, that thing that's not a thing?"

"And now the place has claimed it back too," Amjelle said.

Sylthia nodded. "As it did with the journal. As if whatever wasn't supposed to be... found its way home."

"As if the place is healing itself."

The mystic, still in the barbarian's grip, fidgeted about, shaking his head. "So what? What good does it do?" he crowed. "The world... it's gone! I've scried it. You've been there, and you saw it!" He made some effort to wrench himself free, until the giant had enough of him and allowed the mystic to slip back to the ground, where he crumbled into a heap, still blabbering. "It's too late now. It will always be too late."

"You sure about that?" Whinewaeyn stroked his beard. "You've changed things from a place beyond time and space. Who says things can't be changed back the same way?"

"We'd only make it worse," Zarothaster wailed.

Whinewaeyn looked about. "Have we explored everything here yet?" Somewhere, somehow, the energies that permeated the air were still sizzling. If he couldn't pick them up right now, he surely sensed them doing their thing. They had taken what wasn't meant to be back into their fold, and if they had managed to separate the one from the other, they had to be alive and well, doing their behind-the-world kind of things that only they would ever understand.

Whinewaeyn gestured ahead. "What's over that way?"

"Thimble," Amjelle reminded him.

"Thimble?"

"He went after the cub when he—" But now that her eyes followed Whinewaeyn's into the depths of darkness, she cocked her head and drew her brows together. Her voice faltered. Neither Thimble, nor the cub were anywhere to be seen. She whirled around to face the mystic. "What *is* over there?"

"There?" Zarothaster's lips warped into a laconic smirk. "Our final frontier."

"There you are!"

Thimble's feet painted some final stepping stones into the darkness to reach the fluffball on four legs. He switched the torch into his other hand and reached down to scoop up the distracted runaway, all the while staring at the wheely wall as it curved around and above him.

"What's got into you, anyway?" he scolded the cub. "Thought you were scared of heights! And now you go hunting for… whatever… in a place like this, with all those wheels and a whole lot of nothing just about everywhere else. We're going home."

Home, though, was sort of relative. They'd have to settle for the other side of the abyss, and the cub had already begun to fidget in his hands – prompted, Thimble guessed, by their own magnified reflections thrown back at them by the myriad of cogs. He turned back, but then his torchlight caught something in the wheely wall, and he moved the fire closer.

A piece of metal protruded from the cog before him, out of place in the otherwise smooth mechanical affair. He examined the cog itself, which was meshed with others of its kind – no, just one, he corrected himself – and that one connected to two more, and from there it went on. The piece of metal that stood out looked like nothing much. Like a coat peg maybe, one without a knob.

"A coat peg," Thimble declared, shaking his head. "Would you believe it, Snowy?" His eyes dropped to the cub in his arms. "At the end of the universe… What's there to find? A pot of gold? Nah. Just a coat peg on a cog!"

The cub licked his face.

"Wouldn't even work if that thing it's mounted on was turning. A coat would drop right off. Not even a gnome could make something like—"

Gnomes. Visions of gnomes swam up in his mind: garden gnomes, a bear-wearing gnome, and, mixed in, another gnome's face he could only vaguely remember. His thoughts circled back to Tsynnslin. With another kind of wall in front of him now, Thimble could almost hear the gnome knocking again at the rock wall, trying for some sort of response, before the whole thing transmogrified into a giant mirror. Thimble stared at the odd gathering of cogs before him, his very own version of a mirrored wall, and the distorted reflection of a halfling holding his gaze with rapt awe.

Hey! Thimble shrank back. *What was that?*

Was it just him, or had the wheely wall just wobbled? Just… a tiny wee wiggly wobble? His head tilted back, staring up at the coggy curve bending overhead. Had the wall turned spectral for a moment, or was it just his eyes playing tricks on him? He rubbed them for certainty. The wheely wall stayed wheely, and a wall… for now. But then again, so had the mystic. He'd been a mystic, and then an aardvark. And the moment Thimble hadn't thought of him as an aardvark anymore, he was a mystic again. What if the wheely wall was like the mystic becoming an aardvark? What was the wheely wall if it wasn't a wheely wall? What *could* it be? Twisted thoughts of gnomes and walls and mirrors chased after each other in his mind, and with them came unicorns, cubs and cogs, merging and coalescing as if in a dream.

His gaze dropped to his feet, to the impossible flagstones. And yet there they still were, pledging support. His eyes moved over the abyss, then back to the cog wall, only an arm's length away, and they climbed up and up until they declared whatever they tried to overcome as insurmountable.

If only he could get a grip on what it all meant…

Wait. He could, couldn't he?

He could… get a grip on it. He had seen this before.

Just a little push, said a voice in the back of his mind. *Anyone can do it. Even the smallest person. The rest… is magic.*

This was magic. With wheels. Weaverring Clock Tower magic.

His hand reached forward. Goose bumps ran up his arm.

The smallest person.

"See? This is where it all ends."

The party lined up at the point where the chequerboard floor had called it quits. Even Bormph shuffled forward, taking a peek from the precipice. The guidelight hovered before them, illuminating a row of flagstones reaching into the space ahead, but between the white tiles, the black ones had turned into actual gaps, adding depth to their colour.

"The place must have taken them both by now," Zarothaster said flatly.

"Oh, yeah?" Amjelle pushed past him. She strained her eyes, looking into the abyss, and bent over the tiles' edge, but found neither halfling nor cub hiding underneath.

Sylthia joined her. "This cannot be an end. The Dream works in circles. There's always more horizon behind any horizon. After the darkness, there's always light. After each end, a beginning. Always."

"Works both ways, I guess," Bormph commented facetiously, gesturing abysswards. His eyes searched for the mystic. "Anyway, from all we know, an obstacle like this can't be more than a minor inconvenience, right? Thimble must have found a way."

"We're not meant to cross," Zarothaster said. "There have to be limits to what we can imagine. This is how far we're supposed to go. Your companion's gone."

"If this *is* the Dreamkeep," Sylthia countered, "then there *must* be a way."

"Yeah, what do you know, Toaster?" Bormph added. "We should just do one of your tricks and see where it gets us. Let me think of a bridge or something."

A deep notch dented the dwarf's forehead and his eyes grew focused as his gaze fixed on the abyss. Nothing happened beyond that. Maybe the notch deepened some more, but that was it.

"We're not meant to cross," Zarothaster insisted.

"Guess we *all* need to think of a bridge," Amjelle argued. "On the count of three?"

Ramrok was still busy bending back thumb, forefinger, middle finger, when Amjelle already gave the signal, "One, two, three!"

Still, whatever anyone's mind dreamed up, nothing noteworthy came of it, aside from building anxiety. And just as much when Ramrok threw in a tentative "Four?"

Sylthia squinted across the bridgeless abyss. "Maybe we're not focusing on the right thing. A bridge is supposed to connect two points. If we don't know where we're actually supposed to end up, then how would a bridge know?" She nocked an arrow, released it, and watched it vanish without a sound.

"I could certainly try some magic," Whinewaeyn said, with some confidence. "After all, what am I here for?"

"Yeah. Was wondering about that myself, wizzer." Bormph grimaced. "The thing is, you never seem to get enough of your elements together, or whatever other whizzy-whazzy you spellcasting guys need, so I wouldn't count on it. Also, this place almost cost you your staff, remember?"

Whinewaeyn raised a hand. "There's no shortage of anything here. And I can do magic things... manually.

With my hands." The wizard indicated his guidelight. "Worked with this little fellow, so I might as well try... Well, you just watch me."

After handing the staff over to Amjelle, he made motions as if stirring an invisible cauldron. Very slow, very measured motions. In time, all kinds of multicoloured flashes popped up before and around him and, eventually, a pillar made of what looked like sparkling, revolving air manifested itself. The longer the stirring went on, the larger the flashes became, and the more violent the discharges they unleashed on the space above the abyss. Bush-, tree- and eventually lightning-sized discharges forked off into the distance and were submerged in the gloom, only to flare up again farther away. At one point even the neutrally observing guidelight was sucked into the swirling, crackling, streaks-of-light-throwing spectacle, until—

"Well, so much for that," Whinewaeyn said, in a voice much calmer than the brew he had formed might suggest. He had stopped stirring now, and the crackles of energy fell back little by little into much smaller skeletal versions of themselves. As they toned down, the guidelight they had taken for a whirl was released too, and the former prisoner wove its way tipsily towards a safe space. The party reassembled around the wizard until whatever he had attempted to concoct was no more.

"Just as I thought," Whinewaeyn said. "No elemental shortage. And that's just it. It's all too much of everything. As soon as you put a hand in it, it's too much already."

Bormph swallowed a sigh. "Couldn't you at least have tried a little longer?"

"And get us all killed?" snapped Amjelle, to whom staying alive seemed a reasonable priority. Then another thing entered her mind. "What happens in a place like this when you die, anyway?"

Good question.

"If it's like with the dust..." Whinewaeyn speculated after a bit, "in that we brought the dust *with* us, and that dust still behaves like dust around here even if it isn't *from* here, not as such... Then, well, in analogy, everything considered, if we *are* like that dust, upon our death... we'd be" – he scratched the back of his head – "dust."

"Dust?" Bormph checked back.

"Guess so," Whinewaeyn repeated, almost apologetically. "Dust, in a sense."

There was a stir behind them. "Maybe herein lies your answer." Zarothaster's sparse frame emerged from the shadows, right at the point when everybody seemed to come to the conclusion that there was no simple answer. "Right here." Gazes followed him.

"What... in the dust?" Bormph blinked at the mystic, who had reached the edge of the precipice and was facing the nothingness that stretched away before him.

"We're all but possibilities, travellers," the mystic said, his worn face looking out over nothing much. "Notions born here, destined to be realized elsewhere... Maybe that's how your Dreameress dreams, elf, or how the God of Gods devised things to be." He turned halfway back for a brief glance at Sylthia and Amjelle. "We wouldn't know. We cannot step back. We're not made for looking at the whole. We're part of it ourselves." His gaze locked on the abyss again, his thoughts still drifting. "And here I am, the seeker, the doubter, the renegade who reckoned he could take on the world... But who am I, really? A mere aspect of what's eternal." He leaned forward over the impenetrable blackness. "Yet what's eternal cannot perish." His arms unfolded. "Can one man change the universe? Maybe if he can destroy it, he can rebuild it too... if only he returns what's not his?" For a moment, the mystic looked as though he was about to step off the edge. And then he did.

His own weight ripped him away.

With a start, the guidelight's watchful eye zipped closer to the spot where the mystic had dropped off. It bundled its radiance into a beam and threw it into the abyss, revealing the figure's rapid descent.

The mystic flapped wildly against the forces that tore him down, limbs flailing about in his blue silken robe, the stringy hair fluttering along. He grew ever smaller and smaller. But the shaft of light could only reach so far, and when it was about to lose sight of the figure altogether, the descending vivid shades of blue unfolded, spread out, and whatever they may have contained unravelled with them into a multitude of separate streaks – light, wispy, half-translucent ribbons that shifted, bent, curled and twisted. When the darkness had enough of the ribbons' bizarre dance, it erased them, as if the mystic had never been there in the first place.

Click-click...

The knobless coat peg swung forward, yielding with ease. The tiny cog to which it was attached began to turn.

Clickety-click.

Caught in the wheel's rotation, the peg slipped out of Thimble's fingers and went for another spin, this time all by itself. A fresh sound joined in, a clank of heavy metal that put the first hesitant clicks in their place.

Claaaack-a-TACK.

The adjacent cog turned as well. Then a third creaked into motion, and as it was connected with more of its kin, its kin followed suit. Behind them, even more gears wheezed and shifted.

Cluck. Clock. Ba-TOOOMPH!

Thimble gripped the cub tighter and stood back. Clicks and clacks, hisses and whirrs filled the air, urgent, intense. A grinding noise cut in, punctuated now and again by a series of crude thuds and bangs, hammering away offbeat, until the racket was drowned out by a rending boom from someplace hidden, way up above, coming rumbling, tumbling down into unseen depths. An awful roar of echoes was unleashed along the way. Even more noise erupted around the dome. This time from the sides, as if each single cog – big or small, delicate or massive – wanted to have a say in this. Soon, everything was moving. No matter where Thimble pointed his torch, cogs were ticking, tocking and turning, rattling and rolling. The reflected image of his halfling self had gone for a spin too, and it refused to settle. Thimble stared into the torrent, surrounded by the clangs, and yet he was moving with it somehow, caught in the swirl…

Another boom rattled through the space. His light died. The oily stench went with it.

Thimble groped about in the dark.

A jitter rippled across the flagstones. And yet, despite himself, this time Thimble was far from scared. Maybe because he wasn't all by himself anymore, because he felt Snowflake's warm and fluffy presence, but mostly because a rhythm had emerged amid the ongoing din, and he found the invariable steadiness of it oddly reassuring.

It wasn't altogether dark either. If his torch was gone, a hazy veil still lingered behind. It drifted over the turning cogs, expanding. When the shreds parted, lanes had opened up between the wheels of the giant apparatus, through which Thimble thought he could glimpse a whole other world, where the shadows had pooled together to form their own entity, something that went beyond colour. It seemed separate from the world Thimble knew as his own, but separate too from that other half of things they had stumbled upon here in this place, of which the wheely wall must have been just the latest whim... Beyond it all, Thimble imagined, there must be a third half.

By and by, the hazy veil lifted. The inky sea widened. The turning and churning hadn't ceased, but the starless, velvety beyond rolled nearer, spilling over the wheely schemes, until Thimble, body and mind, was swathed with it. And as he sensed a certain familiarity to that swathy presence, the promise of a new-found whole he had only been vaguely aware of until then, he reached for it, wanting to touch it – no, more than that – to dip into it, swim *with* it... out... out... farther out.

Incandescent streaks bled through that ocean. Thimble, holding the cub in one arm and pushing aside the silky current for him to pass through with the other, watched the streaks grow into distinct shapes as he moved: straight lines, curves, dots, sometimes all at once. At some point they froze in place. He blinked, and then he recognized them for what they were: runes of the Forgotten.

A whole eight-letter sequence had painted itself out of nothing. And yet there was more to it. For whatever arcane, aardvarkish reason that was impossible for Thimble to fathom, they made some sense. They were just letters still, no numbers among them, and maybe he was just seeing things and hearing things in all this pandemonium, but he felt like he could read these runes now too, if he only wanted. If he set his mind to it. If he could convince himself that he was able to see through it all, then he might... see that third half of things. He squinted at the runes in their arrested state.

On second thought, maybe he'd been too ambitious. What pretended to be a word, wasn't. Not as such.

U-P... Well, that part of it made sense, at least... *D-A-T-I-N-G.*

Was it about getting your romantic relationships to the next level?

Or fruit? How to grow better dates?

Something to do with... time?

U-P-D-A-T-I-N-G.

A vertical line slipped into existence underneath rune number one. It didn't remain that way, though. What started out small soon lengthened and, in no time at all, had extended into a horizontal rectangle the breadth of the first two letters put together. After that, the shape froze for a bit, as if thinking, then soldiered on further towards the right, stopping again, dreaming some more. In that unsteady rhythm, observing a glacial, barely perceptible pace, the shape grew little by little into a thick, broad bar that reached across the width of several of the runes. When there were only two letters left, the thing – just for the heck of it – jumped to the final rune, and with that done, underlined the lot.

Thimble glared, and waited.

Then the ground fell out from underneath his feet.

Eeeek-k-k-k-k-k-k-k-eeee-k-k-k-k-k-k-eeee-k-k-k-k-k...

At the end, there was nothing but a grating noise in the Void, a primal jarring screech that reigned supreme. And it was awful. Music of the spheres was yesterday, and it showed. What a blessing that nobody could be listening.

Sometime after the end, however, it came to be that a tiny tinkle entered the worldless Void, so soft and meek that it was hardly perceivable. It had a fresh and sonorous ring to it, and its innocence, once it had asserted itself, clashed with the raucous, all-encompassing grating din. *How about we shake things up a little?* the single note seemed to suggest, and it wove over and under its discordant screechy sibling, as if playing tag with it. Soon it had caught up, whereupon the both of them entangled, twined around each other like threads spun by some cosmic loom until, eventually, they merged into one.

Eeee-aoooo-k-k-k-eeee-aooo-k-k-k-eeee-aoo-k-k...

And lo and behold, the otherworldly shriek mellowed and undulated away into a calmer version of itself, and the calmer version ebbed into something closer to an agitated pulse than to a shriek ringing out across the shadows eternal. Was it a melodious tune yet? A song for the ages as universes are beholden to aspire to? A piece to be remembered till next Doomsday? No, it was not. But it was good enough for now. Change was in the air.

Eeee-aoooo-eeee-aooo-eeee-aoo...

The Void felt inspired. It got the notion that it wanted to be more than just Void banging about. That's why it twisted. It turned. It did the jig. It found its rhythm.

Nobody noticed. Nobody was around who could've. Everything was as black as pitch, and the Void, twisting and jigging in the dark, try as it might, was as good as invisible.

All the same, the Void had some creative ideas to make up for that. It turned itself inside out, as one might turn a coat which can be worn both ways. Now *that* did the trick! The other side was nothing like its reverse, and it gave the Void something to play with. Whereas the darkness was made up of seamless black squares, thus supplying the Void with its distinguished non-look of impenetrability, its reverse was quite the opposite. Tiny dots were laid out across the back of the squares, white ones, as to make a difference. Turned inside out, all of a sudden the Void looked grainy, more like something rather than nothing. It wasn't much yet, but memories started to come back already, and the Void, sensing the possibilities, was eager for more.

Like a painter breaking in a canvas, it scratched a line into the dots, and then it took its meagre palette and scraped some white together – which, accordingly, left other parts dark. Then it expanded on the principle of the dot and formed a sizeable circle, after which – for nobody likes to be called two-dimensional – it made the circle into a ball. So as to keep it from the rest, the Void shoved the ball above a line, and let the grain be grain beneath it. Everything else happened almost by itself. Some dots banded together, first as mere blotches swimming in the haze, then into patches more shadowy than blotchy, and as no shadow is just a shadow by itself, the shadows took on shapes. And what would shaped shadows be without someone to cast them?

The throbbing and thrumming waned into a chirping, buzzing sound almost like beetles enjoying themselves. Maybe because that's what it was.

A universe snapped back into focus.

"*Aaaaaaaaa-a-a-ah—*"

The scream was just one scream in a whole spectrum of screams, some of them high-pitched and sharp, some deep and hollering, and one distinctly bassy.

"*Aaaaaaaaaaaaaaaaaaaargh?*"

Half an eternity of screaming later, the blazing white that had swallowed a halfling whole faded away before his eyes. The flickering fruit-fly-like dots swarming about packed off, or maybe coalesced into something larger – either way, it was all a blur. Most importantly, Thimble felt support underneath his hairy feet again and held off making further expressions. Briefly. Until it occurred to him that whatever his bare feet were relying on was anything but solid ground, and that it was baking hot besides.

"Aaaaaaaaahhh—"

A shadow slid over him… A giant shadow. The shadow of… a giant? Then another shape joined the first, less gigantic. It waddled more than it drifted. Keg-like. Noisy. Murmuring, grousing, cursing. He knew that shape.

"What's happening?" Thimble got out.

Something pushed through his toes. When his eyes had halfway adjusted, he got the message: his feet were buried in… grains and grains of sand!

"What's going on?" Thimble cried as he pulled one foot out, followed by the other. He tried to take a step, and trod into more of the self-same halfling-devouring sand.

"Desert," declared a Bormph-like grumble, and then Thimble's eyes found the dwarf that belonged to the voice, planted next to Ramrok just a pebble's throw ahead, looking out over…

"Desert," Ramrok deadpanned too, looking back at him.

Thimble trudged forward. When he reached his companions, the sweltering heat reached him too, and they shared a view across a bleak and barren wasteland.

"Desert?" he said, incredulous. The desolation looked familiar. Absolute nothingness in the guise of a landscape. No hint of a breeze. *The Joghavri,* Thimble thought. He'd recognize it from miles away. And from right in the middle of it too.

His gaze swept across the featureless plain and came across something blonde and beautiful that stuck out not too far away. He recognized it as the blonde his heart belonged to. The elf knelt a distance off, as if sifting through the sand. Or maybe she wasn't, for now she got up, slowly looking about quizzically like everyone else. She cranked her head back towards the barbarian, dwarf and halfling, and towards a voice that reached them from even farther behind.

"Curious." Indeed, there was the wizard too, looking as bedraggled as ever, and next to him he saw Amjelle. And behind Amjelle, a pitched camp. Horses. And the sky, in a strong, dark, dusky blue.

"*K-rn-tk-prt?*" Thimble put to the universe, tentatively. Nothing happened whatsoever.

Somehow, he knew. The universe was out of teapots.

CHAPTER 25

Apocalypses… and After

Dawn crested the Thourgethrum's ragged peaks. One final push, then sunlight spilled over the lands like a pancake in the making, slow and gentle, as though aiming to get the recipe just right. For lack of a sky-sized pan to keep the expanding brilliance in check, the luminous dough rolled on unhindered, its soft, frothy edges stretching ever westwards, until, by and by, a crunchy gloss enveloped Dimmerskeep and its environs.

The new day greeted a number of early woken faces – among them the bakers, who had stepped outside while waiting for the latest batch of pretzels to rise. The day went on to relieve the night watch from their duties and remind the market people to set up their stalls. Excess rays of sunshine bundled together and pushed past drawn curtains to prod awake anyone still holing up inside. Some reluctant moaning and groaning made its way across town, as it always does when yet another regular morning makes landfall.

"Feeling peckish," Whinewaeyn declared, staring up at the heavenly omelette. His head dropped, drawn to a scent from one of the stalls wafting by. "How about you, little one?"

Thimble's mind was elsewhere. "What if someone recognizes us?" He was a bit uneasy in his own skin.

"Ah, celebrity problems." The wizard winked at him.

"There's not been an announcement yet," Thimble hissed. "Have you forgotten that the Prince put out leaflets searching for us all over the place! You suppose we can just walk around like normal before it's all official?"

"In case you missed it, the apocalypse has been cancelled. In the meantime, if you're still worried… just do something like this." Whinewaeyn turned his hat around.

Thimble failed to notice a difference.

"How about a haircut? A serious one? Nobody has ever seen a bald halfling. You could—"

A sudden clatter hitting the cobbles made them start. It announced a giant of a man in burnished silver armour, gauntlets, greaves and – hence the clatter – pointed, metal-shod steel boots. While the din he was making commanded a respect of its own, he also flaunted an important-looking gait to match his attire.

Thimble gulped, but Whinewaeyn dipped his head in greeting as the noisemaker walked past, and received a well-mannered nod back.

"See?" The wizard gave Thimble a look. "Must be one of the big cheeses around here. Looked me straight in the eye… no reaction. The hat had him fooled."

Thimble was about to reply when a booming voice echoed through the alley.

"For the gods' sakes, Captain!" The very same giant was yelling at a horseman coming up the street. "Would you get rid of those ridiculous plumes? The cavalry is no pony farm! It's been *three days* since Mish-Clash! *Three days!*" Shaking his head, the bear of a man strutted away, taking the clatter with him, while the horseman began fumbling around with the horse's headgear as he rode on.

Thimble wiped his brow. "Geez... I thought..."

"Now, just relax a little. They'll sort things out, Bormph and the big one, while we do the breakfast shopping, as arranged. It's a decent enough plan. The dwarf is well suited to getting the most out of everything money-wise, and the big one will assist him by doing what he does best: looking intimidating."

"But what if they don't get an audience? What if they're thrown straight into the dungeons?"

"Ah, come on. Wouldn't *you* want to know why the world's still standing? And if the suspects turn up to tell the Prince personally that they were the ones who actually saved everyone..."

"But who would believe a wild tale like—"

"The Prince," Whinewaeyn provided. "The Prince is the Prince, isn't he?"

So much was true. The Prince was the Prince.

"As soon as he knows the whole story, he'll declare us heroes in no time," the wizard said confidently, "and then, once we get our accolades, you'd better watch out for underthings being flung at you and the like. Ladies are raving mad for world-savers."

"Yeah?"

"But of course!" Whinewaeyn's eyes shifted towards Dymmling's Hill where the palace crowned the town in its completeness. "The tower is back, the gnomes too, and everyone's busy being alive. His Lunacy the Prince will lavish so much gold and jewels upon us that it hurts!"

"Right..." said Thimble, a little reassured. The wizard had only stated the obvious. The world was still standing.

Or floating. Whatever it did, or used to do, it still did it. For the third time in the three days they'd been back, the spheres had developed a healthy blue, and the earth had refrained from even the slightest quiver. Everything adhered to long-established conventions. Plus, he wouldn't mind a few gems. He wasn't that much into underthings, though, thank you very much.

What surprised him most, however, was that folks were playing it so cool; no one had even mentioned the apocalypse. It was so unlike the Prince too – who surely wouldn't skip a post-apocalyptic feast for anything in the world. *Maybe they're preparing something real big,* Thimble thought. *Big things do take time.* As for now, people appeared to be getting back into the swing of things and enjoying it quite a bit: because they *had* their things to appreciate. People were to-ing and fro-ing everywhere, with the antsy urgency of opening markets. All that scurrying with purpose almost made the halfling feel guilty for just standing about, watching, like someone lost. "What's the holdup?" the faces of the townsfolk seemed to ask. "Get on with it! The world is waiting!"

The world, indeed.

"Isn't it weird how the universe works?"

"Hmm?" Whinewaeyn cocked his head at Thimble. "Hold on to that thought, will you? Oh, and this one too…" He passed the halfling his staff, fumbled about in his sleeve, dug up a handkerchief and blew his nose like an elephant. People started turning heads, though some might just have been wondering if that funny-looking fellow was wearing his hat backwards.

"Ah, nobody knows how the universe really works," Whinewaeyn then replied to Thimble on a quieter note as he stuffed the cloth back up his sleeve. He groped for his staff. "Worked in weird ways before the whole fuss, and works in weird ways after. One might as well just assume it's supposed to. Pretzel?"

They got themselves some pretzels, extra crunchy.

"Still," Thimble groused on as they walked past the stalls, "I wonder why it is that the gods, the Weavers or the Forgotten or whoever, went through all that trouble. Why'd they make ghostholds and secret codes and built wheely machines to operate the universe? Why is it that there's something rather than nothing? If I were a god, I'd be fine with just that: being a god. I'd do nothing much, and I'd have nothing much to worry about. I'd just sit back and enjoy the sunshine on my belly."

"Only there'd be no sun and no belly," Whinewaeyn put his finger on the flaw, "if you didn't create any of it first. And if there was no belly, there'd be no point in having pretzels, and who'd want that?"

True, thought Thimble, nibbling away. *If there isn't anything, it's not that much, considering.*

"But then," he began again, "they make the whole thing with their world machine… and mess it all up!"

"You mean…"

Thimble knew damn well what he meant. A memory of the previous evening whirled up like a cake rising on a ladleful of baking powder: there was Sylthia, and there he was, a dopey halfling, foolish enough to ask for his post-apocalyptic date. Her eyes said it all! And then her mouth: "But… I'm with Am, Thimble!" That's what his ears heard, even if he wished they hadn't. "I thought you knew?" She thought he knew! Would you believe it? It dawned on him then. In the middle of the post-apocalyptic night, it dawned on him.

He'd had it with blondes. For real, this time. The gods, the Weavers, the Forgotten, call them what you will, were watching him from wherever they were hiding, maybe directing him towards one shipwreck after another! Or they weren't. Which would be even worse.

"They've botched things up! Everything!" he blurted out. He was chewing on a lot more than just that one pretzel. "That's why all this happened, isn't it? Whoever made the world could've made things right, could've made it all out of pretzels if they wanted, and they didn't. They botched things up! *We* had to save the world!"

"Isn't it a good thing then that we were here for them?" Whinewaeyn said.

For a time, Thimble went quiet as he munched his pretzel. He had no idea what those world-makers were up to. But then again, he couldn't say he really understood, say, elves either. Or females. Or female elves! The world was just too big for a three-foot halfling, not counting his curls.

The wizard had stopped walking, so Thimble stopped too.

"You think they've already taken down our *wanted* poster?" Whinewaeyn pointed to the roofed notice board in front of them. "I can't see it anywhere."

Oddly enough, he was right. There was no poster like the one Tsynnslin had shown them. Another poster, however, announced in huge, attention-grabbing letters: *THIS AFTERNOON! Big Hero's Welcome!*

Thimble's excitement was limited. "Meh. It's not about us."

"Well, how could it be already?" Whinewaeyn stood back to look at the big poster, which he had failed to notice the first time around, given his penchant for missing the obvious. "What's this one about then?"

"Ah, some all-around great guy from up north. Tracks down lost prize cows, helps the poor and needy, uncovers conspiracies, that sort of thing. Guess that's what he did before the apocalypse, and he's still in business. Now he's going on tour, questing in the south."

"What, like a rocker?[*]"

Thimble put on a wry smile. "I guess so. Might as well be a rocker. Some people get it all – the gold, the girls and the glory."

Whinewaeyn's gaze slid sideways towards misery curdling on two legs. "What's eating you all of a sudden, little one? And just before your big moment?"

"Ah, whoever's out there, whatever they want to call themselves, they can just mind their own business." Thimble grumped. "You go visit them, and they aren't home. I don't even know why we bother with orcs and trolls and dragons and Zarrafandans and goblins armed to their teeth and make ourselves dizzy climbing up ghostholds to save the universe."

As if to make his point, a flea-ridden mongrel limped by, sniffed at one of the wooden posts, lifted a leg, and was off again.

"You know what?" Whinewaeyn said abruptly. "Ever since we're back from saving the world, I've been thinking

---

[*] Rockers (short for "rock artists") are sought-after dwarven star sculptors. They "turn rock faces into faces in the rock", as rock veteran Brooms Steadstone once humbly put it. But as the mountain won't come to the artist, the artist must seek out the mountain and chisel on-site. Thus, mostly to save travel expenses, it has become customary for rock stars to go on tour.

about that Dânthelrân fellow. Ever heard of the seven wisdoms of Dânthelrân?" Thimble didn't look as though he did, so he enlightened him. "The last one goes, 'You always end up where you've been going all along.'"

"Did he say that before or after he went funny in the head?"

"Actually, I'm not quite sure when exactly they put him in the fools' tower. But… can't you see, little one? He was on to something there. It's just that you only know where you've been going all along once you've arrived."

That Dânthelrân was a hell of a fellow, Thimble thought.

"Also" – Whinewaeyn smiled broadly – "you can't miss it."

Thimble looked up again. "Miss what?"

"Where you arrive. You're already there."

Thimble scratched his cheek. He was all out of pretzel now, but tried to take it all in: the sun reconquering its scorching reign, people jostling by up and down the plaza, and the damp dog smell too, which lingered long after the mutt had made off to mark more territory.

"Hmm…" Whinewaeyn said, and Thimble switched back from watching the mongrel to the old geezer beside him.

He almost failed to recognize the brightened face as the wizard's. He was studying a notice:

Fireworks specialist looking for assistant.
Help with coordinated explosions and professional
sky-painting. Alchemical or magical background
not required, but helpful.
Apply now at Postbox 4096, or directly at
Glampatch E. Zaengdaengler Inc.,
Big Blaze Boulevard 256.
We blow things up with style!

Just my luck, Thimble thought. *There goes the wizard.* Maybe that was the universe's way of poking fun at him. Again. His mind kept wandering, settling on nothing in particular when, in midst of the muddle, something washed to the forefront and banged about insistently in the little skull of his.

It's been three days since Mish-Clash! The booming voice rang and rang again in his ear.

Three days. Something... wasn't quite right.

In the palace, Prince Dymmling sat regally on his throne.

Presently, he was wiggling a bit. The fresh upholstery was an improvement over the past twelve attempts, no doubt. Still, the prototype of Paddy Laddy IV was a trace short of absolute perfection. Even though Ruffles, the gerbil in charge, was gambolling on her own throne just as she had done on version twelve, the Prince felt that a certain tenderness was still missing in number thirteen. Maybe an overhaul of the whole throne room was in order? A kind of leisure land with a gnome-constructed recliner in the centre?

There was a rap on the door. Ruffles chittered moodily. In came Princelings Klimbish and Rimfish, bowing, and subsequently lining up at the bottom of the steps leading up to Paddy Laddy IV and its sensitive occupant.

"You called, Your Pricelessness?"

"I was wondering, Klimby..." The Prince seesawed back and forth as he spoke, finishing up the candidate's bobbability probe. "During my morning exercise in the solar, I saw you two walking across the courtyard. I presume you were heading towards your study, about to handle day-to-day business?"

"Yes, Your Majesty. Sorting out audience requests and the like."

"I recall there were two fellows with you. One stocky, broad, hairy…"

"A dwarf," Klimbish confirmed.

"Yes. And his… very different… looking companion?"

Rimfish nodded. "A dwarf and a, shall we say, rougher kind of person."

"Clothed on the light side," the Prince noted. "Exotic. Pecs taut as leather, steely arms, thighs like cannon-barrels. Shiny skin… Supple movements…"

"A barbarian, as they say."

"Big, *big*…"

There were two synchronized stately coughs. "Quite tall, yes," Rimfish said quickly. "A mercenary."

"Fascinating specimen. Even from afar."

"But less verbose than the dwarf," Klimbish opined.

"Both absolutely nuts," Rimfish supplemented.

"Nuts?" the Prince repeated. "What would be the reason for such an unlikely couple to request an audience with My Valued Magnificency?"

"Said they were the ones we've been looking for, Your Majesty."

The Prince thought for a moment. "Remind me, Klimbish, I seem to have forgotten why we've been looking for them."

The princeling shrugged. "We haven't. We had no idea what they were talking about. They said all wasn't as we thought it was, and that they hadn't caused, but had actually averted what they called 'the apocalypse'. They wanted reimbursement for their efforts. The dwarf's words. The other only made ill-mannered noises."

"Go on." This beat throne gymnastics.

"Oh, we wouldn't want to trouble you with the rest of that drivel. They were all over the place." Klimbish rolled his eyes. "Cooked up some story about one of the palace towers absconding to the Oc'potsh orcs. So they reinstalled it for us or something. Also, we should have no more worries about the skies turning pink and gnomes making off, they said. 'And why is that?' I ask. 'Because we crawled under a rock,' says the dwarf, 'had a talk with the man behind the curtain and, most importantly, squished a bug.'"

"Desert grasshopper or something," Rimfish specified.

"People these days!" Klimbish summed up with a controlled amount of indignation. "The insolence! Wasting our precious time! Crackpots everywhere you look!"

"Barbarians…" The Prince's gaze had turned dreamy. "They call them barbarians, you say?"

At the same time, in a dive not too far away. Not a gay bar. Bormph had double-checked.

"You see what I'm saying?"

Ramrok didn't see what the dwarf was saying. But he heard him alright, with his two ears, each of them twice the size of the dwarf's own lugs. "Dwarf say pocalpyps bad business. Make pocalpyps go away for nothing. Is disgrace."

"Right. We make a trip to the end of the world and back, and what is it we get? Bugger all."

"Bugger all," Ramrok echoed.

"Nothing. Not even a few gems from Pinky and his gerbil. No diamonds, no trinkets, no vouchers, no extra-large V-necks for broad-shouldered guys like us. Thankless bunch, the lot of them!"

"The lot of 'em!"

"You know what I'm wondering, though, big one? How…" Bormph paused and started again. "How come the Dymmling's dimwits had no recollection whatsoever about the whole tower thing ever happening? It cannot be!"

The truth was, Ramrok hadn't been wondering. He was a silent supporter of the ignorance-is-bliss faction. But now that the dwarf brought it up, he couldn't help but wonder. He wondered what the dwarf was up to.

"It's almost as if it never… *was*," Bormph pondered on aloud. "As if…" Suddenly he felt an epiphany wash over him, and his voice rose to the occasion. "By Old Groovy and his Grimmlings! That must be it! That explains it! You know what that was, that thing behind the world that the Fumbler thimbled with?"

Ramrok tried to look apprehensive and failed gloriously.

"A *time and space machine!* The world machine is a *time and space machine!*"

Ramrok gave a tentative nod.

"Which makes it a *time machine* too!"

Ramrok still wasn't sure what he was nodding tentatively in agreement with.

"We rolled it all back! That's why nobody has any inkling! We – rolled – it – back!" Bormph's flat, fat hand landed with a smack on the table, sending the glasses dancing. "The whole world, the lot of it, was turned back to *before* it all happened…" A glow had entered Bormph's beard-wreathed cheeks, and his mind was racing now. "Back to *before* the Toaster cocked it all up with his gnomes and bugs, before the tower went on its journey because of it, before the earth started quaking and the sky got confused, before…"

"…pocalpyps!"

"Exactly! See? Even a barbarian gets it. And that's why we must have wound up back in the desert too, at that exact time, because that's where we chanced upon the Toaster's most wretched creation. Except, well, we didn't. Not anymore."

Ramrok mumbled something. Sorting through thoughts was tough business for a Northlander, especially on an advanced level. Fortunately, the dwarf was better at it. And he was already signalling for a wench to bring more ale to oil his brain.

"Trouble is," Bormph concluded on a less enthusiastic note, "how then could anyone remember the world ending...? Apart from us, that is. It's all been undone. And now we can't just go round telling everybody and their dog that we've done all that world-saving for them, because they have no idea about it ending in the first place!"

"Hmm?" Ramrok's thoughts had slipped towards... dogs. Why was it that everybody else had one, and they didn't?

"So, where do we go from here then, big one?"

The barbarian shrugged. He once had a mutt, Soggysheep, when he was a wee baby barbarian. A very special creature. Never since had he come across another mutt that bleated just like it.

"Now, here's the thing..." Bormph leaned closer once he had enough alcohol in him. "We both know you're not the sharpest knife in the drawer. So just let me do the thinking for the both of us. And what I'm thinking's this..."

Ramrok harrumphed, but he gave the dwarf a queer look as well. Civilized people sometimes talked strange. He wasn't a knife, though people sometimes called him a sword, a sellsword. And he wore no drawers, barbarian's honour. Loincloth tops.

"We've saved the world, but made no profit," Bormph grunted. "But any adventurer needs to earn a living. So, next time round, we should skip the world-saving. It's a distraction. If the world needs saving, let's leave that to others, and we'll focus on what you and I... well, er... I can count. Gold. You get me?"

Ramrok muttered his approval in barbaric.

"So here's what we'll do." Bormph unfolded a piece of paper. A map stretched over it, ranging from the Groo'cae'tran mines in the south up to the Amcalladams. The dwarf's calloused thumb tapped somewhere near the top. "This is the place." A sea of snow-caked peaks made off towards the map's edge. "That's the spot mentioned on the tapestry back in Toastertown. The one that had all those gold and gem symbols. Right here." His finger came to a rest on a particularly high summit that jutted up like a claw. "Treasure's all over the place here. Just needs picking up. And we're halfway there already anyway, now that we've been able to sneak a peek at its secret location. That must have been the true purpose of our little excursion. Everything happens for a reason!"

The barbarian's brow knitted into a deep crevice. "Is dangerous?"

"Piece of cake. Nothing we haven't seen before."

"With wizzy?" Ramrok asked. "And black-mane and elfy and little Fumbler?"

"Might need a little convincing. I can see why this could look like a step down for the one or the other if there's no world ending involved."

Ramrok squinted at the map. "H-E…" he spelled, tracing the letters with an enormous finger. "He… reb…ed," he ploughed on. "…R-A-G…" The barbarian looked up. "*Herebedragons.* Funny name!"

Elsewhere, on a pier in the Harbour Quarter.

"Feels like a dream, Am." Sylthia leaned back, her eyes on the healer.

Amjelle looked out over the silver-blue vastness that was Grand Lake, and watched the gentle ripples roll towards where her feet dangled from the landing. The water lapped playfully against the poles, for the most part disappearing with low-key murmurs under the planks, with some more elaborate gurgles mixed in.

She stirred. "A dream, yes. But isn't it a Dream you elves believe in anyway?" Then she turned. "Your Dreameress must be dreaming this moment too."

Sylthia stared ahead. "I can't help thinking about it, about the Dreamkeep. If that's what it was, what it is, out there somewhere, somehow… *behind* things, behind *us*… between the Dreameress's eternity and our fleeting world."

"You think the Dreameress dreamed up Zarothaster too?"

"Why, she must have. And Tsynnslin."

"And now they're both… where?"

The elf shrugged her shoulders. "Only the Dreameress knows everybody's place, and her Dream goes in a circle, so that nothing is ever lost. Whatever is gone, whoever is no more, everything and everyone's still part of where we are now, *how* we are. *What* we are."

Amjelle didn't speak. She *felt* them too, those ripples coming in, licking from time to time at the tips of her toes, unhurried, cool and fresh, regular as breaths – the breaths of something she knew intimately, and yet would never quite understand.

"That place…" Sylthia talked on, "wasn't it like a dream in itself? Just as the mystic told us? As we imagined it, whether we knew it or not? And then…" The elf raised her chin skywards, where the sun was doing its rounds, and blinked. "Then we imagined that we'd succeed, that we could make the end of the world go away… and so it did. We *wanted* it, Am, and perhaps that's why it worked, why we're now sitting here. It's as if we've just stepped out of a dream, right into another, one of our own making." She caught Amjelle's sidelong glance back at her, the long black hair tumbling over the healer's forehead. "As if we've dreamed us back, Am." Sylthia brushed the strand behind the healer's ear to search her eyes. "Or maybe we're still in the Keep, merely dreaming that we're here. If we both had the same dream, we wouldn't even know."

The corners of Amjelle's mouth drew up, just a little, and she slipped the elf's hand into her own. The slender fingers closed around hers. "We're dreamers, either way, Syl. When the world comes apart, what else but a dream could save it? Maybe one has to reach that place at the end of everything, before one truly can believe."

They fell silent for a while and just sat there overlooking the water. The lake was calm and busy at the same time. It lay before them unmoving, one single, boundless entity that stretched as far as the horizon, and yet, close by, the giant azure body felt alive in so many ways – the breeze played with it, spawning shudders on its surface, and the sun sparkled off it as though it had burst into a million tiny stars that skipped perkily from wave to wave before returning to their post-dusk jobs.

Amjelle felt Sylthia's hand clasp hers tighter.

They leaned against each other, staring out at the lake, a white furry something snuggled between them, perhaps dreaming of something too. Something like… icebergs?

Elsewhere in space… and time… A ripple away.

The dwarf dodged a fireball.

"You know what?" he shouted over the sound of lava bubbles bursting in rapid succession. "I've just had the oddest sensation!"

"This is not the time and place to have odd sensations!" an agitated snarl answered. "It's over!" The dark-skinned elf swerved away from another projectile the pyromagical harm-doer on the other end of the cavern aimed at her. Busy with that, she almost stumbled into the fiery pool that ringed the crumbling platform, of which she was now the only occupant. "But… you know what?" the elf shouted back at the dwarf on his very own crumbling platform. She leaned to the side, fixing the lich and his dragon in her sights.

"What?"

"I've just had the oddest sensation too!"

Dormhelm Humhammer and Ilvith Irwithswing turned to look at each other. Their eyes delved into their counterparts and swam a few rounds.

"As if…" they said as one. Another fireball dropped by. It missed them by a hair, but then chanced upon some magical residue.

WOOOOM!

The blast rearranged the lava sea, rocked the cavern and consigned Dormhelm Humhammer and Ilvith Irwithswing to history. As it should have been.

A ripple away.

Vensk Stormraiser was snoring like a whole pigsty. At times, when shifting his weight, he would start to puff and blow, rock back and forth, roll left or right, fish for a pillow gone astray. After a while though, he'd settle back to where he had started and the grunts would cease again.

A mumbled word or two slipped in between the groans. "*Chr-chr*-ba-*chr*-entrance! *Chr-chr*... tow-*chr*? *Chr*-daga-*chr*... *Chr*-arra-*chr*-ANDANS!" He startled himself awake. "ALL-OUT-WAR!" he heard himself caw, and the fright his own voice gave him made his pudgy hand grapple for his blanketside bell. Which wasn't there. It looked back at him from the corner to which it had escaped earlier, fleeing the prospect of mistreatment. Vensk was alarmingly alarmless. Ghosts of a conspiracy swayed in his head.

A door creaked open. The sound reached gingerly into the room, but not gingerly enough for Vensk not to have noticed. He flapped his hands and managed to prop himself on his elbows. The only trouble was that getting up the rest of the way was out of the question without the help of half a dozen of his staff. And as he was expecting to get floored by an assassin at any moment, the sensible thing to do was to stay put. Pretend he had it all under control.

"It's me, Master," said a hushed voice. "You must have had another nightmare!"

"K'lhonk?" Vensk's bulging eyes found the shape of a goblin peering over the perfect rim of his belly, a steaming bowl in his hands.

"Courier Thromp-da-glomph just reported that there's... er... nothing to report," K'lhonk informed him.

The mouth behind the belly opened.

The goblin was faster. "But not to worry, Master... It's all been taken care of already. I've provided him with suggestions on where we could optimize our reporting process. Breakfast?"

"Oh, alright then," Vensk puffed, easily persuaded. "How many courses?"

The goblin just smiled, snapped with his fingers, and the queue of serving trolleys waiting outside got rattling.

A ripple away.

Empress Jesmarine relaxed in her royal deckchair. The sky was an unblemished blue, the sun was blazing, and the Grand Empress was baking. However...

"Juvdor, I've got a problem."

The Grand Empress's personal servant leaned over, close to collapse from the heat. Nobody had warned him that a visit to the palace gardens might extend into a lethal affair. But who was he to question the Empress's tangled mind?

"Your Excellency?" he managed.

"How am I supposed to reconcile blue blood with a tan?"

"I beg your pardon?" Juvdor dabbed his brow with an already soaked handkerchief.

"Just look at me, Juffy!"

He looked at her in her long-sleeved, high-collared dress – a prudish oven on legs.

"Our sort is supposed to leave the whole toiling thing to the smallfolk and remain as pale as a ghost," she said. "Am I right or am I right?"

Juvdor nodded, for where Her Excellency was right, she was right.

"Then why is it that all kinds of stories go round court that Baron This or Duke That was seen with a sweaty maid or an exotic dancer, while at the same time he's known to shun the official house ghost for wedlock-ordained rumpy-pumpy?"

Juvdor struggled to come up with something. Anything. Like an appeal for reticence.

"Well, I'll tell you why!" the Empress interrupted his brooding. "It's because pale is boooring. See, I've thought about this. There are two ways to conquer the world, Juffy. Mommy was the campaigner. She dealt with armies. *I'll* go straight for hearts. I've decided I'm gonna charm my way through the rest of the known world. And for that" – she shook her hair loose, ripped open her blouse, corset and bustier – "I need a tan."

Juvdor staggered about, hit by the sun and something else.

"They say the Zarrafandan prince is quite fetching." The Empress leaned back. "Useless as a ruler, but fetching. Precisely what we need. He could wear my crown." She aligned her bust with the sun. "I've heard, he's particularly hard to get. Well, Juffy… Let's see."

Juvdor saw. He tried to nod, or shake his head, but whatever it was, it didn't go so well. He twitched, tilted sideways and – entirely unceremoniously for once – collapsed.

A ripple away.

Normi Stargazer was about to make a breakthrough. He was only a matter of minutes away from pinpointing the exact time of the end of the world. Of that he was certain. If only he were able to figure out how to extract a square root with his standard-edition abacus… For a little breather between problems, as he so often did, he stole a peek into his skyglass, and that's when he suddenly saw it – what he could only describe as… a grand nebula.

Something didn't add up. Or multiply. The nebula had drawn up out of nowhere, between the very moment he was peeking and the last time he had done so, about a minute ago. And already the mist stretched all over the place! Taking its size, density and the speed of its appearance into the equation, the cosmic proportions of the discovery were staggering. Its consequences… unfathomable. Most likely world-changing. Even – did he dare to think it? Yes, he did! – *apocalyptic!*

"Dolm!" Normi's shout reached out for his gnome colleague, but he dared not leave the eyepiece for an instant. "DOLM! Where are you when you're needed? THE WORLD IS ENDING!"

The nebula intensified. Next thing he knew, an enormous unidentifiable flying object half the size of the lens, a thing of a most peculiar structure that shifted as it moved – organic he assumed – cut through the ghostly image and gobbled it up as if there was nothing to it. It emanated a squeak so high-pitched, so blood-curdling and universe-penetrating that it resounded shriek-like even within the very walls of the observatory. Normi backed away, screeching with it.

But the moment he did, one of his out-of-sync eyes caught something else. Something up there, still, but more inside than outside, and quite close by rather than a cosmos away.

Dorky Dolm was balanced on the upper end of a ladder, a rag in one hand and a bucket in the other. A dotty cloth was wrapped around his head, tied neatly into a bow above his brow.

"What is it now?" he shouted down. "Can't you see I'm busy? Someone has to clean this thing!"

A ripple away.

There was bubbling, hissing, sizzling and lots of steam. Then a staccato of brazen, metallic sounds. When the last ring wasn't broken by any further noises, it hung around in the company of the bubbles for a bit, but eventually died a natural death. By and by the fumes lifted, revealing a reddish-brown mass, still whirling, but more with deliberation than vigour. Various chunks drifted by in the seething mass, dancing in the brew until it settled for good. The reflection that had been lingering withdrew: the reflection of a ladle.

"Ahhhh…" came a nearby voice, with relish.

The contents of the pot darkened again, and in its surface the mirror image of a furry head with jutting, rounded ears swam up. A snout and a row of teeth appeared, flanked by two dangerous-looking spiky canines. Beneath it was yet another head, one sporting bushy eyebrows, a prow nose and a goatee.

The lower set of eyes twinkled when they spotted something bobbing up, and the ladle dipped in to fish for it.

"Gotcha!" The ladle rose. Loud slurping ensued.

Tsynnslin turned. Chewing on the piece of not-quite-fully-cooked-yet squirrel, he looked around the perfect emptiness of the cavernous space around him, and wondered: What the *shmodork* was he doing up here?

A ripple away.

"There you are!"

Thimble tilted his head and squinted up at the voice chiming from above. In return, a nasty sunbeam stabbed

525

into his one open eye. *Thank you very much,* he thought. Screwing up his face, he held up a hand and blinked, a little puzzled, at the slender body at his side. When he saw the long blonde hair dangling in front of his nose, he brushed it away and turned back towards the street, his mood firmly slanting towards glum.

"Ah, well," he said. The elf was the last person he needed right now. "Had to see what that hoopla was all about."

"Oh, me too… Don't get a hero passing through every day."

"Nothing better to do, so…" His eyes roved over the masses crowding the sides of the street. "Just look at all the fuss! *So* overrated! And this one hasn't even saved the world yet!"

"Well, who has?"

"I'm going to tell them who! Gonna write it all down. How I was in the middle of it all, how I went to World's End and back. Now all I need is a proper quill, 'cause mine blotches all over the place."

"A story about how *you* saved the world?"

Thimble rubbed his nose and craned his neck to catch what was happening at the end of the street. But the hero wasn't on his way yet. "Okay, fair enough. I'll put you in it too." He forced a smile.

"Ah, you're funny!" She tittered away. "What's your name, little adventurer? I'll have to look out for it in the bookshops."

Thimble was somewhat stumped by this one. They journey all the way to wherever and back, and she'd already forgotten his name…? His hand rose to his brow again, which was his way of inviting the sun to take her shine somewhere else, and having settled that, he peered up at the blonde once more, making sure to get a proper look.

"I'm Aurora," said the voice up there for some reason, and he must have given his own name in reply, for the voice then said, "Glad to meet you properly, Thimble. But you're much taller than a thimble!" Another giggle escaped from the round lips, light and tinkling. "I thought I would never get the chance to thank you." She tilted her head. "So… without further ado… thank you," she said, mock-curtseying. After a small reflective pause, she added, "Ha, did I do a rhyme there?"

Thimble looked at the hand held out to him, and as the creature it belonged to was so perplexingly straightforward, he shook it, still in a daze.

"Um… er… nothing to thank me for," he managed, but in such a low voice that he wasn't sure words made it out of his mouth at all. For safety, he said them again. Some of them. "Nothing… er… at all."

A memory struck him. It whacked him over the head like his first encounter with the Toaster's tome. The fortune-teller's caravan! He saw the long-legged blonde rapping at the door in his mind's eye, heard the jingling coins in his mind's ears, and climbed the crate with, well, his mind's hands probably. There he was again, arms flailing for balance on top of that questionable construct. The next thing he remembered was a hurting bottom.

"So you're in the world-saving business then, huh?" The blonde's hazel eyes shone as they narrowed.

"Oh… er, yes… You could say that," Thimble stammered. He stared up and got as far as the button nose. "I mean, I was. But… that's a long story. There was something wrong with the universe, you see."

"Isn't there always?"

"Er… Is there?"

"There's *always* something wrong with everything, one way or another," said the blonde with the name reminiscent of morning dew and a voice like a summer's breeze. "That's what my granny says anyway, and that getting something right depends on how you look at it. Can't cut meat with a spoon now, can you?"

"Suppose not." That made culinary sense.

"It's not so much about the big things anyway. It's all about the little ones, isn't it? There wouldn't be anything big without them."

Thimble squinted up at her from his halfling perspective.

"Oh, I'm sorry," she said, "I'm talking too much. I was just wondering: care for a cup of tea at the Weary Traveller? I sure do owe you one. And you still haven't told me that story yet."

"Ah, you're not gonna believe me anyway. It's pretty far out there. I mean, far out there and then some. Really. I mean it."

She smiled. "Try me. I'll bring my hiking boots."

"But… you'll miss the hero's welcome!"

Murmurings had picked up. The latest news on the knight's imminent arrival was rippling through the crowds, prompting restless chatter to bubble up at every corner.

"Any minute now!" a portly fellow announced as he shouldered his way through a throng of people, keen to retake his front row position. "He's already in town. *In town!*"

"What you think he's gonna look like?" someone asked.

"What's he about to do?" asked another. "Hold a speech?"

"You think he'll shake hands with the crowd?" said a third, hopeful.

"Who knows if he'll even show up," said Aurora. "Everyone's been here for hours!"

The portly fellow scoffed at her. "He stops for autographs along the way, hence the delay, milady. Maybe you'll get lucky too! He's here, trust me. He's here!" Already he had turned his back on her, his eyes fixed on the street where the gilded bridle of the hero's mighty warhorse was expected to appear anytime now.

Certainly, the road looked prepared enough for someone important to pass through: branches littered the street, and many a devotee had spread a cloak across the cobbles in reverence of the esteemed visitor. Street vendors with pushcarts peddled souvenirs and finger food, from hot pies and sausages in a bun to bespoke snacks named things like "Hero's balls" and "Swingerwings".

The halfling had fallen silent as cheers around them grew louder and louder. They were so loud and urgent now that when Thimble raised his voice again, it was drowned out instantly by the cheering crowd.

"What was that?" Aurora shouted back, her button-nosed face appearing down at his height, wreathed in the likeness of undulating moonbeams. "You said something, Thimble?"

"How about hot chocolate?" he repeated, louder, and a whole lot firmer. "CHO-CO-LATE?" His eyes searched hers.

She seemed to think for a bit, then asked back, "And a biscuit?"

Acknowledgments

I owe a heartfelt thank you to everyone who helped to make this novel possible, first and foremost to my editors, Kate Nascimento and Emma Parfitt. Kate and Emma were invaluable in ensuring that the fun in the text was also grammatically correct and readable on top of it, so kudos for their meticulous care for the written word in general and the author's unruly brainchild in particular.

I'm equally indebted to the various beta readers, who had to bear with the book's early stages, at a time that felt about a century ago. They laughed in the right places (mostly), spotted holes in the plot (rarer, but still) and commented tirelessly (always). Most notably among my dedicated betas were Eric Wheeler, Lella Flaekja Colacurcio and Sally Hill, but there were many, many others too. Each one of them contributed in one way or another to keep the project on course. You've all been a great source of feedback and, not to forget, motivation.

There's also the artist's contribution. Right from the moment of its inception, this novel with its far-ranging ideas was meant to be illustrated. Santiago Iborra, a long-time friend and no doubt an undisputed wizard with the digital brush, took care of giving the madness shape, digging into the respective passages and expanding on the ideas in his own creative way. Cover, chapter headers, and website graphics, all of it reflect the spirit of the written word to a T. You can see more of these masterpieces in the fully illustrated edition. Great work, Santi!

A big shout-out also has to go to all the former members of Santharia, a cooperative online worldbuilding project, which accompanied my journey as a storyteller for several decades. The project was fun, yet ambitious at the same time, it fostered friendships around the globe and helped me personally to hone my skills as a writer. Good times, fellas, good times.

Finally, I'm grateful to every friend, family member, colleague or pet who provided moral, technical or emotional support and encouragement. Thanks a bunch for all the listening, caring, sharing, advising, researching, suggesting, correcting and the rest of it. Most importantly, however, thanks for providing me with inspiration by just being there, or – in the case of pets – mostly in the way, which is good enough for me. I couldn't have done it without you.

About the Author

Art was born and raised somewhere in the idyllic countryside of Austria back in 1972 when phones were still stationary, the capital letters A and I, when placed side by side, were just two vowels looking all wrong and books never, ever, required a recharge.

He studied Philosophy and Communication Arts in Vienna before moving on to join the local newspaper, where he made headlines without being in them and got a couple of football scores wrong. Deciding that the gruelling, sleep-depriving news world was not for him after all, he moved on to a no less stressful desk job, which involved coding sales management systems, database queries, drawing up reports and still not getting enough sleep. Despite the latter, Art headed a cooperative online fantasy world-building effort on the side for several years, turned into an arthouse movie expert and wrote stories: fairy tales, spooky stuff, parables and novellas, including plots and code for self-developed adventure- and role-playing games.

Getting his epic debut novel underway was only a matter of time. Also only a matter of time was how long it took him to finish. But well, there you are.

🌐 artimidor.com
🅕 /artimidor.avennay

A Final Note

Thank you for reading. If you enjoyed this novel, why not recommend it to a friend? Or write a review. Or do both and pat yourself on the back for it.

Also, as a rule of thumb, remember that a yawning gap on your bookshelf is best filled with – you guessed it! – a book. Buy one, solve your gap problem and support an independent author, all in one. If you need options, feel free to sign up for the newsletter at artimidor.com, where you can learn about upcoming fantastic tales or the fully illustrated version of this novel.

It's people like you who make the world go round.

Printed in Great Britain
by Amazon

42274054R00310